AN UNOFFICIAL GRAPHIC NOVEL FOR MINECRAFTERS

LEGEND OF THE CORAL CAVES

THE S.Q.U.I.D. SQUAD #1

MEGAN MILLER

SKY PONY PRESS

New York

Copyright © 2020 by Hollan Publishing, Inc.

Minecraft® is a registered trademark of Notch Development AB.

The Minecraft game is copyright © Mojang AB.

Sky Pony Press books may be purchased in bulk at special discounts for sales promotion, corporate gifts, fund-raising, or educational purposes. Special editions can also be created to specifications. For details, contact the Special Sales Department, Sky Pony Press, 307 West 36th Street, 11th Floor, New York, NY 10018 or info@ skyhorsepublishing.com.

Sky Pony® is a registered trademark of Skyhorse Publishing, Inc.®, a Delaware corporation.

Minecraft® is a registered trademark of Notch Development AB.
The Minecraft game is copyright © Mojang AB.

Visit our website at www.skyponypress.com.

10 9 8 7 6 5 4 3 2 1

Library of Congress Cataloging-in- Publication Data is available on file.

Cover design by Brian Peterson
Cover and interior art by Megan Miller

Print ISBN: 978-1-5107-4732-6
Ebook ISBN: 978-1-5107-4743-2

Printed in the United States of America

LEGEND OF THE CORAL CAVES

THE S.Q.U.I.D. SQUAD #1

Prologue

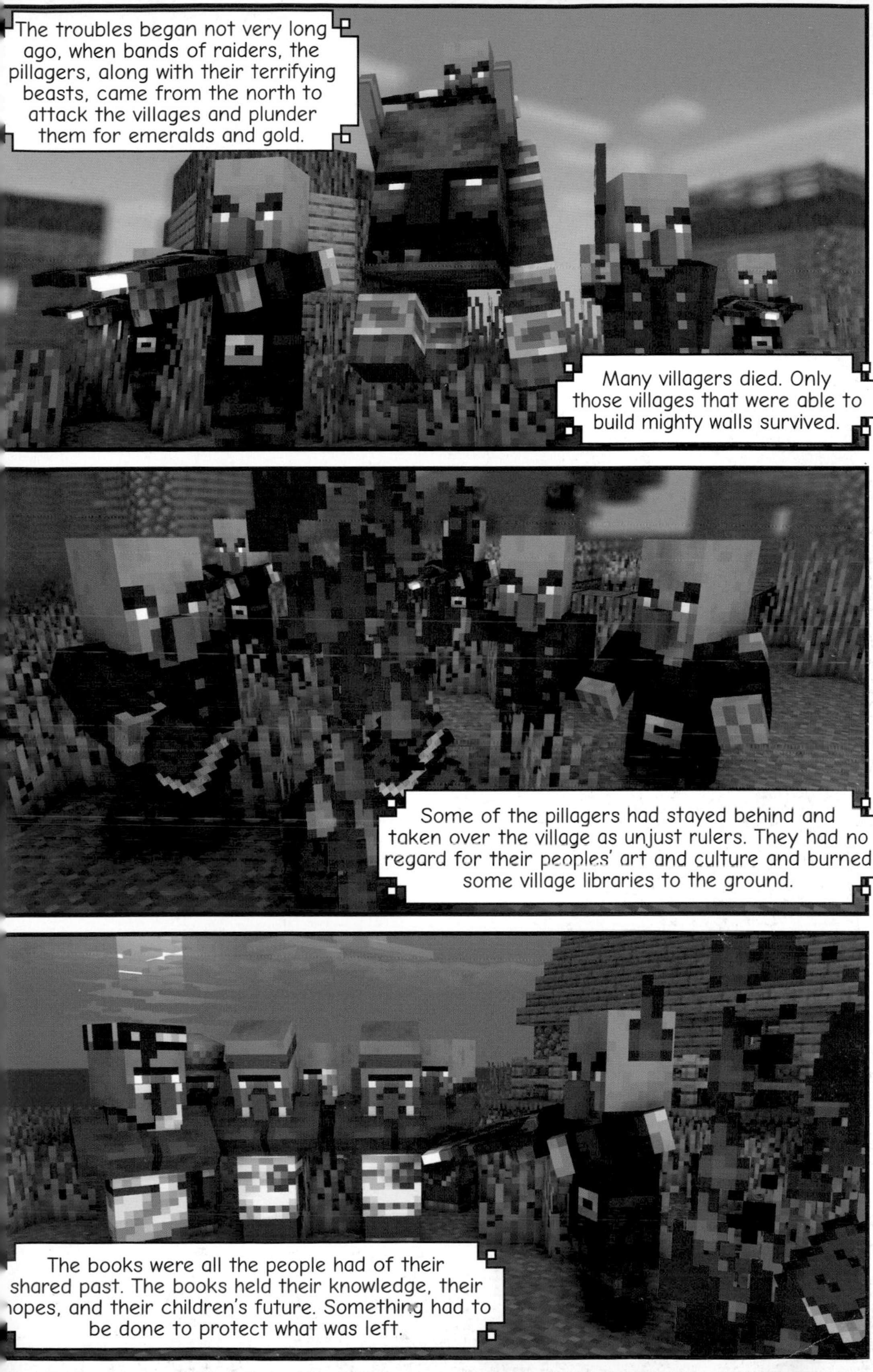
The troubles began not very long ago, when bands of raiders, the pillagers, along with their terrifying beasts, came from the north to attack the villages and plunder them for emeralds and gold.
Many villagers died. Only those villages that were able to build mighty walls survived.
Some of the pillagers had stayed behind and taken over the village as unjust rulers. They had no regard for their peoples' art and culture and burned some village libraries to the ground.
The books were all the people had of their shared past. The books held their knowledge, their hopes, and their children's future. Something had to be done to protect what was left.

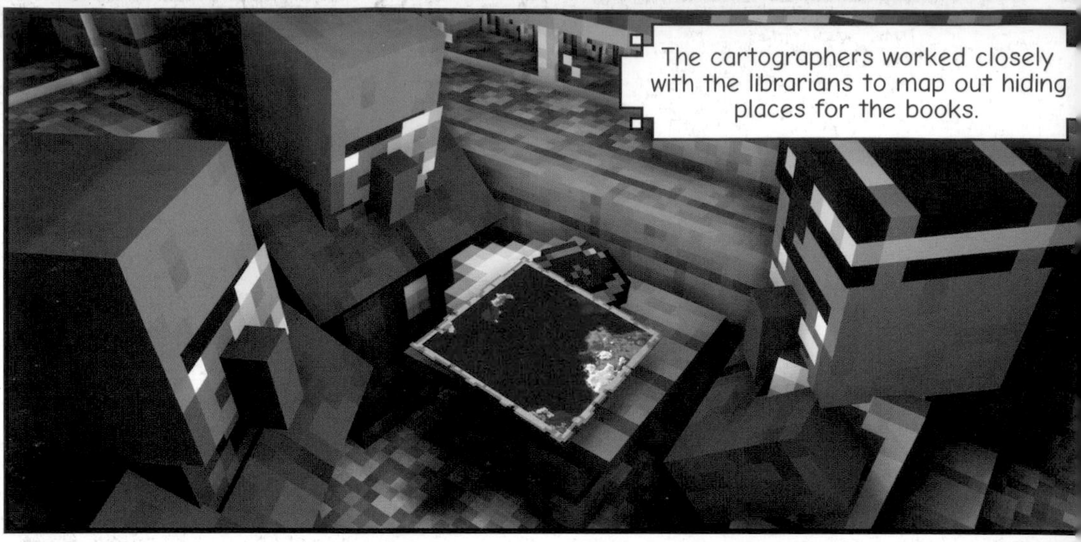
The cartographers worked closely with the librarians to map out hiding places for the books.

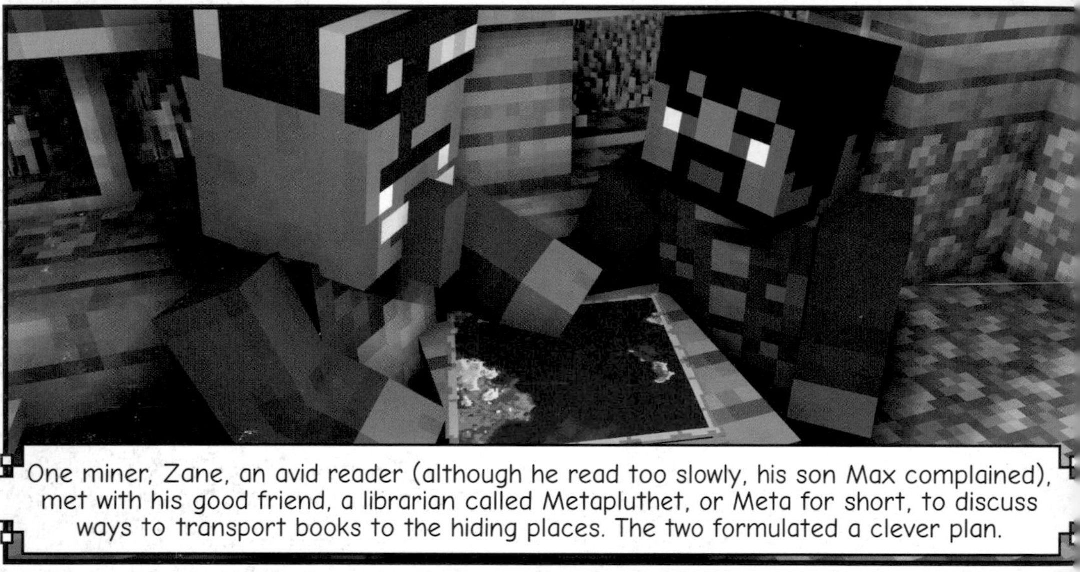
One miner, Zane, an avid reader (although he read too slowly, his son Max complained), met with his good friend, a librarian called Metapluthet, or Meta for short, to discuss ways to transport books to the hiding places. The two formulated a clever plan.

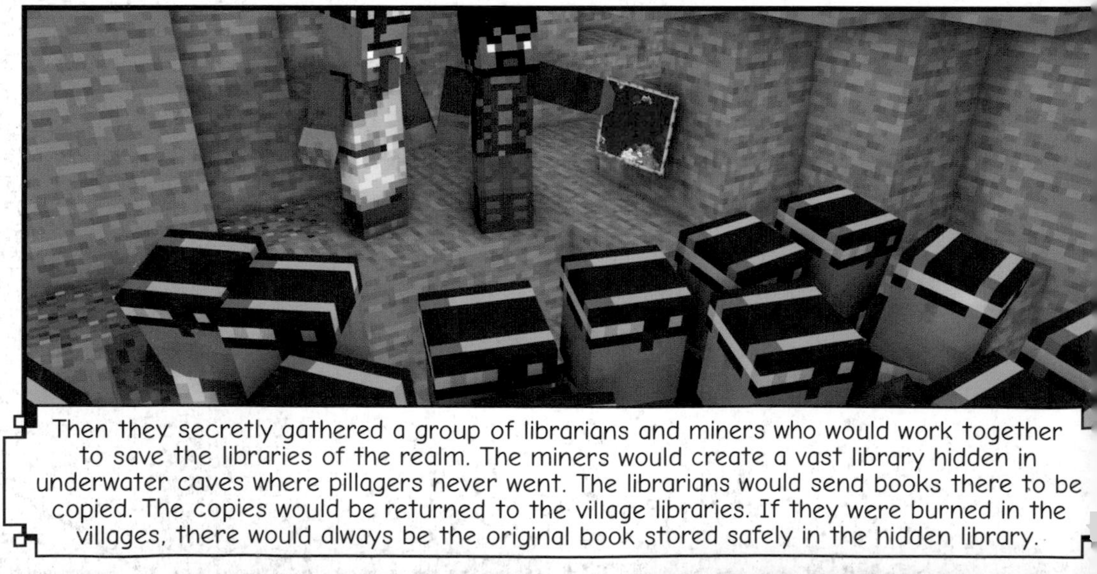
Then they secretly gathered a group of librarians and miners who would work together to save the libraries of the realm. The miners would create a vast library hidden in underwater caves where pillagers never went. The librarians would send books there to be copied. The copies would be returned to the village libraries. If they were burned in the villages, there would always be the original book stored safely in the hidden library.

Chapter 1
Trouble

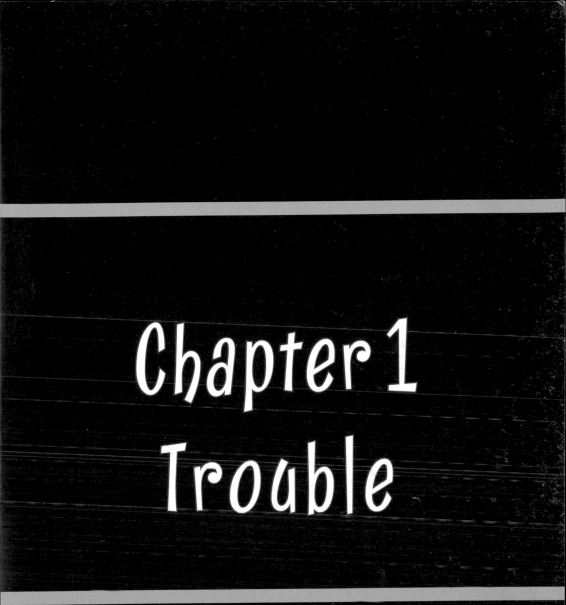

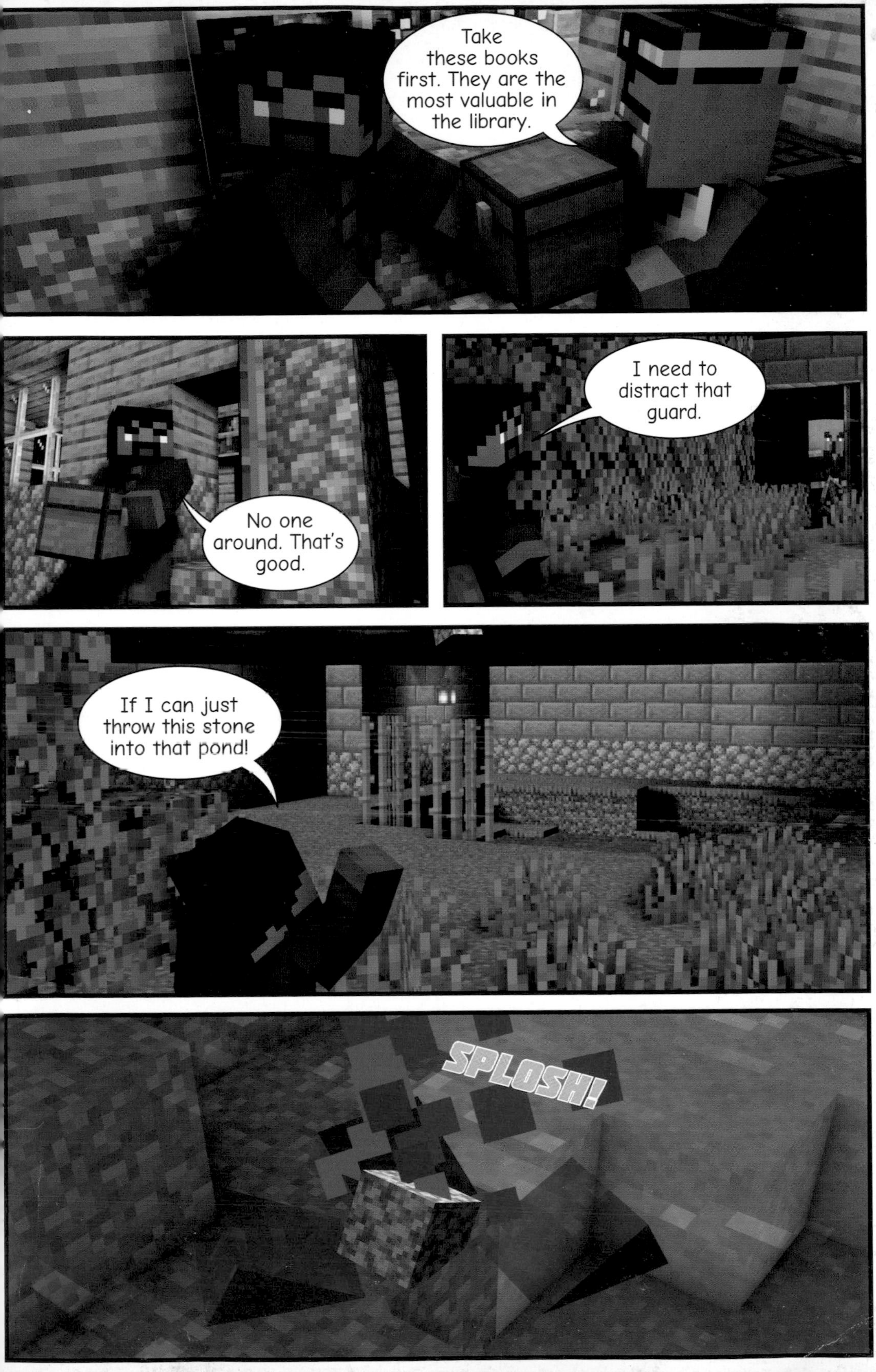
Take these books first. They are the most valuable in the library.
No one around. That's good.
I need to distract that guard.
If I can just throw this stone into that pond!
SPLOSH!

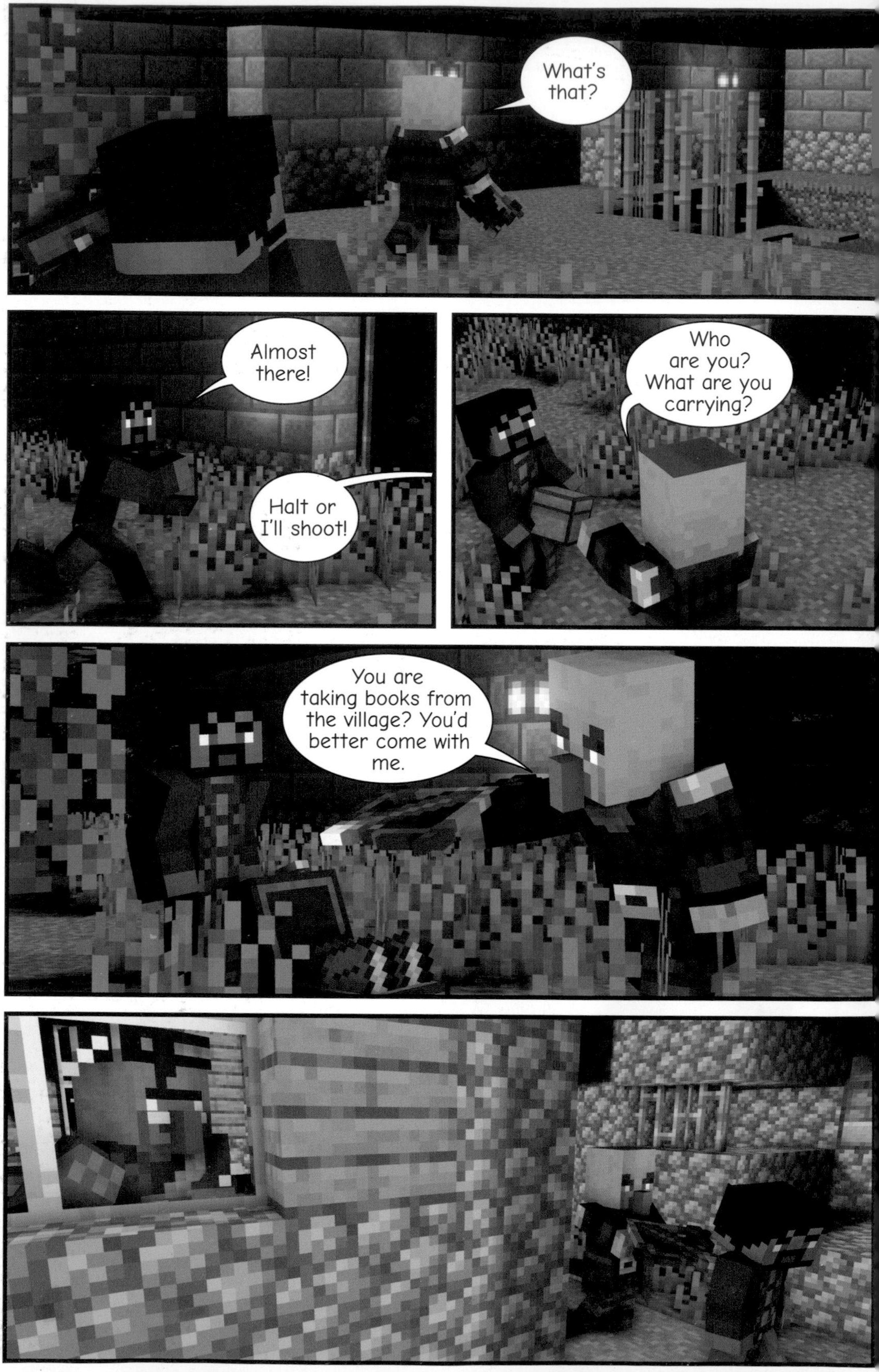
What's that?
Almost there!
Halt or I'll shoot!
Who are you? What are you carrying?
You are taking books from the village? You'd better come with me.

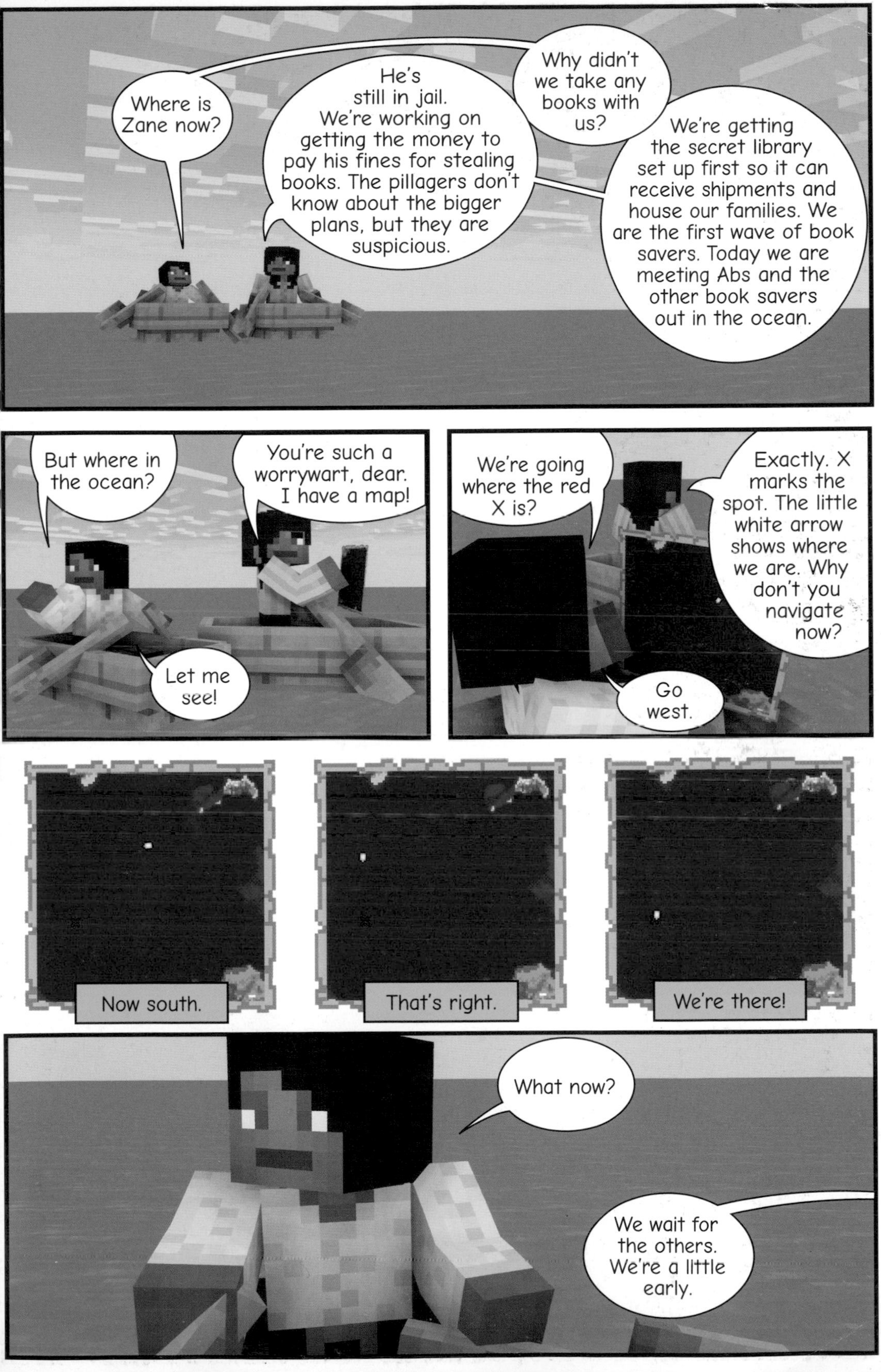
Where is Zane now?
He's still in jail. We're working on getting the money to pay his fines for stealing books. The pillagers don't know about the bigger plans, but they are suspicious.
Why didn't we take any books with us?
We're getting the secret library set up first so it can receive shipments and house our families. We are the first wave of book savers. Today we are meeting Abs and the other book savers out in the ocean.
But where in the ocean?
You're such a worrywart, dear. I have a map!
Let me see!
We're going where the red X is?
Exactly. X marks the spot. The little white arrow shows where we are. Why don't you navigate now?
Go west.
Now south.
That's right.
We're there!
What now?
We wait for the others. We're a little early.

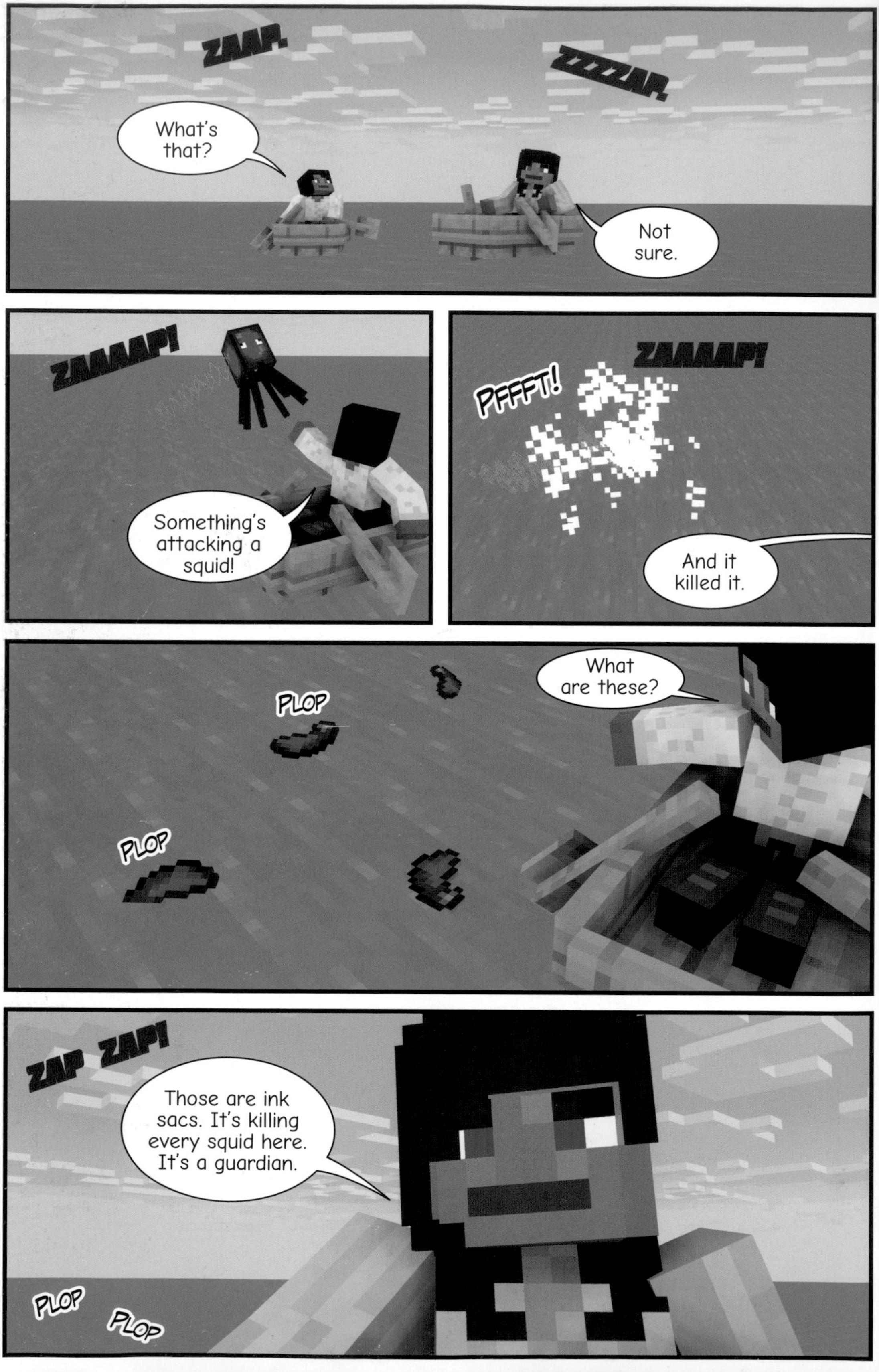
ZAAP.
ZZZZAP.
What's that?
Not sure.
ZAAAAP!
Something's attacking a squid!
ZAAAAP!
PFFFT!
And it killed it.
PLOP
What are these?
PLOP
ZAP ZAP!
Those are ink sacs. It's killing every squid here. It's a guardian.
PLOP
PLOP

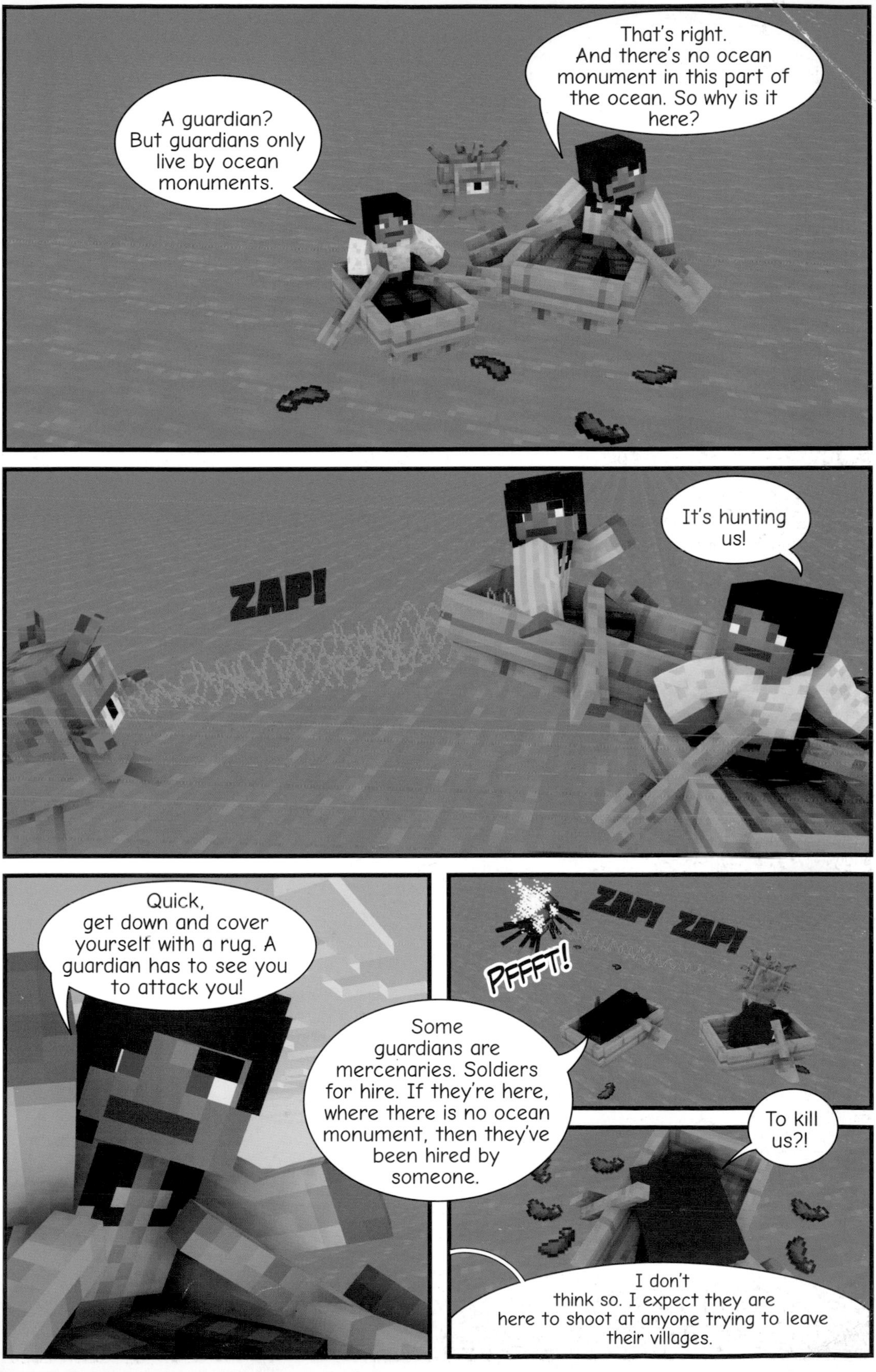
A guardian? But guardians only live by ocean monuments.
That's right. And there's no ocean monument in this part of the ocean. So why is it here?
ZAP!
It's hunting us!
Quick, get down and cover yourself with a rug. A guardian has to see you to attack you!
ZAP! ZAP!
PFFFT!
Some guardians are mercenaries. Soldiers for hire. If they're here, where there is no ocean monument, then they've been hired by someone.
To kill us?!
I don't think so. I expect they are here to shoot at anyone trying to leave their villages.

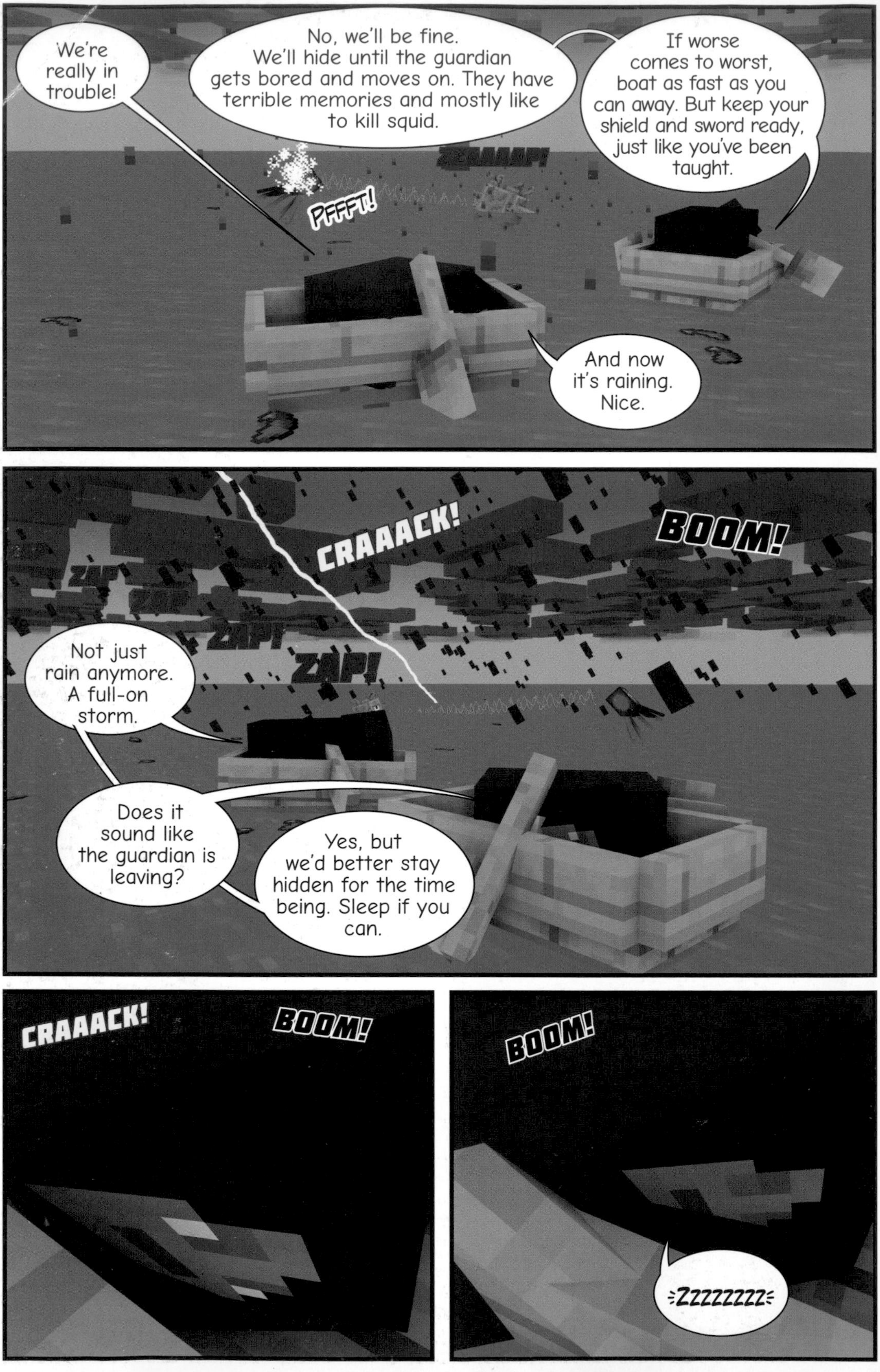

We're really in trouble!
No, we'll be fine. We'll hide until the guardian gets bored and moves on. They have terrible memories and mostly like to kill squid.
If worse comes to worst, boat as fast as you can away. But keep your shield and sword ready, just like you've been taught.
PFFFT!
And now it's raining. Nice.
CRAAACK!
BOOM!
ZAP!
ZAP!
Not just rain anymore. A full-on storm.
Does it sound like the guardian is leaving?
Yes, but we'd better stay hidden for the time being. Sleep if you can.
CRAAACK!
BOOM!
BOOM!
ZZZZZZZZ

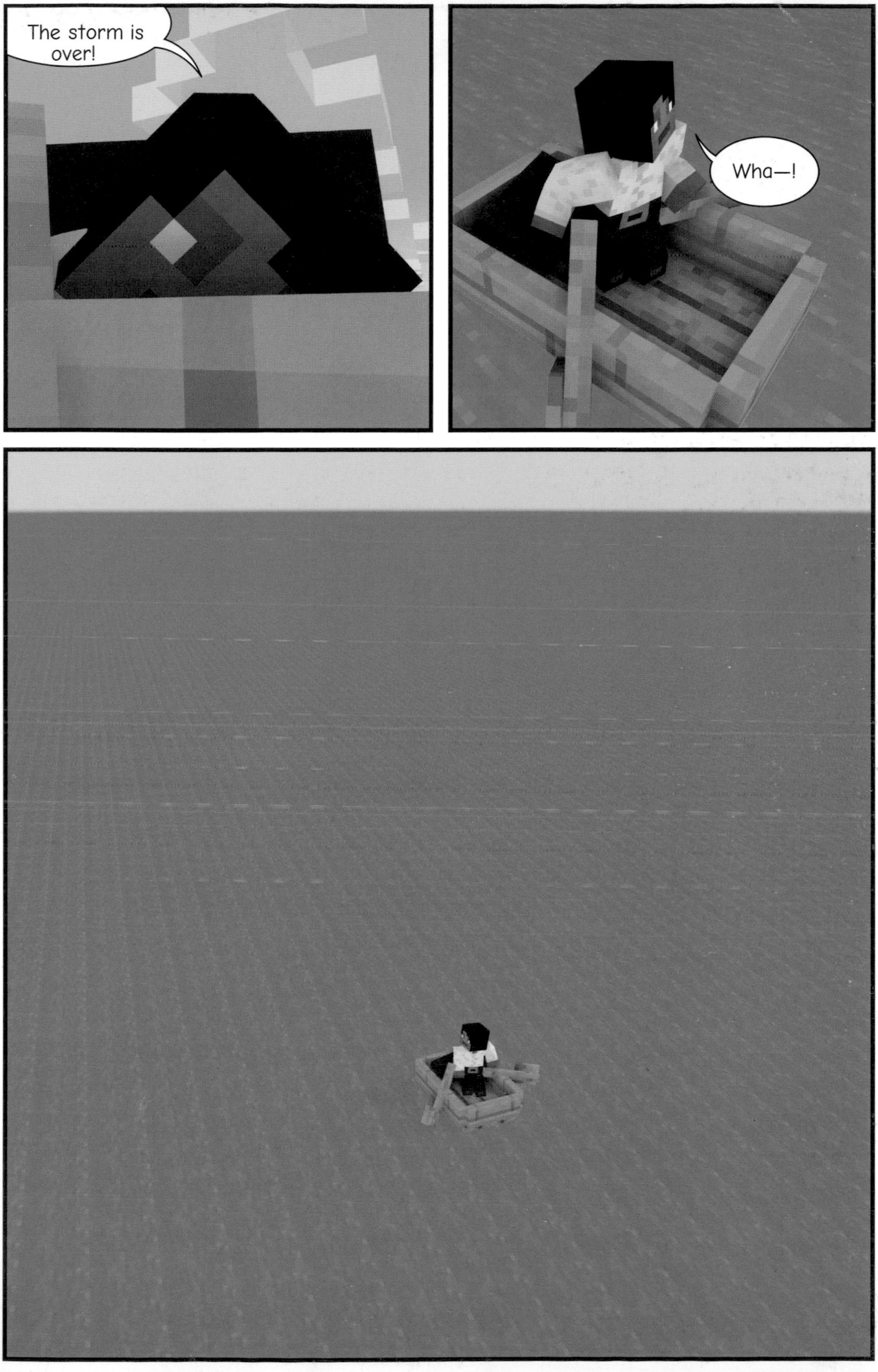
The storm is over!
Wha—!

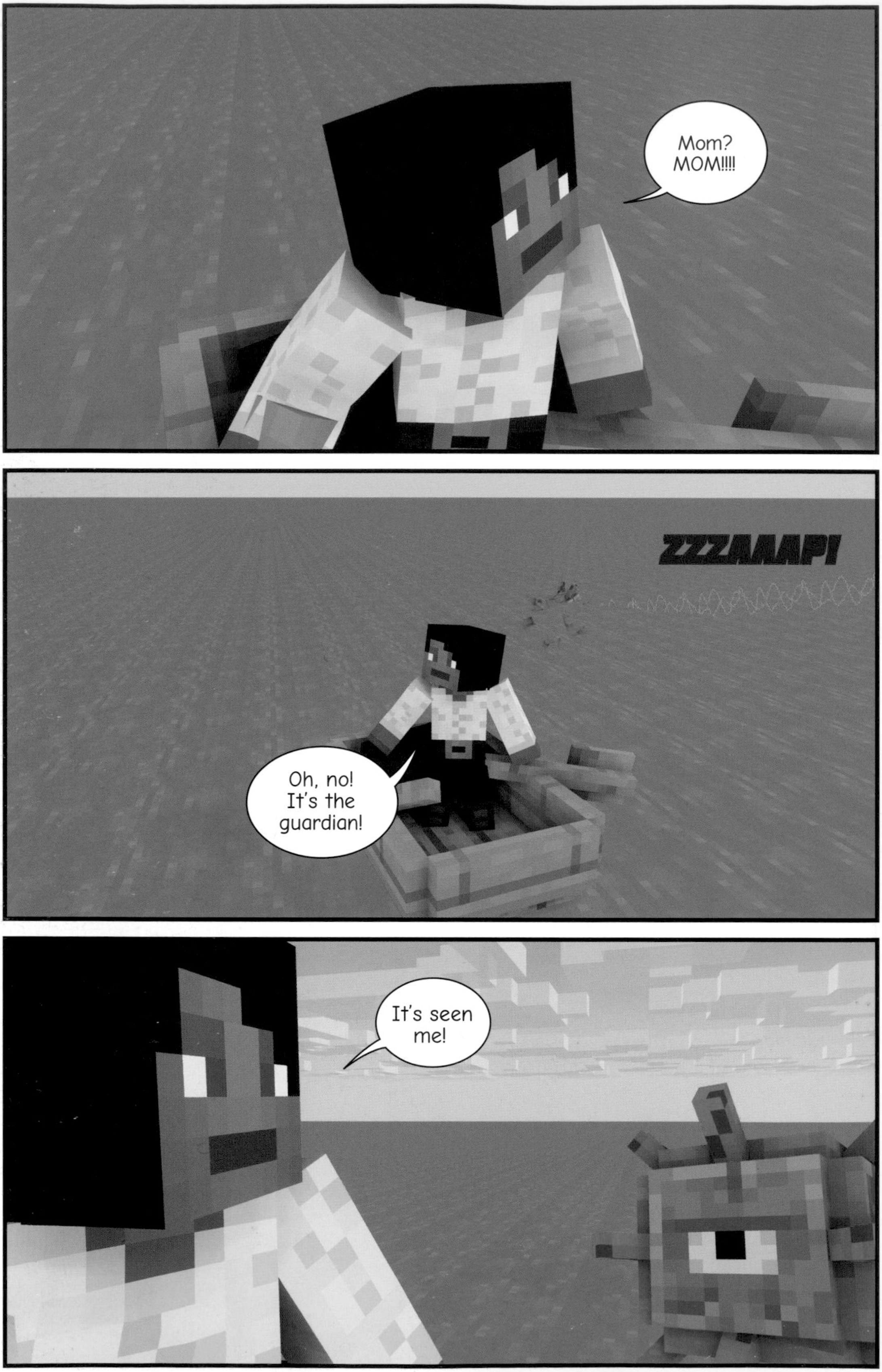
Mom?
MOM!!!!
ZZZAAAP!
Oh, no! It's the guardian!
It's seen me!

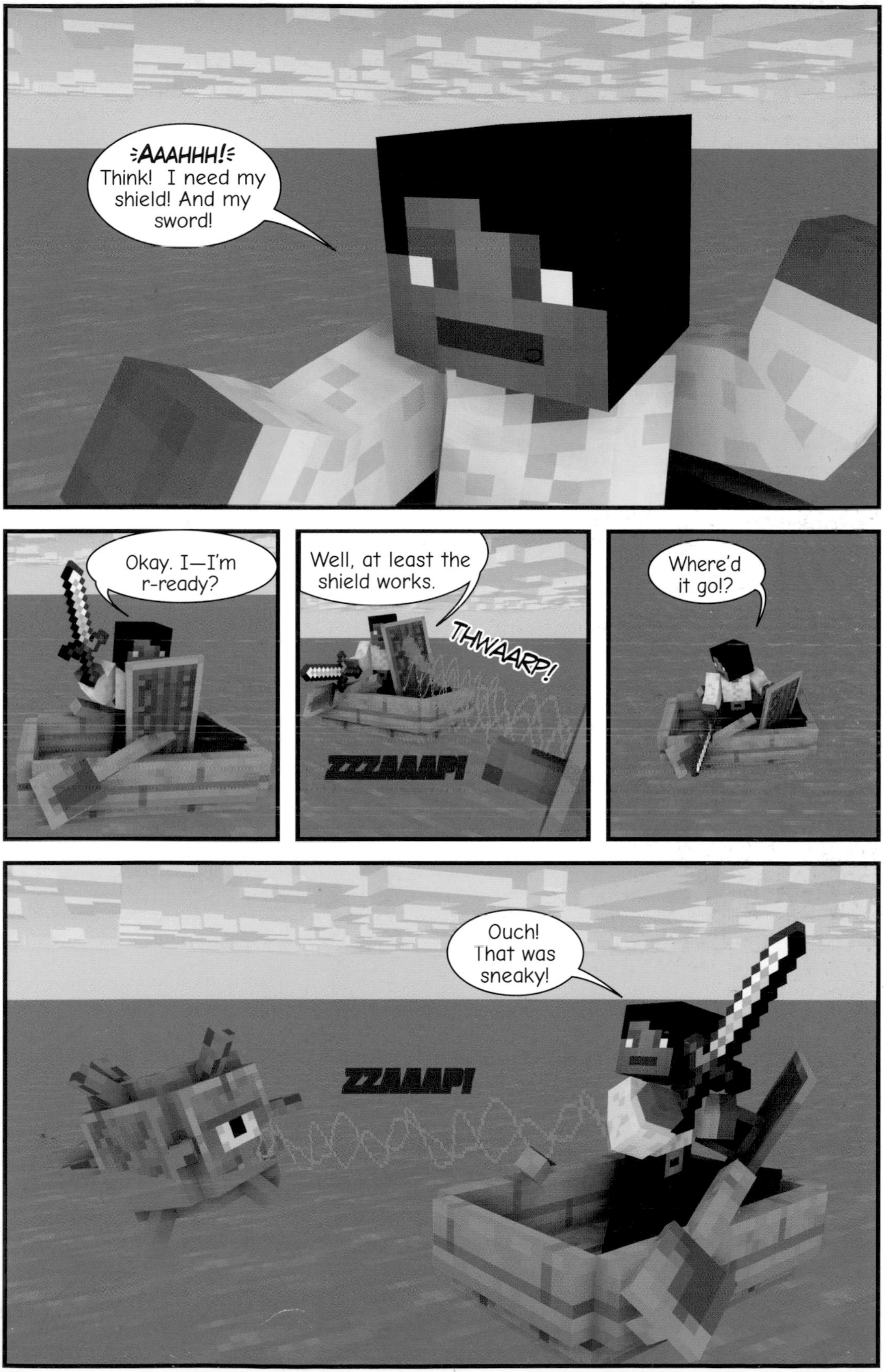
AAAHHH!
Think! I need my shield! And my sword!
Okay. I—I'm r-ready?
Well, at least the shield works.
THWAARP!
ZZZAAAAP!
Where'd it go!?
Ouch! That was sneaky!
ZZAAAP!

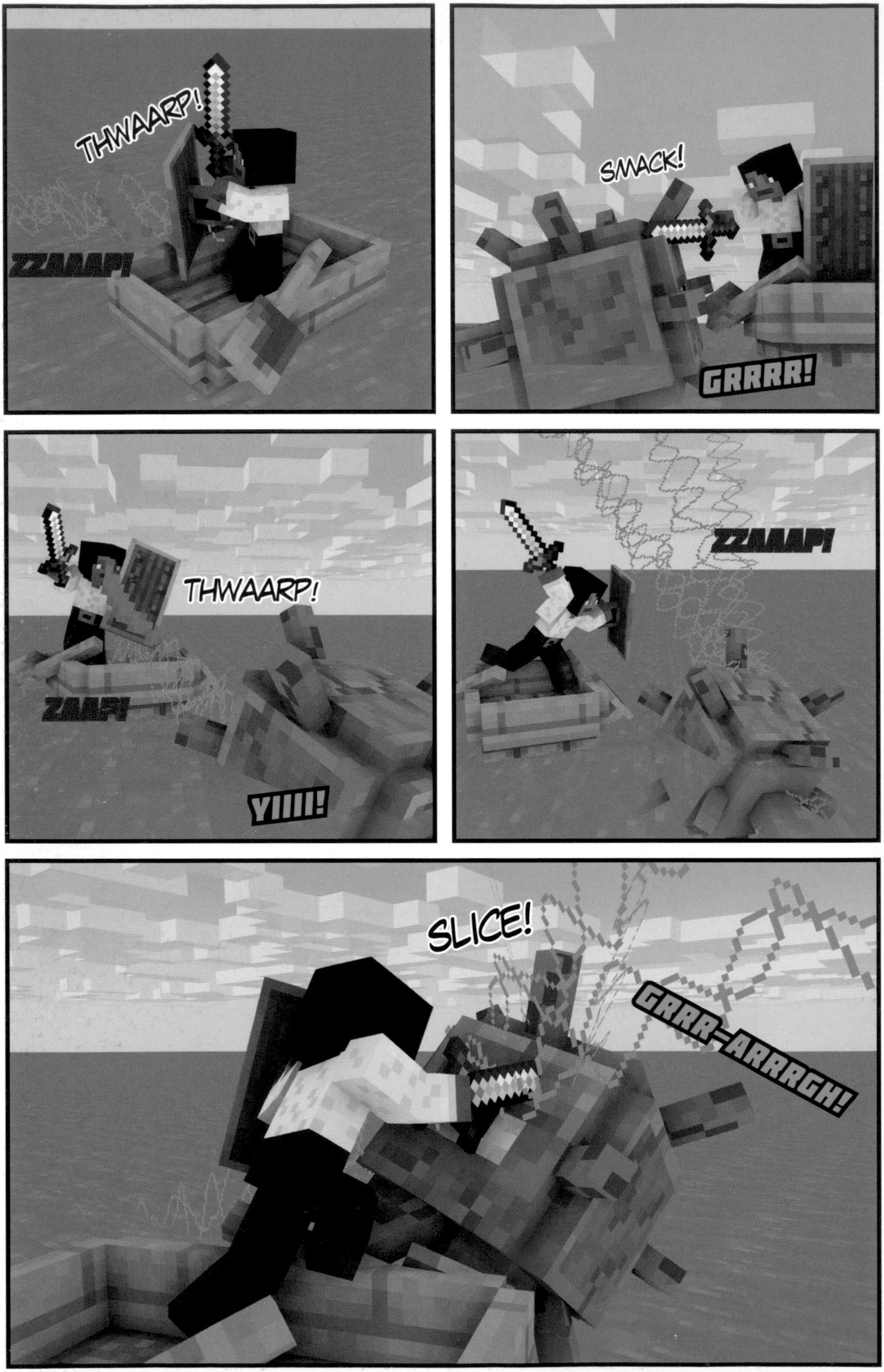
THWAARP!
ZZAAAP!
SMACK!
GRRRR!
THWAARP!
ZAAP!
YIIII!
ZZAAAP!
SLICE!
GRRR-ARRRGH!

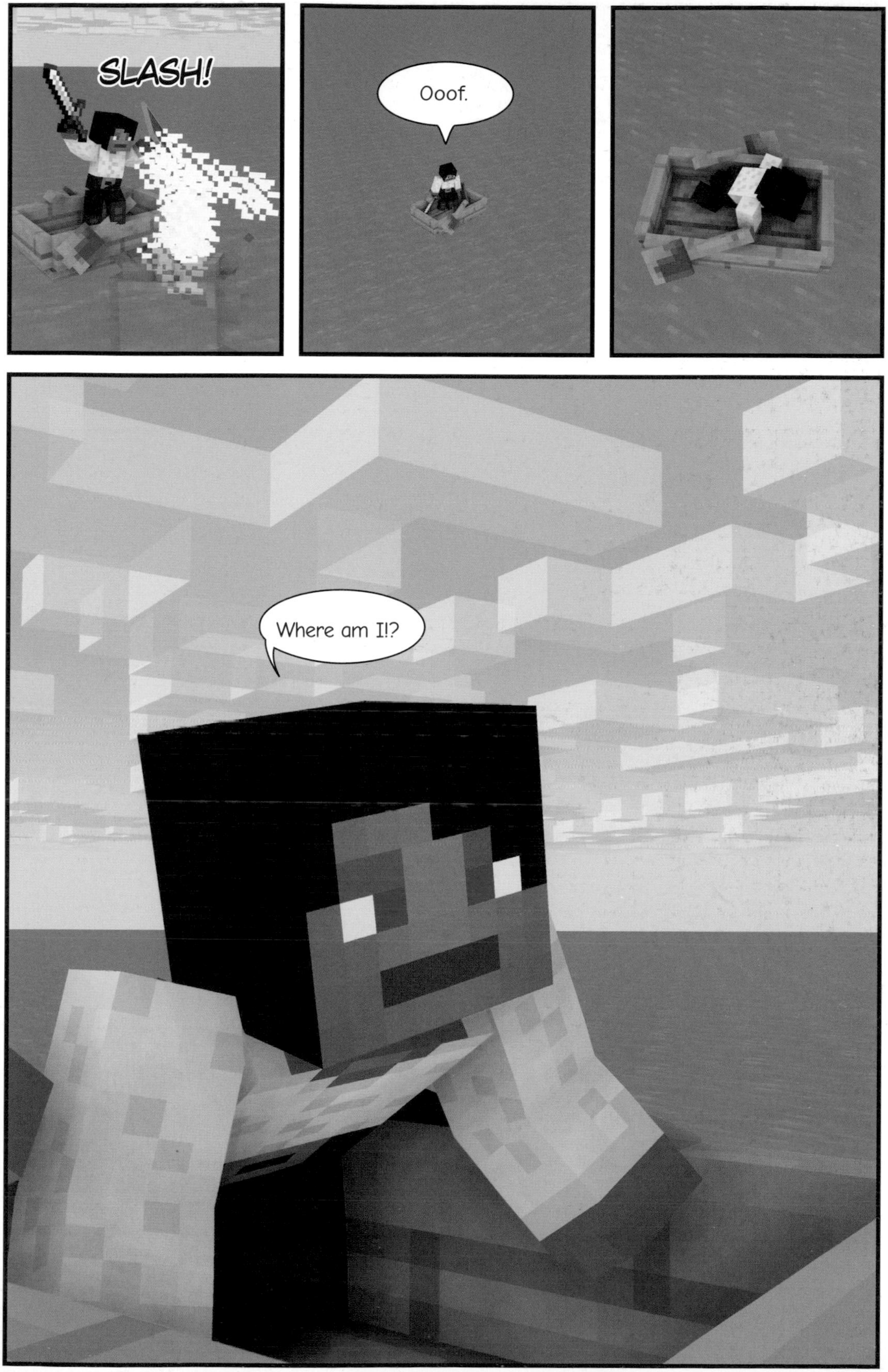
SLASH!
Ooof.
Where am I!?

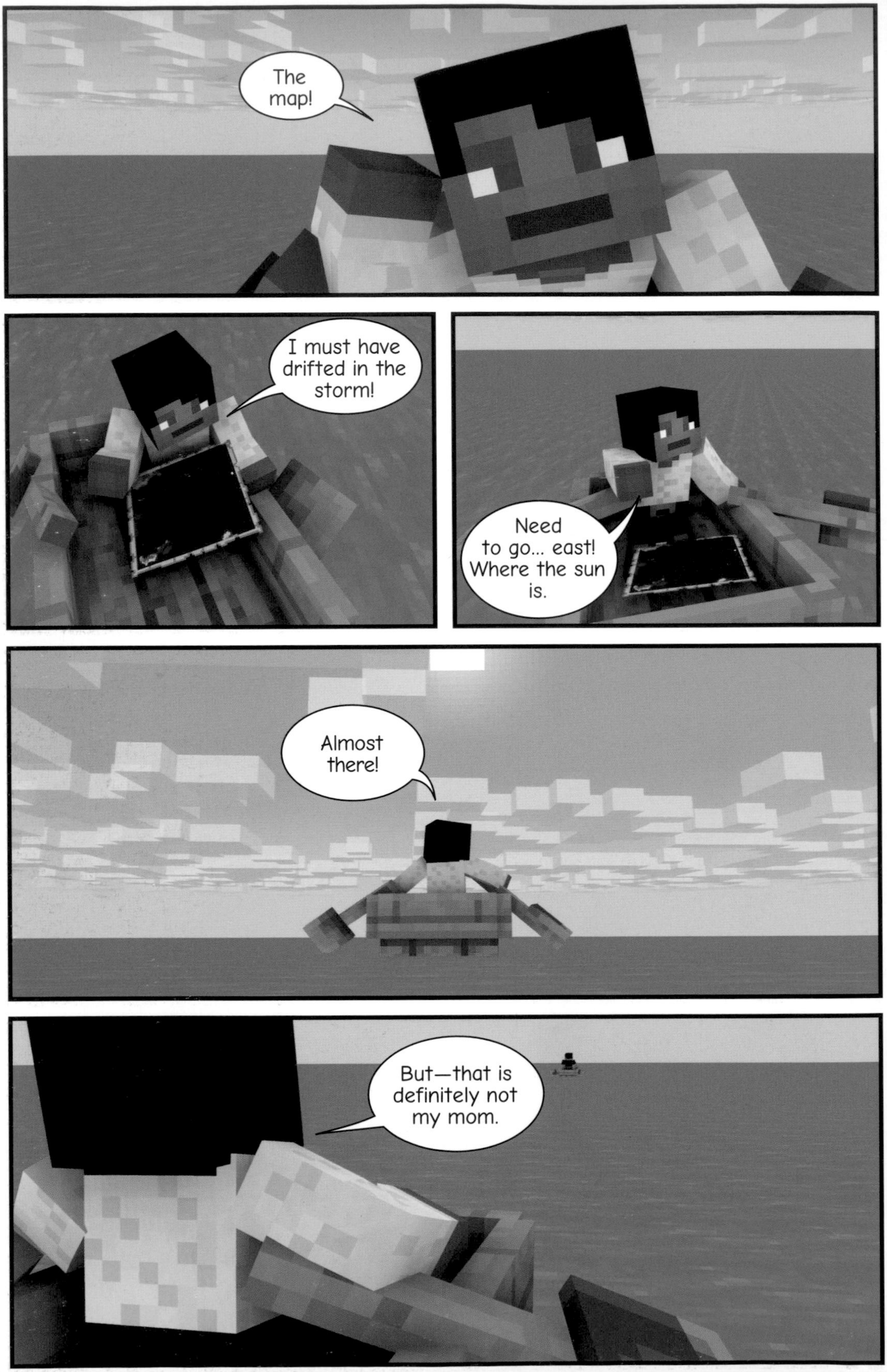
The map!
I must have drifted in the storm!
Need to go... east! Where the sun is.
Almost there!
But—that is definitely not my mom.

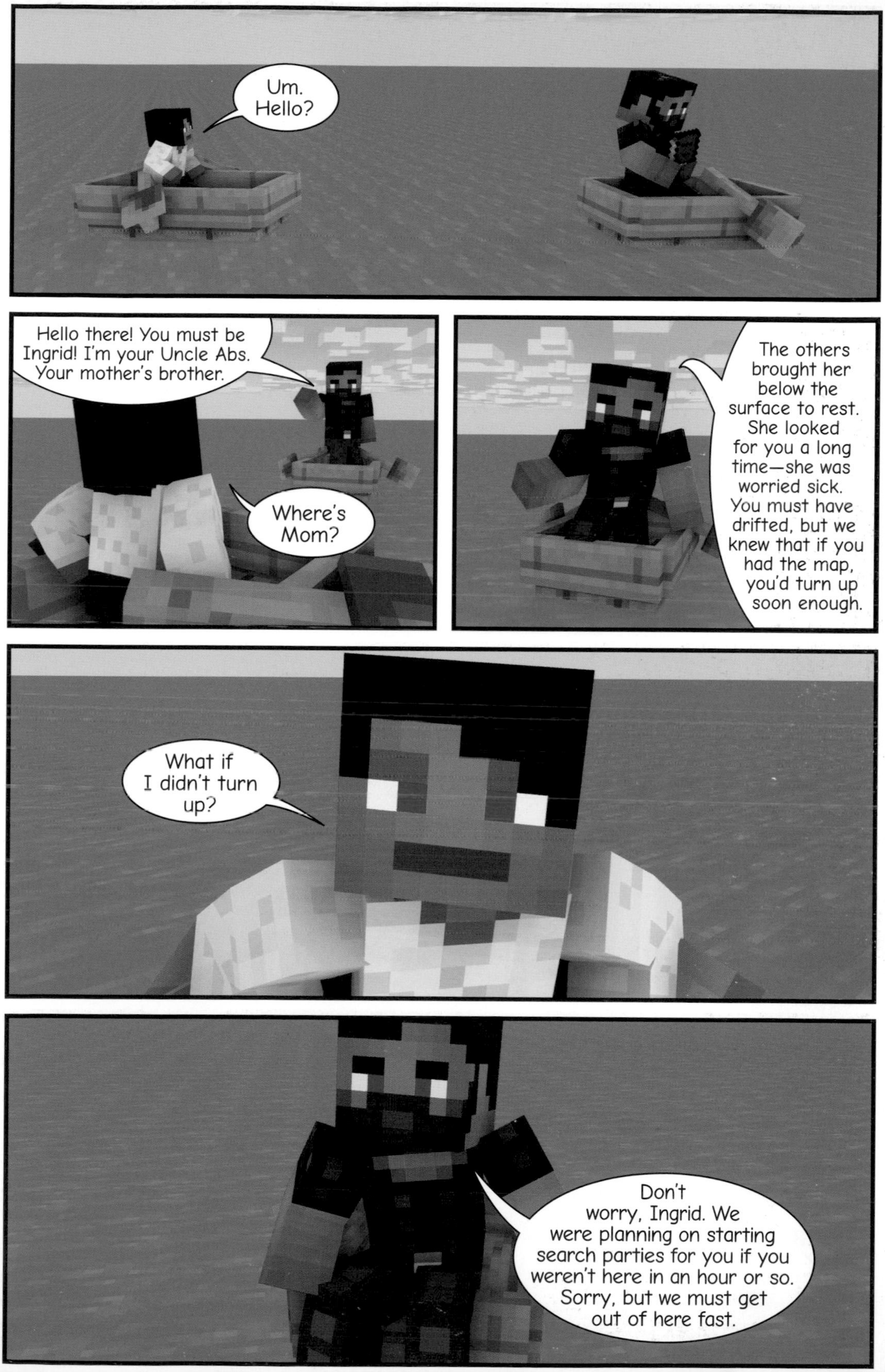
Um. Hello?
Hello there! You must be Ingrid! I'm your Uncle Abs. Your mother's brother.
Where's Mom?
The others brought her below the surface to rest. She looked for you a long time—she was worried sick. You must have drifted, but we knew that if you had the map, you'd turn up soon enough.
What if I didn't turn up?
Don't worry, Ingrid. We were planning on starting search parties for you if you weren't here in an hour or so. Sorry, but we must get out of here fast.

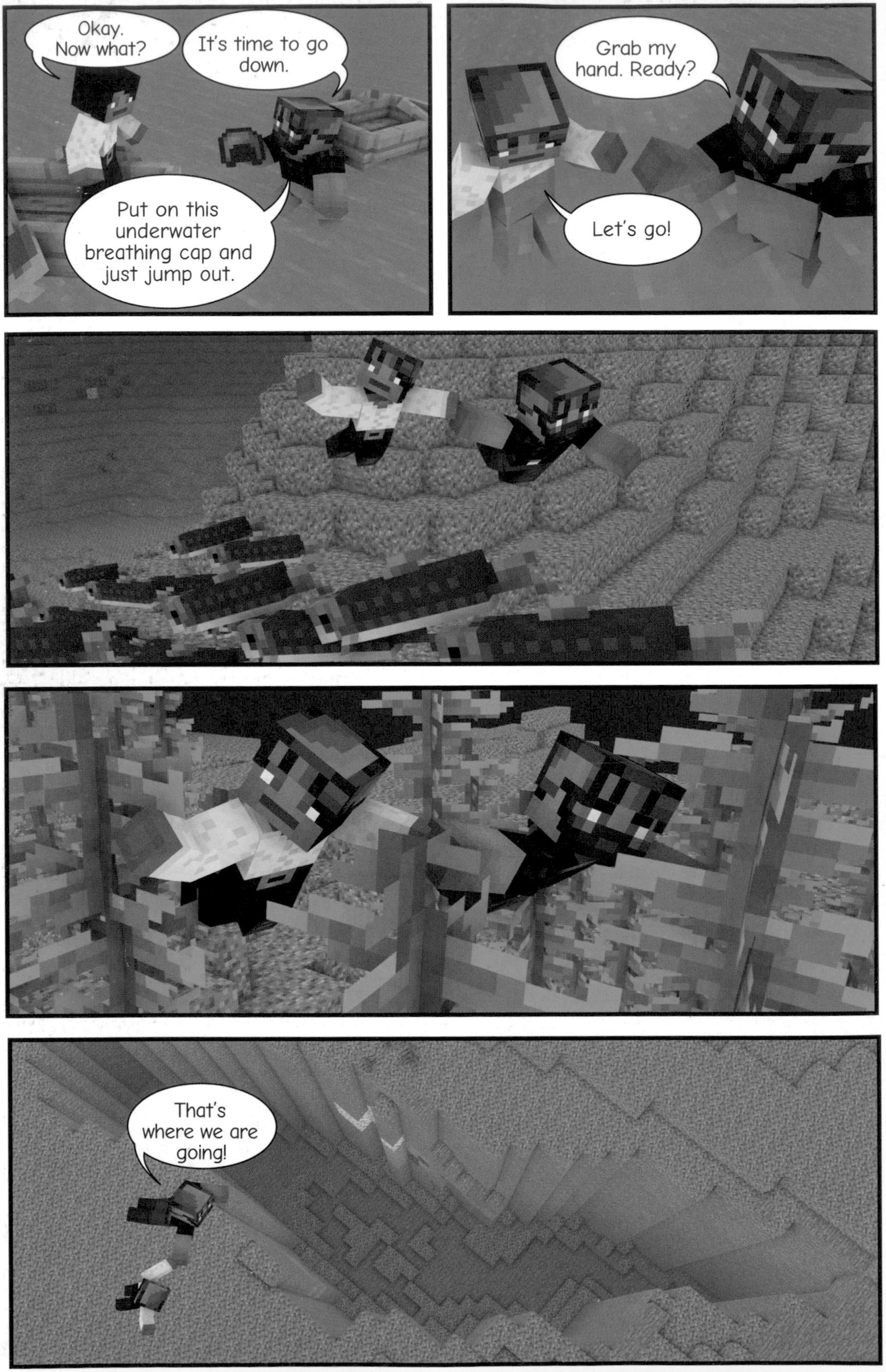
Okay. Now what?
It's time to go down.
Put on this underwater breathing cap and just jump out.
Grab my hand. Ready?
Let's go!
That's where we are going!

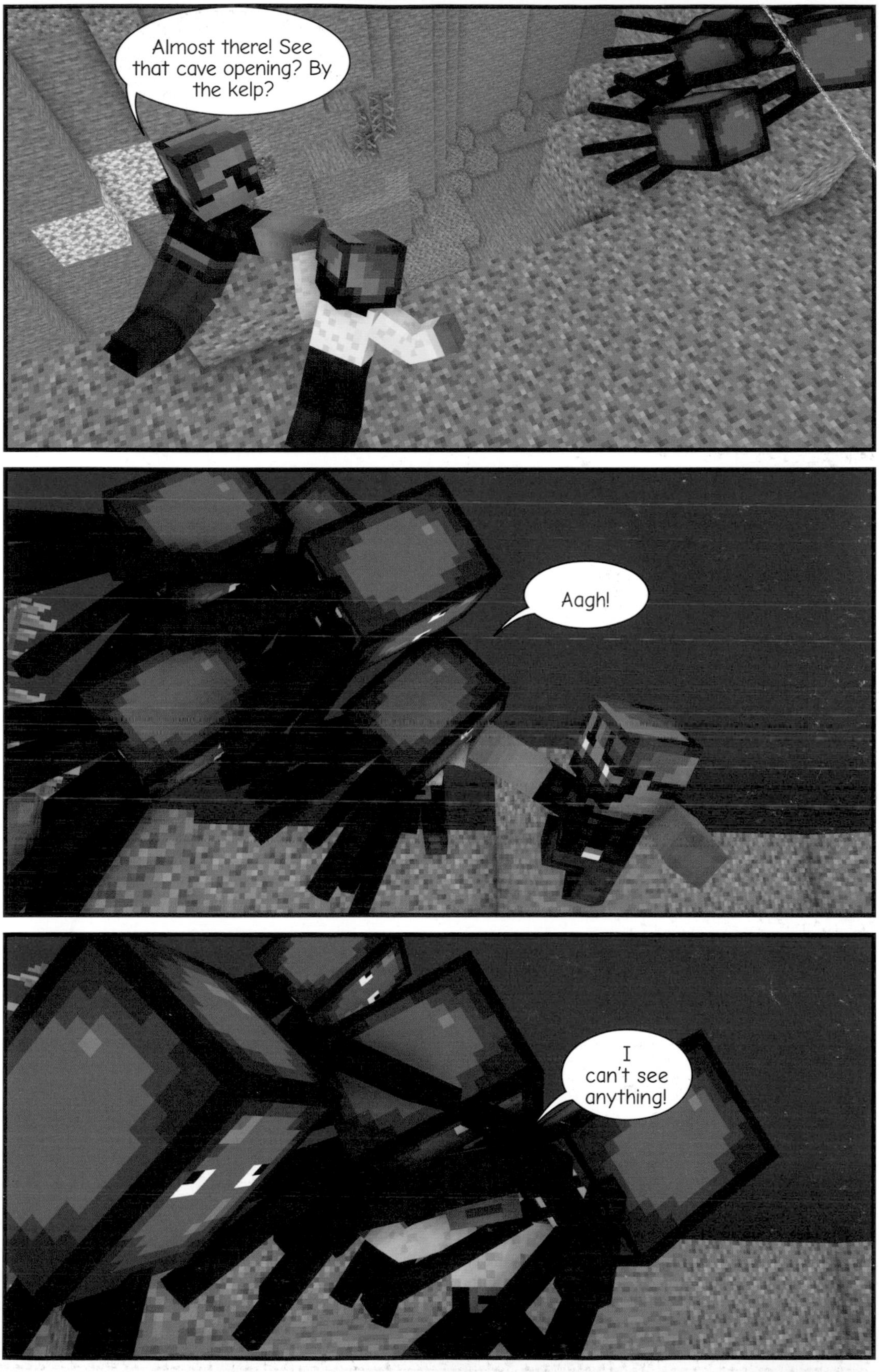
Almost there! See that cave opening? By the kelp?
Aagh!
I can't see anything!

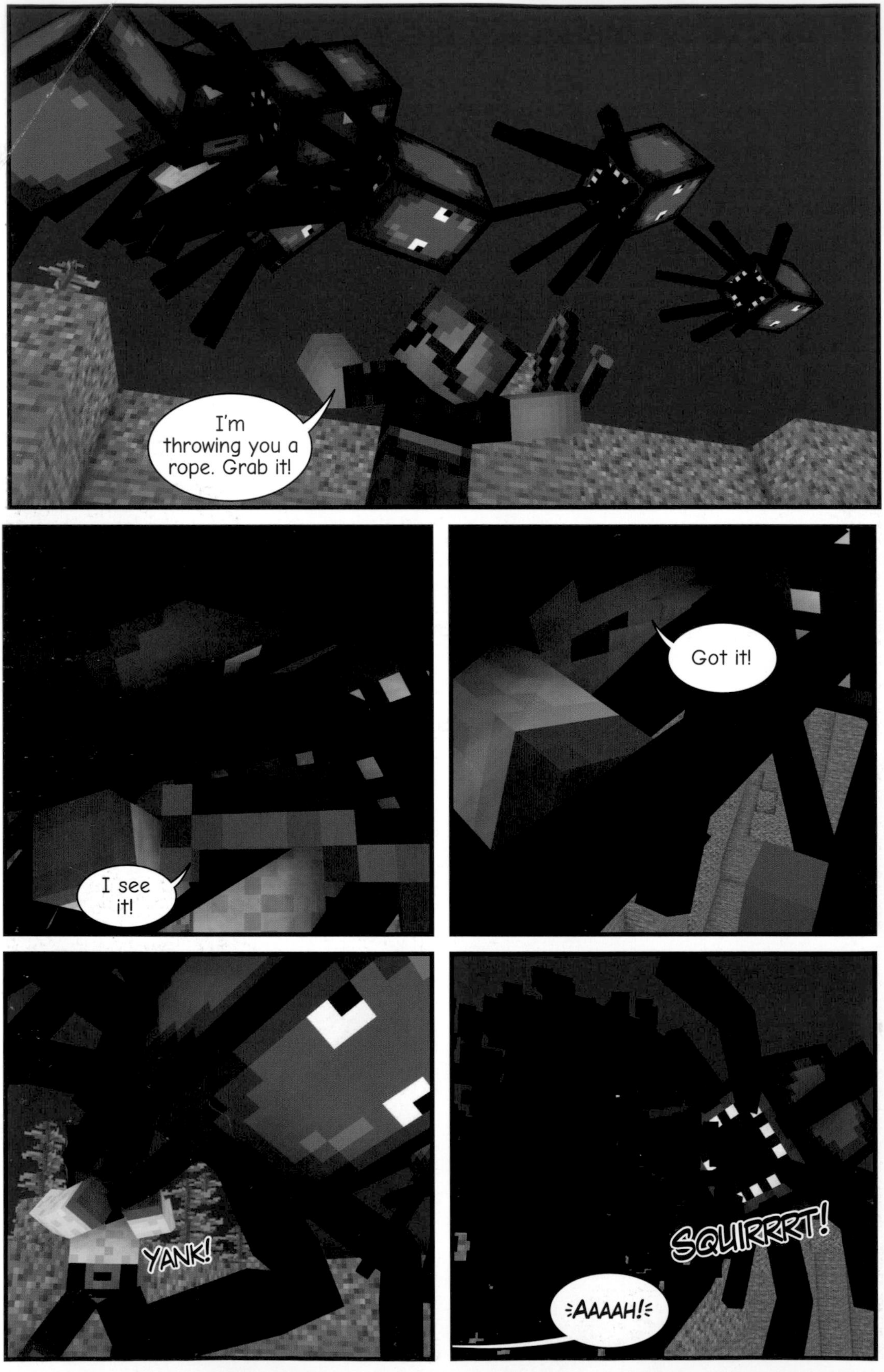
I'm throwing you a rope. Grab it!
I see it!
Got it!
YANK!
SQUIRRRT!
AAAAH!

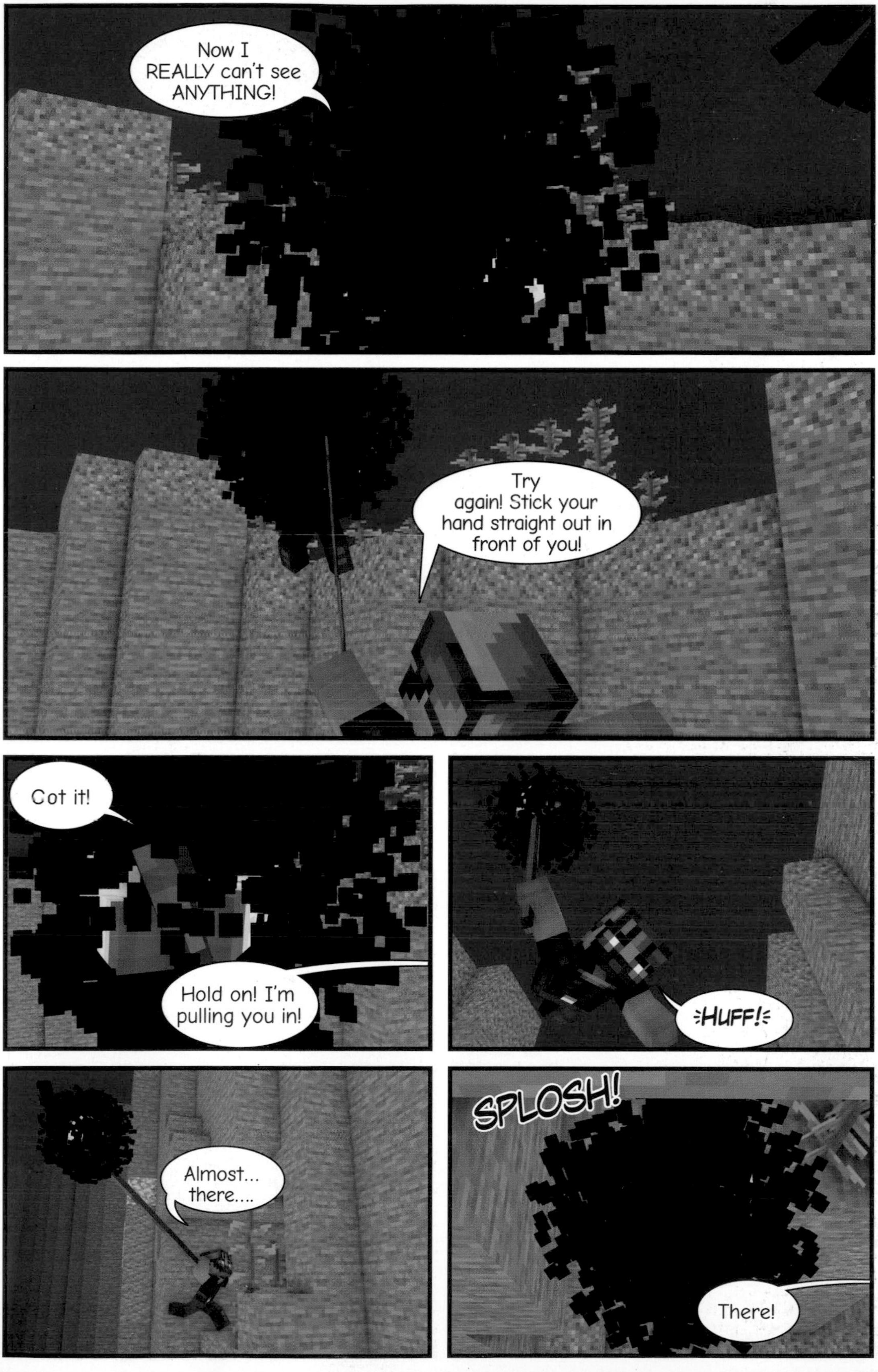
Now I REALLY can't see ANYTHING!
Try again! Stick your hand straight out in front of you!
Cot it!
Hold on! I'm pulling you in!
HUFF!
Almost... there....
SPLOSH!
There!

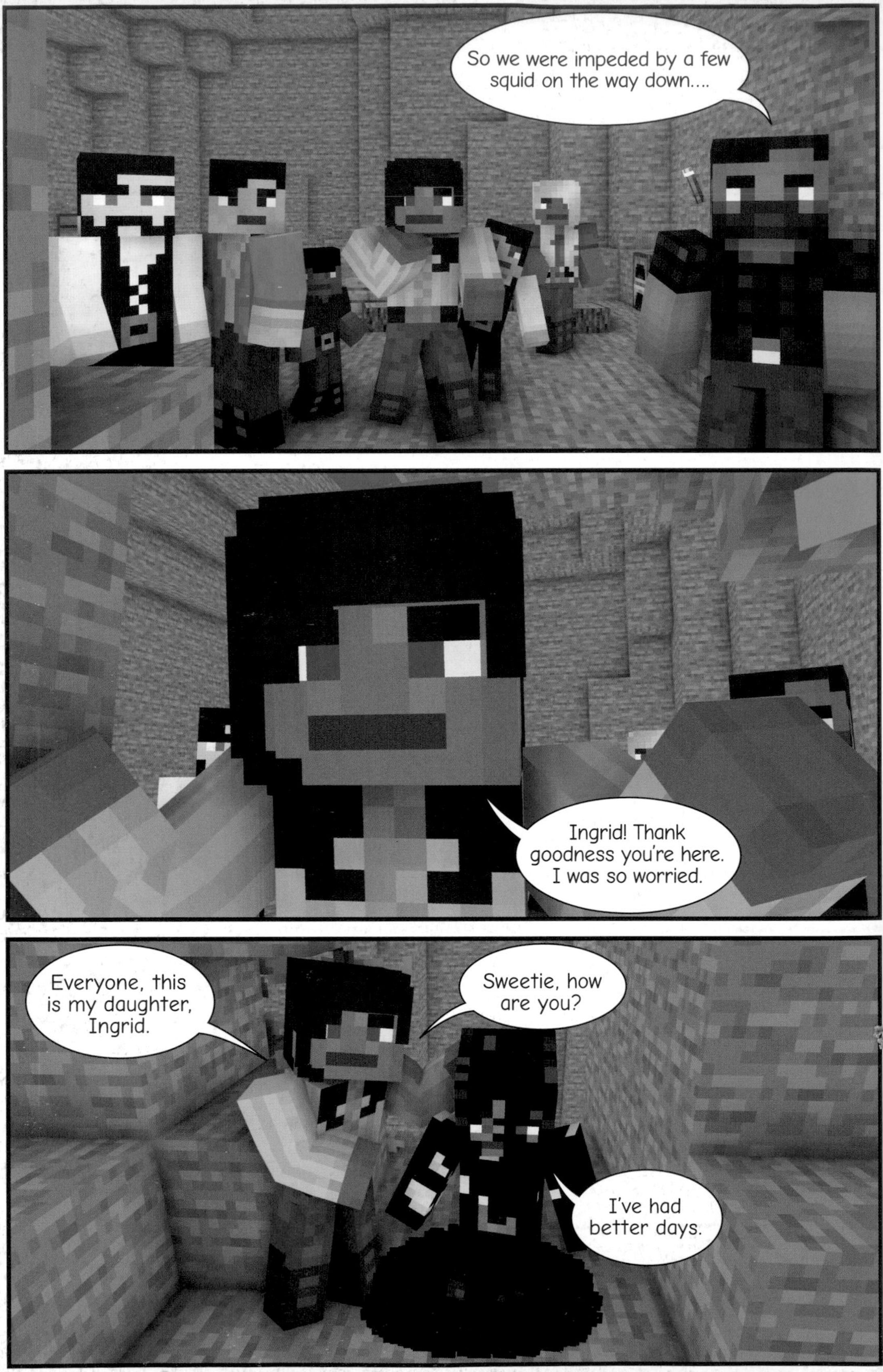
So we were impeded by a few squid on the way down....
Ingrid! Thank goodness you're here. I was so worried.
Everyone, this is my daughter, Ingrid.
Sweetie, how are you?
I've had better days.

Chapter 2
The Ocean Dwellers

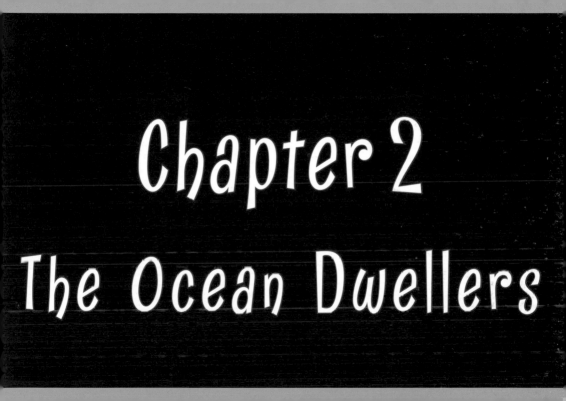

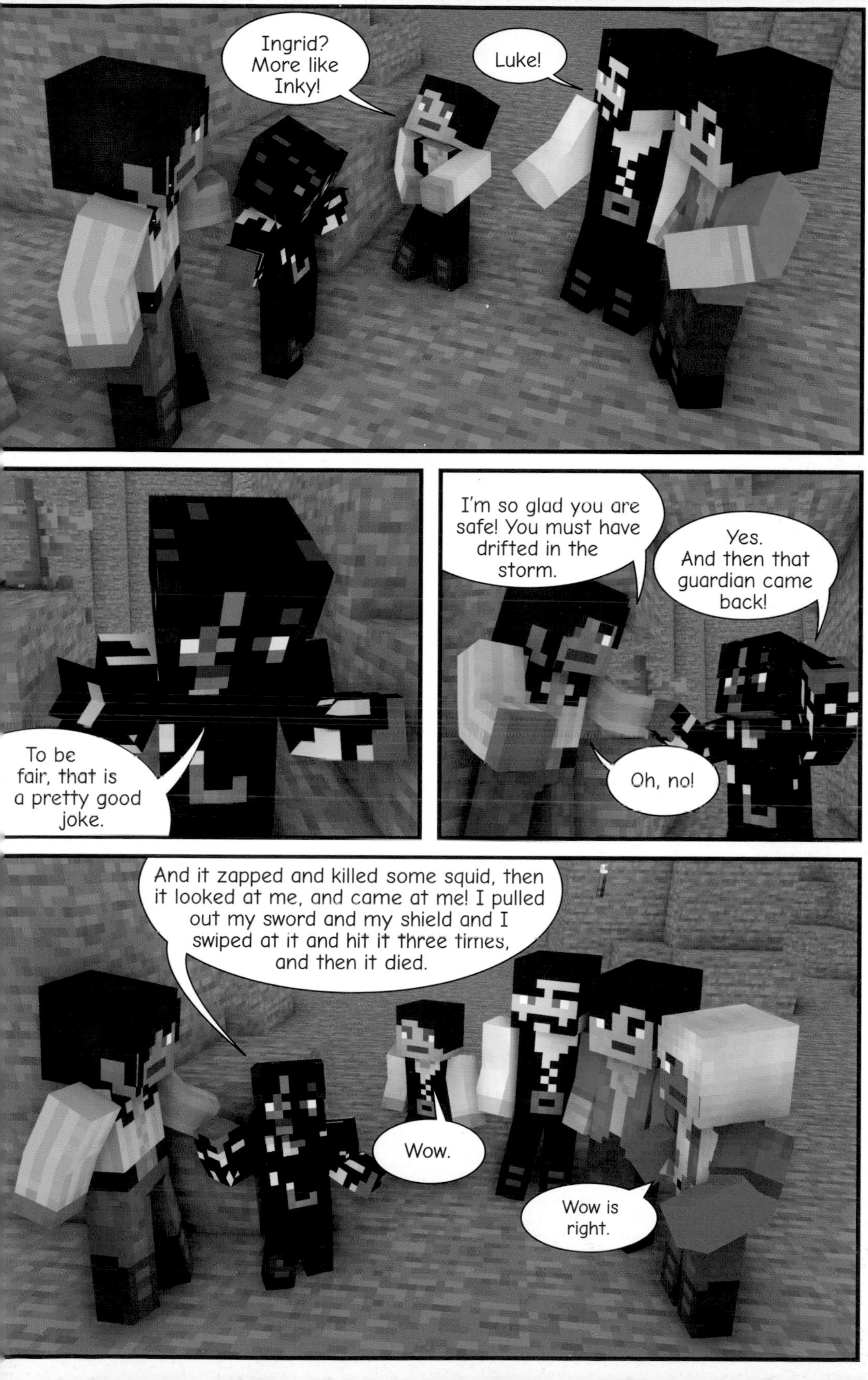
Ingrid? More like Inky!
Luke!
To be fair, that is a pretty good joke.
I'm so glad you are safe! You must have drifted in the storm.
Yes. And then that guardian came back!
Oh, no!
And it zapped and killed some squid, then it looked at me, and came at me! I pulled out my sword and my shield and I swiped at it and hit it three times, and then it died.
Wow.
Wow is right.

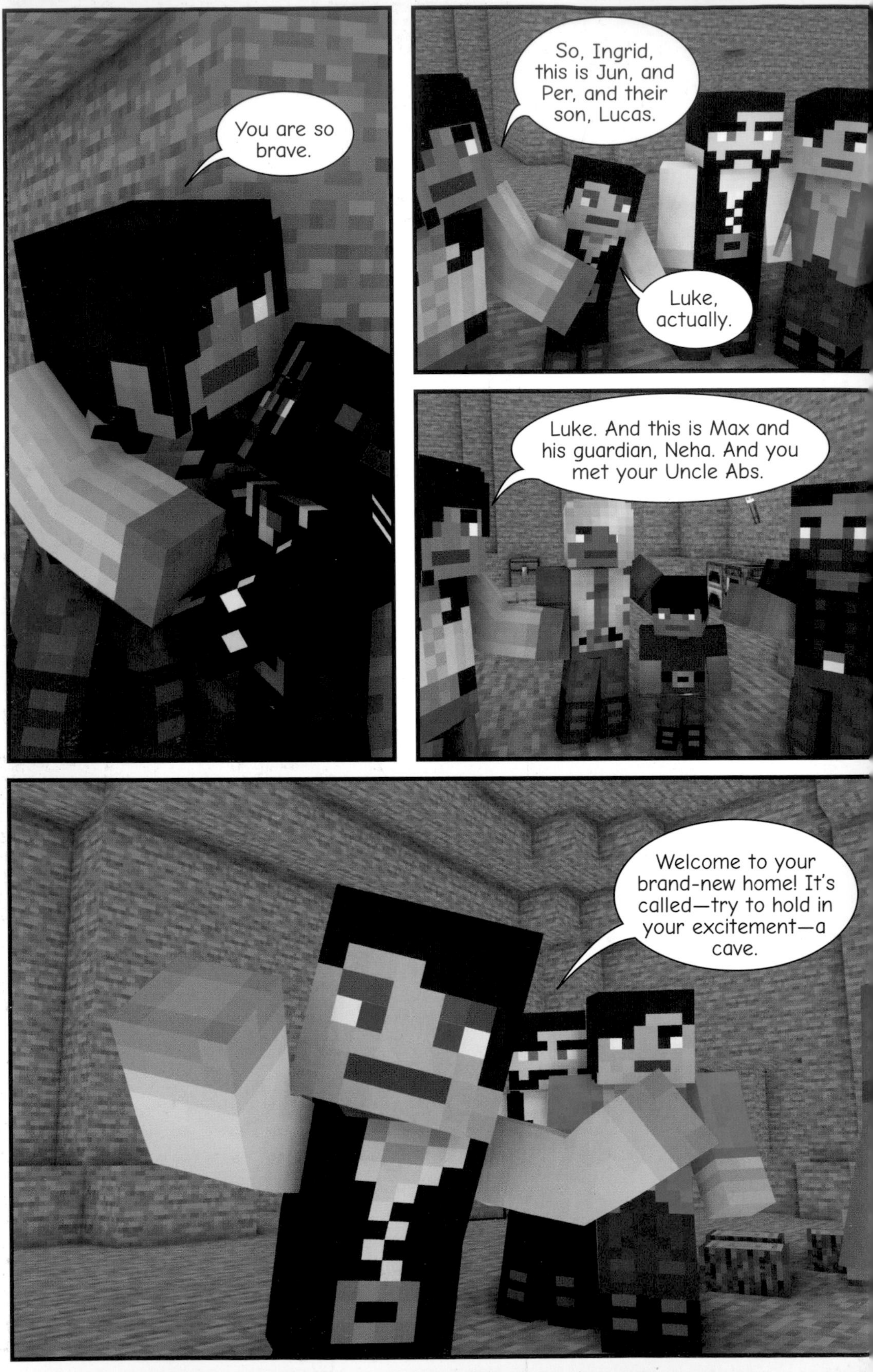
You are so brave.
So, Ingrid, this is Jun, and Per, and their son, Lucas.
Luke, actually.
Luke. And this is Max and his guardian, Neha. And you met your Uncle Abs.
Welcome to your brand-new home! It's called—try to hold in your excitement—a cave.

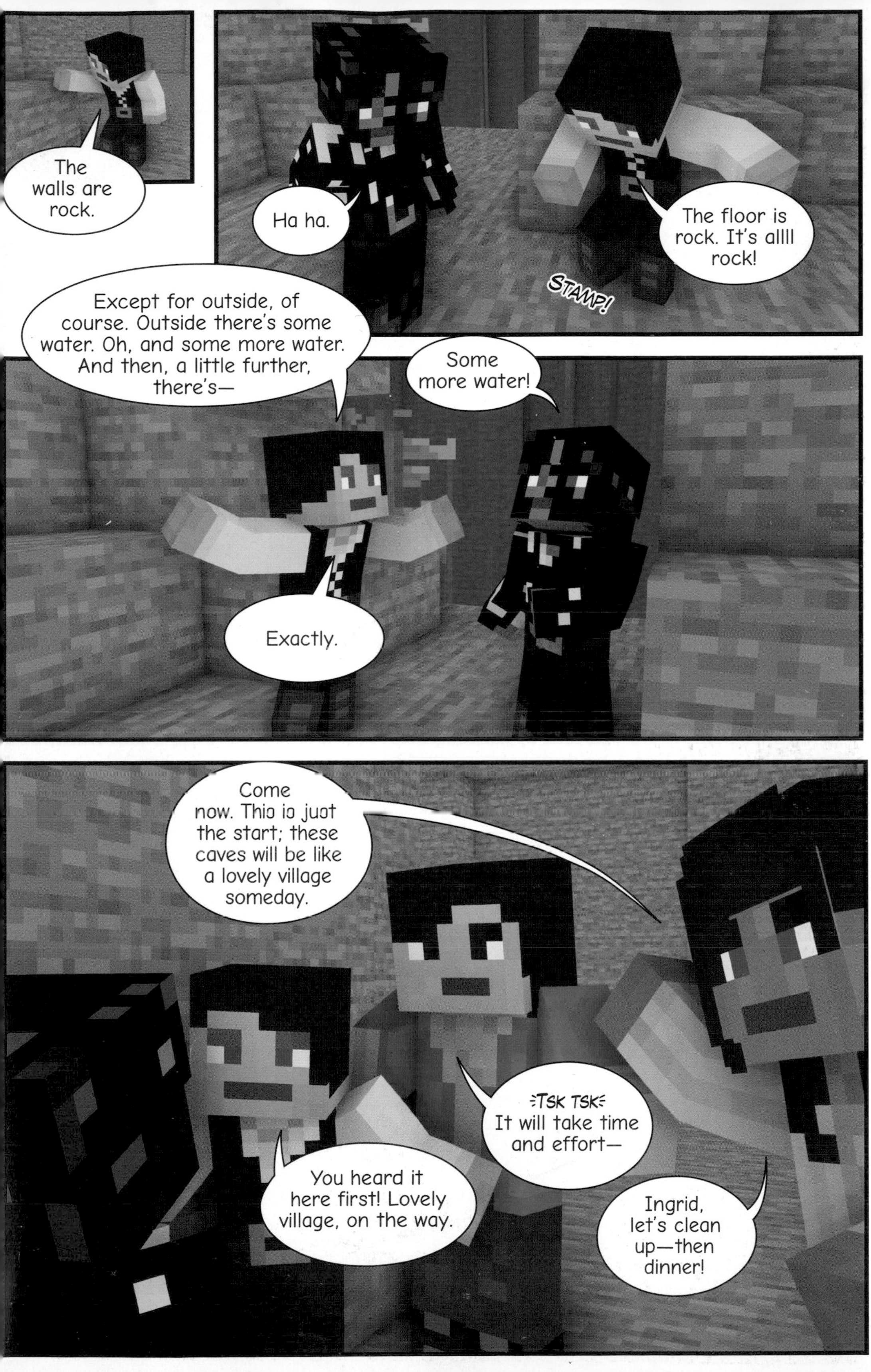
The walls are rock.
Ha ha.
The floor is rock. It's allll rock!
STAMP!
Except for outside, of course. Outside there's some water. Oh, and some more water. And then, a little further, there's—
Some more water!
Exactly.
Come now. Thio io juot the start; these caves will be like a lovely village someday.
TSK TSK
It will take time and effort—
You heard it here first! Lovely village, on the way.
Ingrid, let's clean up—then dinner!

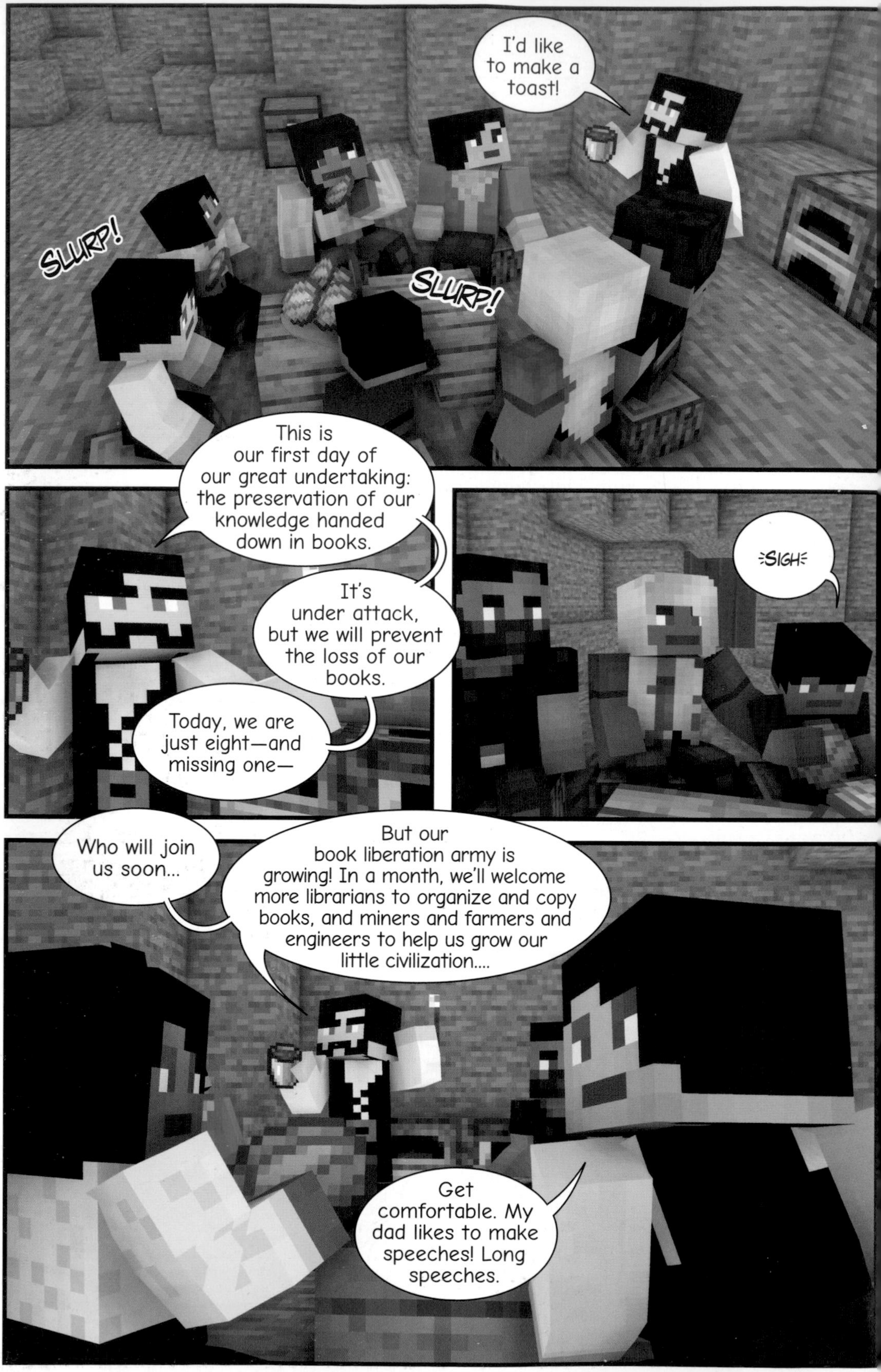
I'd like to make a toast!
SLURP!
SLURP!
This is our first day of our great undertaking: the preservation of our knowledge handed down in books.
It's under attack, but we will prevent the loss of our books.
Today, we are just eight—and missing one—
SIGH
Who will join us soon...
But our book liberation army is growing! In a month, we'll welcome more librarians to organize and copy books, and miners and farmers and engineers to help us grow our little civilization....
Get comfortable. My dad likes to make speeches! Long speeches.

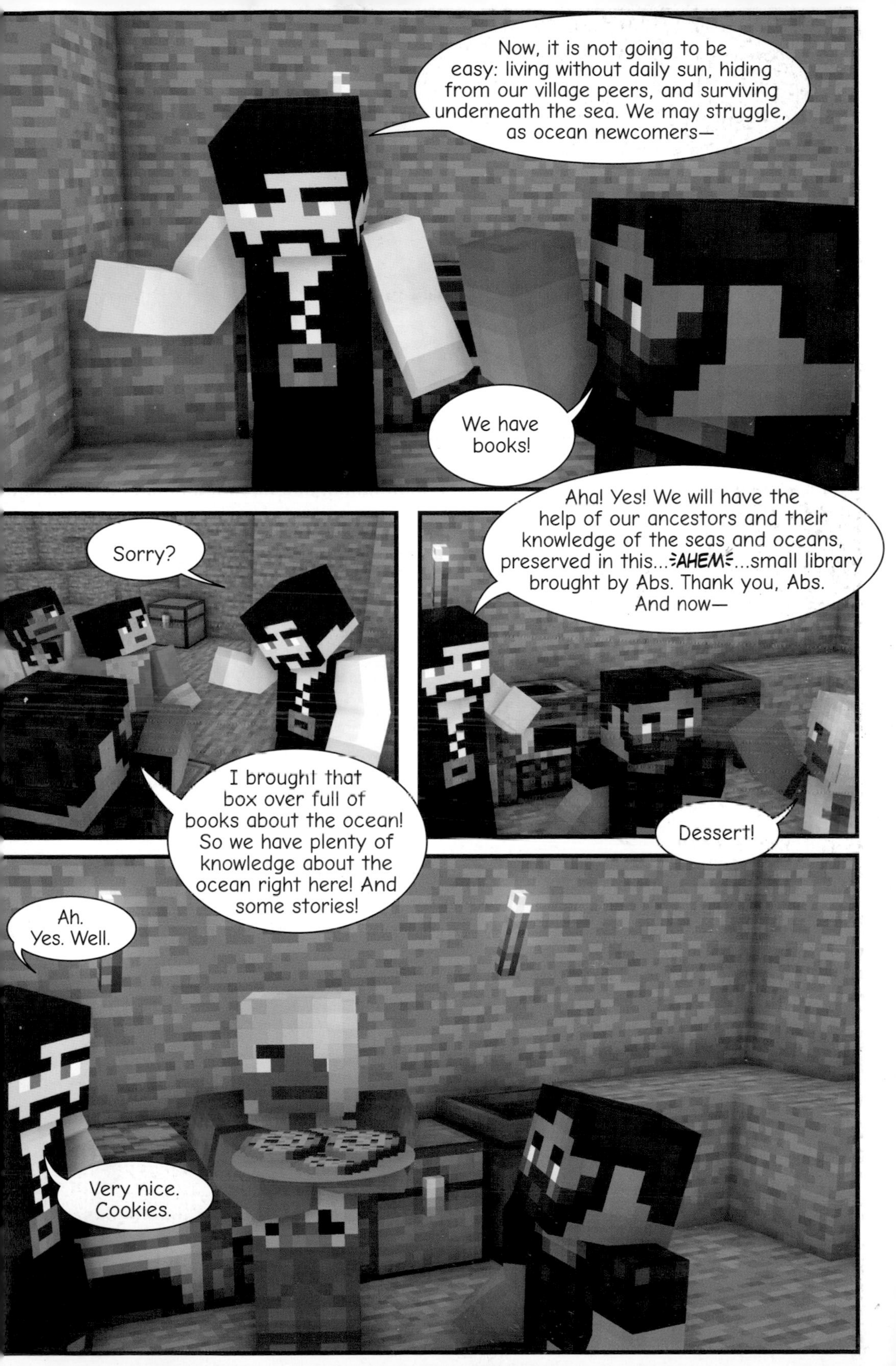
Now, it is not going to be easy: living without daily sun, hiding from our village peers, and surviving underneath the sea. We may struggle, as ocean newcomers—
We have books!
Sorry?
I brought that box over full of books about the ocean! So we have plenty of knowledge about the ocean right here! And some stories!
Aha! Yes! We will have the help of our ancestors and their knowledge of the seas and oceans, preserved in this... AHEM ...small library brought by Abs. Thank you, Abs. And now—
Dessert!
Ah. Yes. Well.
Very nice. Cookies.

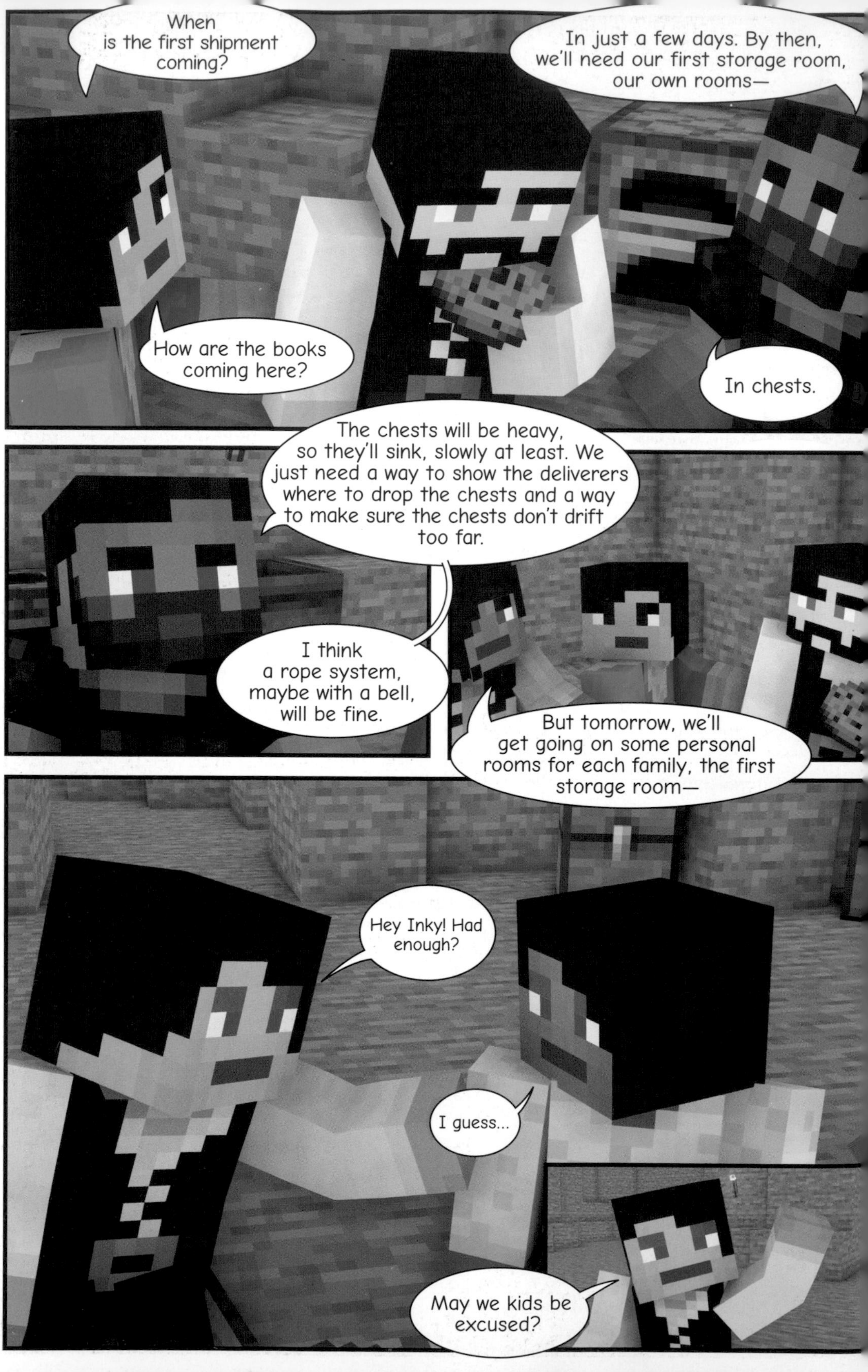
When is the first shipment coming?
In just a few days. By then, we'll need our first storage room, our own rooms—
How are the books coming here?
In chests.
The chests will be heavy, so they'll sink, slowly at least. We just need a way to show the deliverers where to drop the chests and a way to make sure the chests don't drift too far.
I think a rope system, maybe with a bell, will be fine.
But tomorrow, we'll get going on some personal rooms for each family, the first storage room—
Hey Inky! Had enough?
I guess...
May we kids be excused?

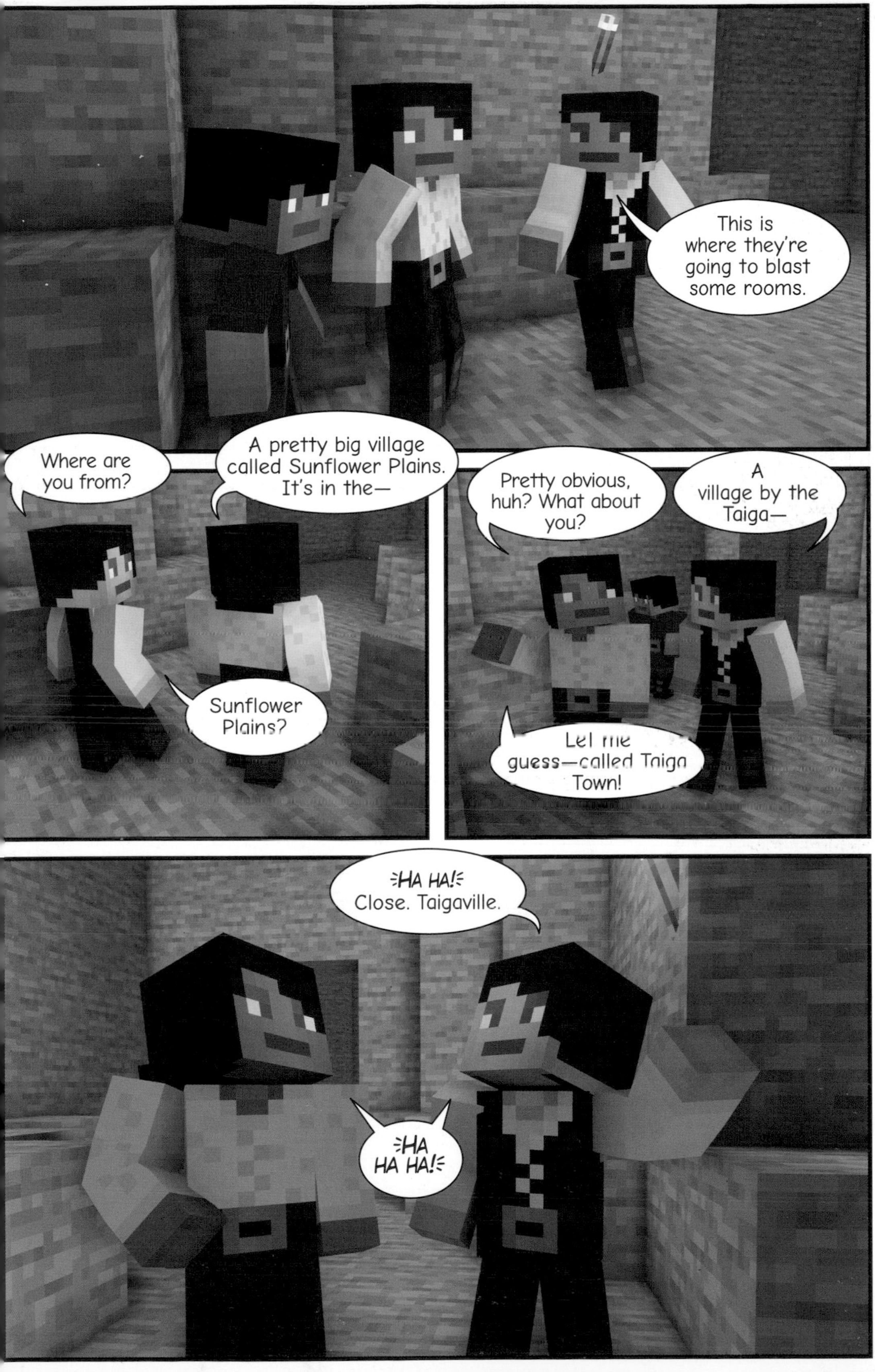
This is where they're going to blast some rooms.
Where are you from?
A pretty big village called Sunflower Plains. It's in the—
Sunflower Plains?
Pretty obvious, huh? What about you?
A village by the Taiga—
Let me guess—called Taiga Town!
HA HA! Close. Taigaville.
HA HA HA!

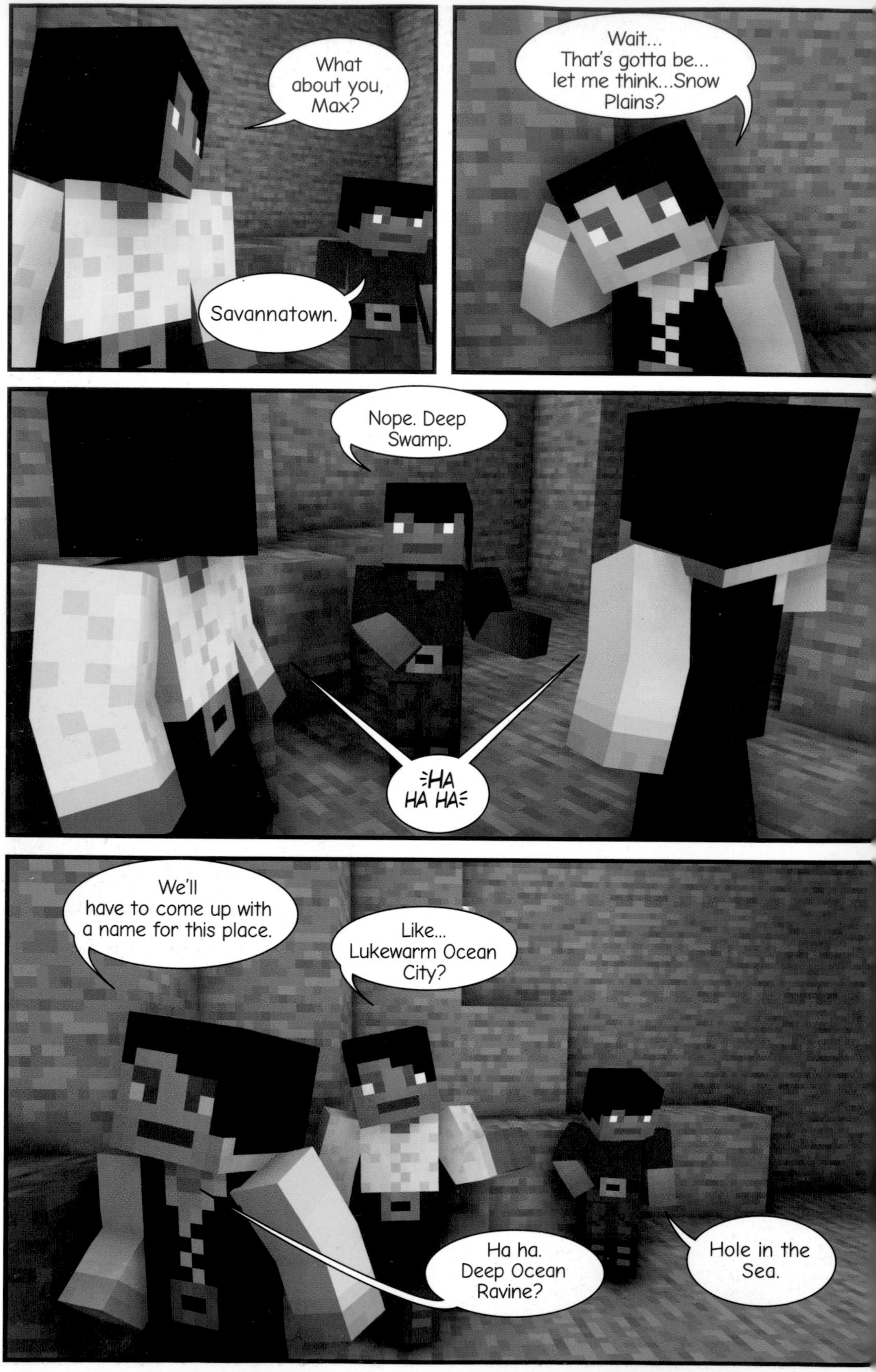
What about you, Max?
Savannatown.
Wait... That's gotta be... let me think...Snow Plains?
Nope. Deep Swamp.
HA HA HA
We'll have to come up with a name for this place.
Like... Lukewarm Ocean City?
Ha ha. Deep Ocean Ravine?
Hole in the Sea.

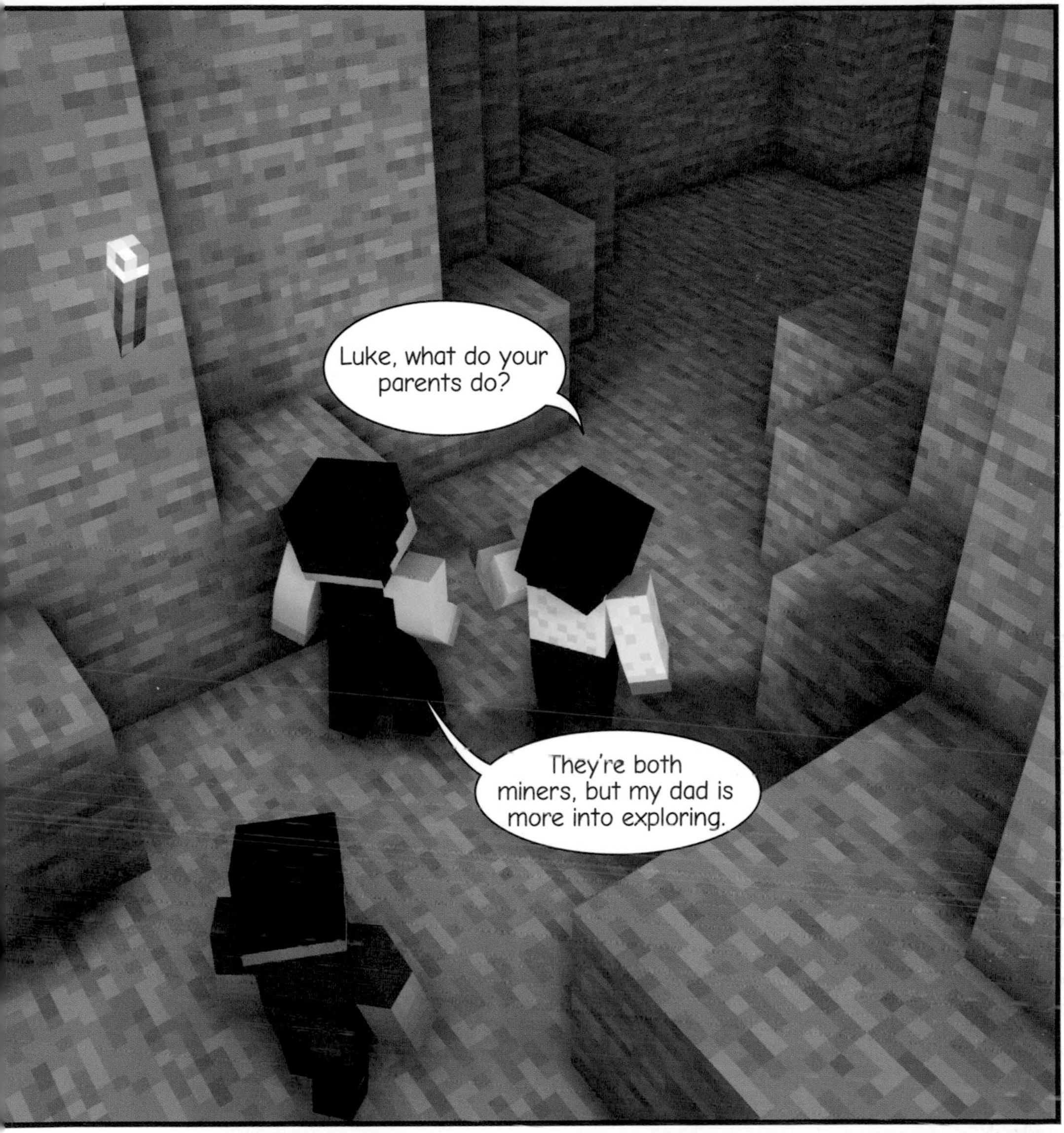
Luke, what do your parents do?
They're both miners, but my dad is more into exploring.

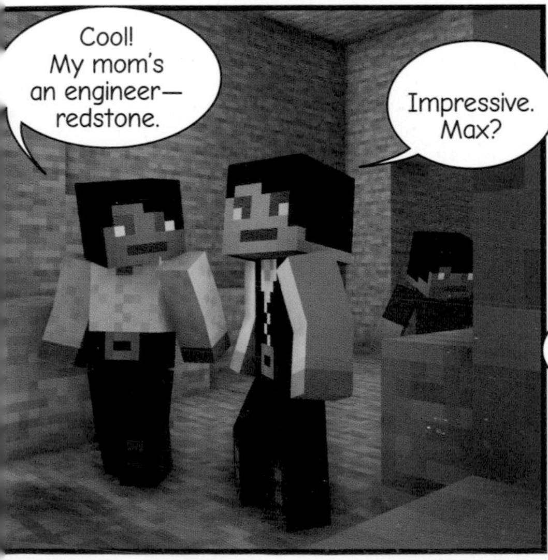
Cool! My mom's an engineer—redstone.
Impressive. Max?

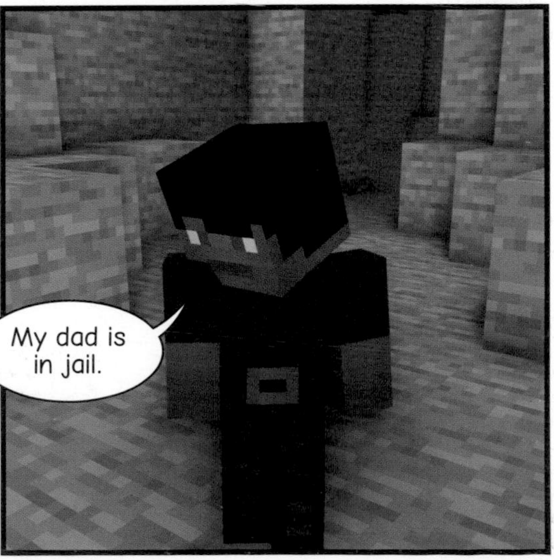
My dad is in jail.

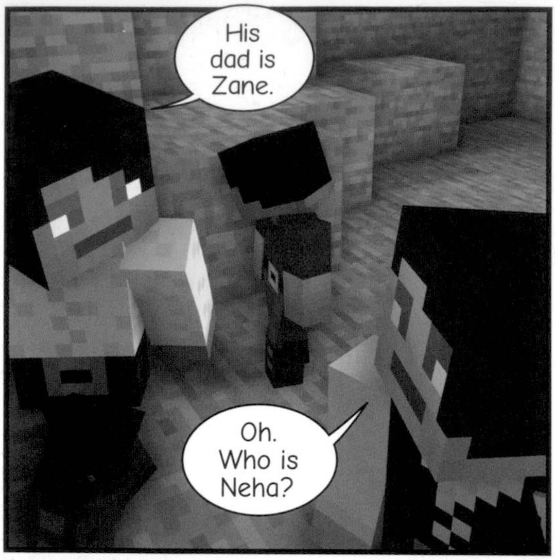
His dad is Zane.
Oh. Who is Neha?

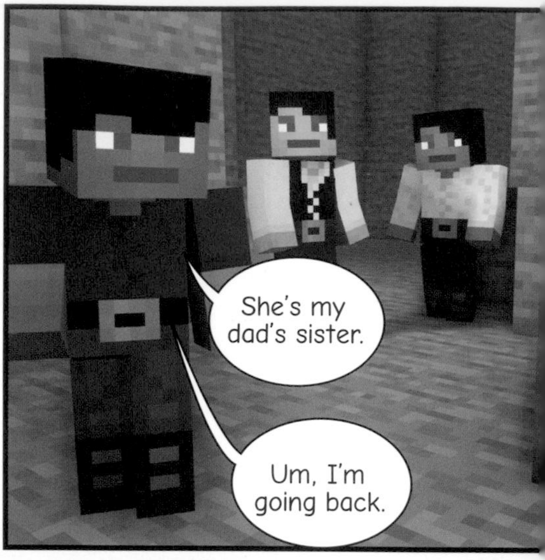
She's my dad's sister.
Um, I'm going back.

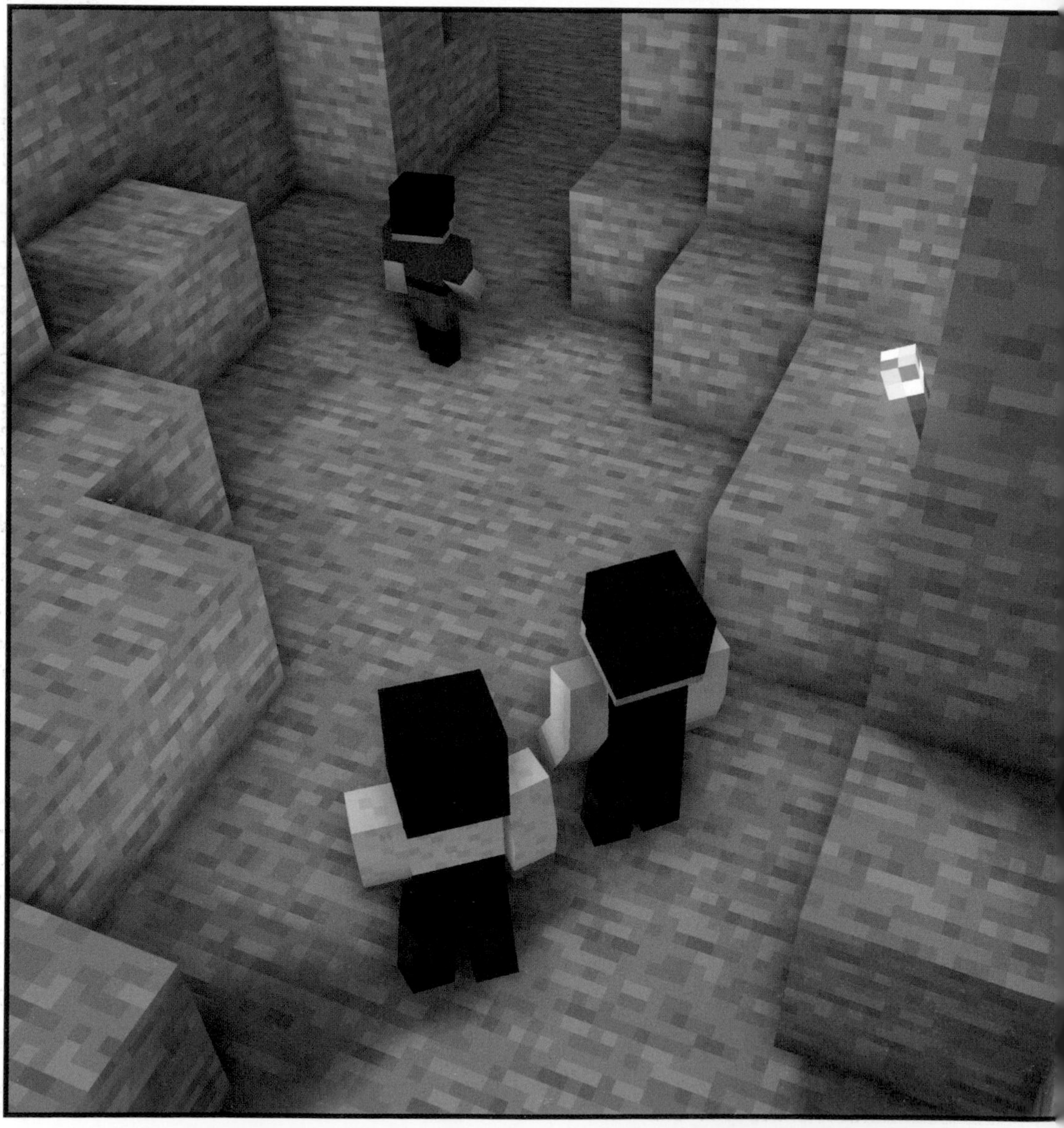

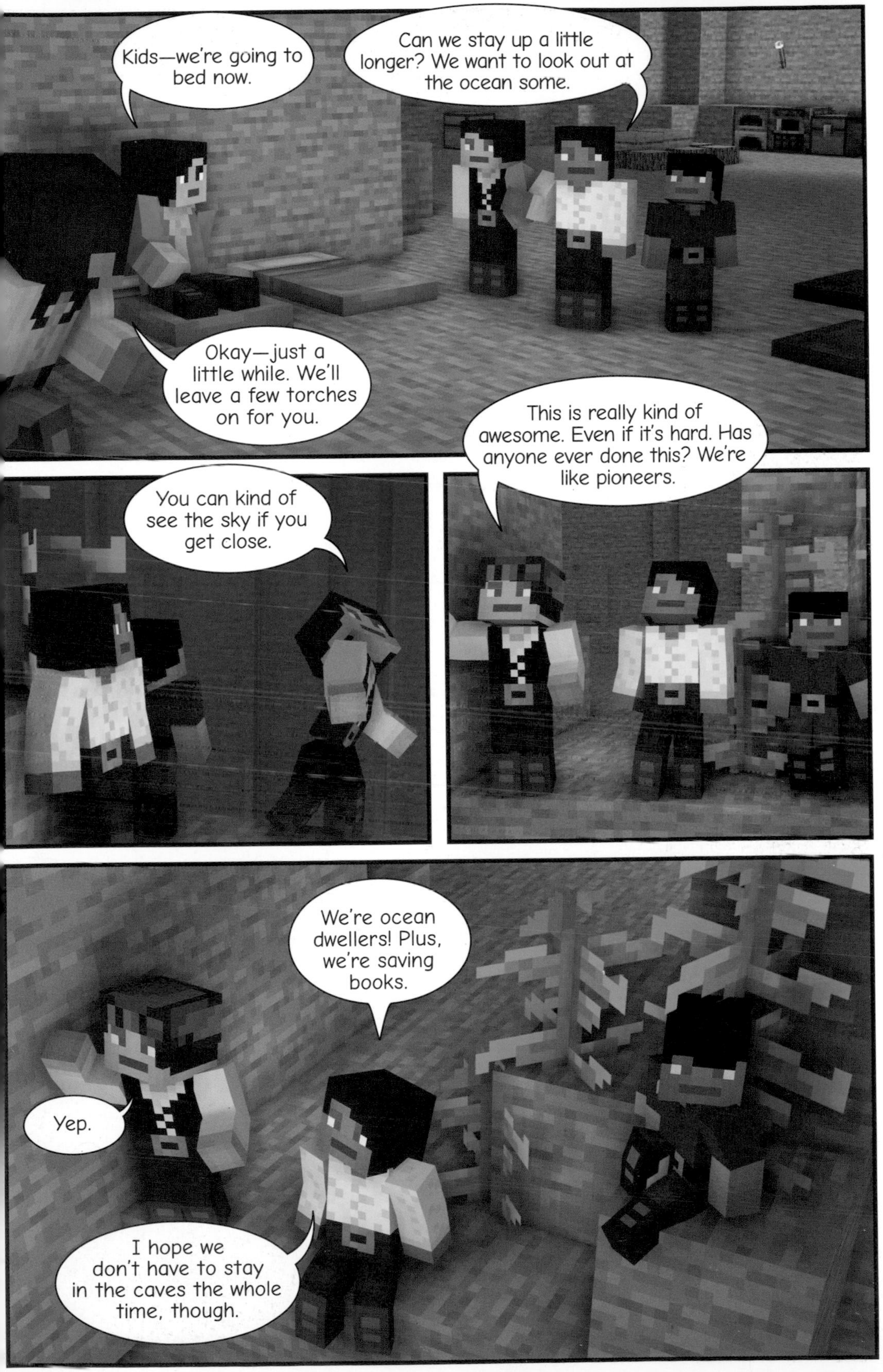
Kids—we're going to bed now.
Can we stay up a little longer? We want to look out at the ocean some.
Okay—just a little while. We'll leave a few torches on for you.
You can kind of see the sky if you get close.
This is really kind of awesome. Even if it's hard. Has anyone ever done this? We're like pioneers.
We're ocean dwellers! Plus, we're saving books.
Yep.
I hope we don't have to stay in the caves the whole time, though.

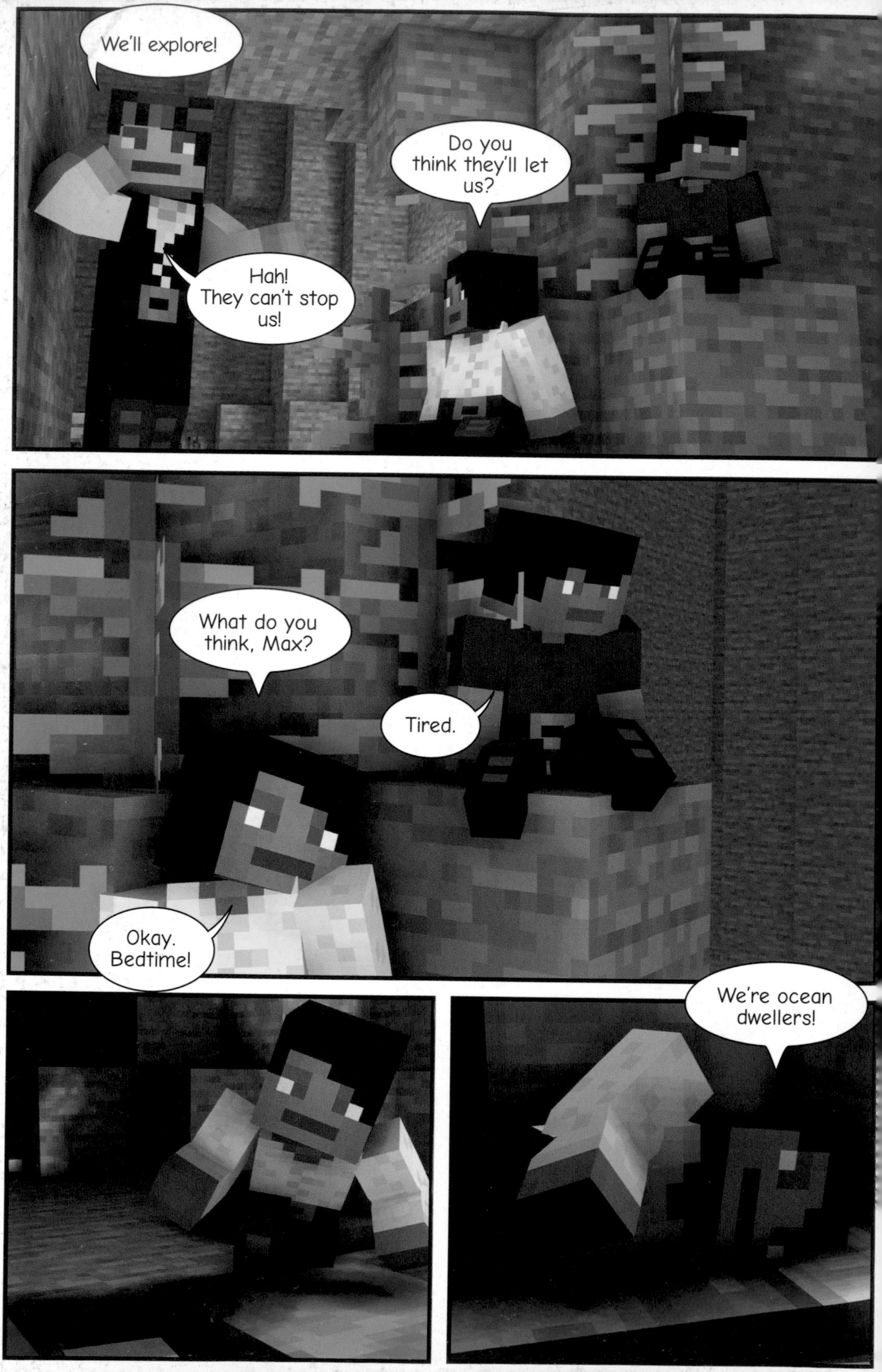

We'll explore!
Do you think they'll let us?
Hah! They can't stop us!
What do you think, Max?
Tired.
Okay. Bedtime!
We're ocean dwellers!

Chapter 3
The Legend

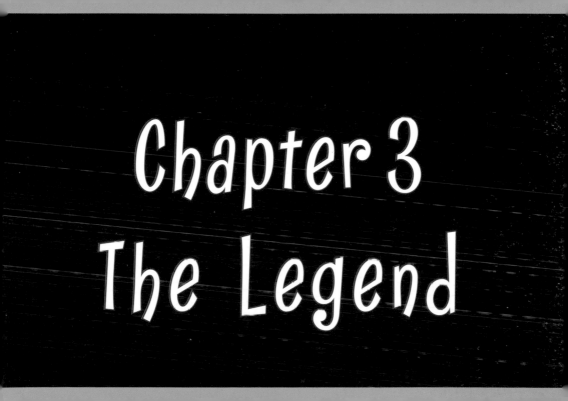

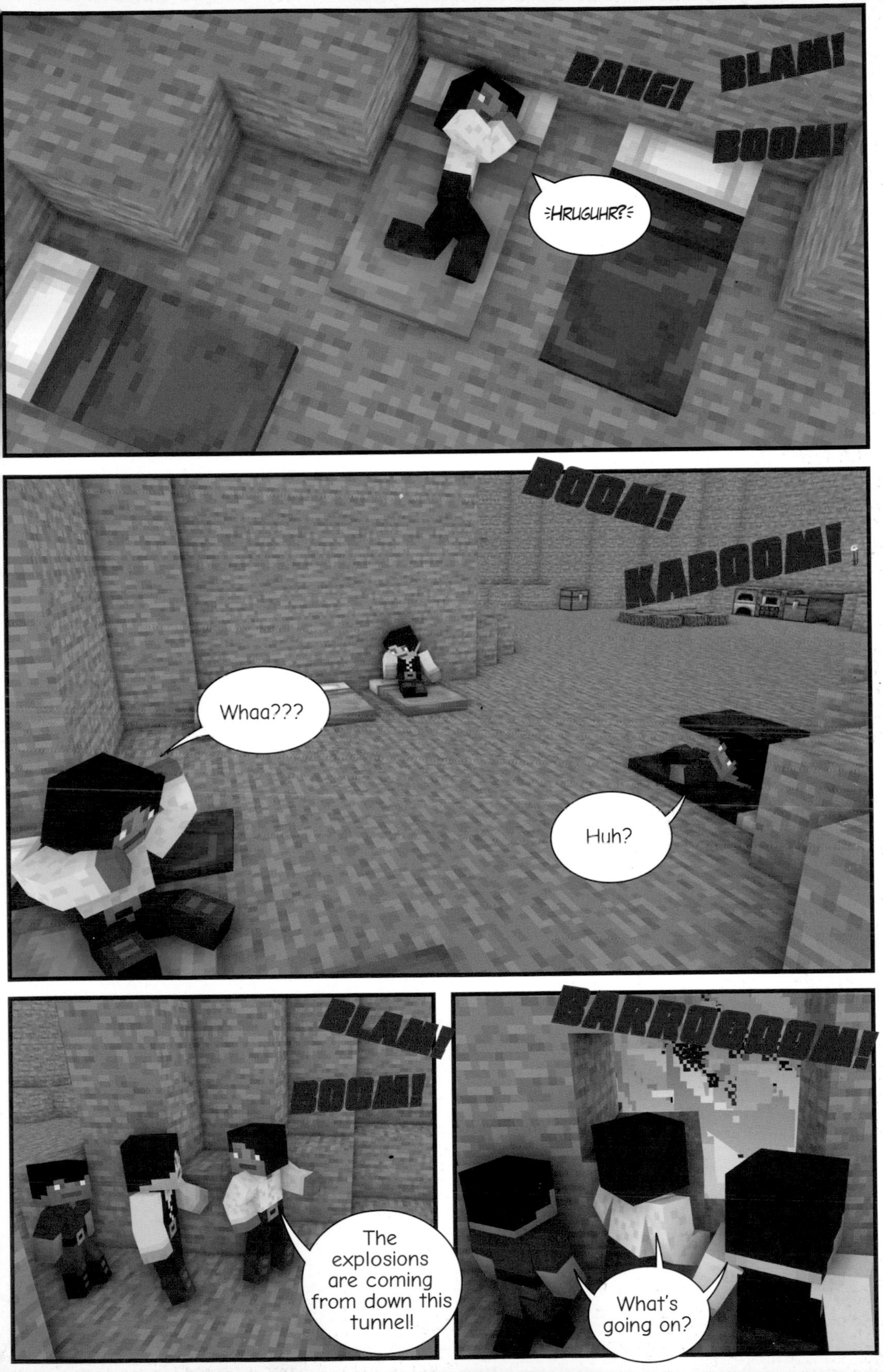
BANG!
BLAM!
BOOM!
HRUGUHR?
BOOM!
KABOOM!
Whaa???
Huh?
BLAM!
BOOM!
The explosions are coming from down this tunnel!
BARROOOOM!
What's going on?

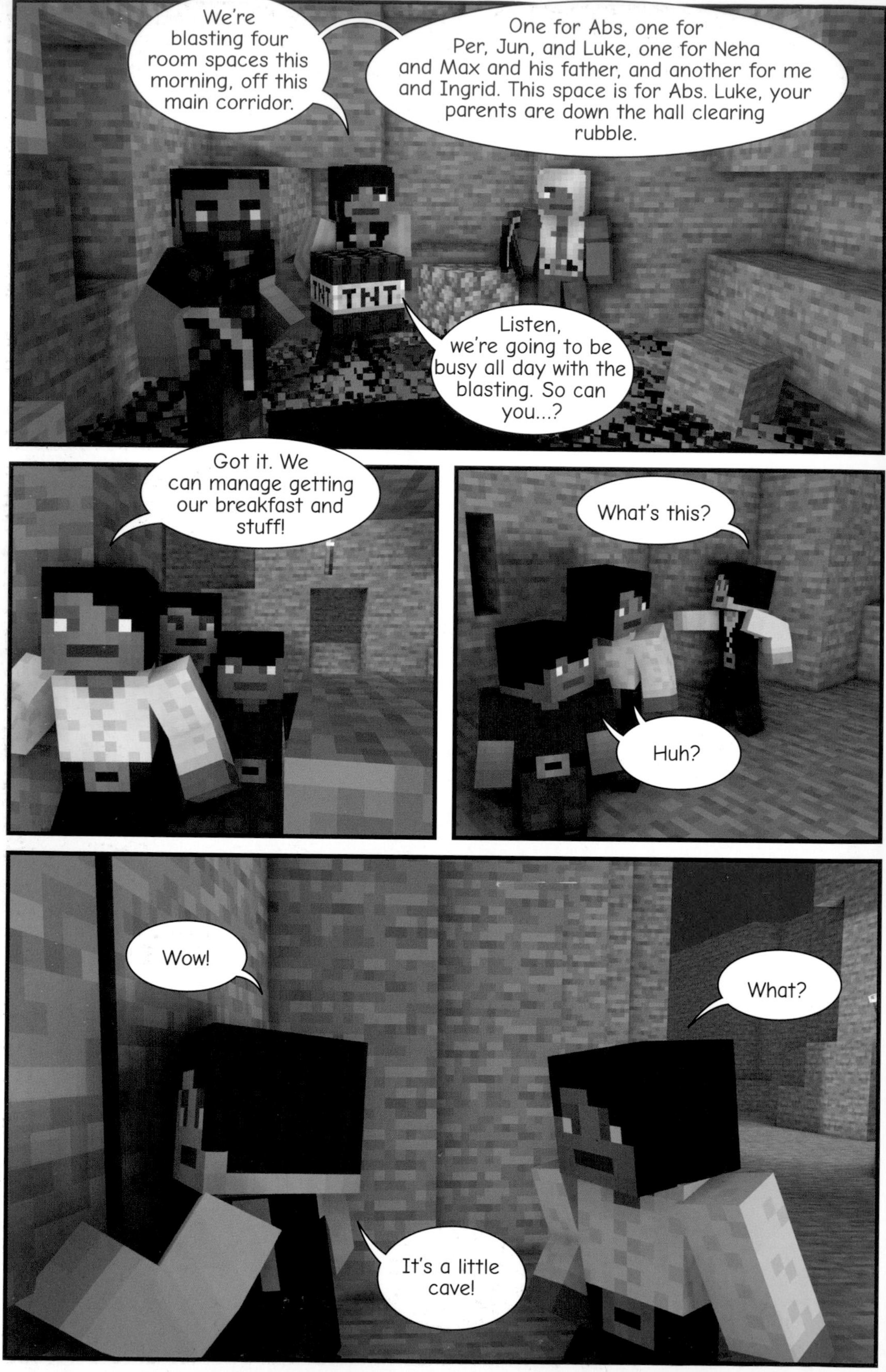
We're blasting four room spaces this morning, off this main corridor.
One for Abs, one for Per, Jun, and Luke, one for Neha and Max and his father, and another for me and Ingrid. This space is for Abs. Luke, your parents are down the hall clearing rubble.
TNT TNT
Listen, we're going to be busy all day with the blasting. So can you...?
Got it. We can manage getting our breakfast and stuff!
What's this?
Huh?
Wow!
What?
It's a little cave!

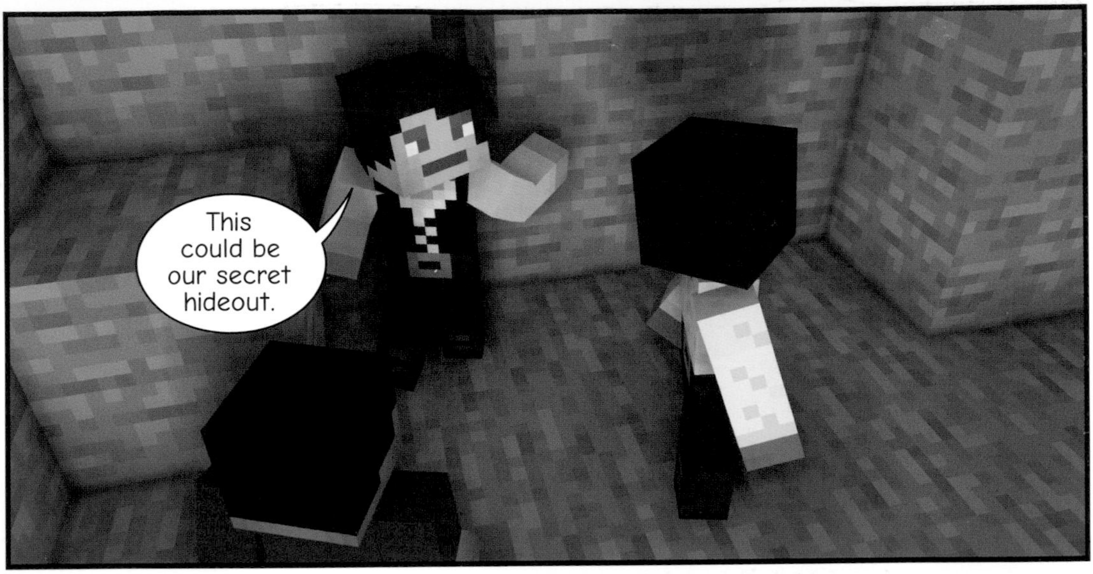
This could be our secret hideout.

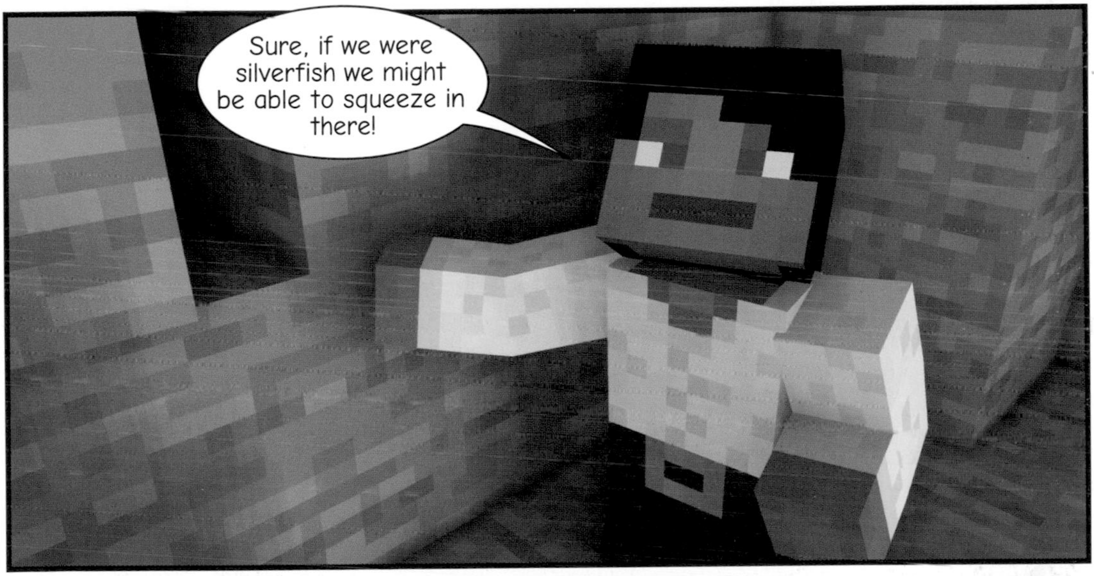
Sure, if we were silverfish we might be able to squeeze in there!

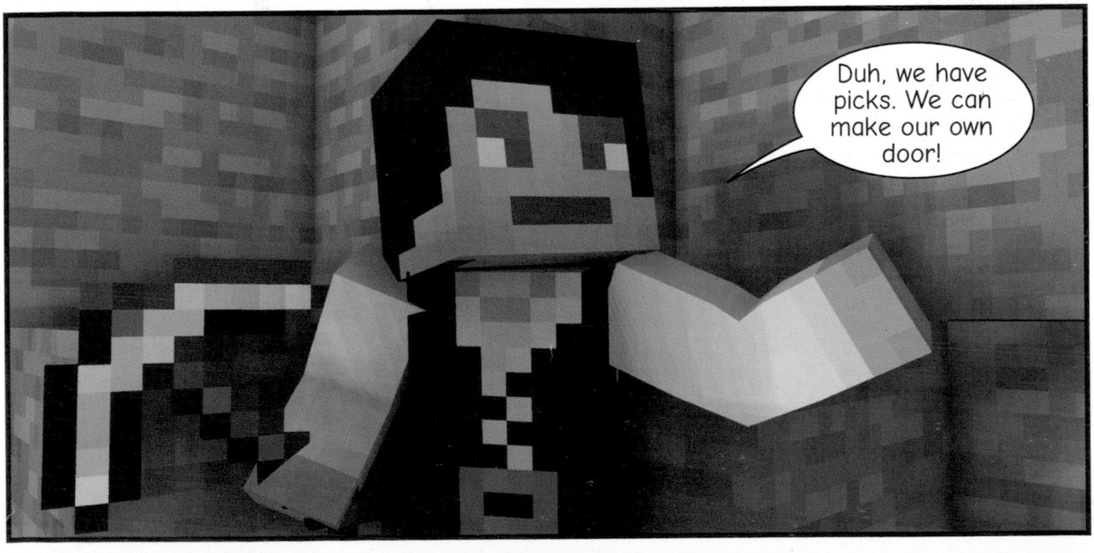
Duh, we have picks. We can make our own door!

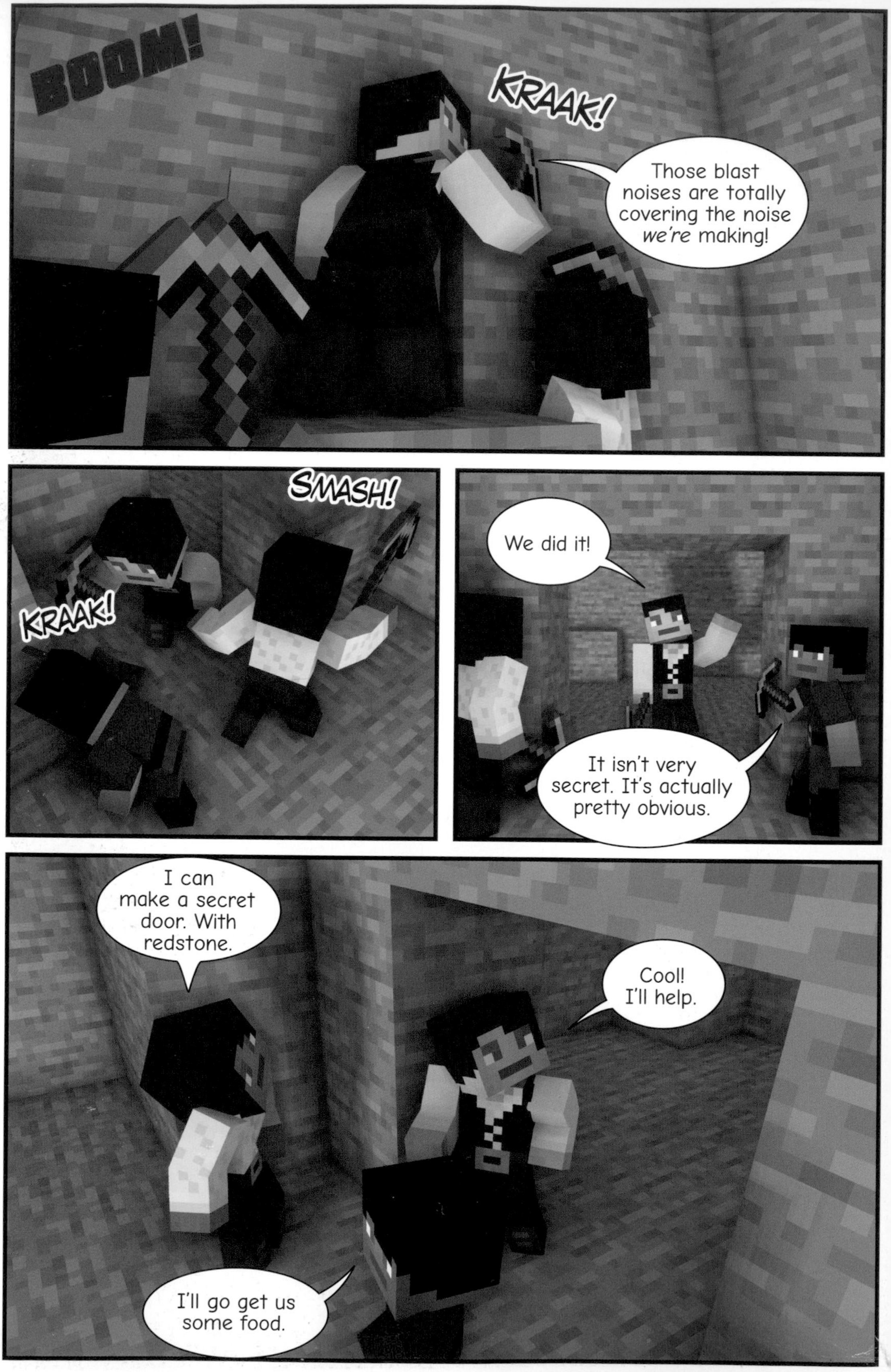
BOOM!
KRAAK!
Those blast noises are totally covering the noise *we're* making!
SMASH!
KRAAK!
We did it!
It isn't very secret. It's actually pretty obvious.
I can make a secret door. With redstone.
Cool! I'll help.
I'll go get us some food.

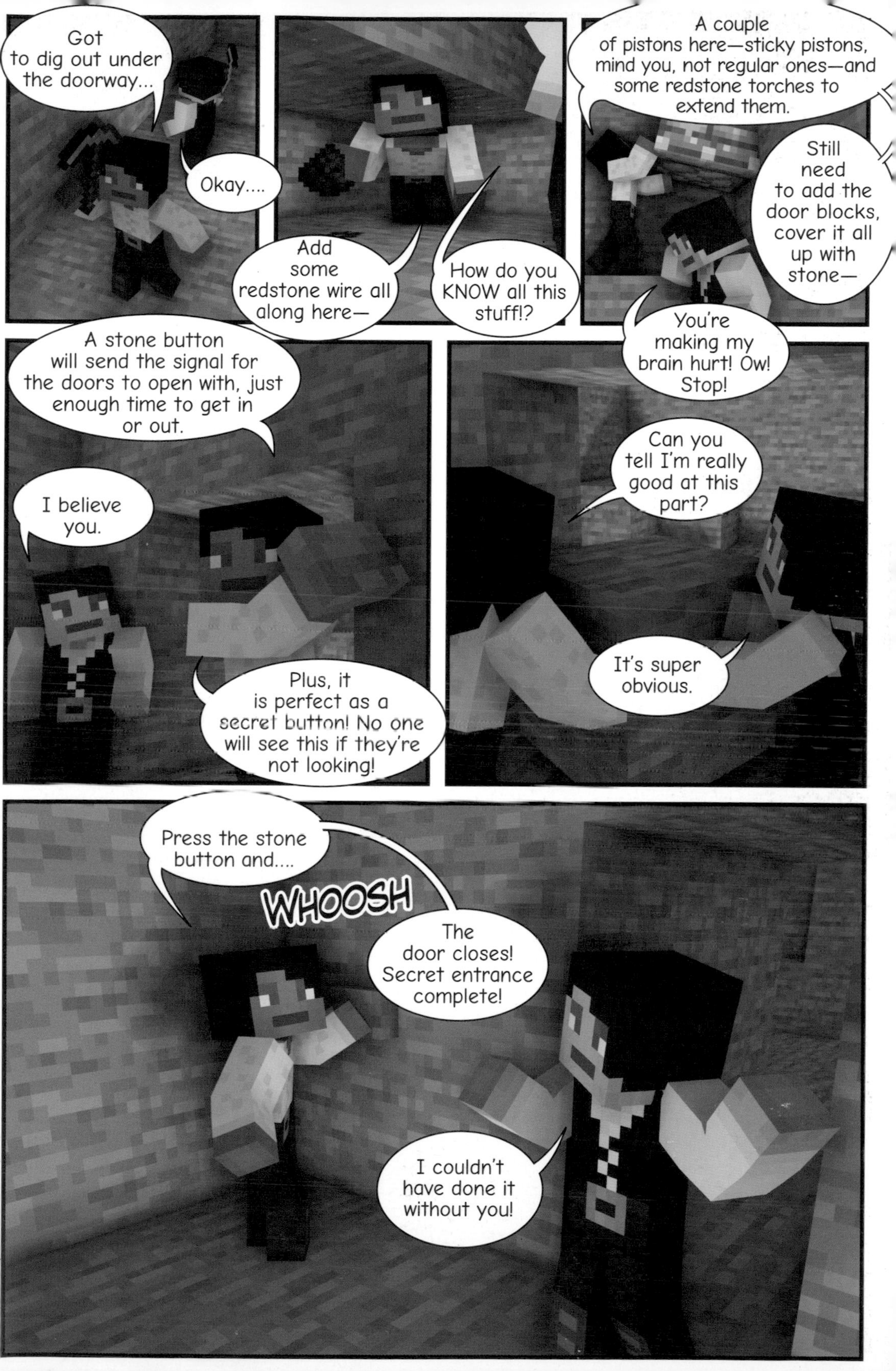

Got to dig out under the doorway...
Okay....
Add some redstone wire all along here—
How do you KNOW all this stuff!?
A couple of pistons here—sticky pistons, mind you, not regular ones—and some redstone torches to extend them.
Still need to add the door blocks, cover it all up with stone—
You're making my brain hurt! Ow! Stop!
A stone button will send the signal for the doors to open with, just enough time to get in or out.
I believe you.
Plus, it is perfect as a secret button! No one will see this if they're not looking!
Can you tell I'm really good at this part?
It's super obvious.
Press the stone button and....
WHOOSH
The door closes! Secret entrance complete!
I couldn't have done it without you!

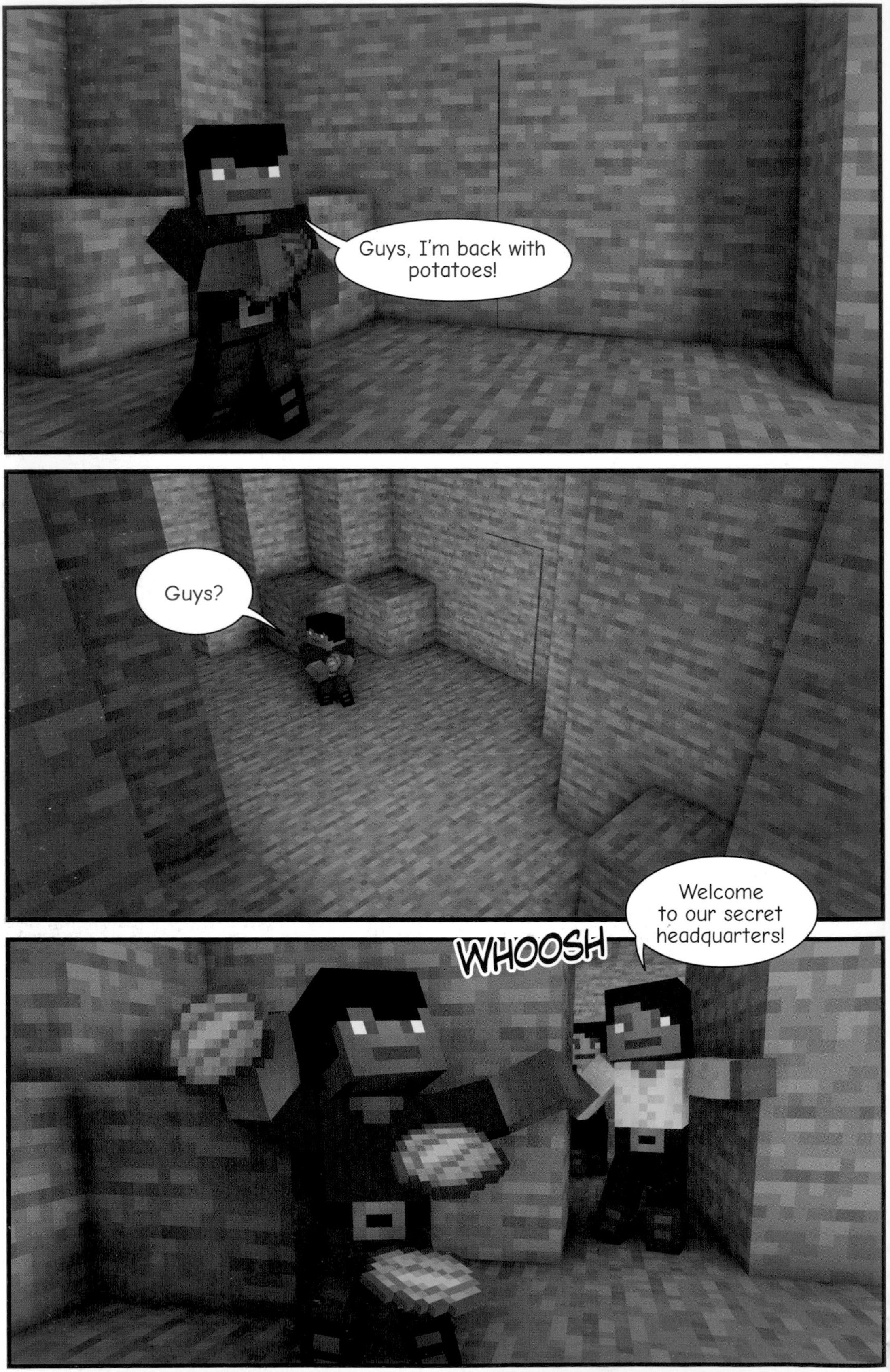
Guys, I'm back with potatoes!
Guys?
WHOOSH
Welcome to our secret headquarters!

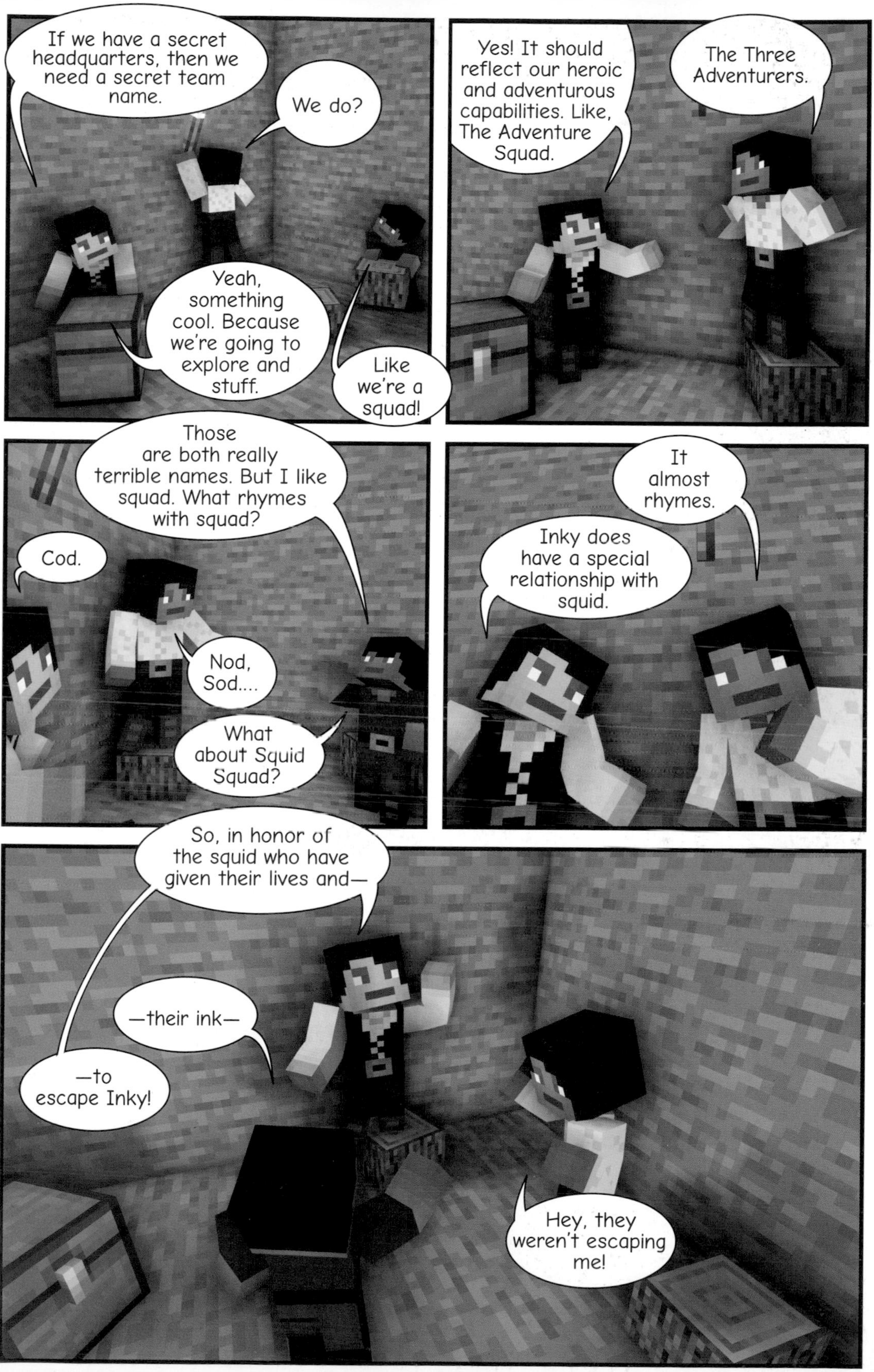
If we have a secret headquarters, then we need a secret team name.
We do?
Yeah, something cool. Because we're going to explore and stuff.
Like we're a squad!
Yes! It should reflect our heroic and adventurous capabilities. Like, The Adventure Squad.
The Three Adventurers.
Those are both really terrible names. But I like squad. What rhymes with squad?
Cod.
Nod, Sod....
What about Squid Squad?
It almost rhymes.
Inky does have a special relationship with squid.
So, in honor of the squid who have given their lives and—
—their ink—
—to escape Inky!
Hey, they weren't escaping me!

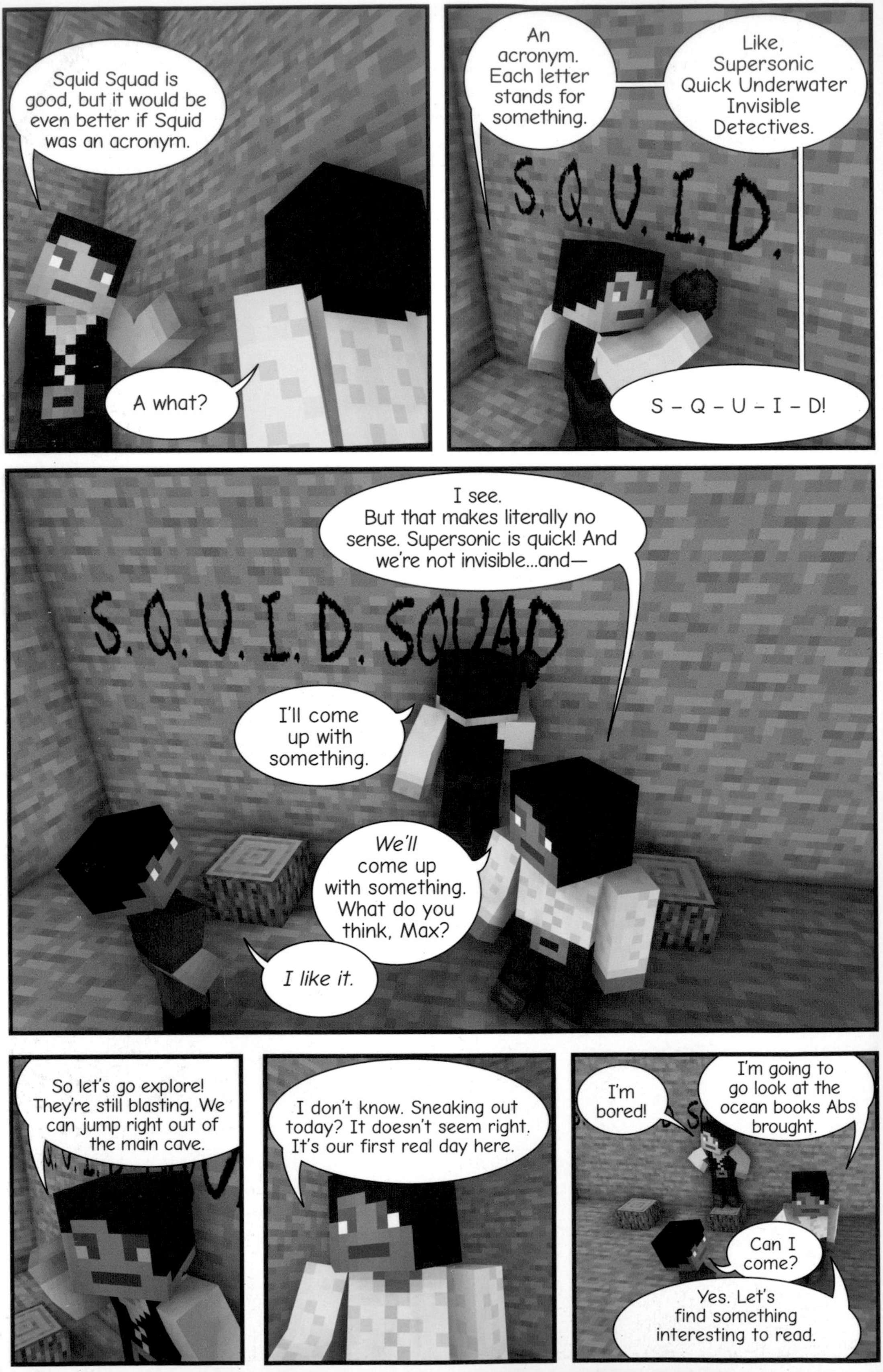
Squid Squad is good, but it would be even better if Squid was an acronym.
A what?
An acronym. Each letter stands for something.
Like, Supersonic Quick Underwater Invisible Detectives.
S.Q.U.I.D.
S – Q – U – I – D!
I see. But that makes literally no sense. Supersonic is quick! And we're not invisible...and—
S.Q.U.I.D. SQUAD
I'll come up with something.
We'll come up with something. What do you think, Max?
I like it.
So let's go explore! They're still blasting. We can jump right out of the main cave.
I don't know. Sneaking out today? It doesn't seem right. It's our first real day here.
I'm bored!
I'm going to go look at the ocean books Abs brought.
Can I come?
Yes. Let's find something interesting to read.

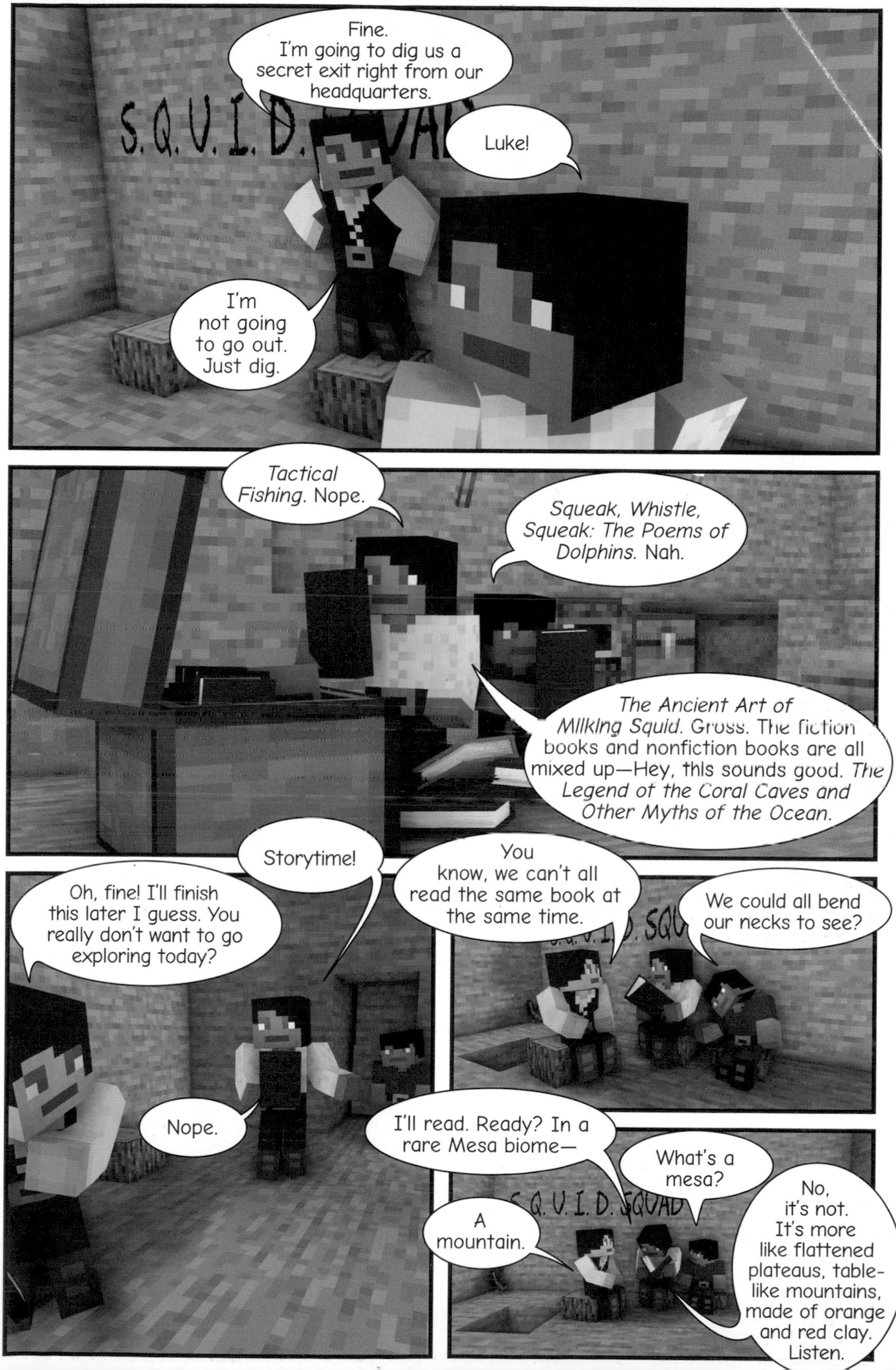
S.Q.U.I.D.
Fine. I'm going to dig us a secret exit right from our headquarters.
Luke!
I'm not going to go out. Just dig.
Tactical Fishing. Nope.
Squeak, Whistle, Squeak: The Poems of Dolphins. Nah.
The Ancient Art of Milking Squid. Gross. The fiction books and nonfiction books are all mixed up—Hey, this sounds good. *The Legend of the Coral Caves and Other Myths of the Ocean*.
Storytime!
Oh, fine! I'll finish this later I guess. You really don't want to go exploring today?
Nope.
You know, we can't all read the same book at the same time.
We could all bend our necks to see?
I'll read. Ready? In a rare Mesa biome—
What's a mesa?
S.Q.U.I.D. SQUAD
A mountain.
No, it's not. It's more like flattened plateaus, table-like mountains, made of orange and red clay. Listen.

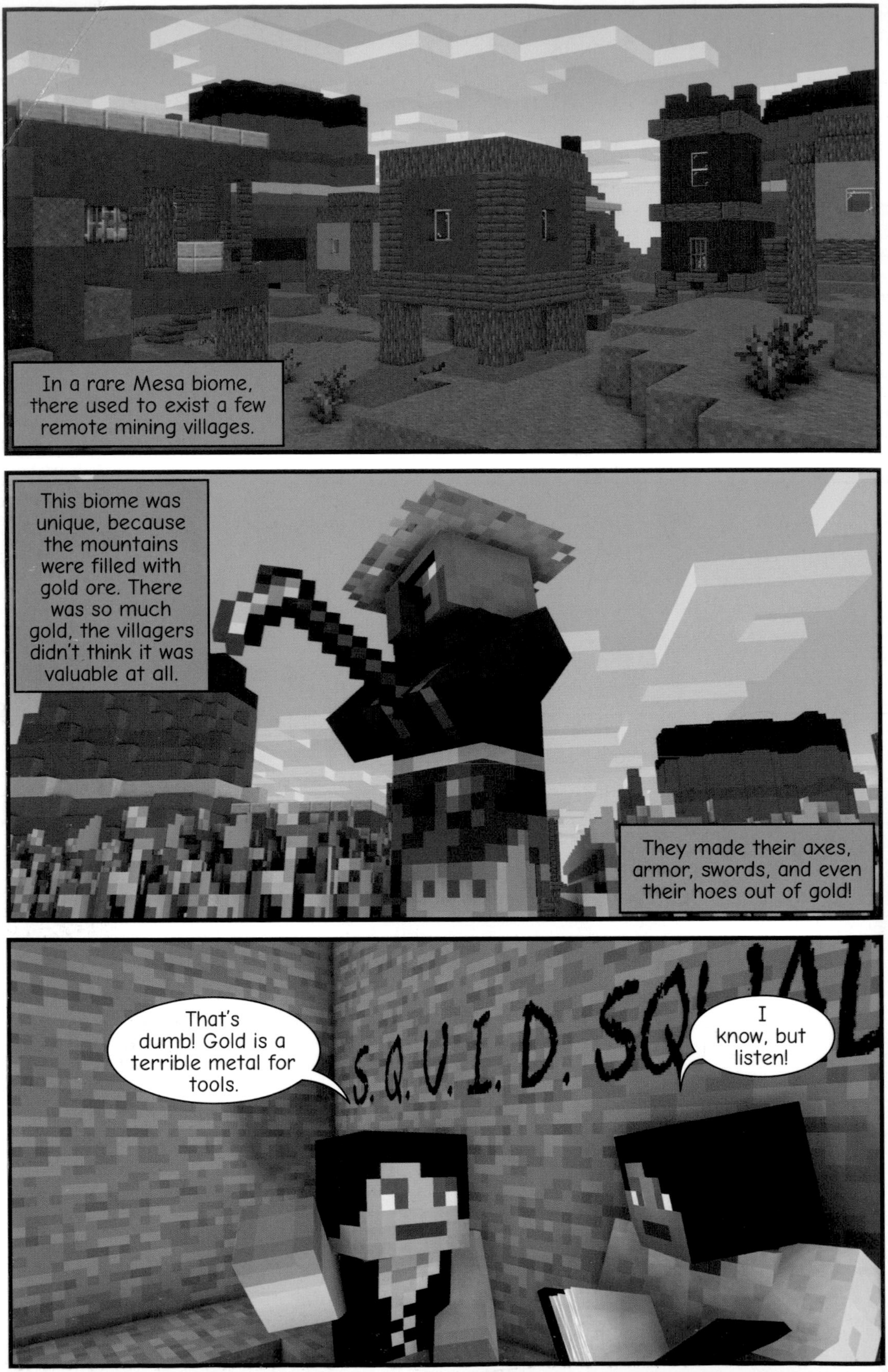
In a rare Mesa biome, there used to exist a few remote mining villages.
This biome was unique, because the mountains were filled with gold ore. There was so much gold, the villagers didn't think it was valuable at all.
They made their axes, armor, swords, and even their hoes out of gold!
S.Q.U.I.D. SQUAD
That's dumb! Gold is a terrible metal for tools.
I know, but listen!

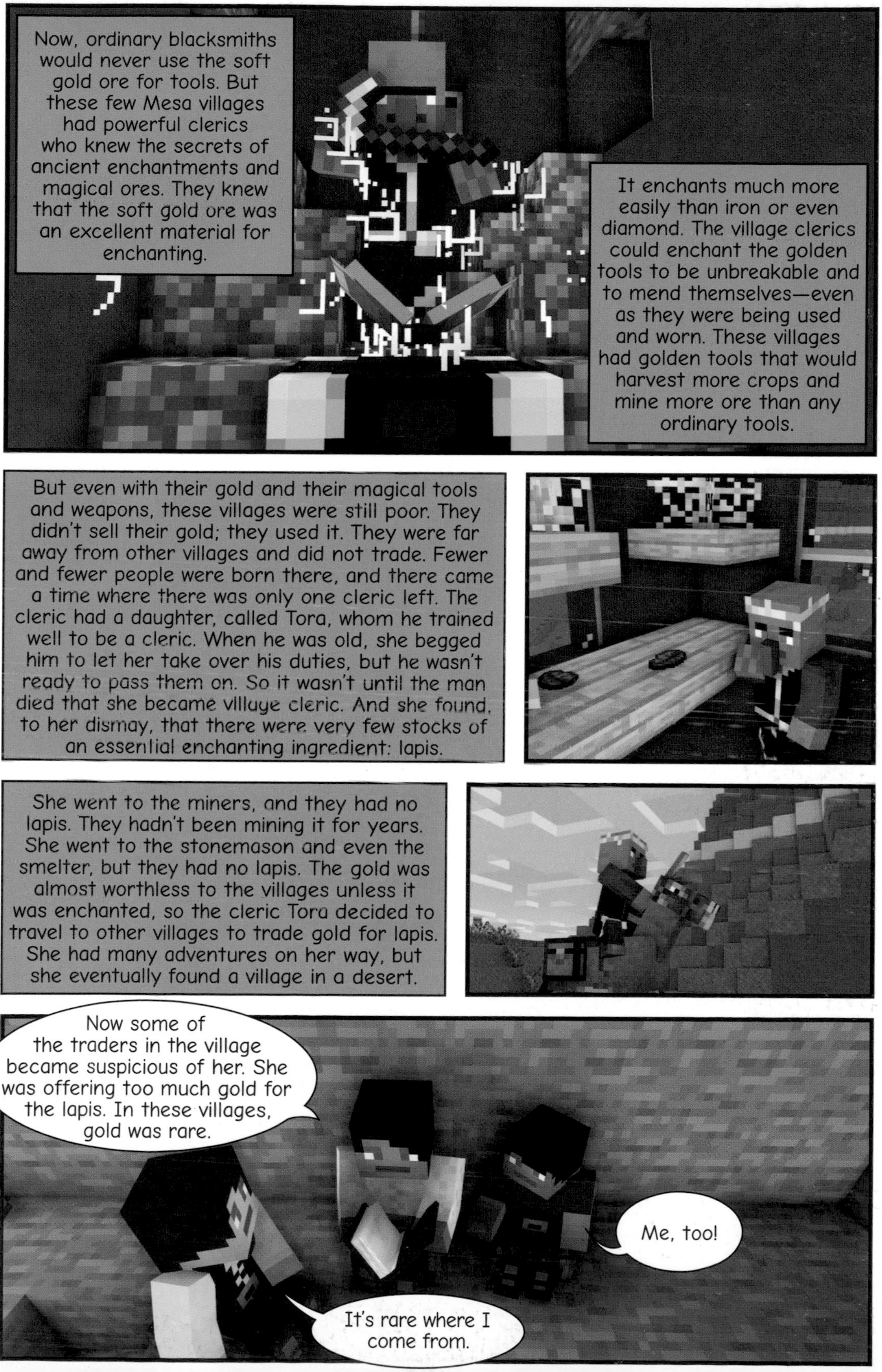
Now, ordinary blacksmiths would never use the soft gold ore for tools. But these few Mesa villages had powerful clerics who knew the secrets of ancient enchantments and magical ores. They knew that the soft gold ore was an excellent material for enchanting.
It enchants much more easily than iron or even diamond. The village clerics could enchant the golden tools to be unbreakable and to mend themselves—even as they were being used and worn. These villages had golden tools that would harvest more crops and mine more ore than any ordinary tools.
But even with their gold and their magical tools and weapons, these villages were still poor. They didn't sell their gold; they used it. They were far away from other villages and did not trade. Fewer and fewer people were born there, and there came a time where there was only one cleric left. The cleric had a daughter, called Tora, whom he trained well to be a cleric. When he was old, she begged him to let her take over his duties, but he wasn't ready to pass them on. So it wasn't until the man died that she became village cleric. And she found, to her dismay, that there were very few stocks of an essential enchanting ingredient: lapis.
She went to the miners, and they had no lapis. They hadn't been mining it for years. She went to the stonemason and even the smelter, but they had no lapis. The gold was almost worthless to the villages unless it was enchanted, so the cleric Tora decided to travel to other villages to trade gold for lapis. She had many adventures on her way, but she eventually found a village in a desert.
Now some of the traders in the village became suspicious of her. She was offering too much gold for the lapis. In these villages, gold was rare.
Me, too!
It's rare where I come from.

Well, these merchants were suspicious, so they followed her at night to the place where she had set up camp with her donkey... and the next morning when she left to go trading, they looked through her belongings. She had so much gold, they were shocked. They thought at first she might have stolen it, but they had not heard of any gold thefts. Then they thought, what if she had found a huge store of gold, perhaps buried treasure? They decided to find out where the gold was from.

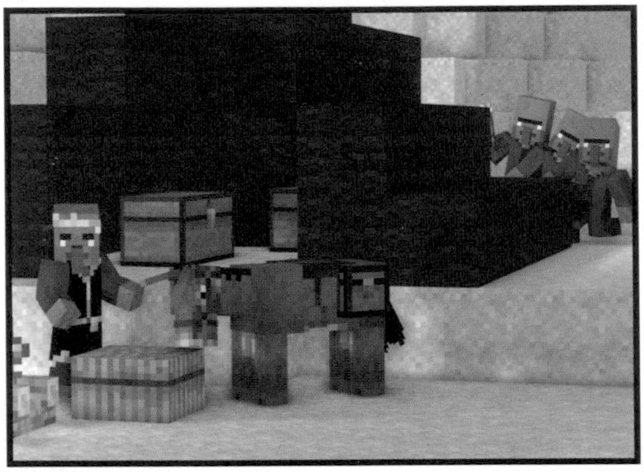

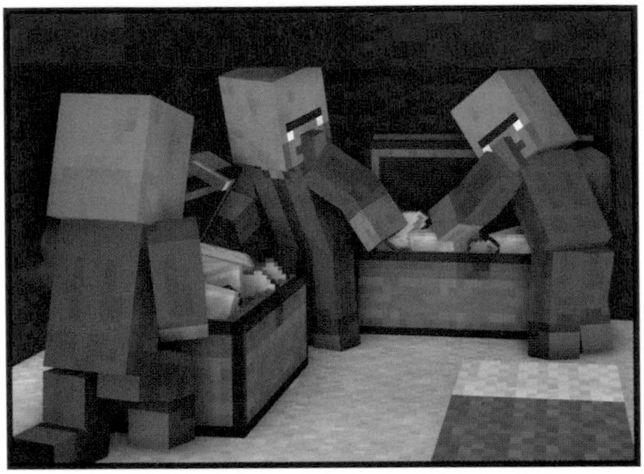

Later that morning, one of the merchants told her, "My fellow merchants and I will trade you lapis, but only if you provide enough gold so that we can hire more miners to mine the lapis." He told her the amount of gold he required. She agreed happily, and assured them that she'd return with the gold. She had to return to her village to get it.

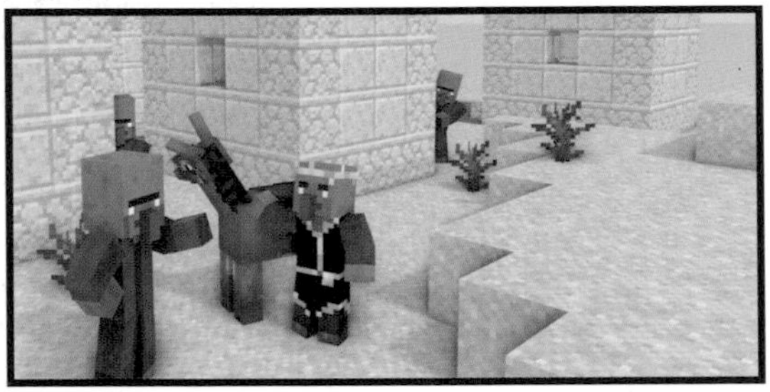

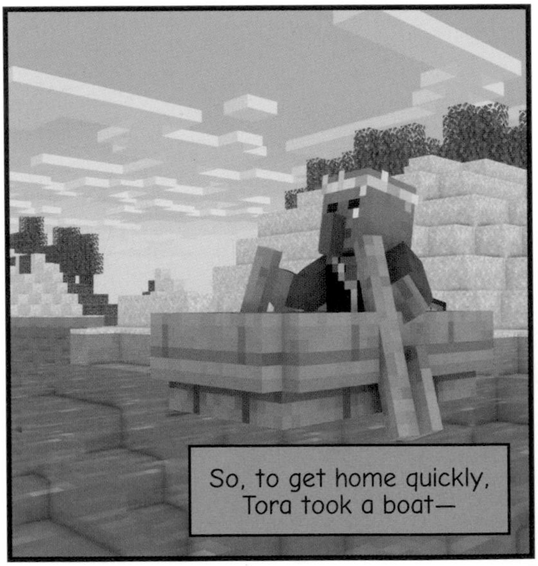
So, to get home quickly, Tora took a boat—

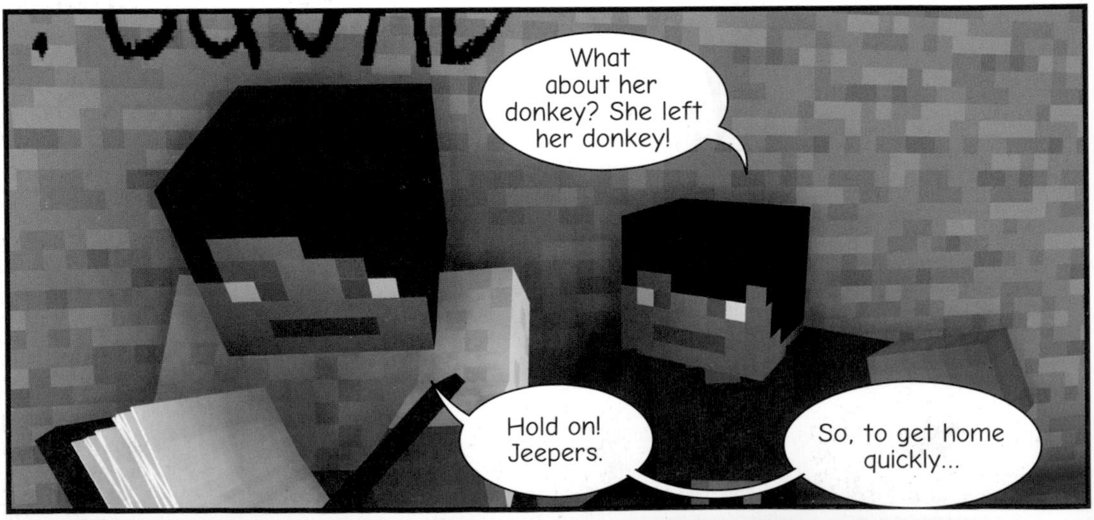
What about her donkey? She left her donkey!
Hold on! Jeepers.
So, to get home quickly...

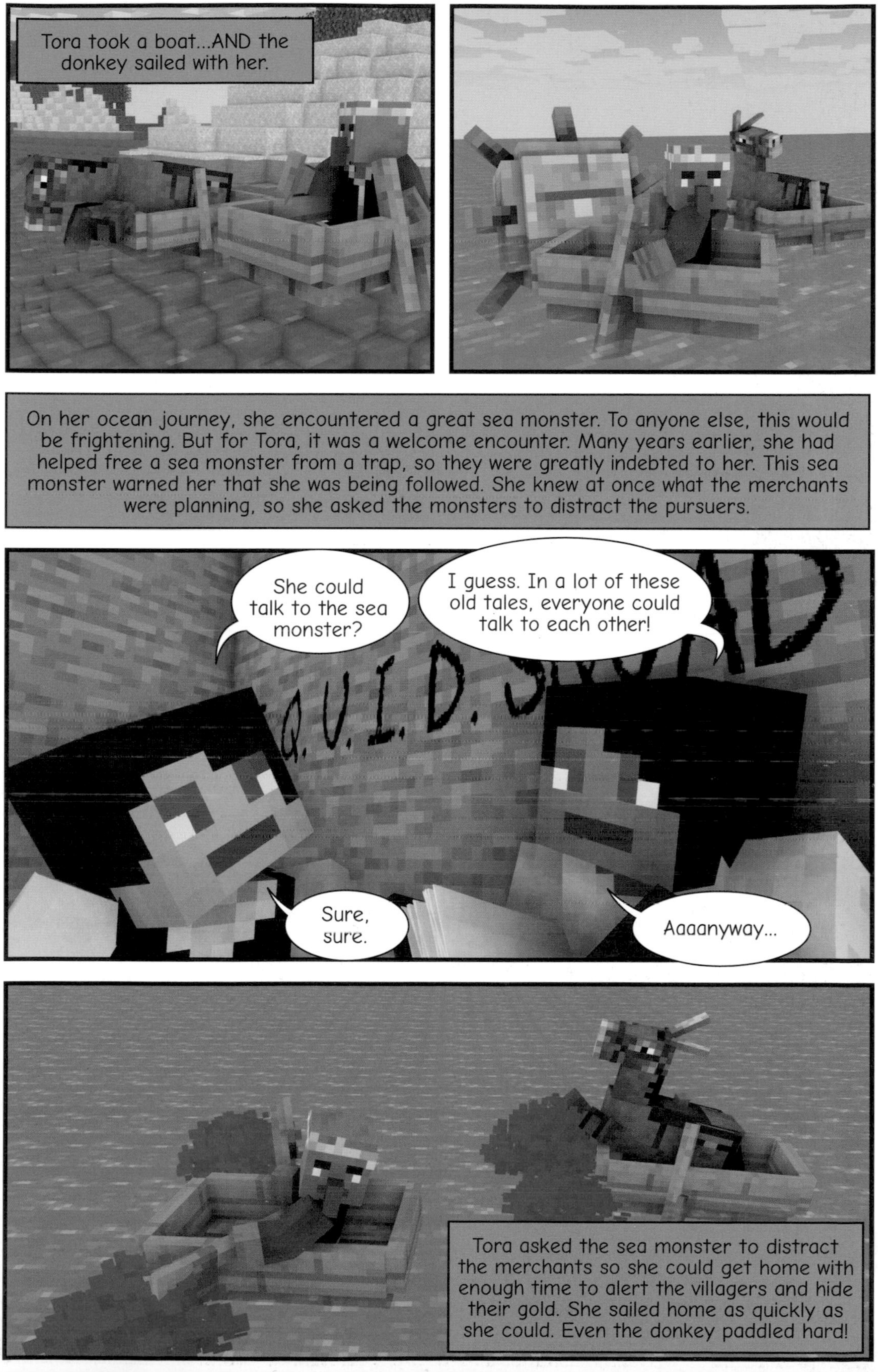
Tora took a boat...AND the donkey sailed with her.
On her ocean journey, she encountered a great sea monster. To anyone else, this would be frightening. But for Tora, it was a welcome encounter. Many years earlier, she had helped free a sea monster from a trap, so they were greatly indebted to her. This sea monster warned her that she was being followed. She knew at once what the merchants were planning, so she asked the monsters to distract the pursuers.
She could talk to the sea monster?
I guess. In a lot of these old tales, everyone could talk to each other!
Sure, sure.
Aaaanyway...
Tora asked the sea monster to distract the merchants so she could get home with enough time to alert the villagers and hide their gold. She sailed home as quickly as she could. Even the donkey paddled hard!

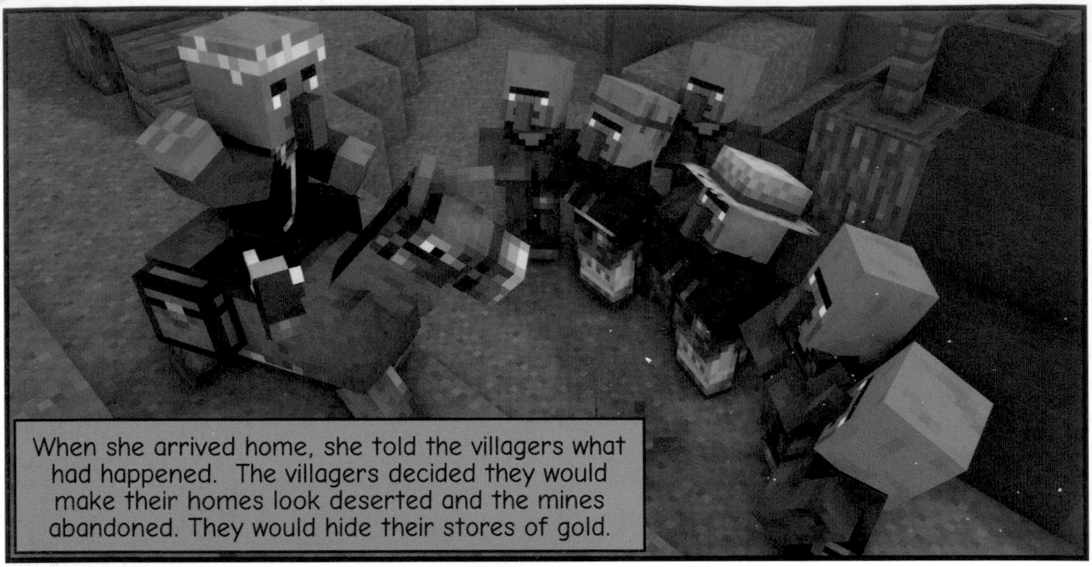
When she arrived home, she told the villagers what had happened. The villagers decided they would make their homes look deserted and the mines abandoned. They would hide their stores of gold.

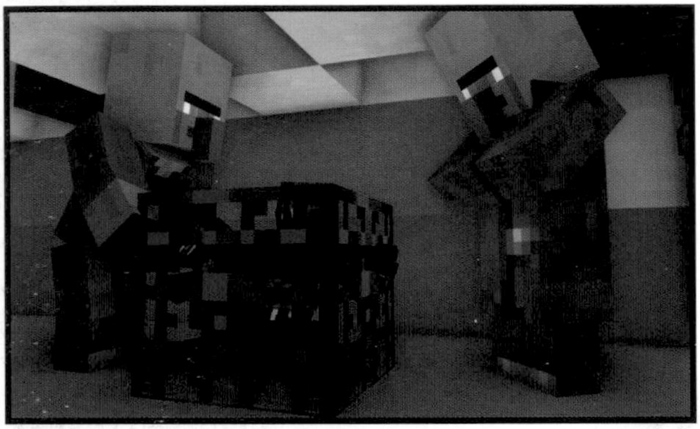

They enchanted spiders to lurk in the mines and poison anyone who entered. The villagers and Tora's donkey would hide in the mountains, away from the mines and the village buildings, and return when it was safe. They agreed that Tora should hide the gold at sea. Tora enchanted a cap so that she could breathe underwater.

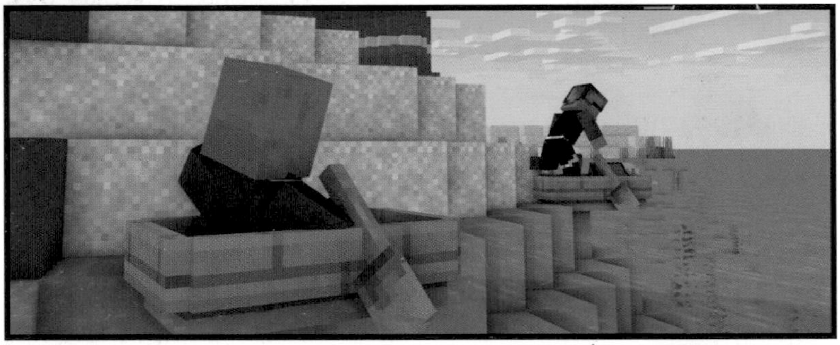

However, one of the traders had escaped from the sea monsters and was sailing past the Mesa when he saw Tora get in her boat. He hid while she sailed off.

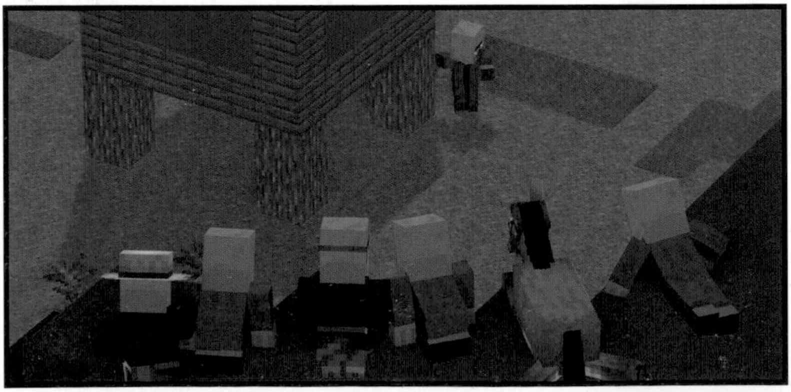

He searched the town quickly and saw that it was abandoned. He decided that she had found all her gold in this abandoned town, and was now leaving with it.

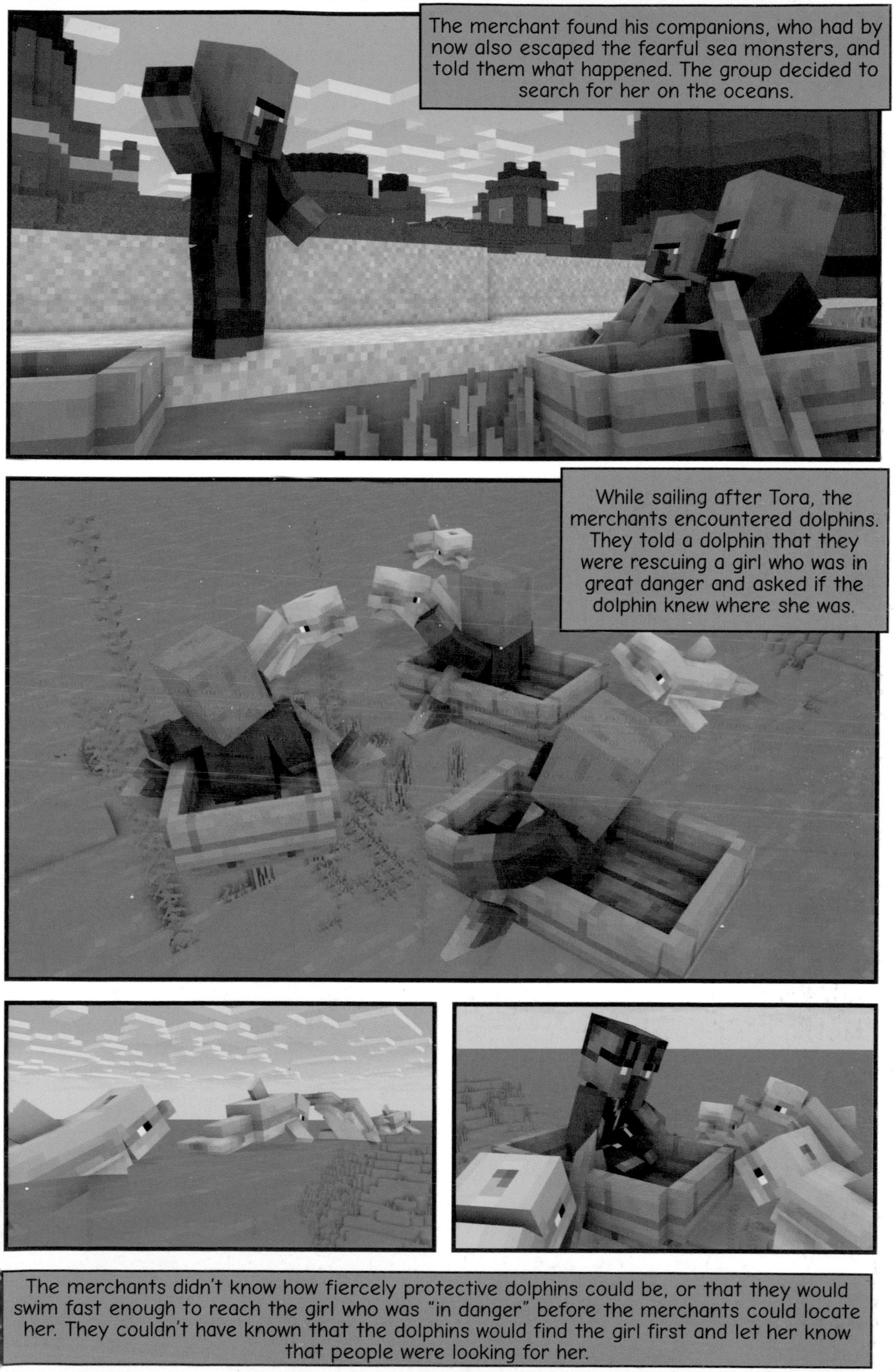

The merchant found his companions, who had by now also escaped the fearful sea monsters, and told them what happened. The group decided to search for her on the oceans.
While sailing after Tora, the merchants encountered dolphins. They told a dolphin that they were rescuing a girl who was in great danger and asked if the dolphin knew where she was.
The merchants didn't know how fiercely protective dolphins could be, or that they would swim fast enough to reach the girl who was "in danger" before the merchants could locate her. They couldn't have known that the dolphins would find the girl first and let her know that people were looking for her.

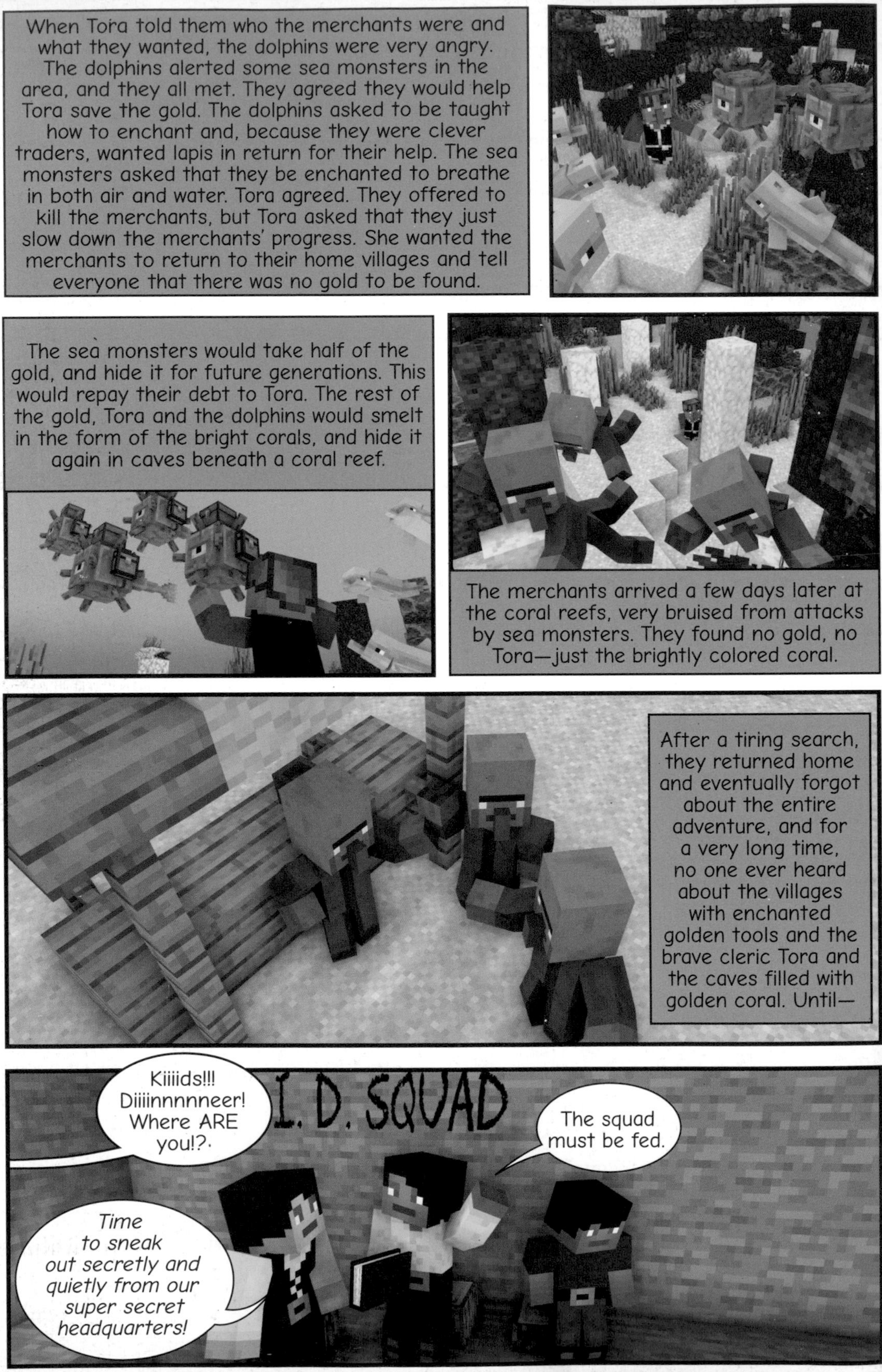
When Tora told them who the merchants were and what they wanted, the dolphins were very angry. The dolphins alerted some sea monsters in the area, and they all met. They agreed they would help Tora save the gold. The dolphins asked to be taught how to enchant and, because they were clever traders, wanted lapis in return for their help. The sea monsters asked that they be enchanted to breathe in both air and water. Tora agreed. They offered to kill the merchants, but Tora asked that they just slow down the merchants' progress. She wanted the merchants to return to their home villages and tell everyone that there was no gold to be found.
The sea monsters would take half of the gold, and hide it for future generations. This would repay their debt to Tora. The rest of the gold, Tora and the dolphins would smelt in the form of the bright corals, and hide it again in caves beneath a coral reef.
The merchants arrived a few days later at the coral reefs, very bruised from attacks by sea monsters. They found no gold, no Tora—just the brightly colored coral.
After a tiring search, they returned home and eventually forgot about the entire adventure, and for a very long time, no one ever heard about the villages with enchanted golden tools and the brave cleric Tora and the caves filled with golden coral. Until—
Kiiiids!!! Diiiinnnnneer! Where ARE you!?.
I. D. SQUAD
The squad must be fed.
Time to sneak out secretly and quietly from our super secret headquarters!

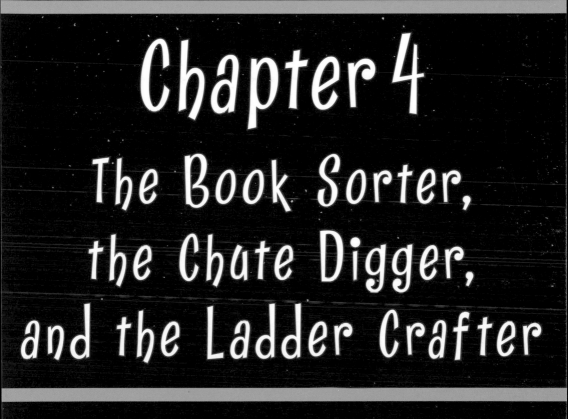

Chapter 4
The Book Sorter,
the Chute Digger,
and the Ladder Crafter

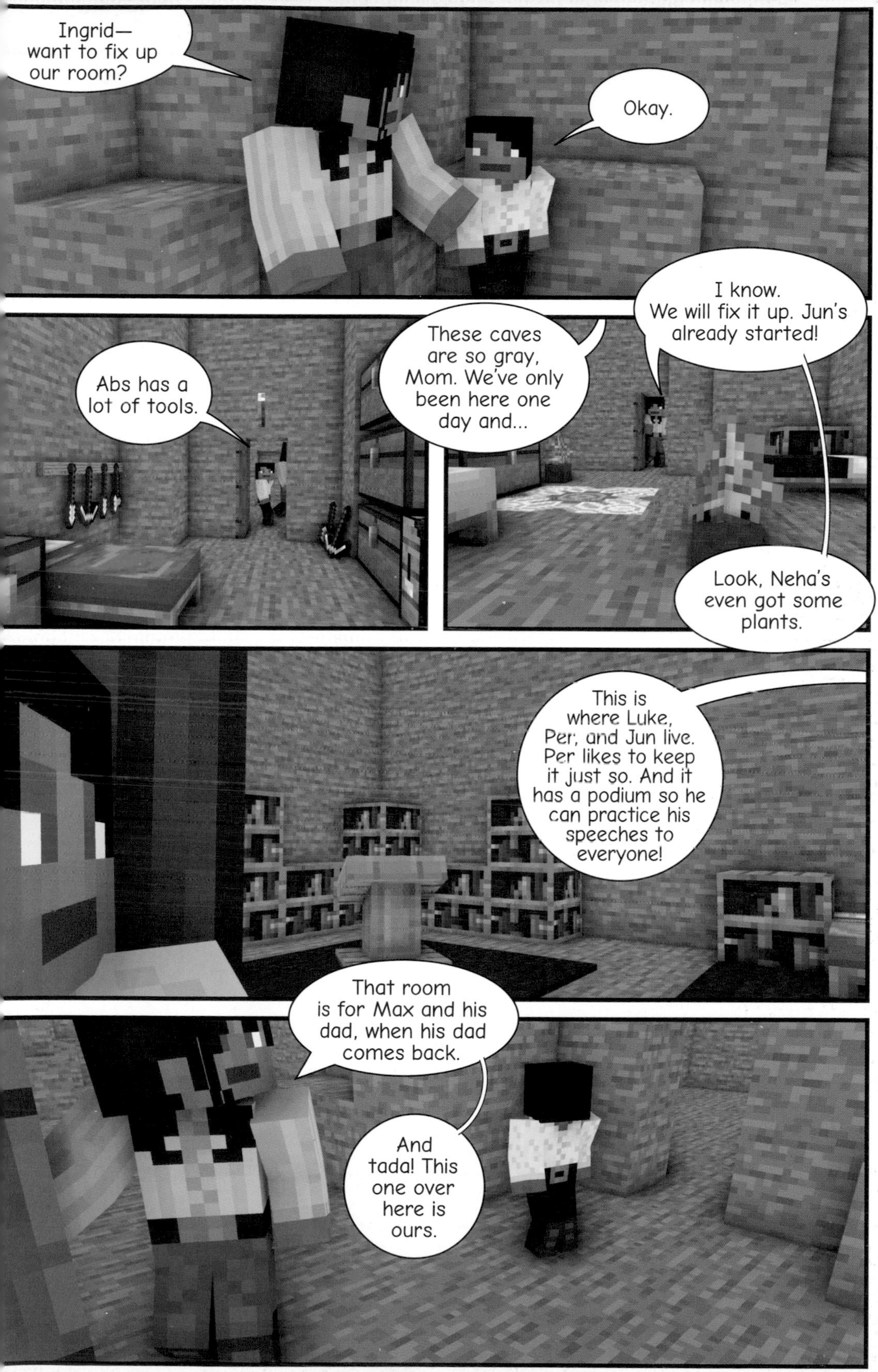
Ingrid—want to fix up our room?
Okay.
Abs has a lot of tools.
These caves are so gray, Mom. We've only been here one day and...
I know. We will fix it up. Jun's already started!
Look, Neha's even got some plants.
This is where Luke, Per, and Jun live. Per likes to keep it just so. And it has a podium so he can practice his speeches to everyone!
That room is for Max and his dad, when his dad comes back.
And tada! This one over here is ours.

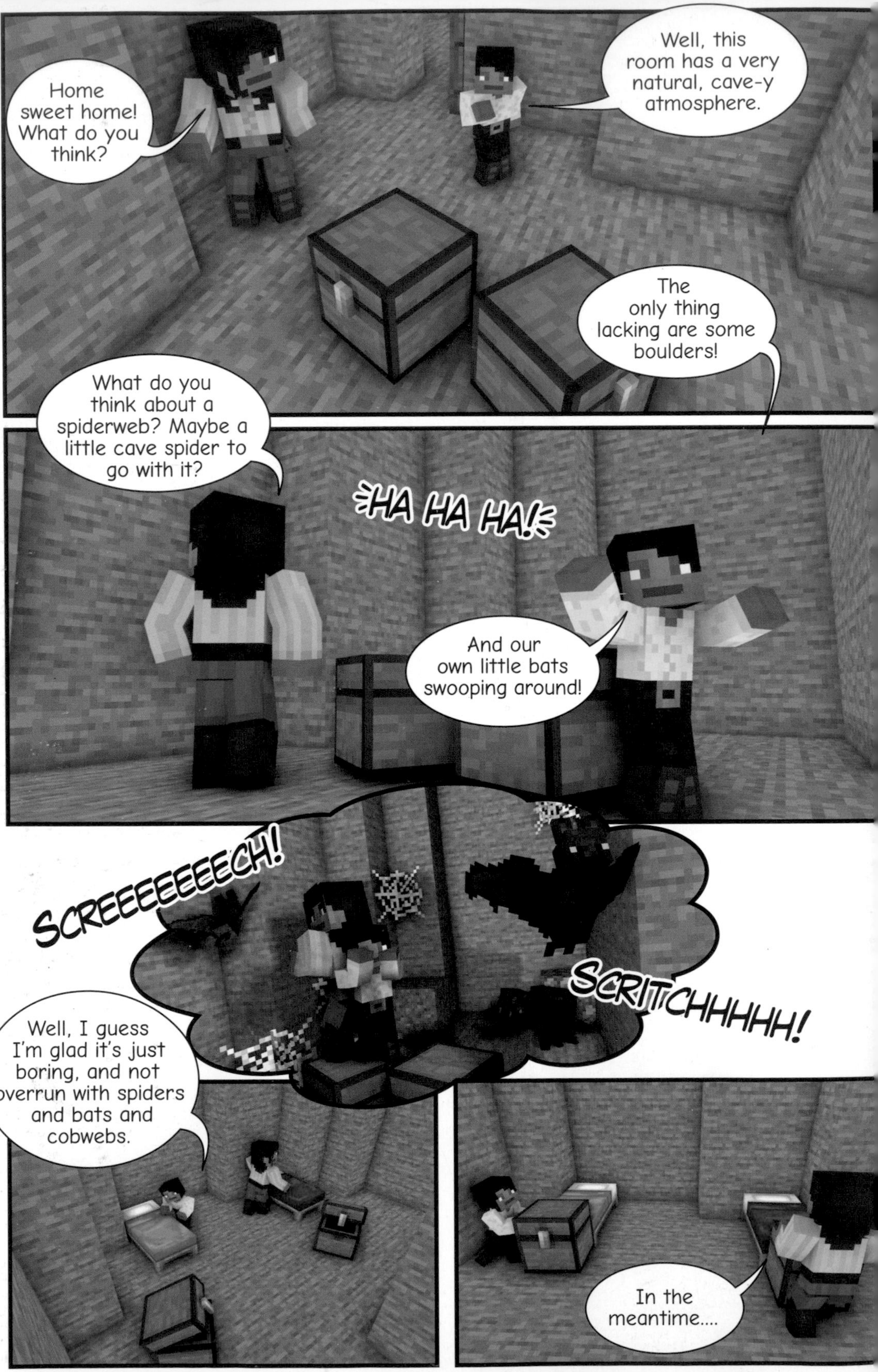
Home sweet home! What do you think?
Well, this room has a very natural, cave-y atmosphere.
The only thing lacking are some boulders!
What do you think about a spiderweb? Maybe a little cave spider to go with it?
HA HA HA!
And our own little bats swooping around!
SCREEEEEEEECH!
SCRITCHHHHH!
Well, I guess I'm glad it's just boring, and not overrun with spiders and bats and cobwebs.
In the meantime....

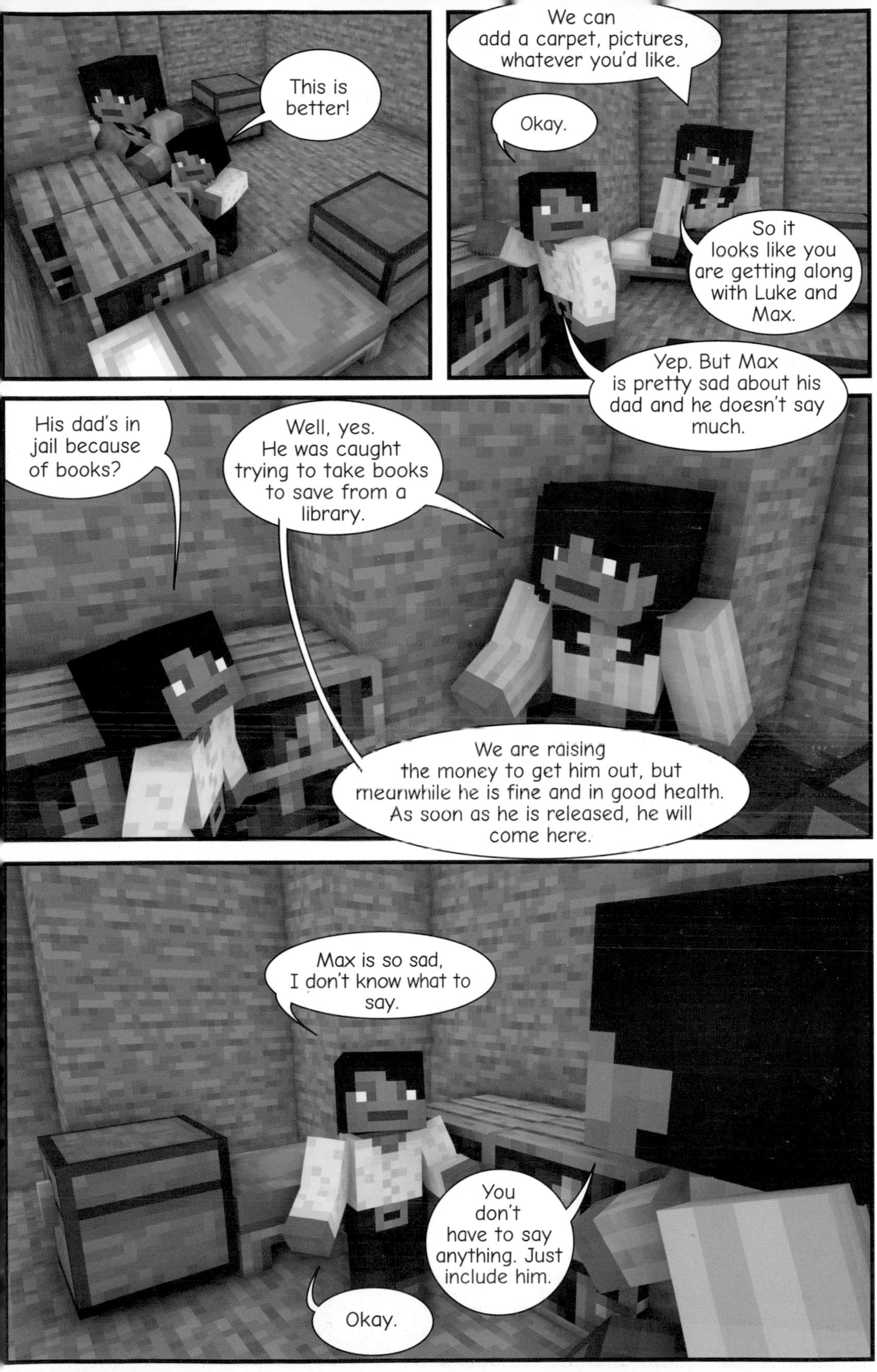
This is better!
We can add a carpet, pictures, whatever you'd like.
Okay.
So it looks like you are getting along with Luke and Max.
Yep. But Max is pretty sad about his dad and he doesn't say much.
His dad's in jail because of books?
Well, yes. He was caught trying to take books to save from a library.
We are raising the money to get him out, but meanwhile he is fine and in good health. As soon as he is released, he will come here.
Max is so sad, I don't know what to say.
You don't have to say anything. Just include him.
Okay.

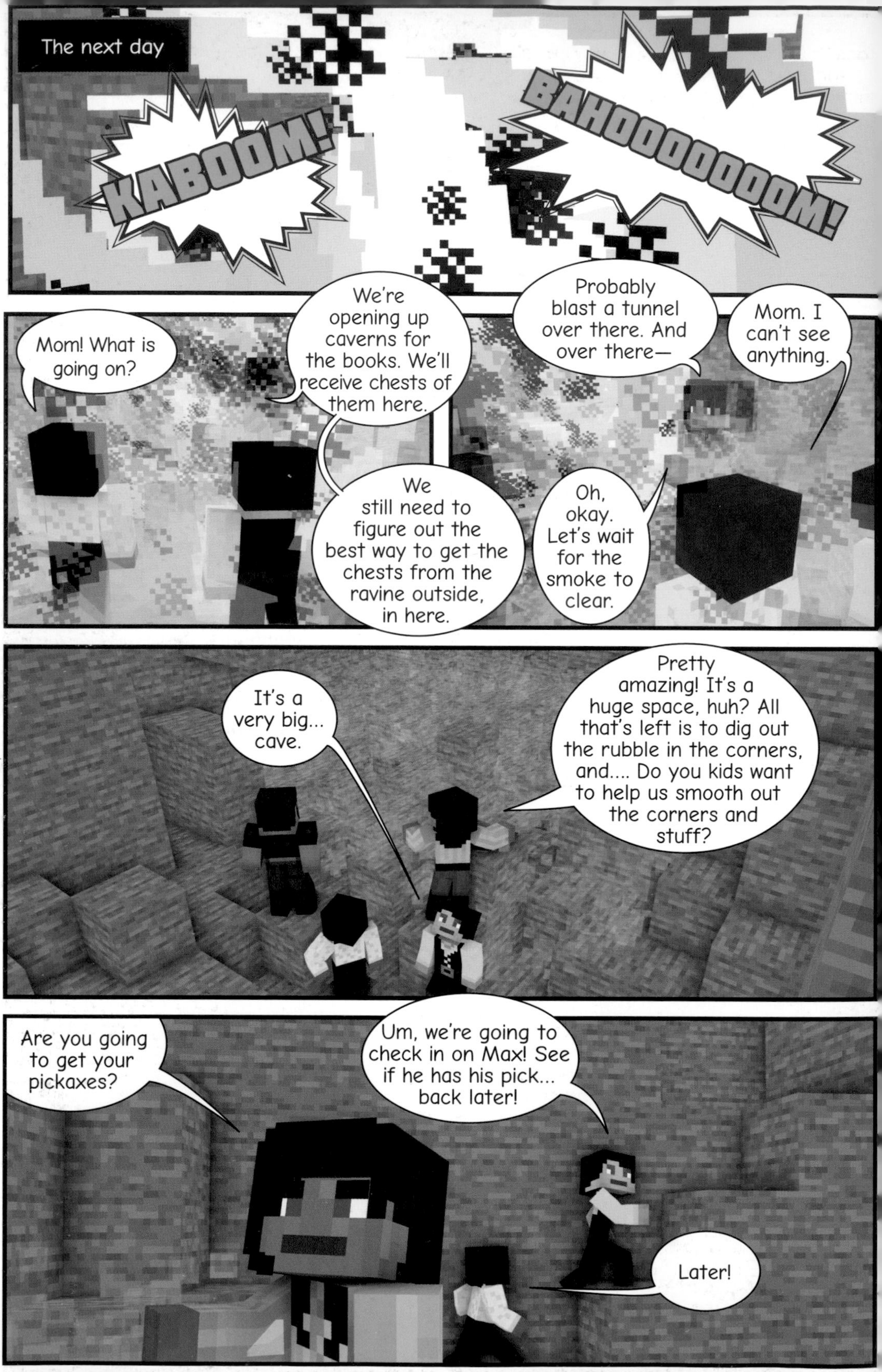
The next day
KABOOM!
BAHOOOOOOOOM!
Mom! What is going on?
We're opening up caverns for the books. We'll receive chests of them here.
We still need to figure out the best way to get the chests from the ravine outside, in here.
Probably blast a tunnel over there. And over there—
Mom. I can't see anything.
Oh, okay. Let's wait for the smoke to clear.
It's a very big... cave.
Pretty amazing! It's a huge space, huh? All that's left is to dig out the rubble in the corners, and.... Do you kids want to help us smooth out the corners and stuff?
Are you going to get your pickaxes?
Um, we're going to check in on Max! See if he has his pick... back later!
Later!

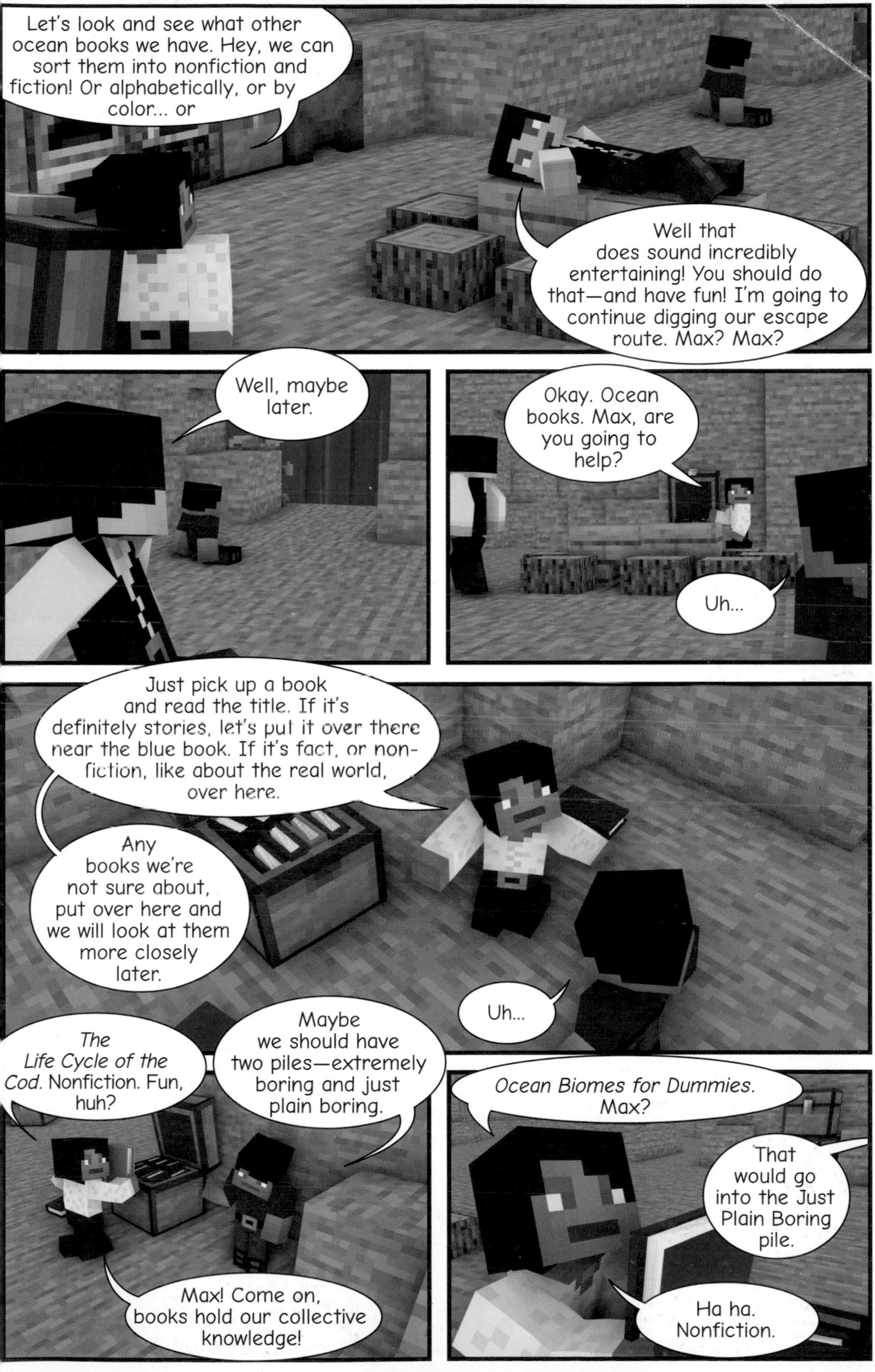

Let's look and see what other ocean books we have. Hey, we can sort them into nonfiction and fiction! Or alphabetically, or by color... or
Well that does sound incredibly entertaining! You should do that—and have fun! I'm going to continue digging our escape route. Max? Max?
Well, maybe later.
Okay. Ocean books. Max, are you going to help?
Uh...
Just pick up a book and read the title. If it's definitely stories, let's put it over there near the blue book. If it's fact, or non-fiction, like about the real world, over here.
Any books we're not sure about, put over here and we will look at them more closely later.
Uh...
The Life Cycle of the Cod. Nonfiction. Fun, huh?
Maybe we should have two piles—extremely boring and just plain boring.
Max! Come on, books hold our collective knowledge!
Ocean Biomes for Dummies. Max?
That would go into the Just Plain Boring pile.
Ha ha. Nonfiction.

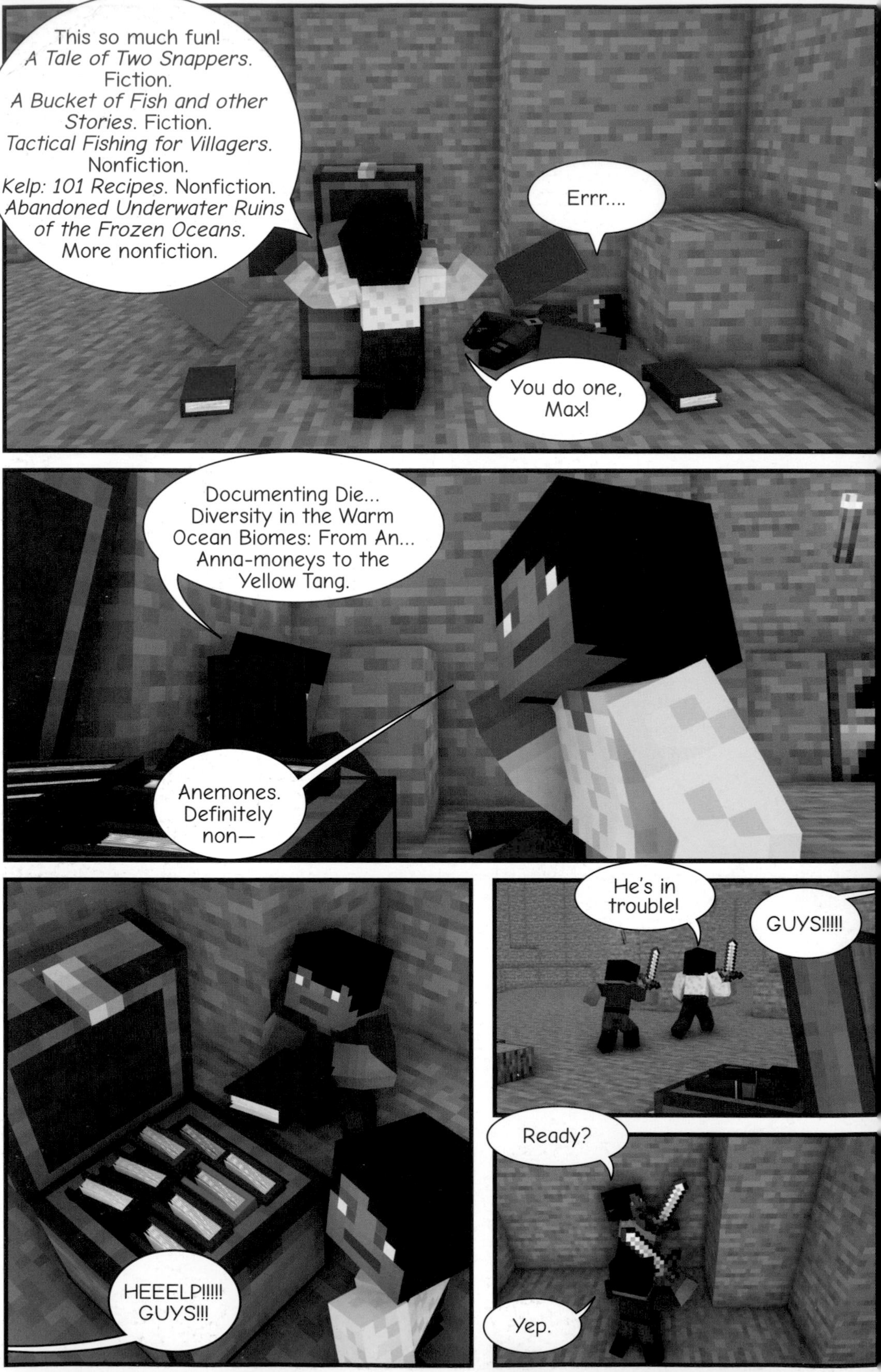
This so much fun!
A Tale of Two Snappers. Fiction.
A Bucket of Fish and other Stories. Fiction.
Tactical Fishing for Villagers. Nonfiction.
Kelp: 101 Recipes. Nonfiction.
Abandoned Underwater Ruins of the Frozen Oceans. More nonfiction.
Errr....
You do one, Max!
Documenting Die... Diversity in the Warm Ocean Biomes: From An... Anna-moneys to the Yellow Tang.
Anemones. Definitely non—
HEEELP!!!!! GUYS!!!
He's in trouble!
GUYS!!!!!
Ready?
Yep.

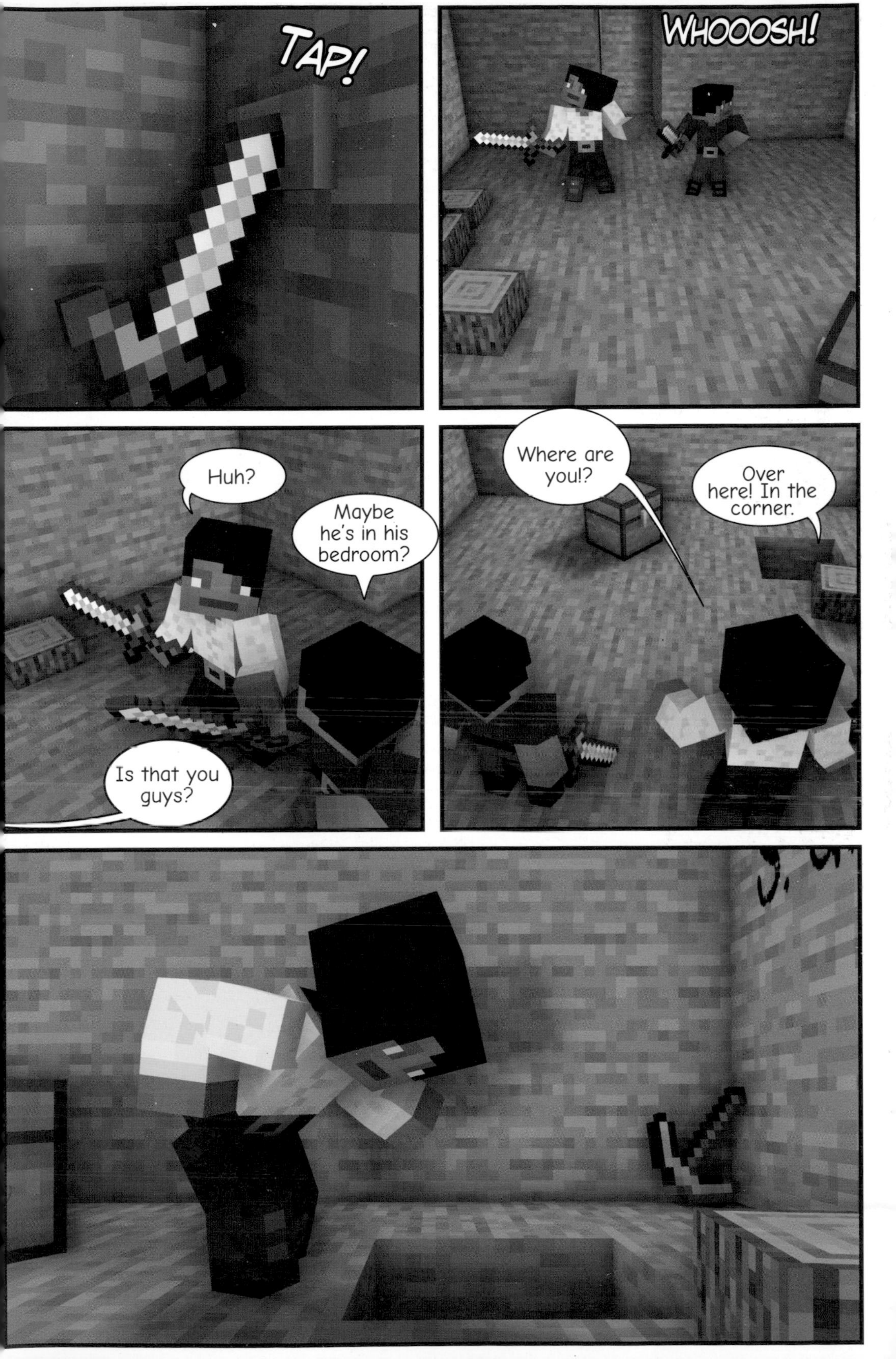
TAP!
WHOOOSH!
Huh?
Maybe he's in his bedroom?
Is that you guys?
Where are you!?
Over here! In the corner.

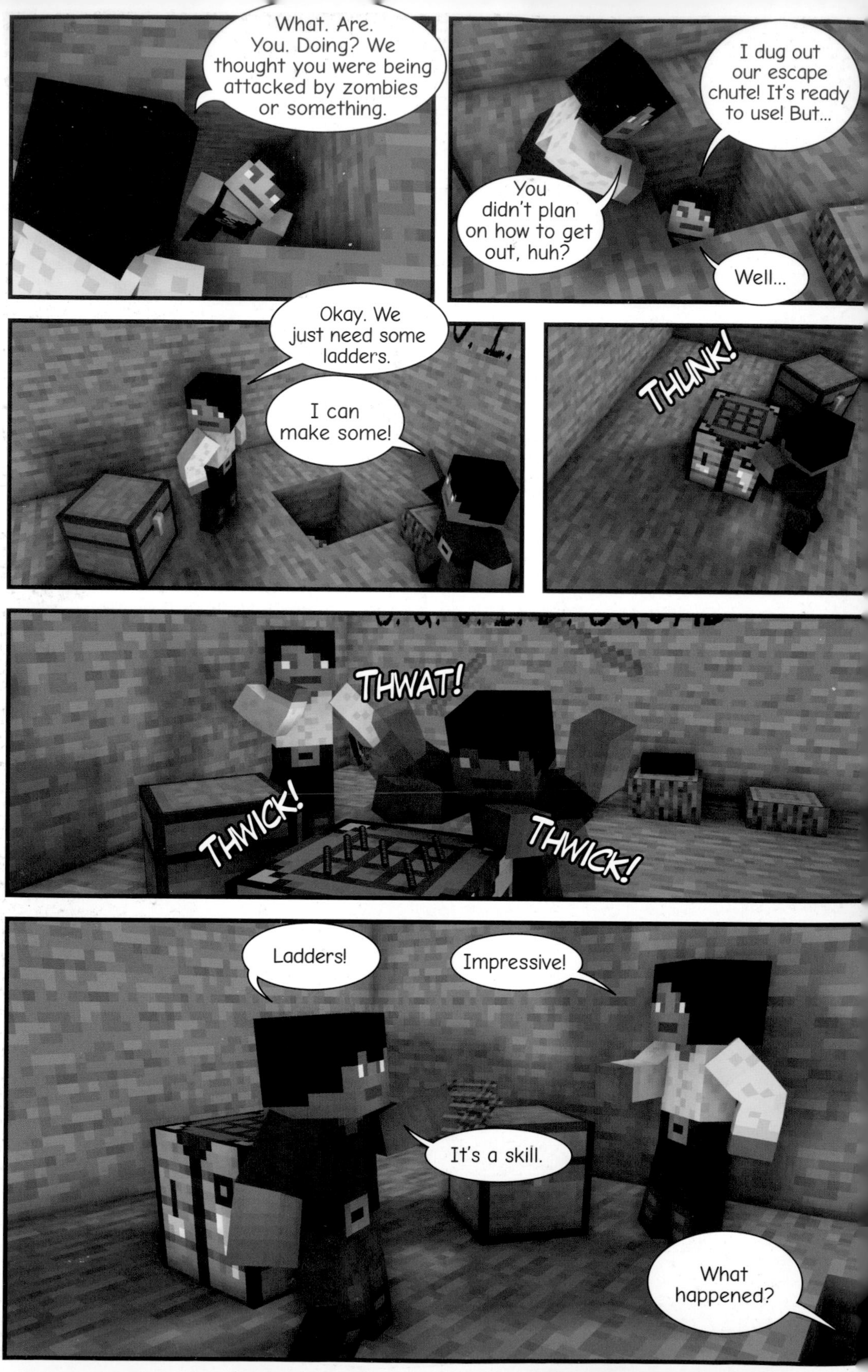
What. Are. You. Doing? We thought you were being attacked by zombies or something.
I dug out our escape chute! It's ready to use! But...
You didn't plan on how to get out, huh?
Well...
Okay. We just need some ladders.
I can make some!
THUNK!
THWAT!
THWICK!
THWICK!
Ladders!
Impressive!
It's a skill.
What happened?

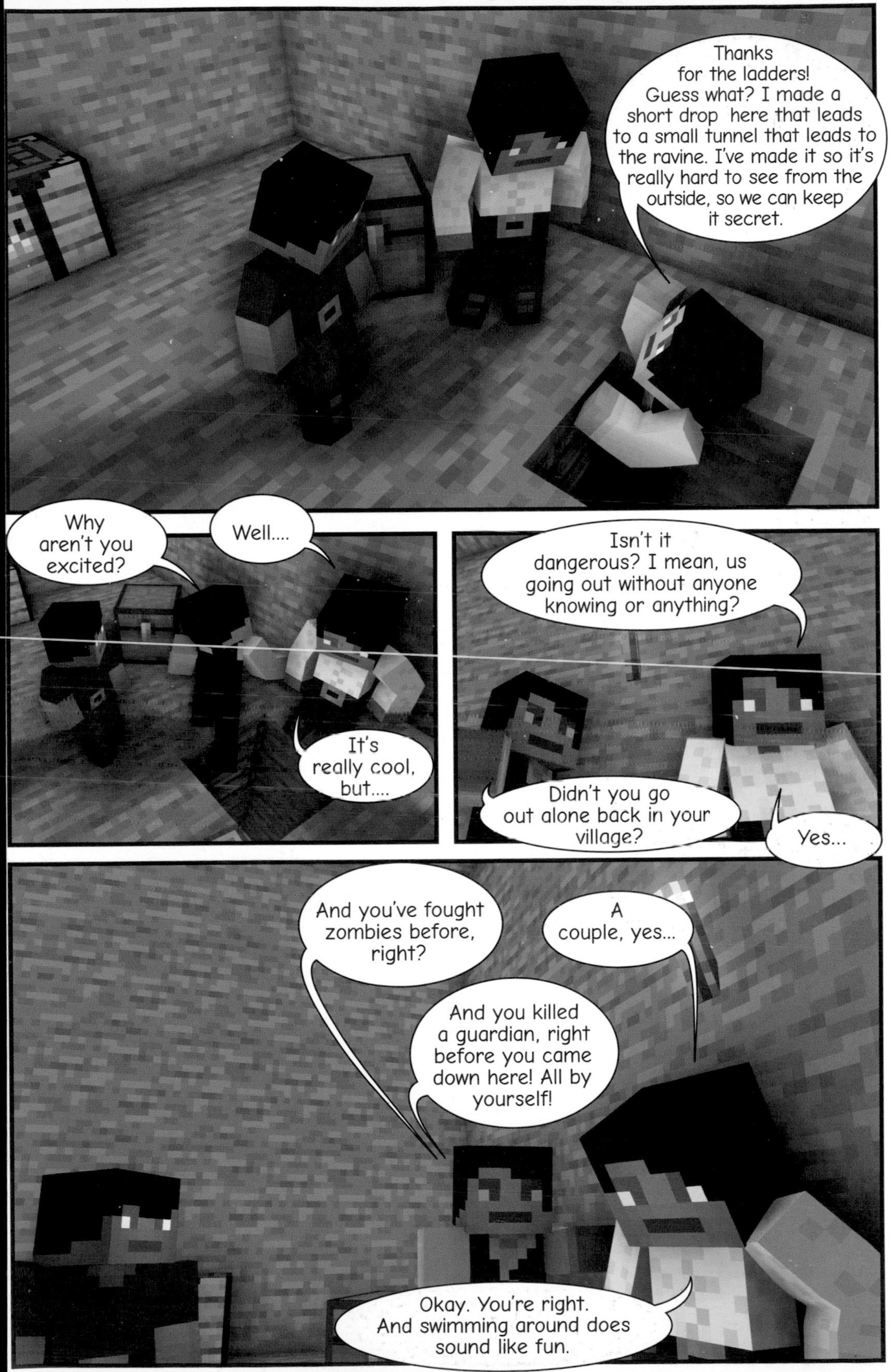
Thanks for the ladders! Guess what? I made a short drop here that leads to a small tunnel that leads to the ravine. I've made it so it's really hard to see from the outside, so we can keep it secret.
Why aren't you excited?
Well....
It's really cool, but....
Isn't it dangerous? I mean, us going out without anyone knowing or anything?
Didn't you go out alone back in your village?
Yes...
And you've fought zombies before, right?
A couple, yes...
And you killed a guardian, right before you came down here! All by yourself!
Okay. You're right. And swimming around does sound like fun.

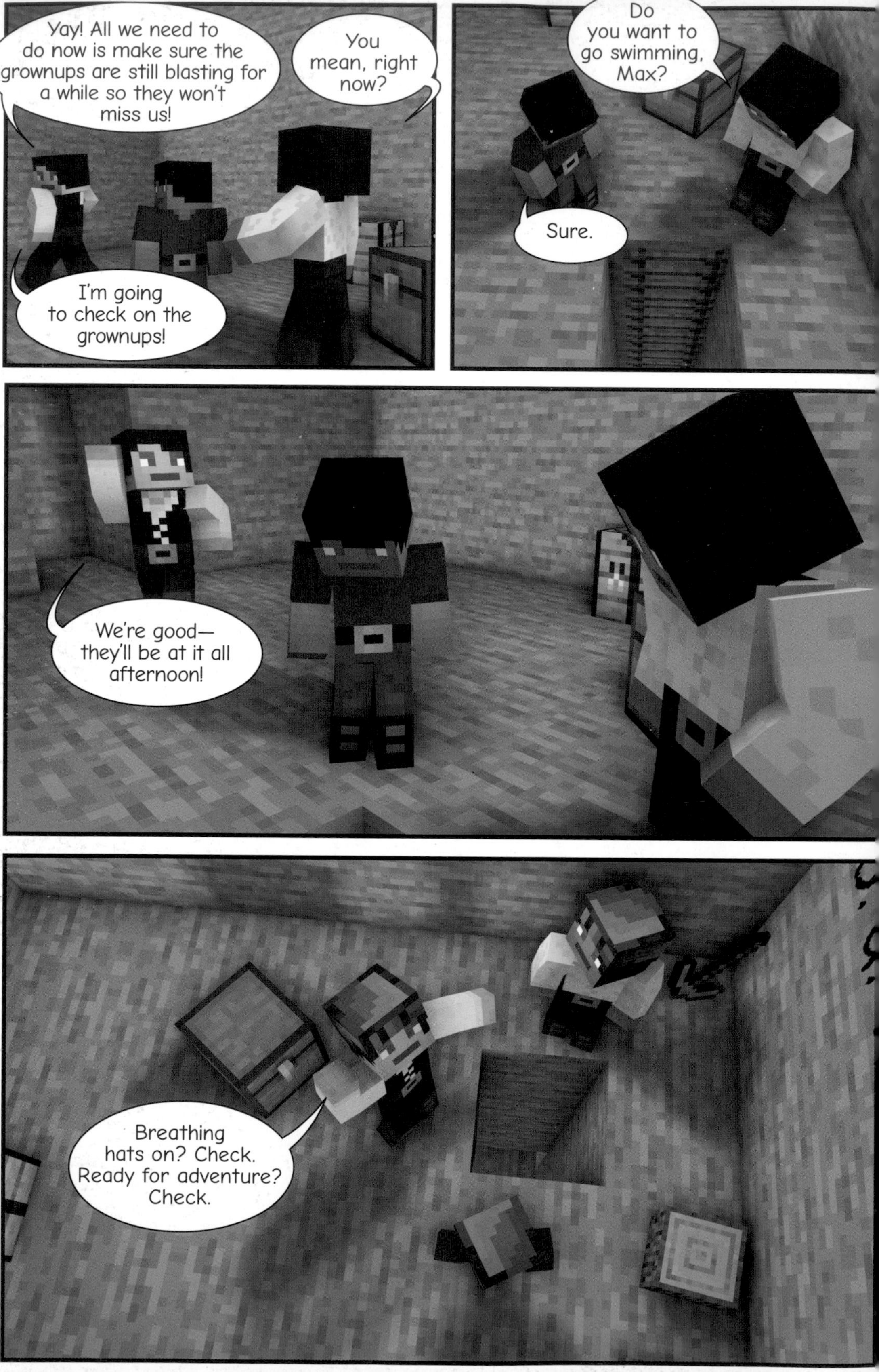
Yay! All we need to do now is make sure the grownups are still blasting for a while so they won't miss us!
You mean, right now?
I'm going to check on the grownups!
Do you want to go swimming, Max?
Sure.
We're good—they'll be at it all afternoon!
Breathing hats on? Check. Ready for adventure? Check.

Chapter 5

Skeleton Flowers and Bubblevators

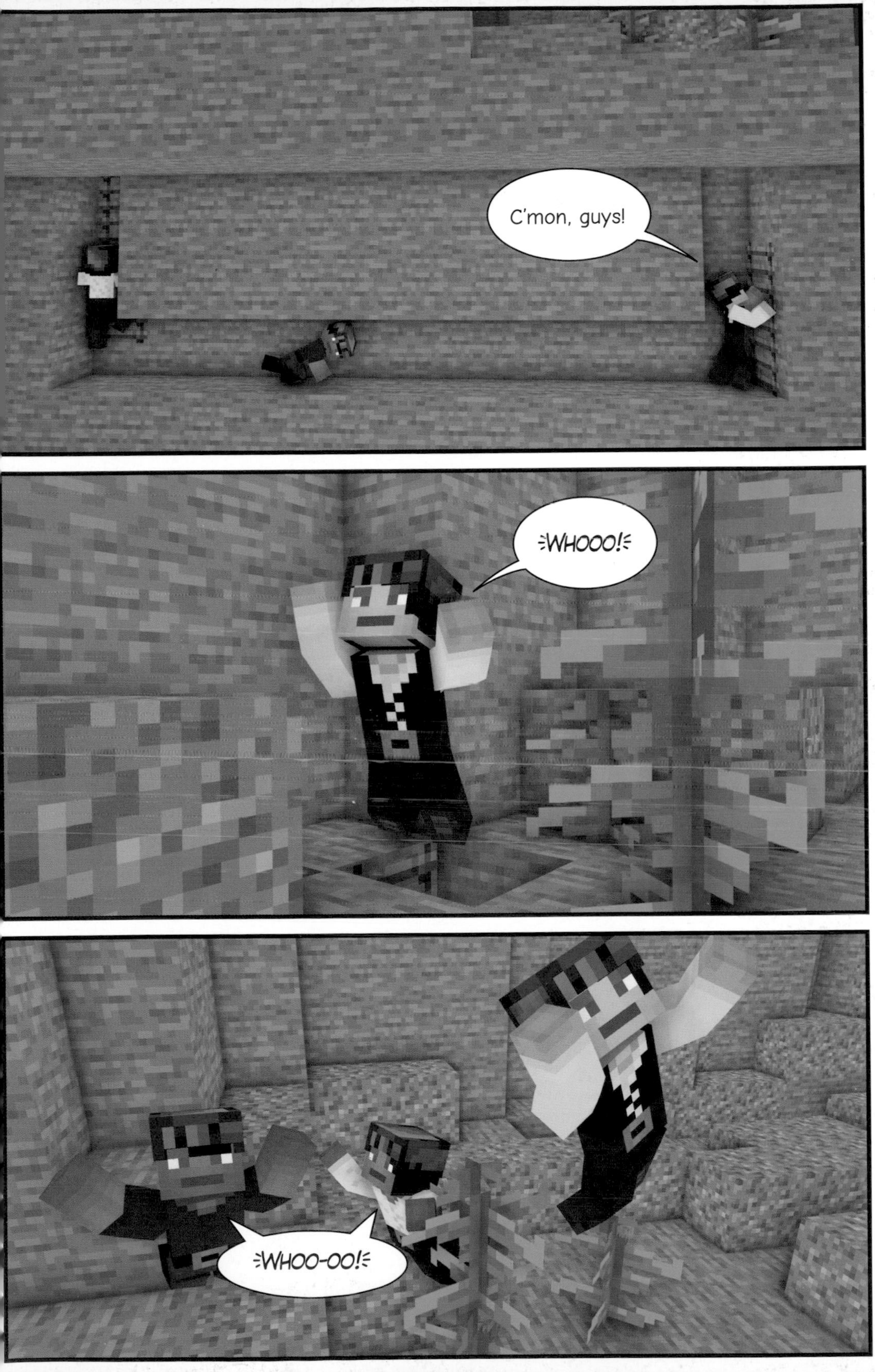
C'mon, guys!
WHOOO!
WHOO-OO!

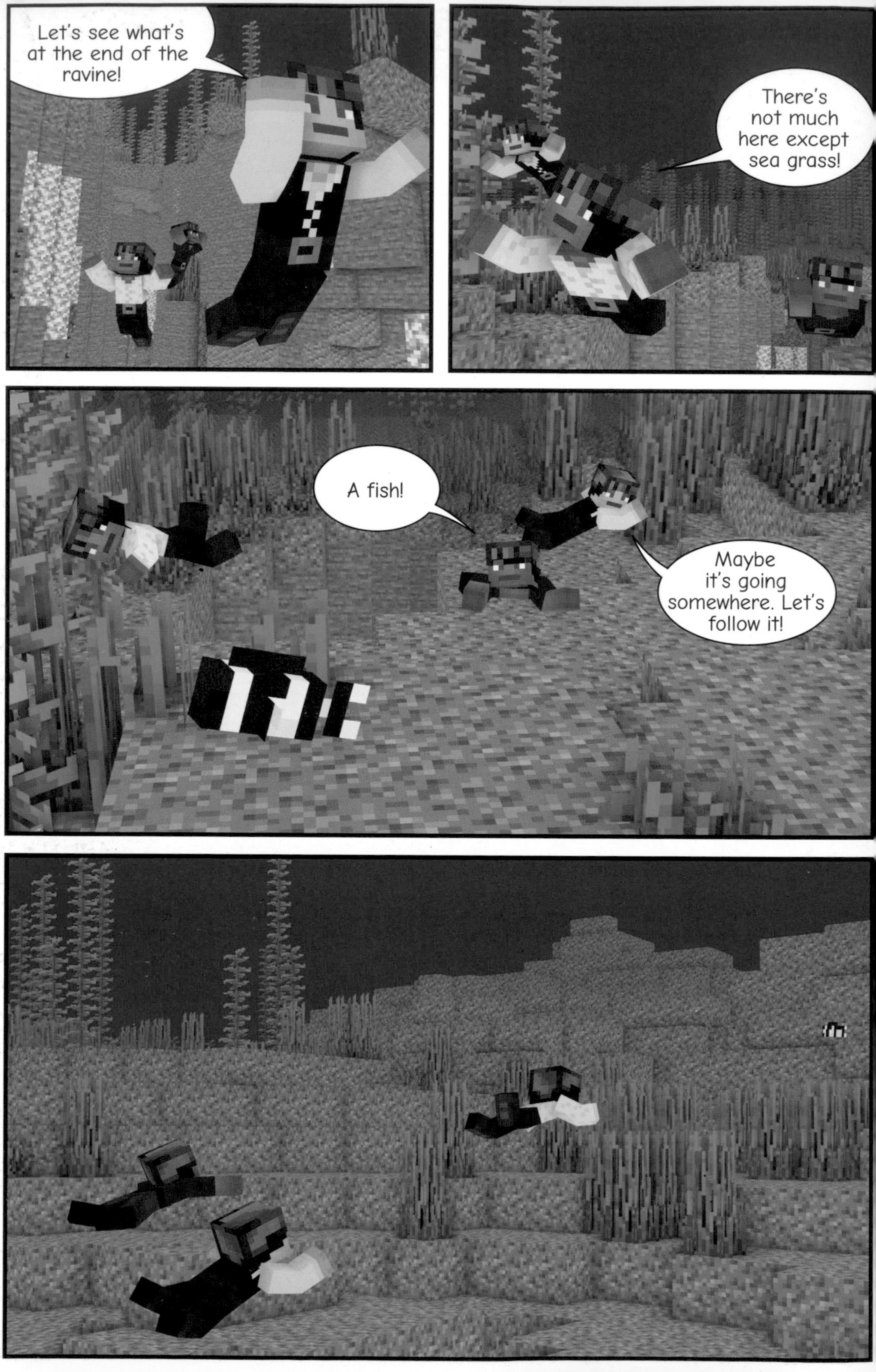
Let's see what's at the end of the ravine!
There's not much here except sea grass!
A fish!
Maybe it's going somewhere. Let's follow it!

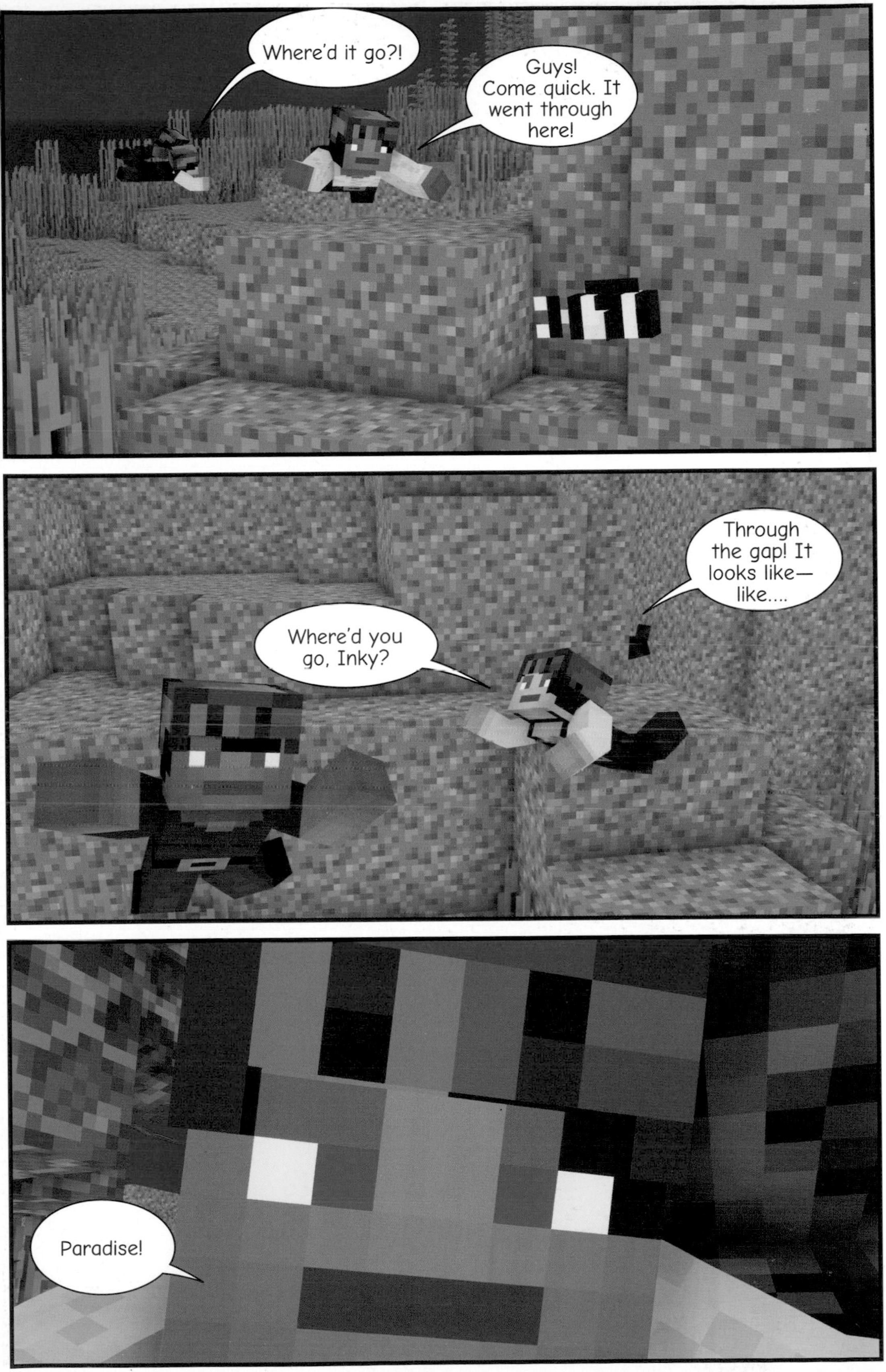
Where'd it go?!
Guys! Come quick. It went through here!
Where'd you go, Inky?
Through the gap! It looks like—like....
Paradise!

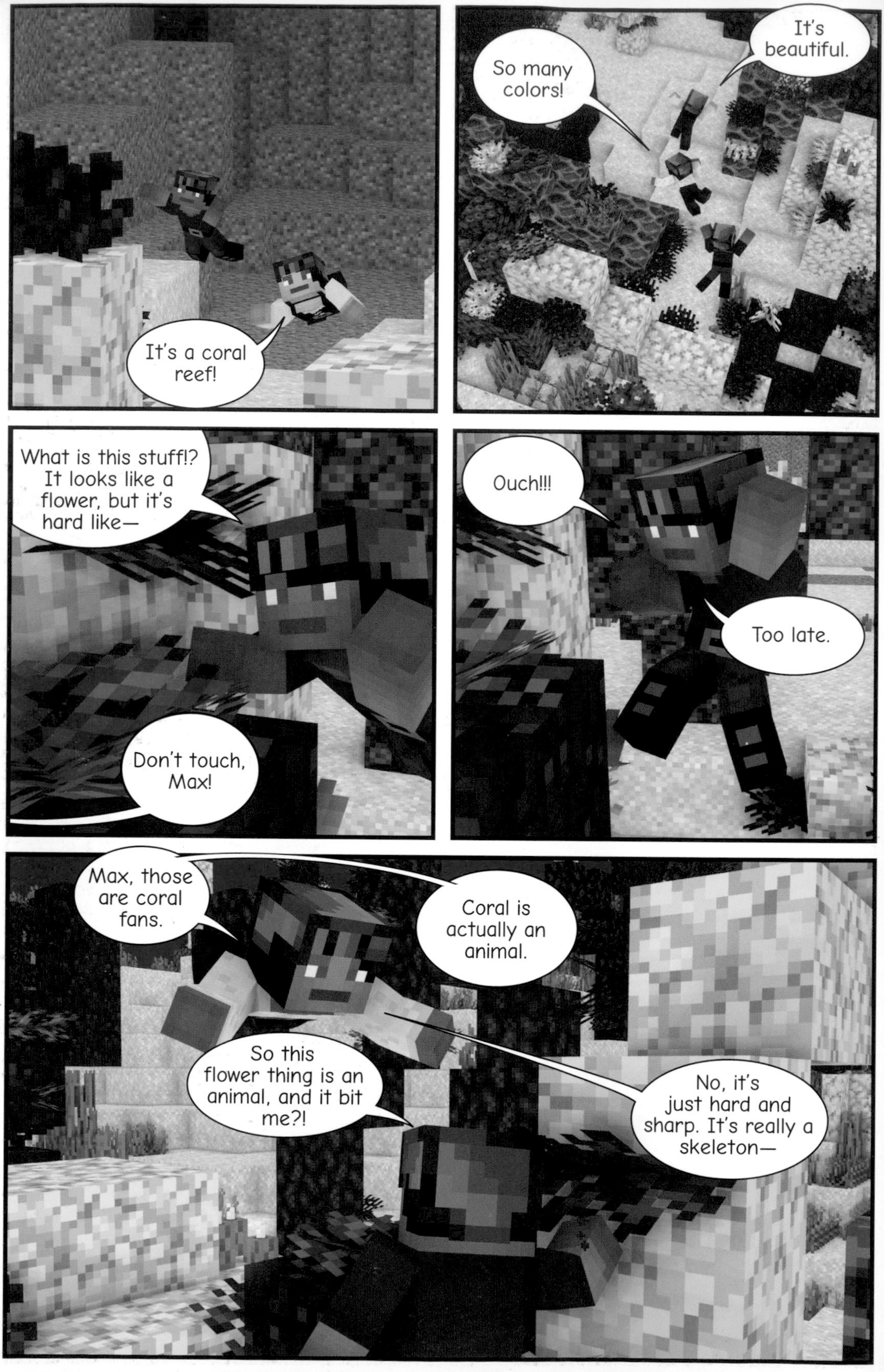
It's a coral reef!
So many colors!
It's beautiful.
What is this stuff!? It looks like a flower, but it's hard like—
Don't touch, Max!
Ouch!!!
Too late.
Max, those are coral fans.
Coral is actually an animal.
So this flower thing is an animal, and it bit me?!
No, it's just hard and sharp. It's really a skeleton—

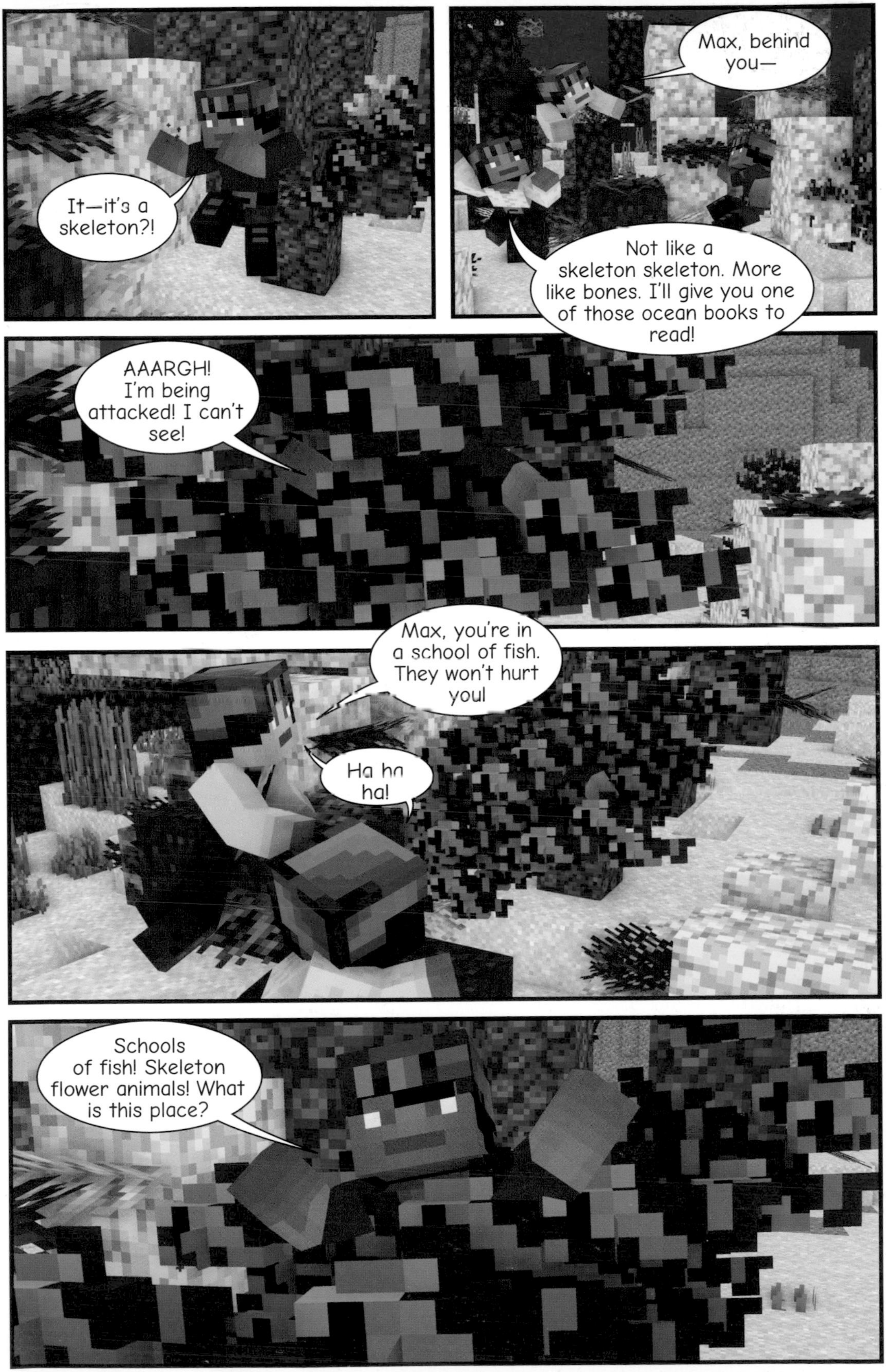
It—it's a skeleton?!
Max, behind you—
Not like a skeleton skeleton. More like bones. I'll give you one of those ocean books to read!
AAARGH! I'm being attacked! I can't see!
Max, you're in a school of fish. They won't hurt you!
Ha ha ha!
Schools of fish! Skeleton flower animals! What is this place?

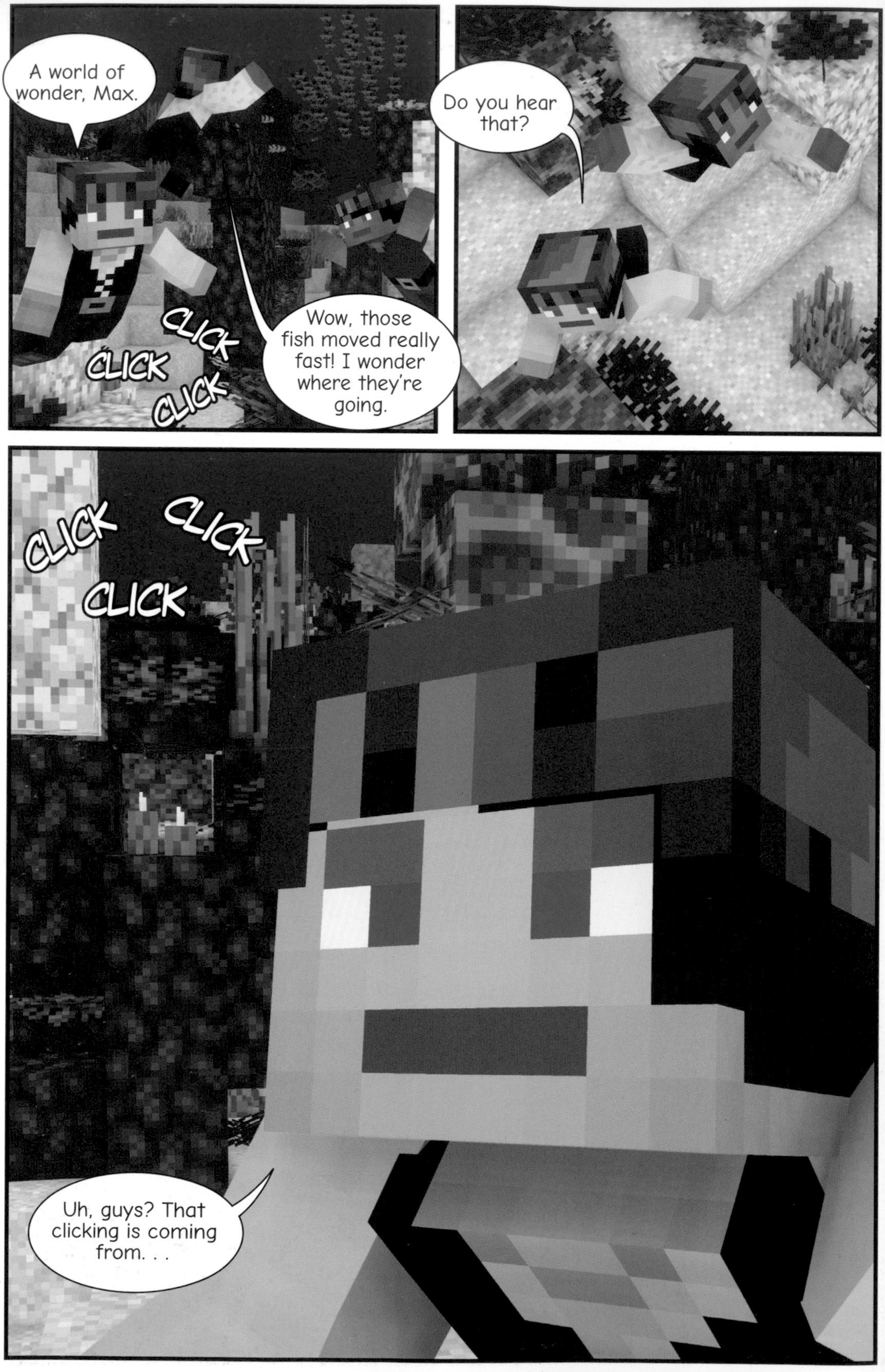
A world of wonder, Max.
CLICK
CLICK
CLICK
Wow, those fish moved really fast! I wonder where they're going.
Do you hear that?
CLICK
CLICK
CLICK
Uh, guys? That clicking is coming from. . .

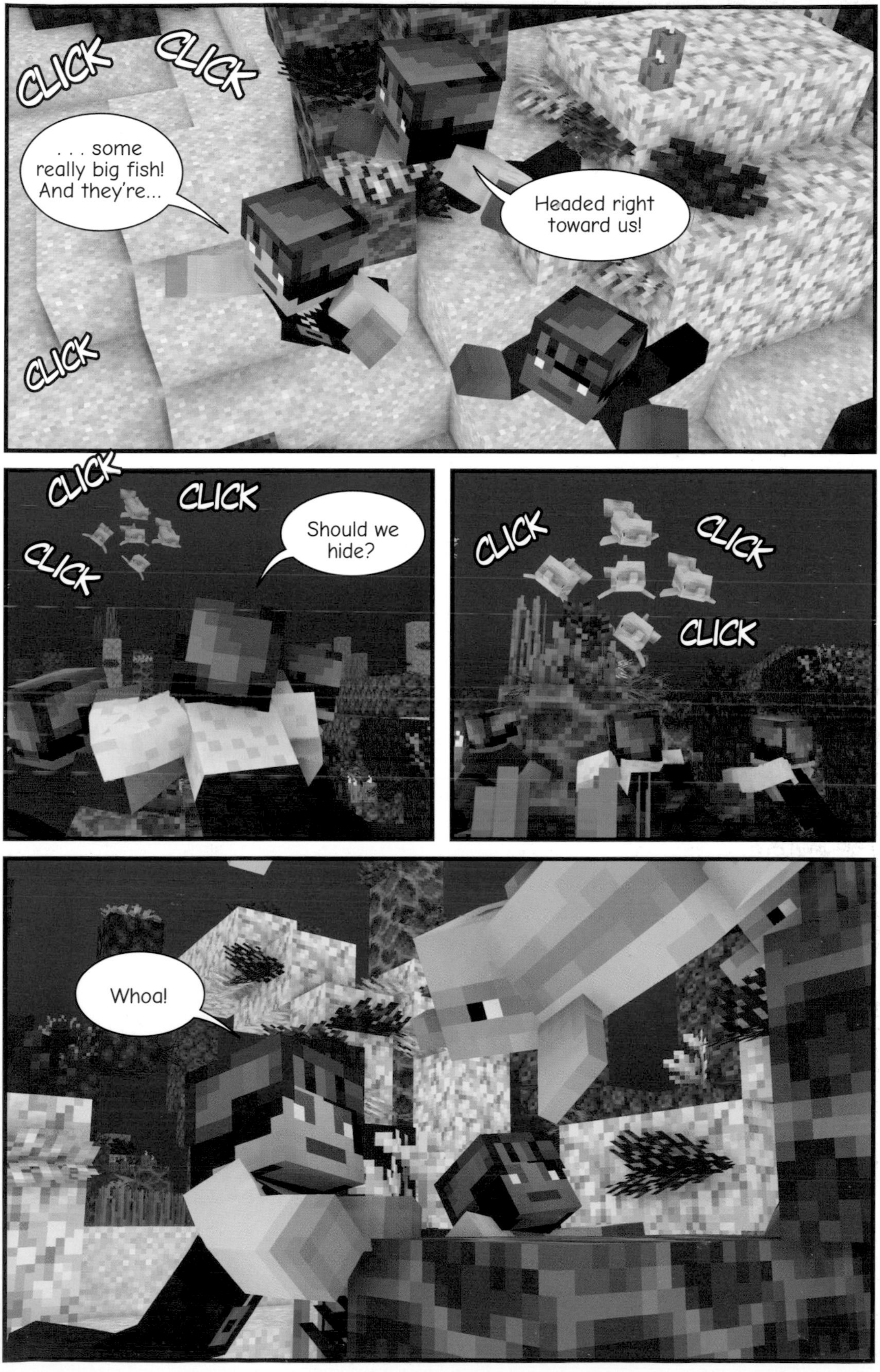
CLICK
CLICK
. . . some really big fish! And they're...
Headed right toward us!
CLICK
CLICK
CLICK
CLICK
Should we hide?
CLICK
CLICK
CLICK
Whoa!

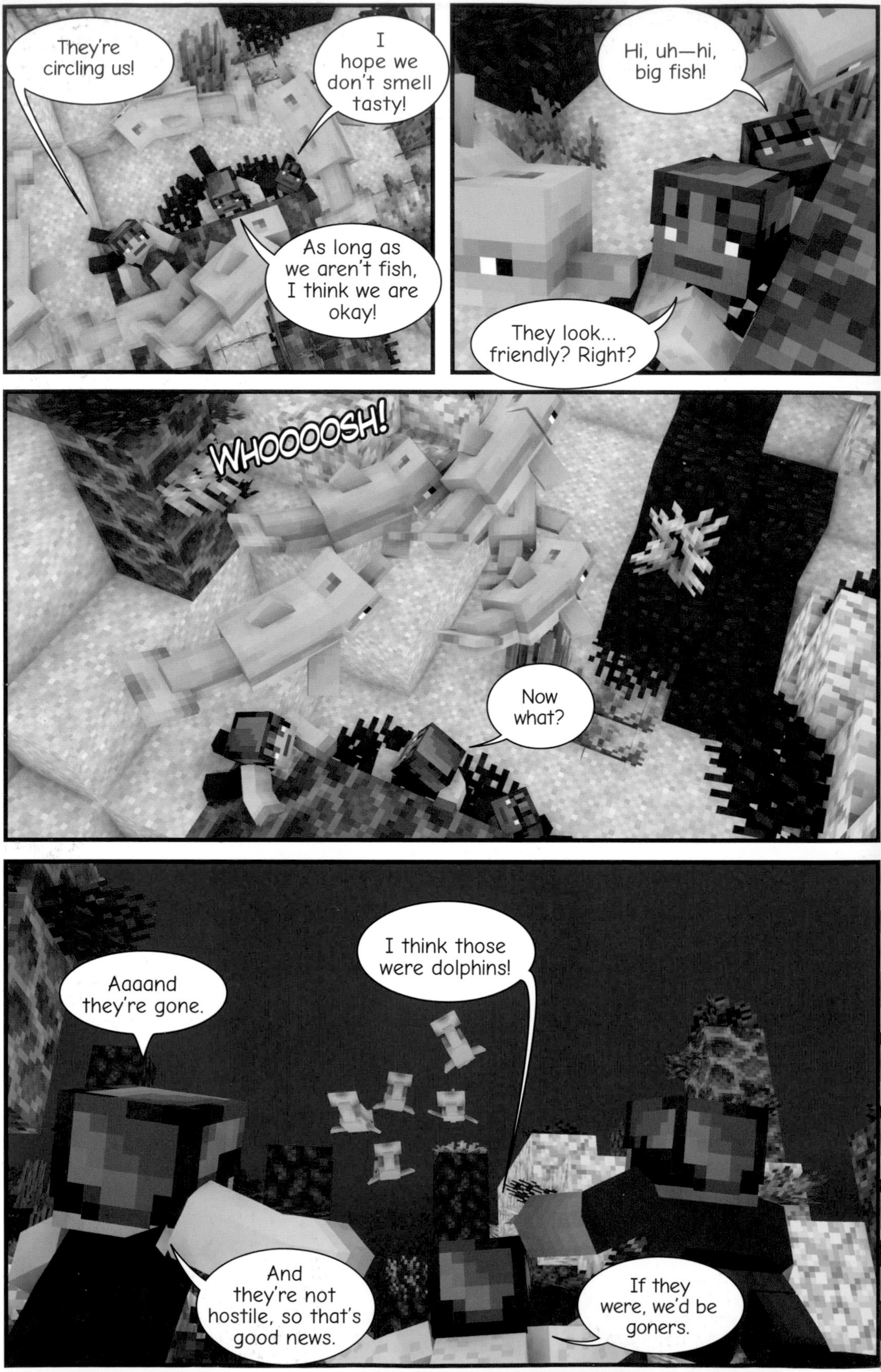
They're circling us!
I hope we don't smell tasty!
As long as we aren't fish, I think we are okay!
Hi, uh—hi, big fish!
They look... friendly? Right?
WHOOOOOSH!
Now what?
Aaaand they're gone.
I think those were dolphins!
And they're not hostile, so that's good news.
If they were, we'd be goners.

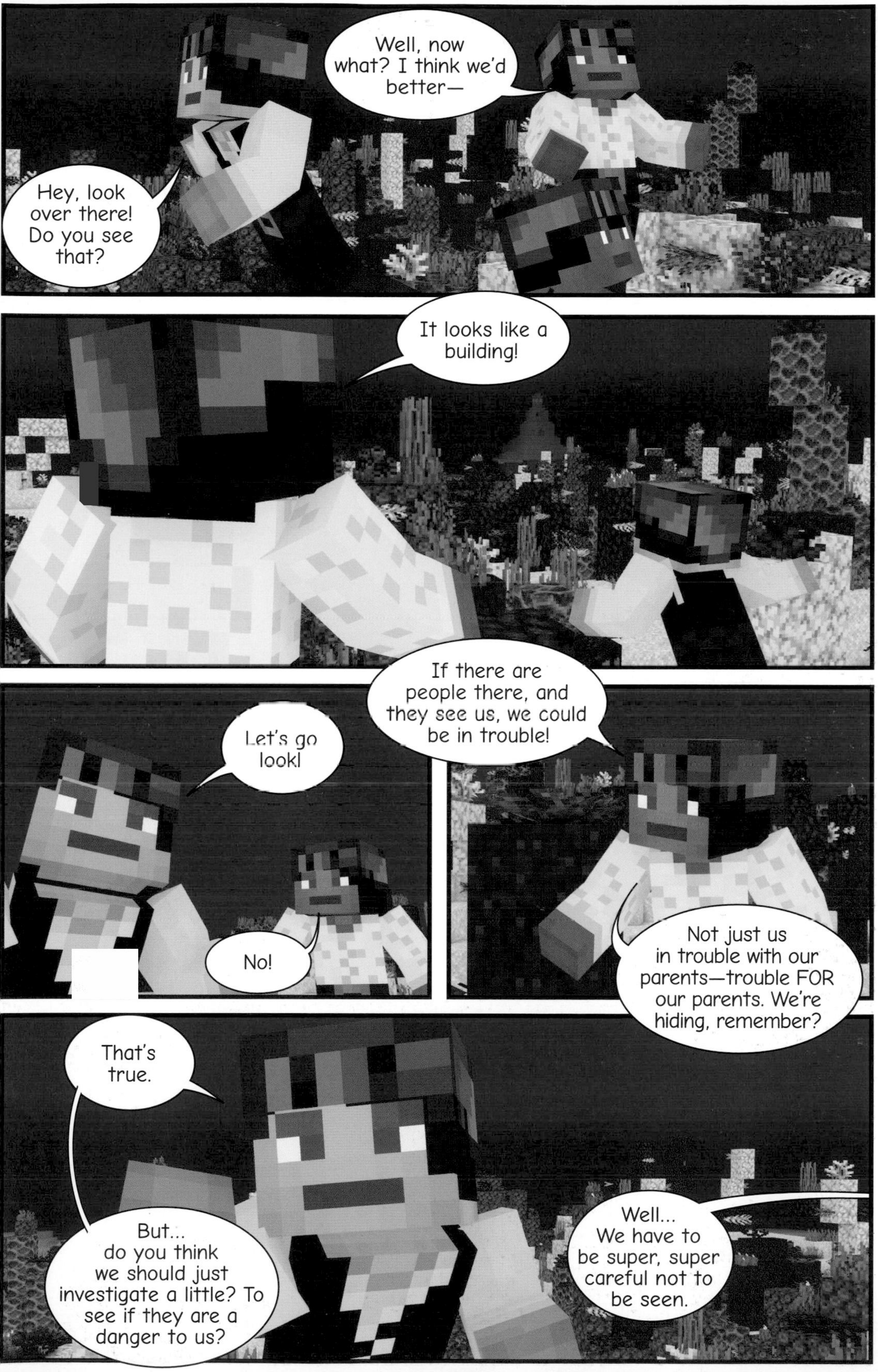
Well, now what? I think we'd better—
Hey, look over there! Do you see that?
It looks like a building!
Let's go look!
No!
If there are people there, and they see us, we could be in trouble!
Not just us in trouble with our parents—trouble FOR our parents. We're hiding, remember?
That's true.
But... do you think we should just investigate a little? To see if they are a danger to us?
Well... We have to be super, super careful not to be seen.

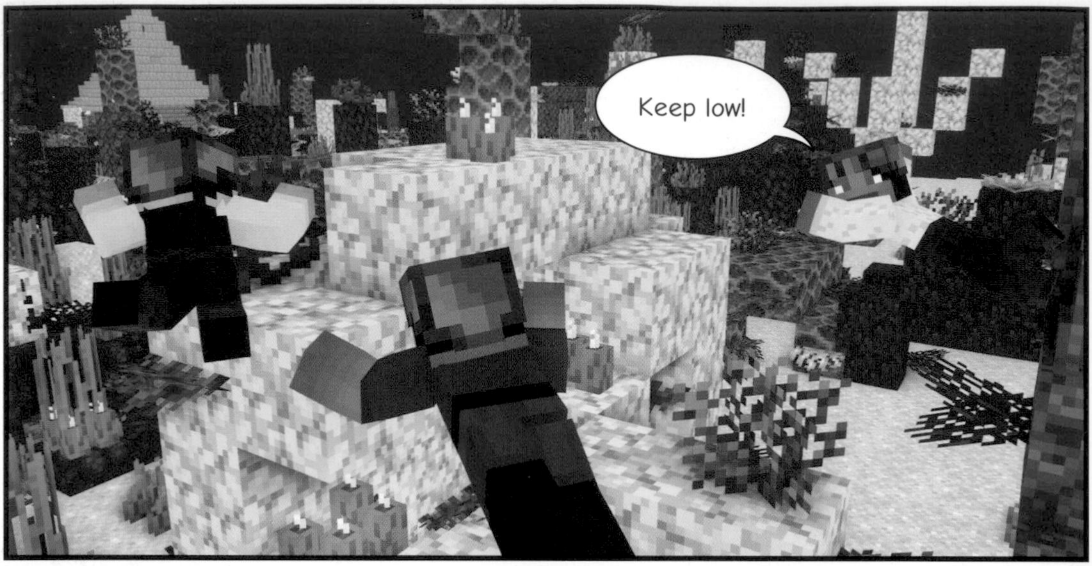
Keep low!

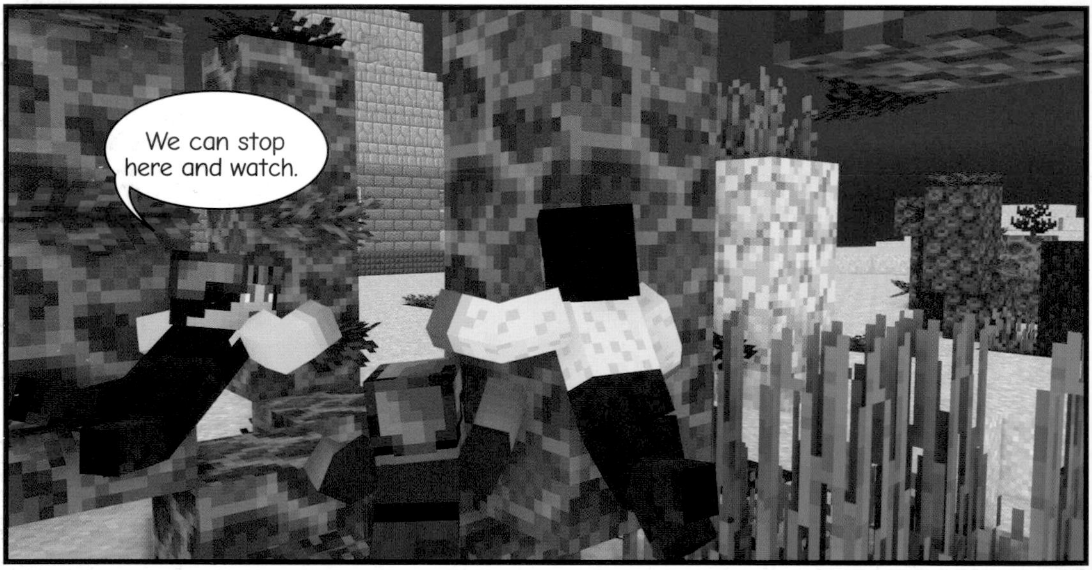
We can stop here and watch.

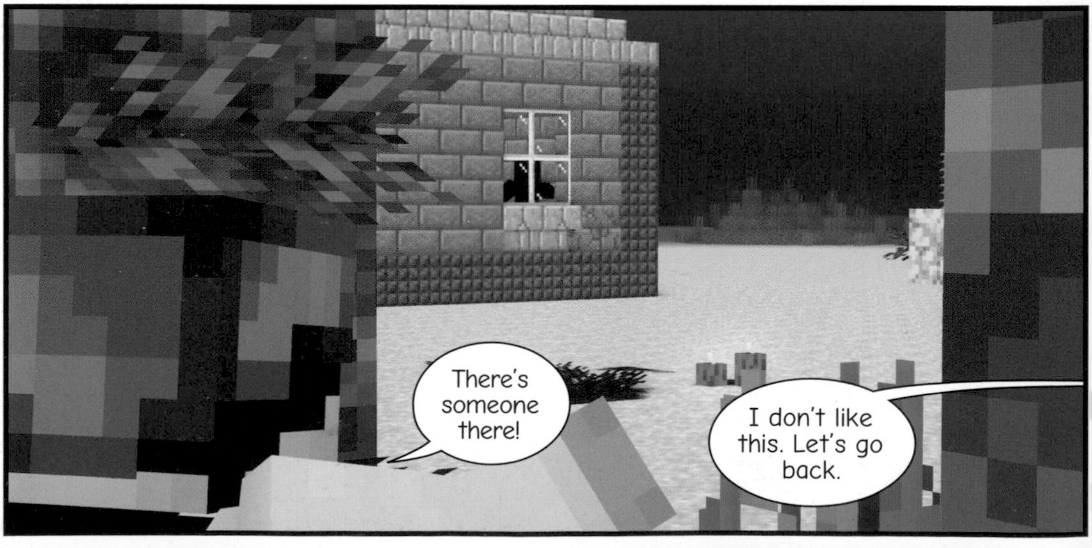
There's someone there!
I don't like this. Let's go back.

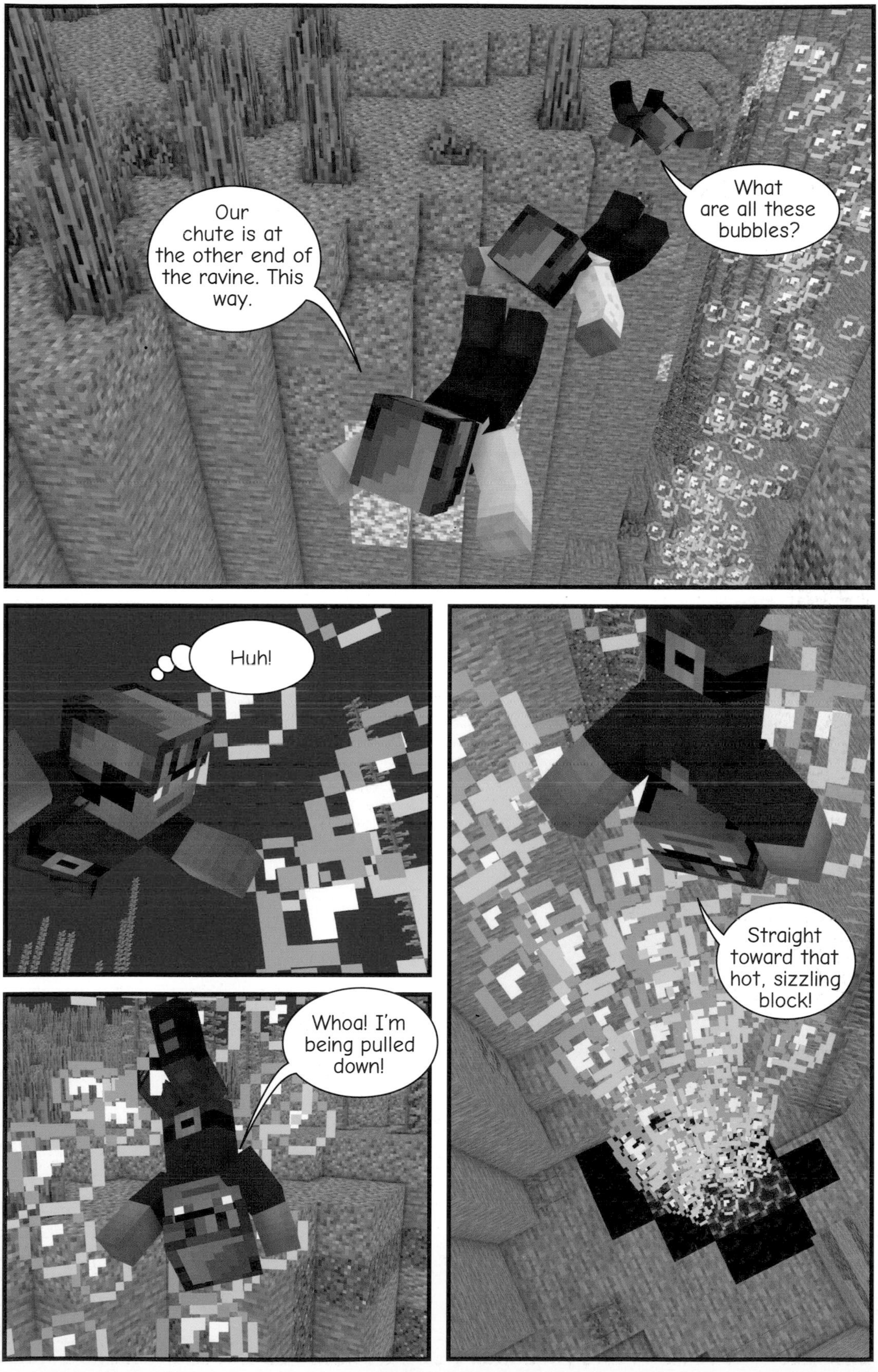
Our chute is at the other end of the ravine. This way.
What are all these bubbles?
Huh!
Whoa! I'm being pulled down!
Straight toward that hot, sizzling block!

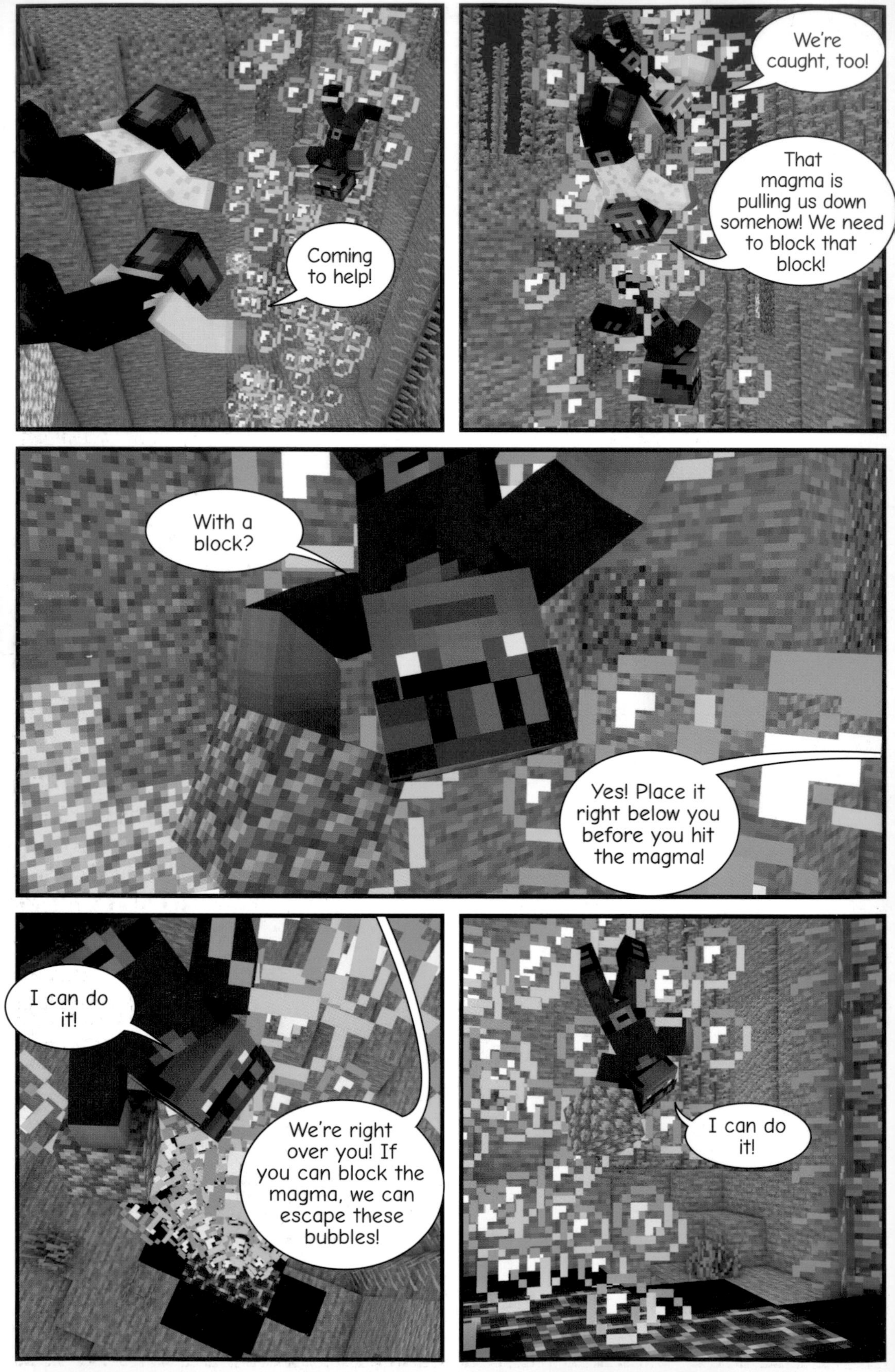
Coming to help!
We're caught, too!
That magma is pulling us down somehow! We need to block that block!
With a block?
Yes! Place it right below you before you hit the magma!
I can do it!
We're right over you! If you can block the magma, we can escape these bubbles!
I can do it!

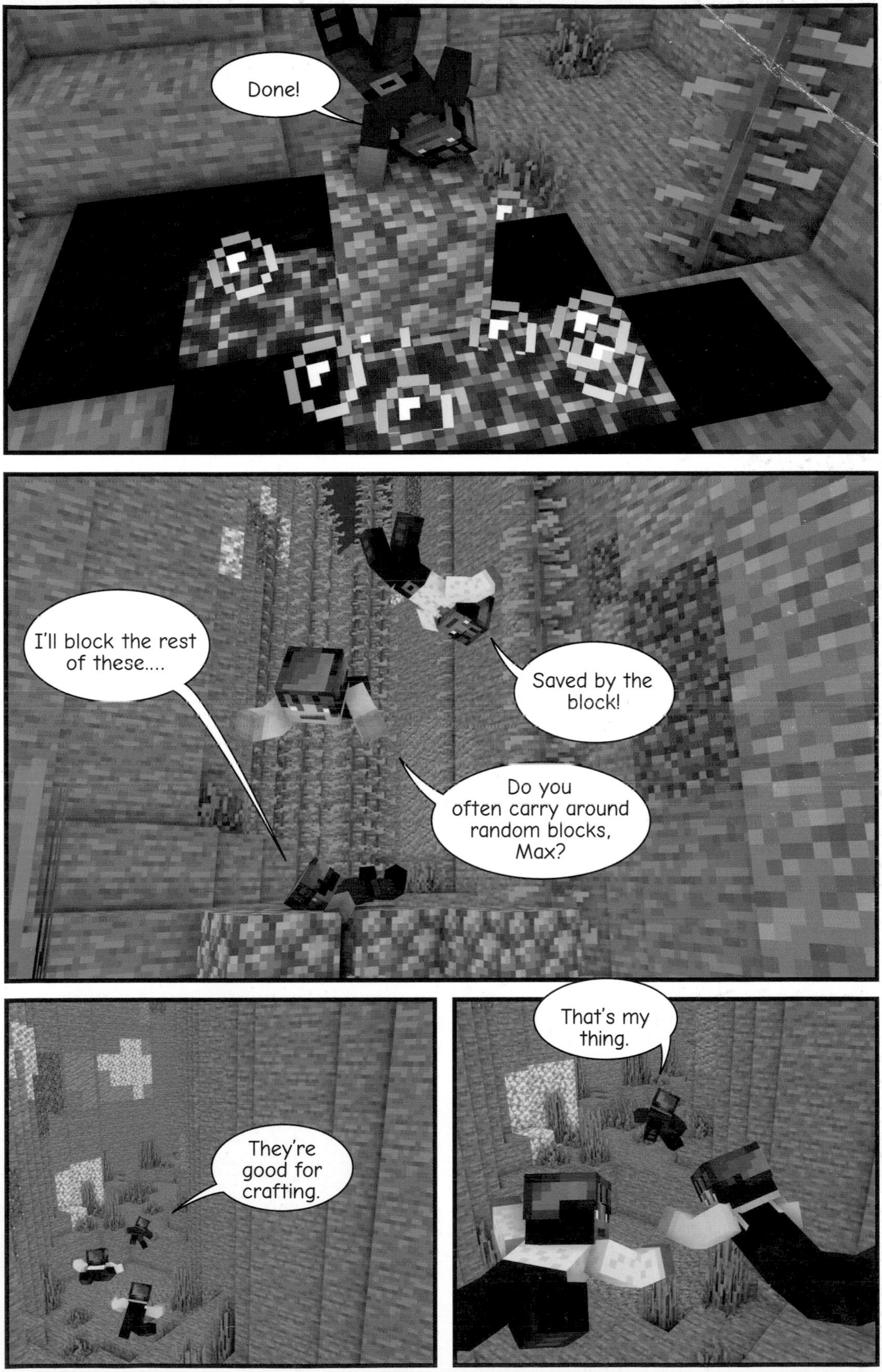
Done!
I'll block the rest of these....
Saved by the block!
Do you often carry around random blocks, Max?
They're good for crafting.
That's my thing.

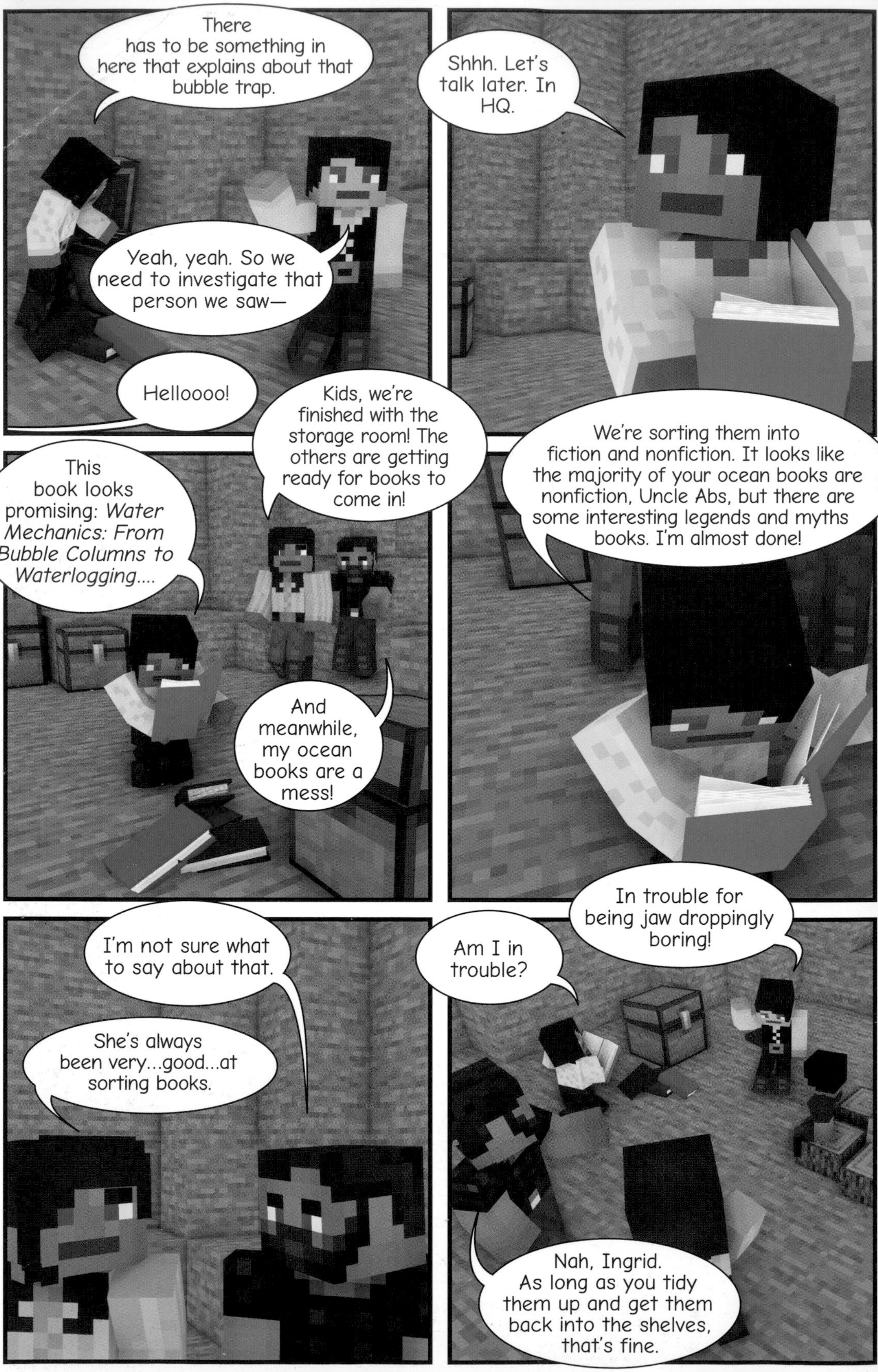
There has to be something in here that explains about that bubble trap.
Yeah, yeah. So we need to investigate that person we saw—
Helloooo!
Shhh. Let's talk later. In HQ.
Kids, we're finished with the storage room! The others are getting ready for books to come in!
This book looks promising: *Water Mechanics: From Bubble Columns to Waterlogging*....
And meanwhile, my ocean books are a mess!
We're sorting them into fiction and nonfiction. It looks like the majority of your ocean books are nonfiction, Uncle Abs, but there are some interesting legends and myths books. I'm almost done!
I'm not sure what to say about that.
She's always been very...good...at sorting books.
Am I in trouble?
In trouble for being jaw droppingly boring!
Nah, Ingrid. As long as you tidy them up and get them back into the shelves, that's fine.

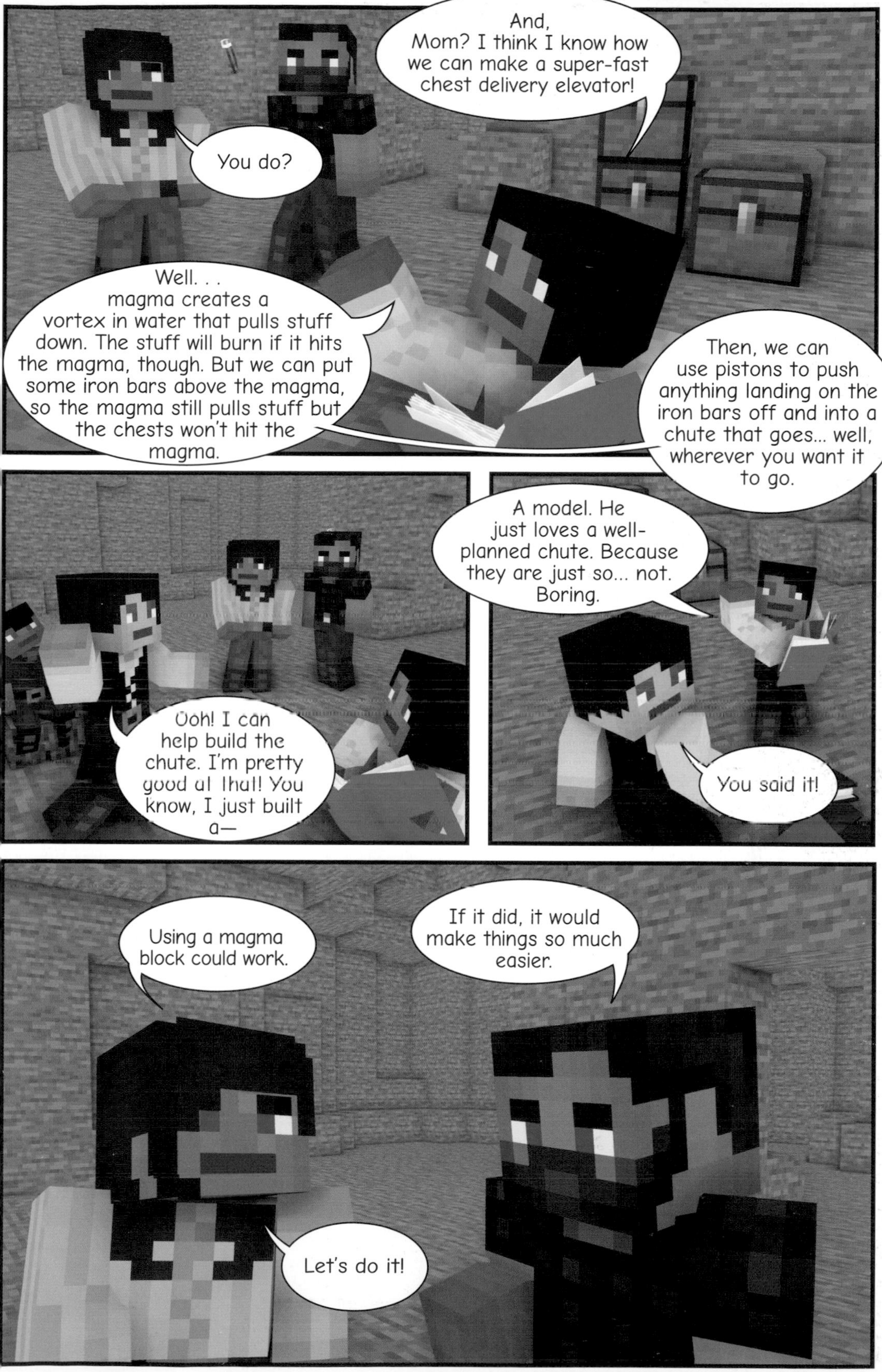
And, Mom? I think I know how we can make a super-fast chest delivery elevator!
You do?
Well. . . magma creates a vortex in water that pulls stuff down. The stuff will burn if it hits the magma, though. But we can put some iron bars above the magma, so the magma still pulls stuff but the chests won't hit the magma.
Then, we can use pistons to push anything landing on the iron bars off and into a chute that goes... well, wherever you want it to go.
Ooh! I can help build the chute. I'm pretty good at that! You know, I just built a—
A model. He just loves a well-planned chute. Because they are just so... not. Boring.
You said it!
Using a magma block could work.
If it did, it would make things so much easier.
Let's do it!

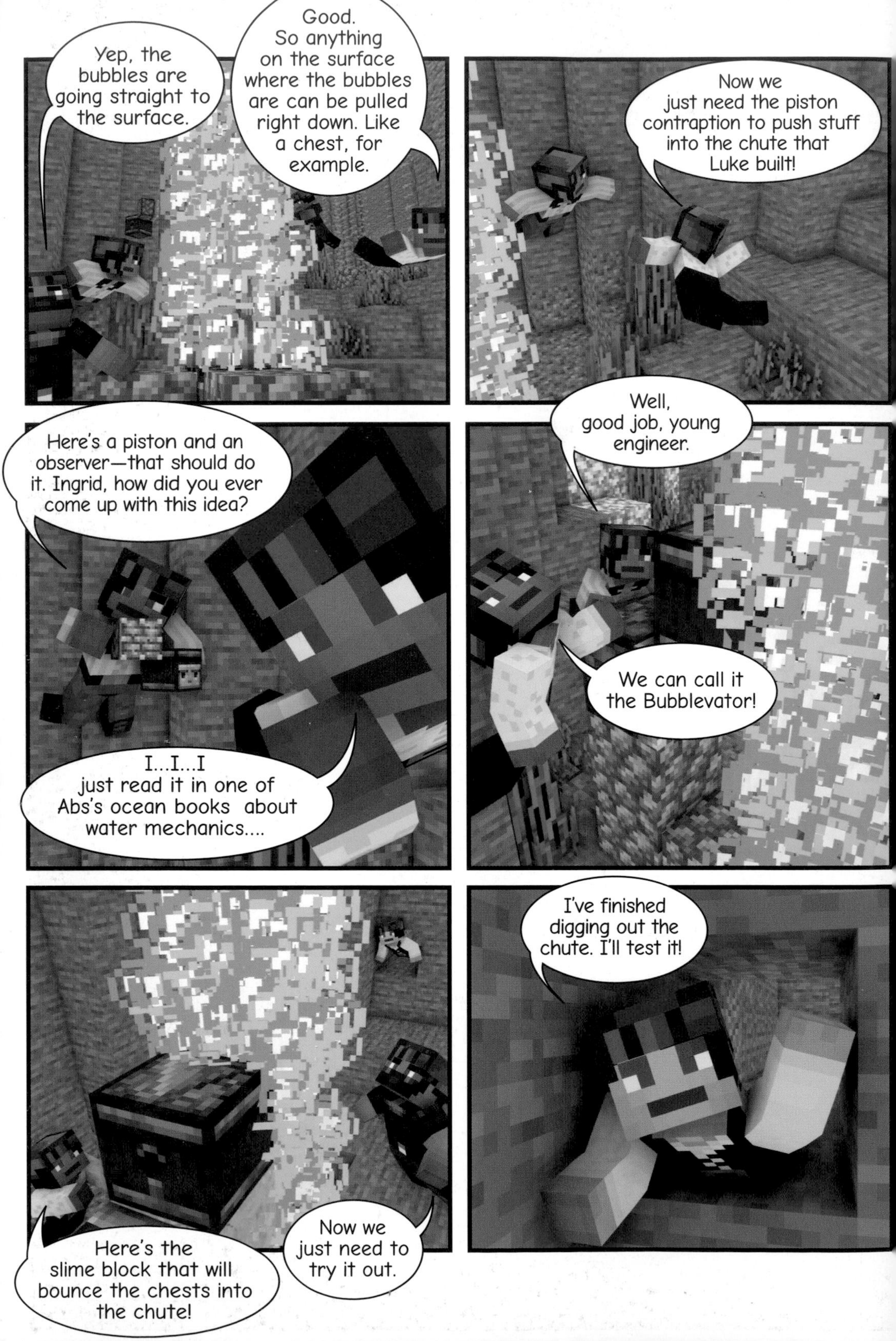
Yep, the bubbles are going straight to the surface.
Good. So anything on the surface where the bubbles are can be pulled right down. Like a chest, for example.
Now we just need the piston contraption to push stuff into the chute that Luke built!
Here's a piston and an observer—that should do it. Ingrid, how did you ever come up with this idea?
I...I...I just read it in one of Abs's ocean books about water mechanics....
Well, good job, young engineer.
We can call it the Bubblevator!
Here's the slime block that will bounce the chests into the chute!
Now we just need to try it out.
I've finished digging out the chute. I'll test it!

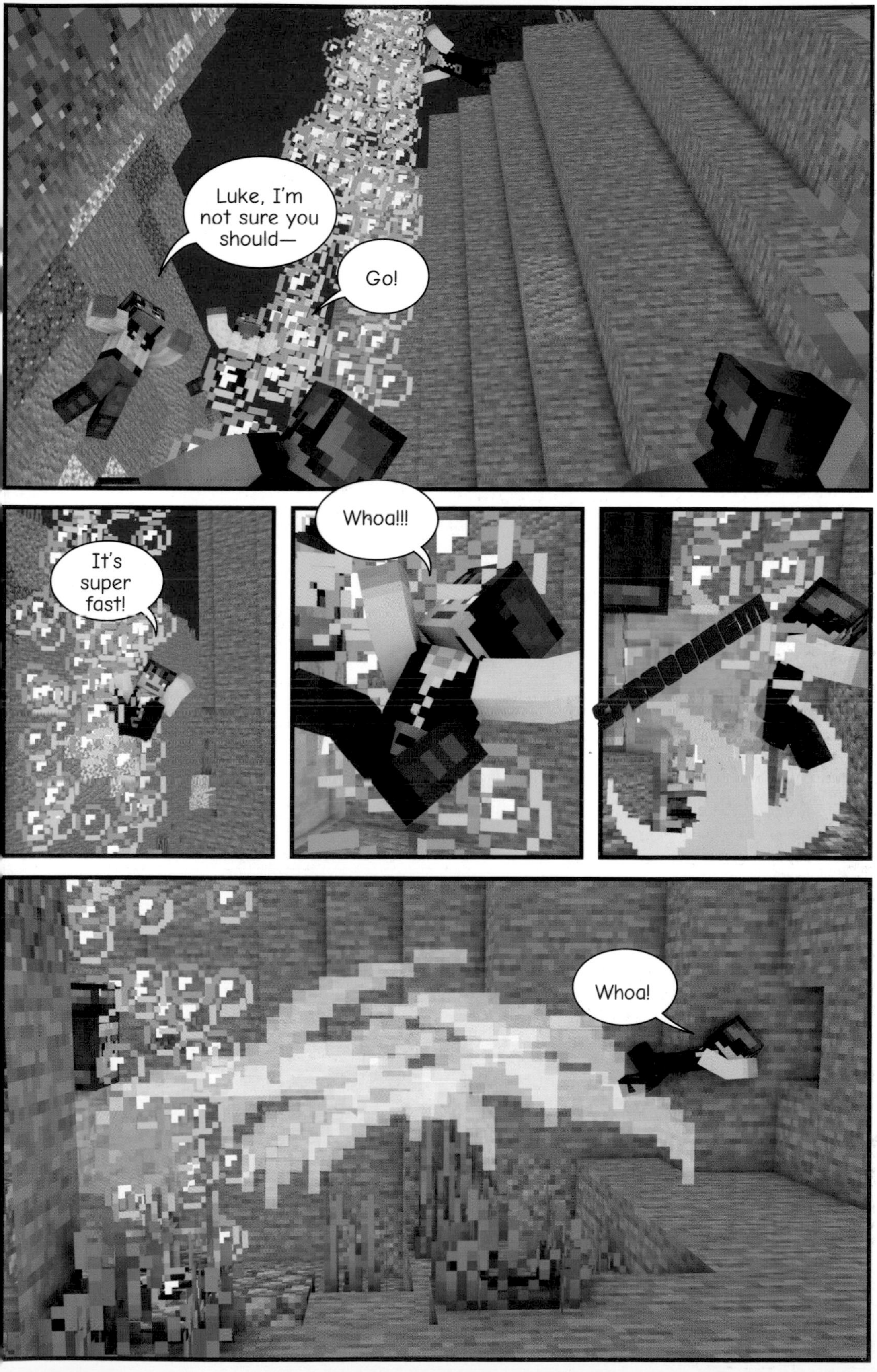
Luke, I'm not sure you should—
Go!
It's super fast!
Whoa!!!
Whoa!

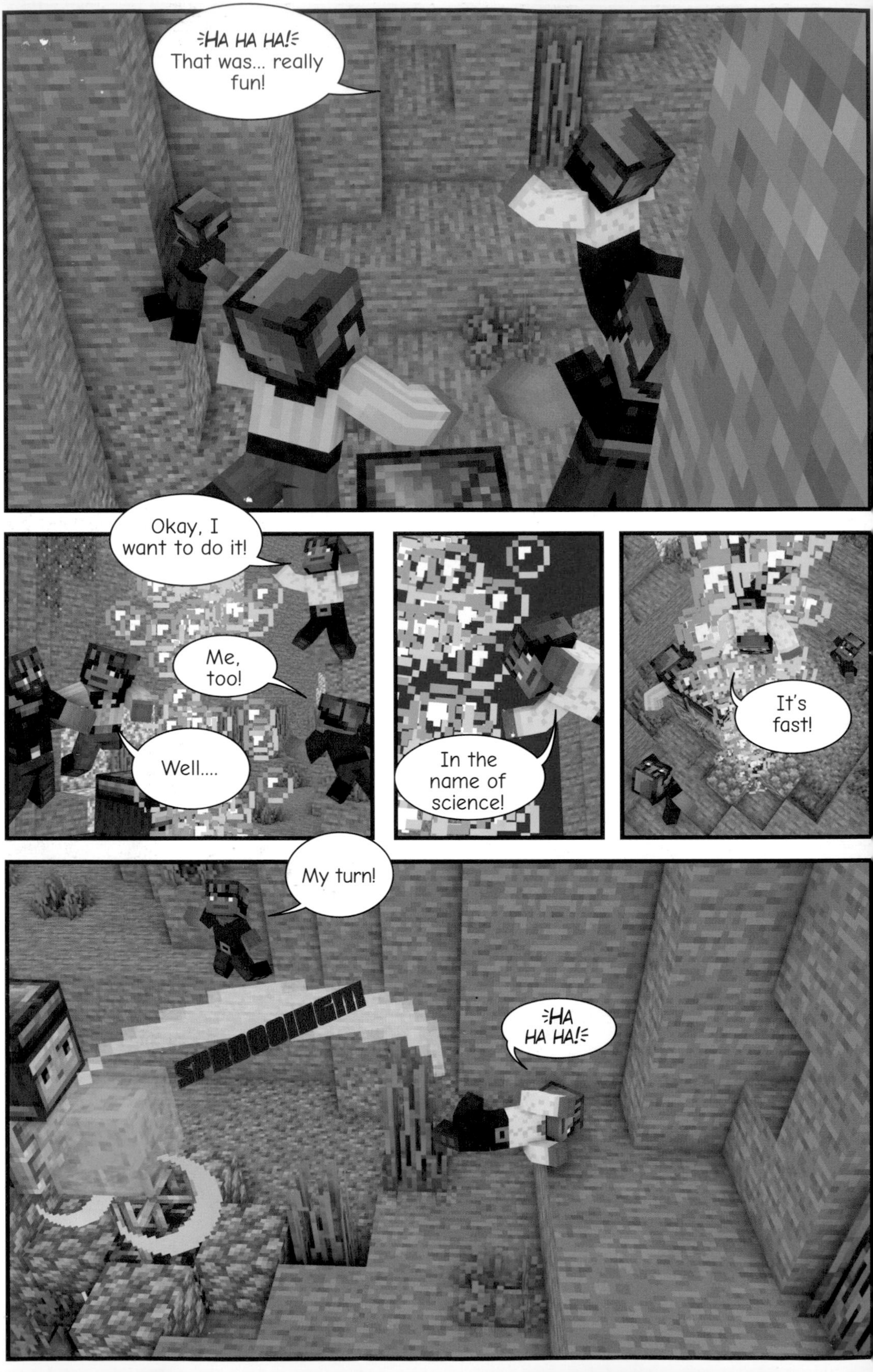
HA HA HA! That was... really fun!
Okay, I want to do it!
Me, too!
Well....
In the name of science!
It's fast!
My turn!
SPROOOINGM
HA HA HA!

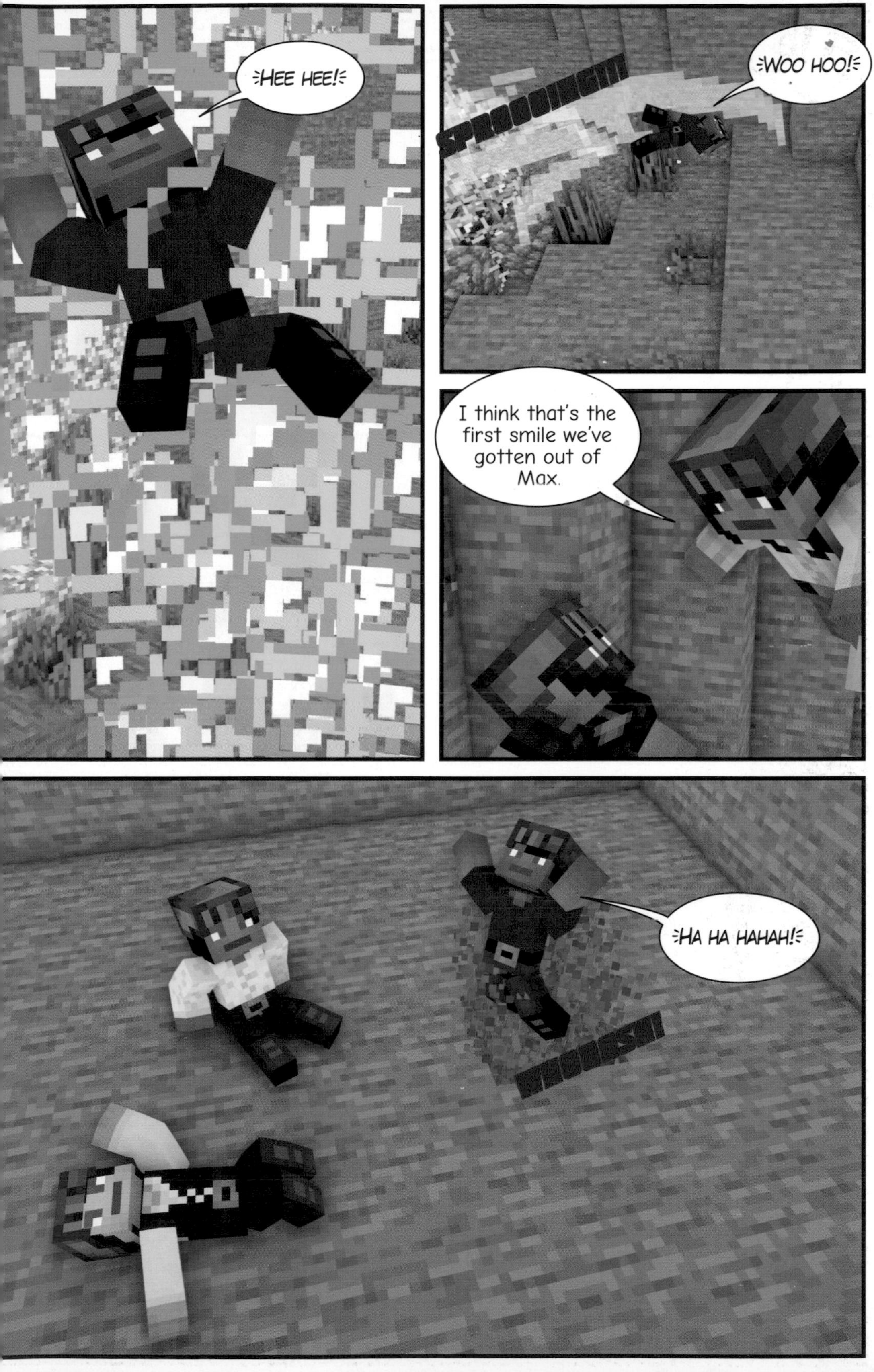
HEE HEE!
SPROOOINGH
WOO HOO!
I think that's the first smile we've gotten out of Max.
HA HA HAHAH!

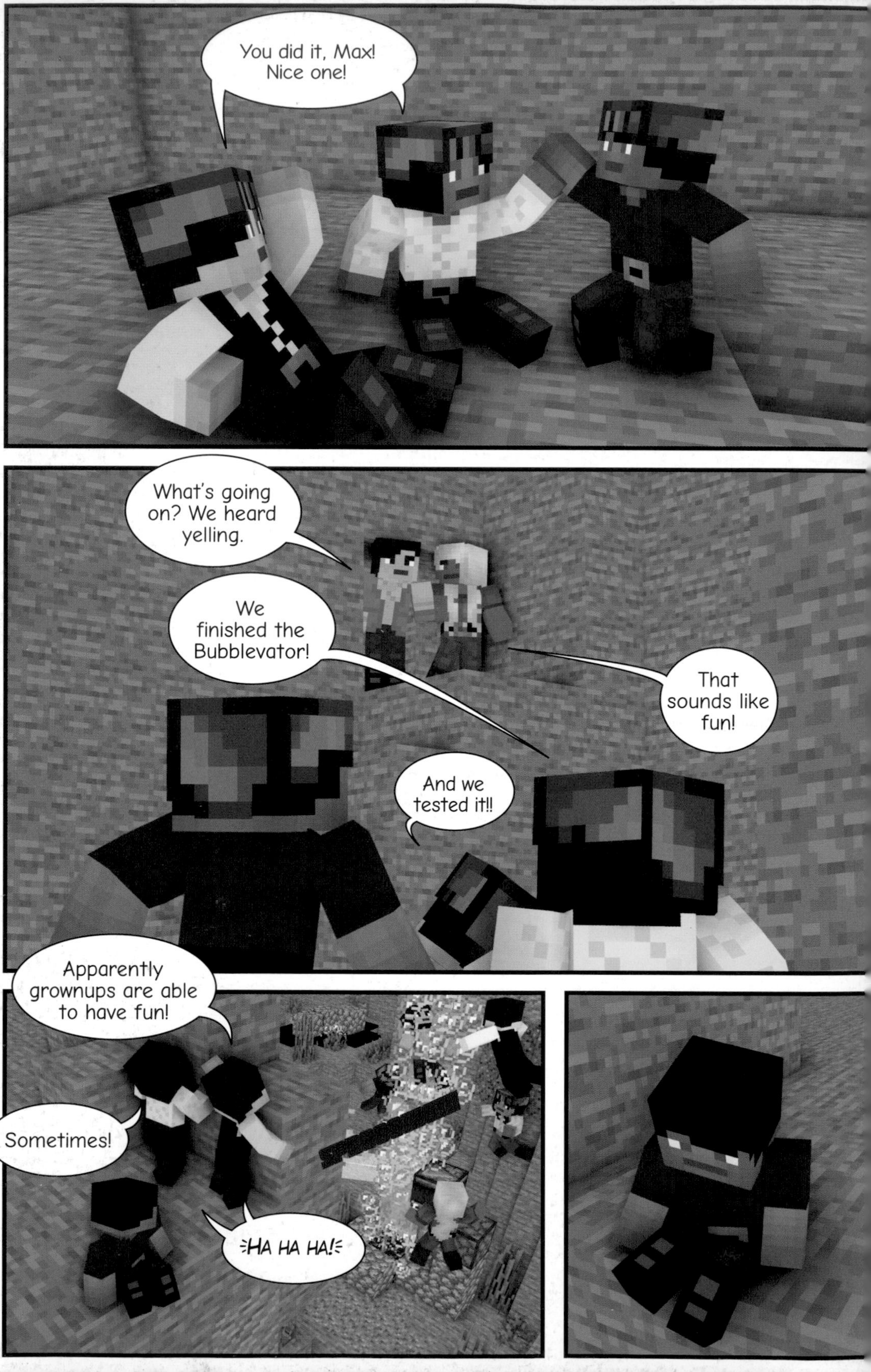
You did it, Max! Nice one!
What's going on? We heard yelling.
We finished the Bubblevator!
That sounds like fun!
And we tested it!!
Apparently grownups are able to have fun!
Sometimes!
HA HA HA!

Chapter 6
Emi

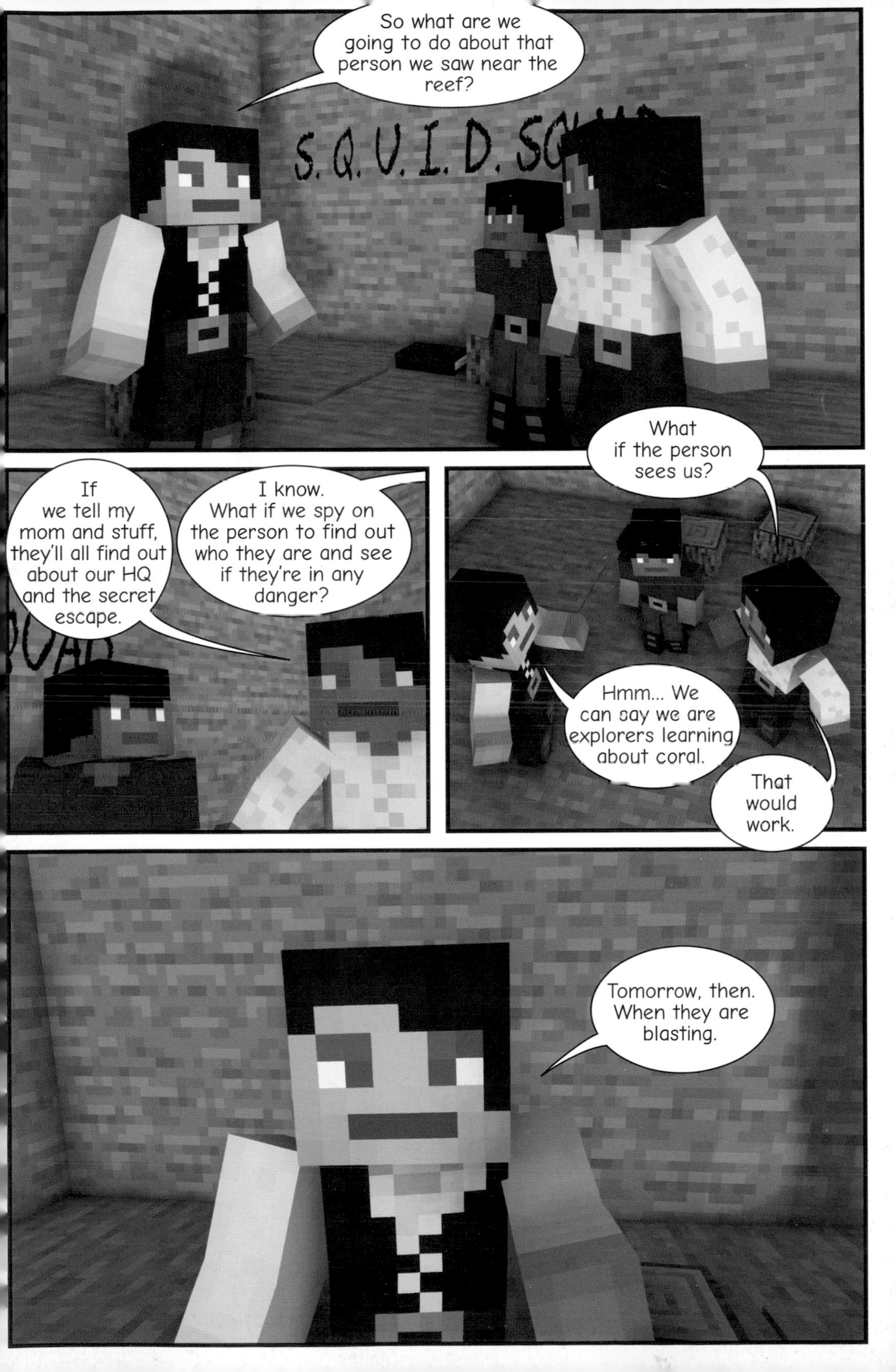
S.Q.U.I.D. SQ
So what are we going to do about that person we saw near the reef?
If we tell my mom and stuff, they'll all find out about our HQ and the secret escape.
I know. What if we spy on the person to find out who they are and see if they're in any danger?
What if the person sees us?
Hmm... We can say we are explorers learning about coral.
That would work.
Tomorrow, then. When they are blasting.

The next day,
as the grownups work ...

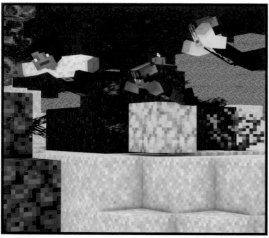

Shhhh!

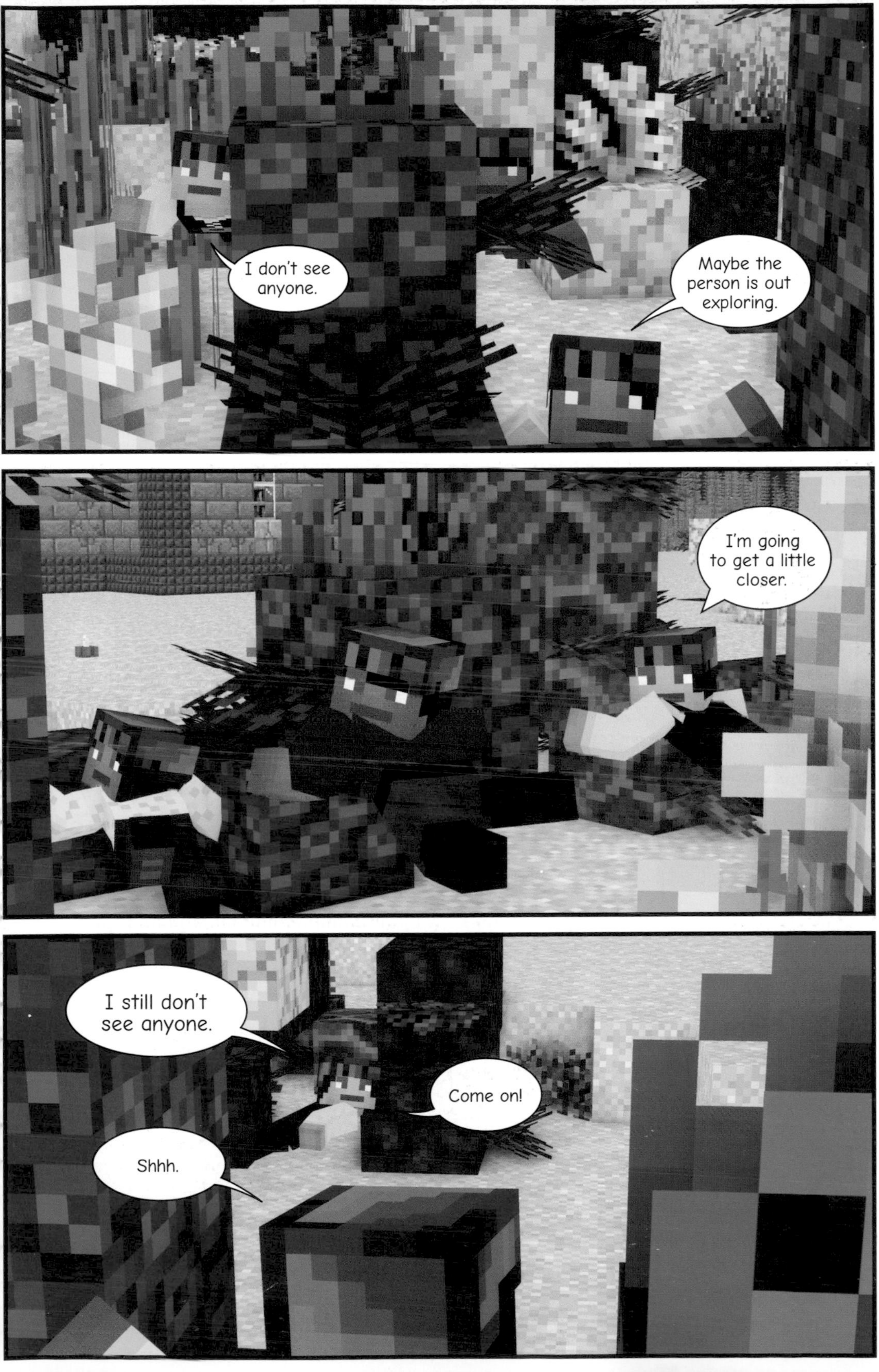

I don't see anyone.
Maybe the person is out exploring.
I'm going to get a little closer.
I still don't see anyone.
Come on!
Shhh.

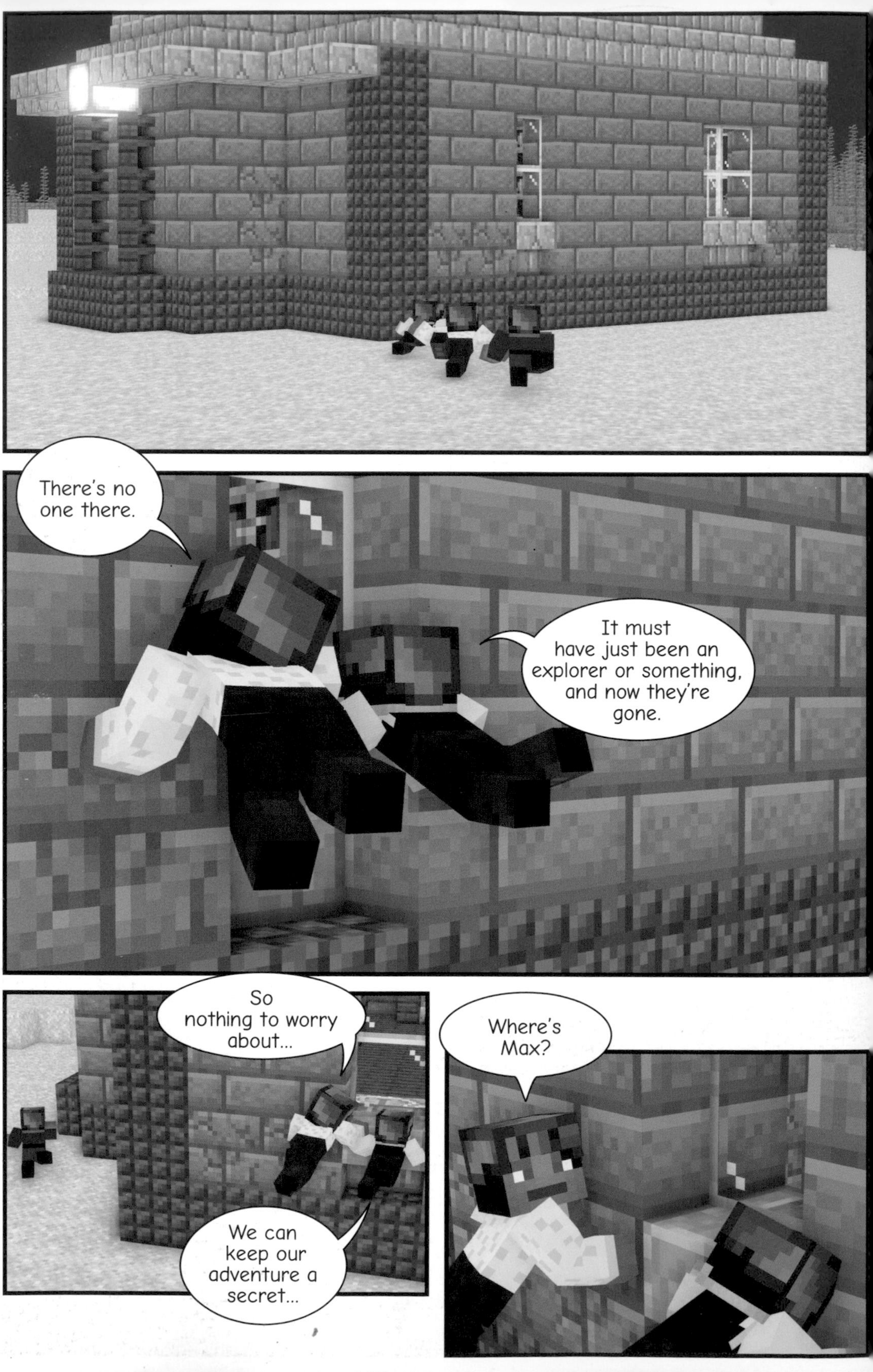
There's no one there.
It must have just been an explorer or something, and now they're gone.
So nothing to worry about...
We can keep our adventure a secret...
Where's Max?

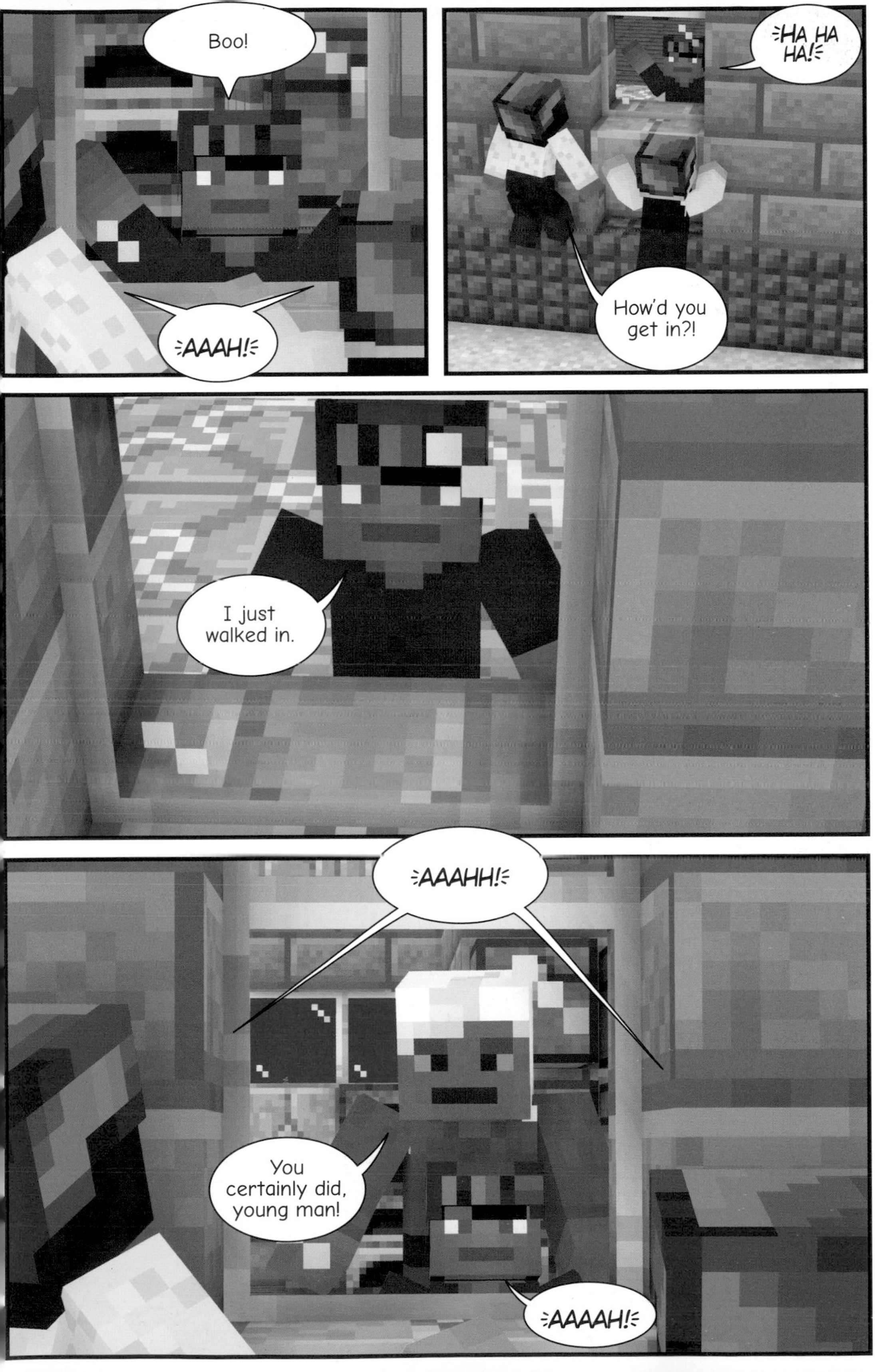
Boo!
AAAH!
HA HA HA!
How'd you get in?!
I just walked in.
AAAHH!
You certainly did, young man!
AAAAH!

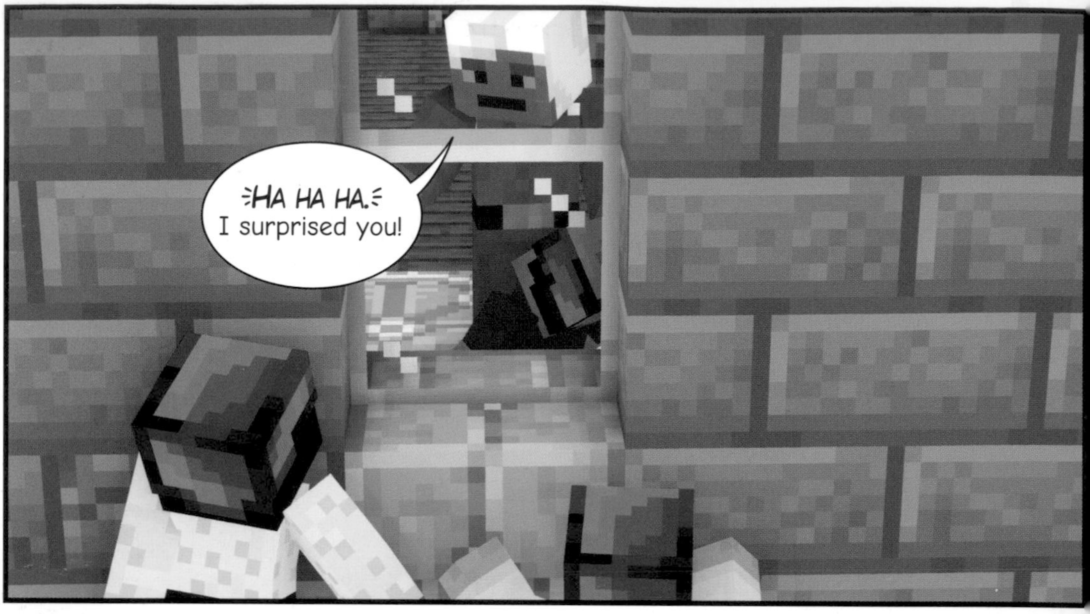
HA HA HA.
I surprised you!

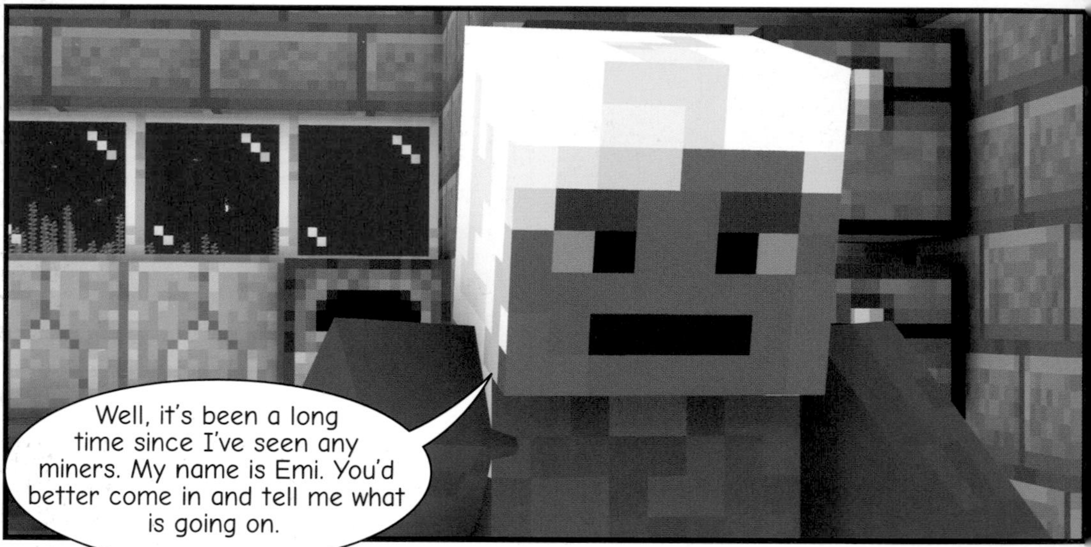
Well, it's been a long time since I've seen any miners. My name is Emi. You'd better come in and tell me what is going on.

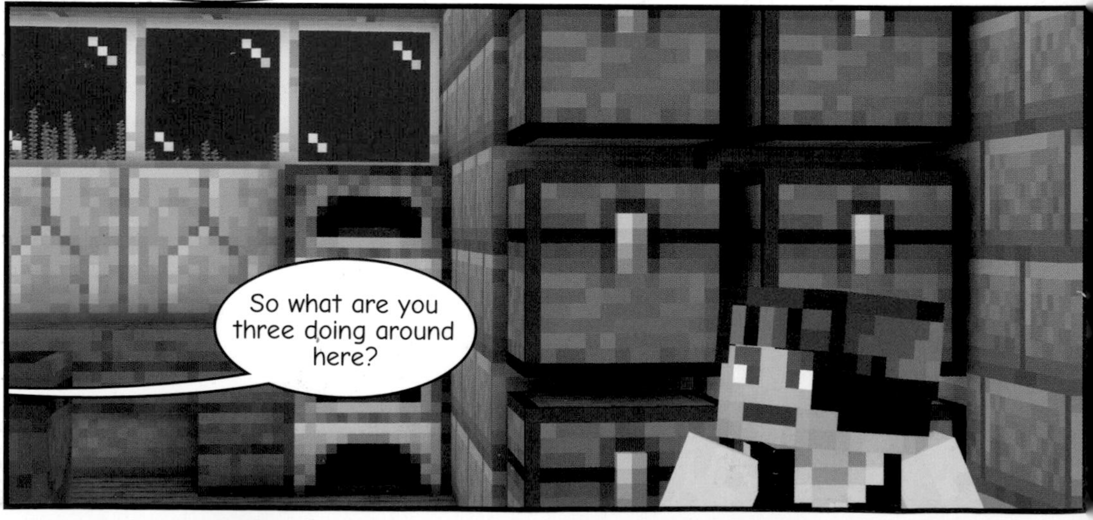
So what are you three doing around here?

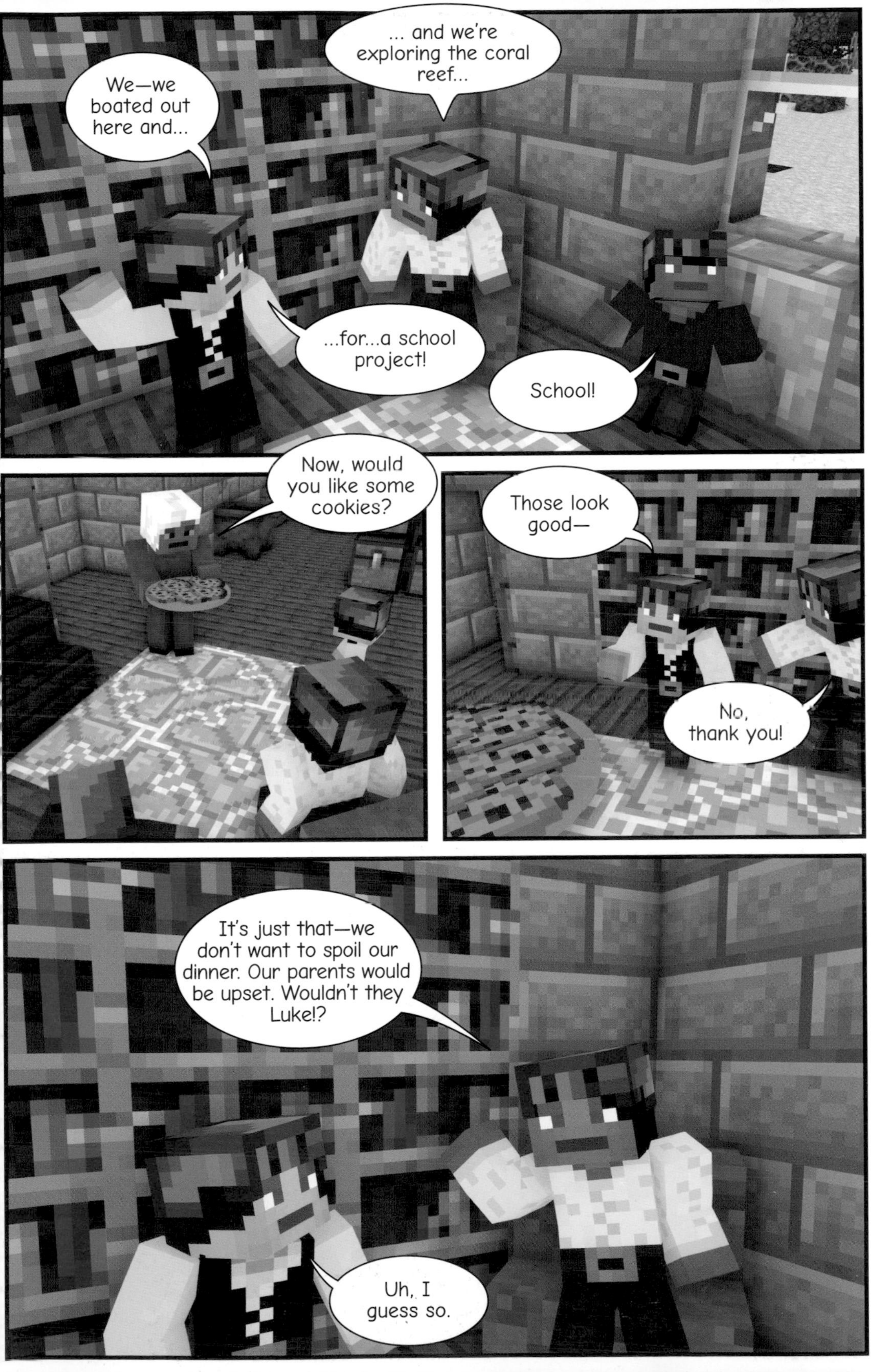
We—we boated out here and...
... and we're exploring the coral reef...
...for...a school project!
School!
Now, would you like some cookies?
Those look good—
No, thank you!
It's just that—we don't want to spoil our dinner. Our parents would be upset. Wouldn't they Luke!?
Uh, I guess so.

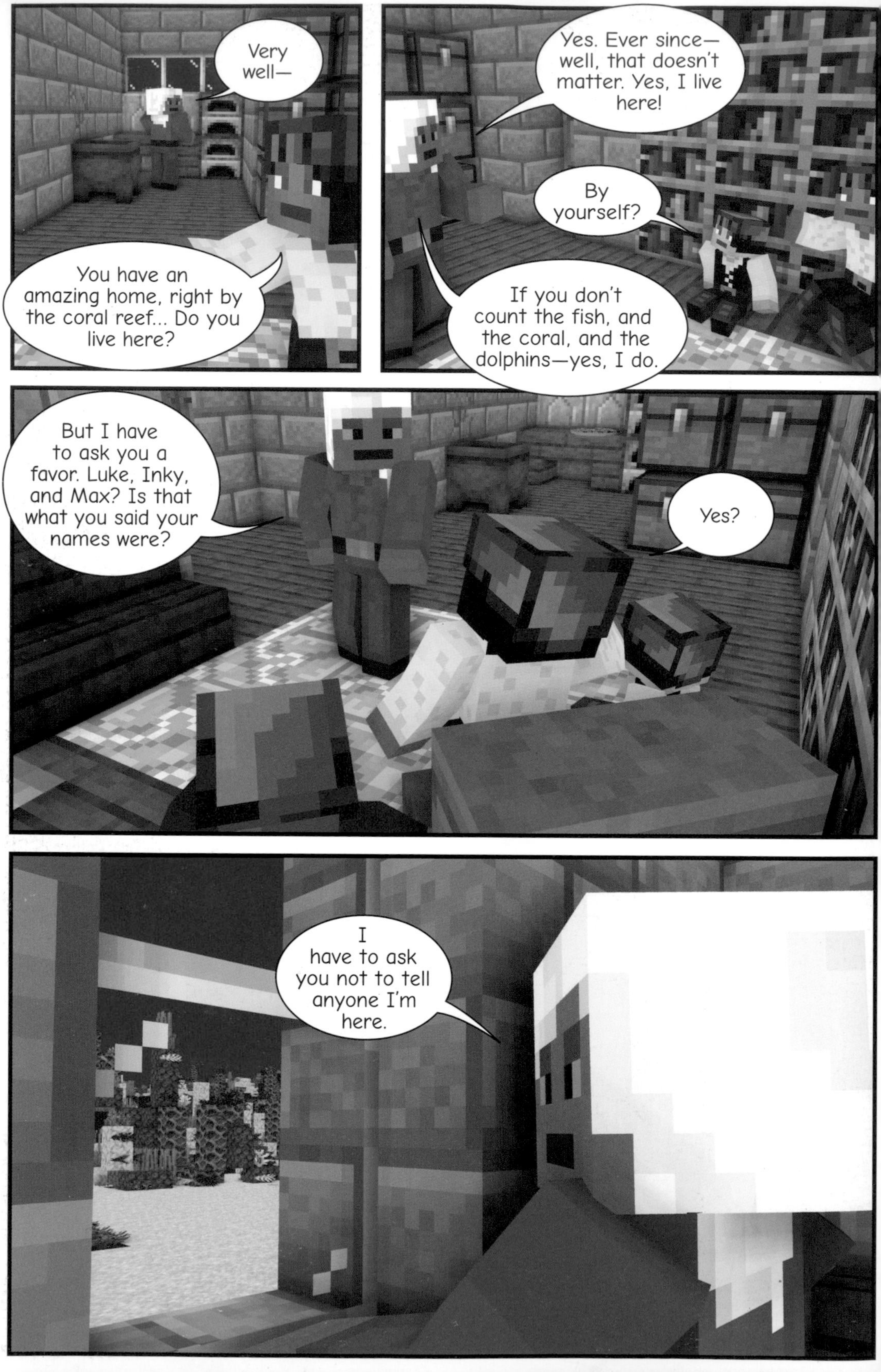
Very well—
You have an amazing home, right by the coral reef... Do you live here?
Yes. Ever since— well, that doesn't matter. Yes, I live here!
By yourself?
If you don't count the fish, and the coral, and the dolphins—yes, I do.
But I have to ask you a favor. Luke, Inky, and Max? Is that what you said your names were?
Yes?
I have to ask you not to tell anyone I'm here.

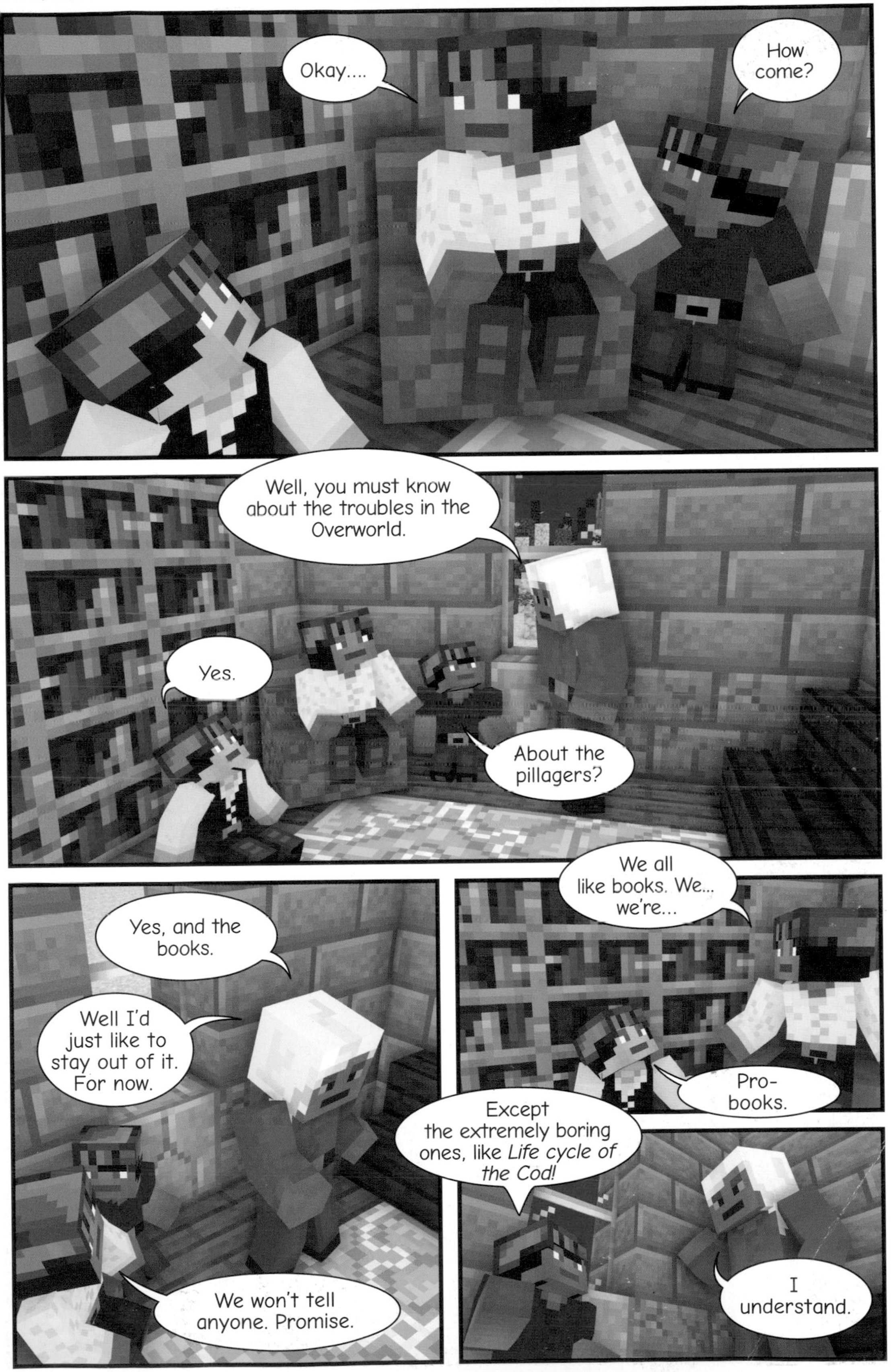
Okay....
How come?
Well, you must know about the troubles in the Overworld.
Yes.
About the pillagers?
Yes, and the books.
Well I'd just like to stay out of it. For now.
We won't tell anyone. Promise.
We all like books. We... we're...
Pro-books.
Except the extremely boring ones, like *Life cycle of the Cod!*
I understand.

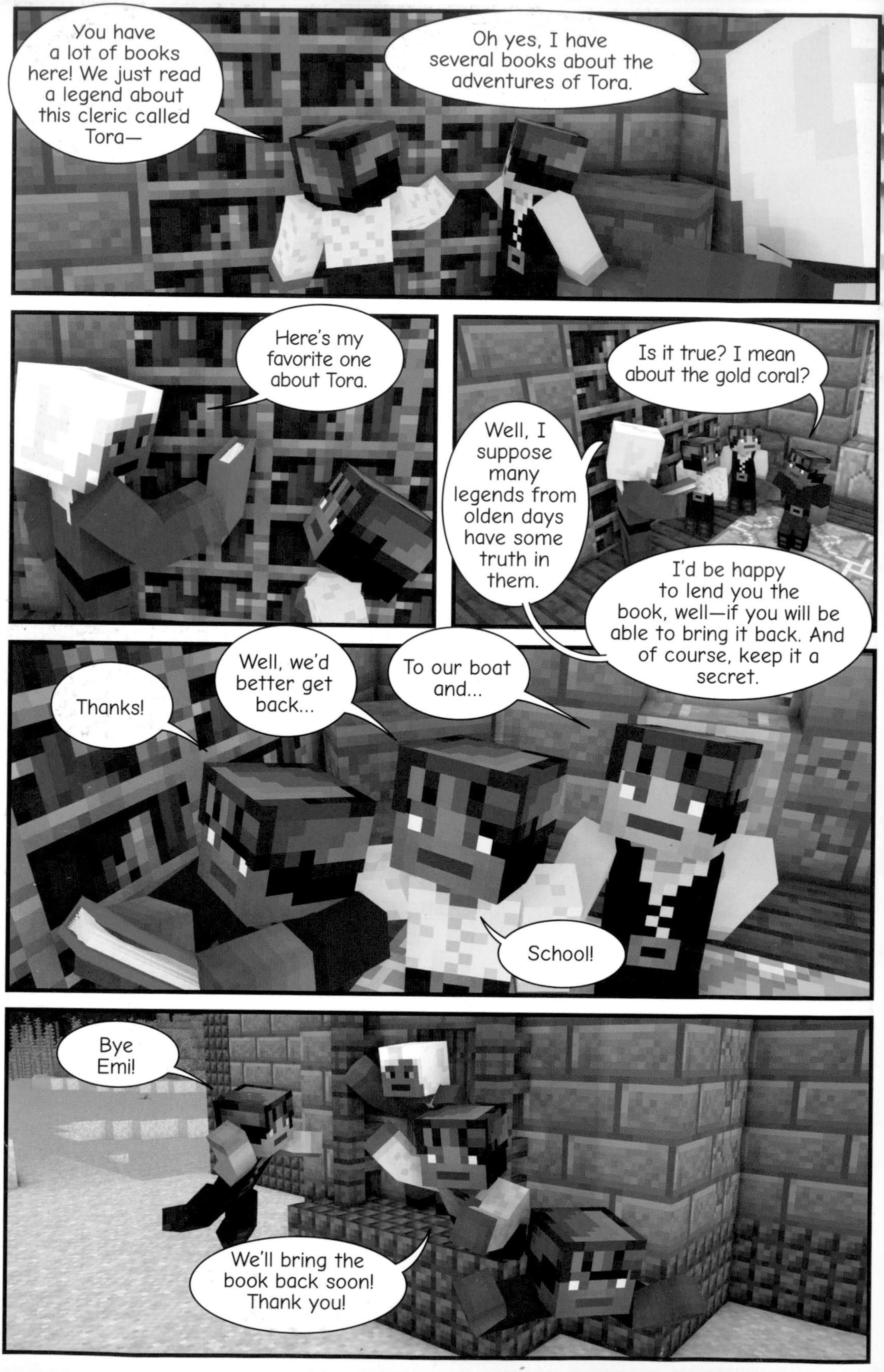
You have a lot of books here! We just read a legend about this cleric called Tora—
Oh yes, I have several books about the adventures of Tora.
Here's my favorite one about Tora.
Is it true? I mean about the gold coral?
Well, I suppose many legends from olden days have some truth in them.
I'd be happy to lend you the book, well—if you will be able to bring it back. And of course, keep it a secret.
Thanks!
Well, we'd better get back...
To our boat and...
School!
Bye Emi!
We'll bring the book back soon! Thank you!

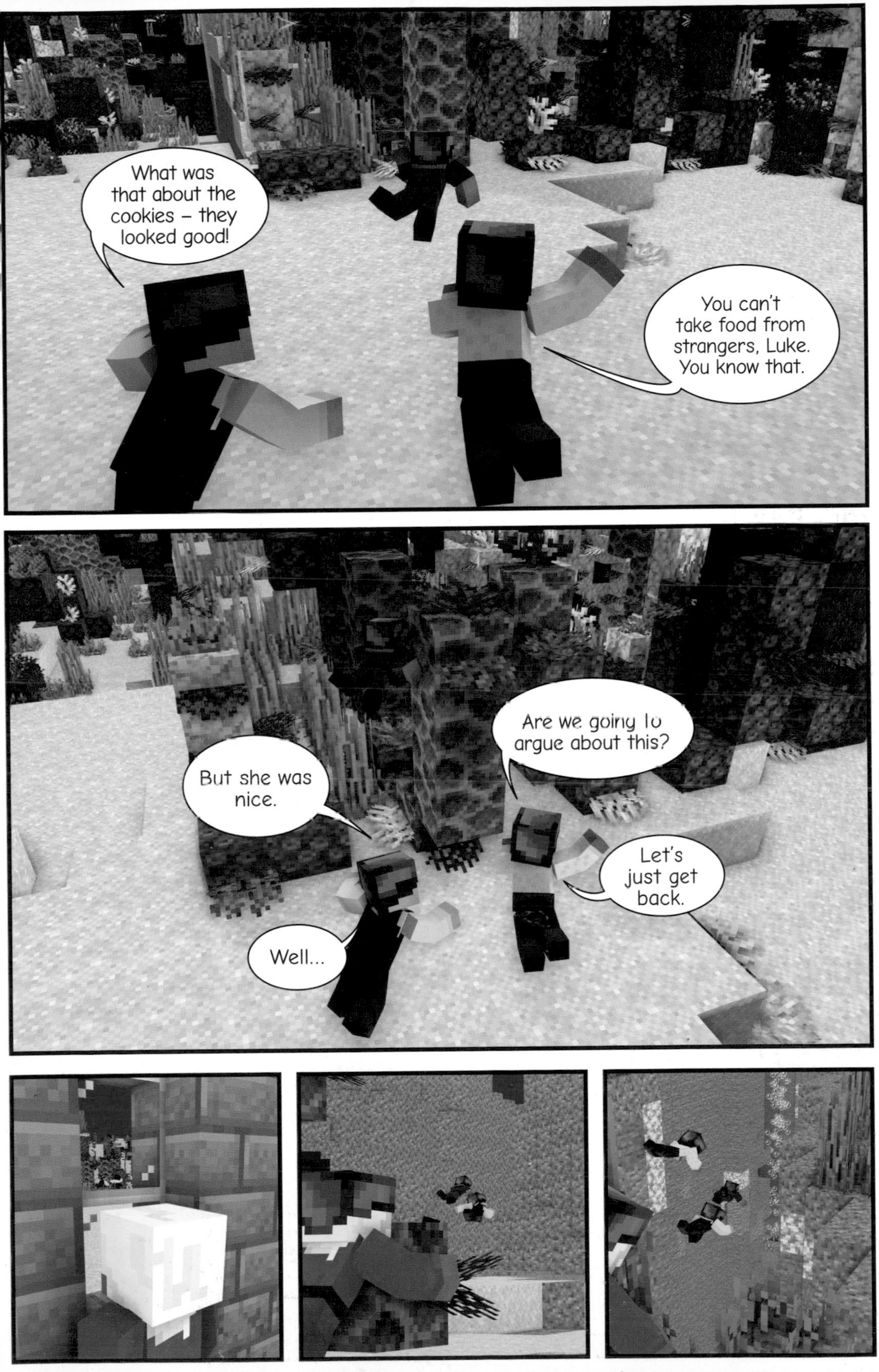
What was that about the cookies – they looked good!
You can't take food from strangers, Luke. You know that.
But she was nice.
Are we going to argue about this?
Let's just get back.
Well...

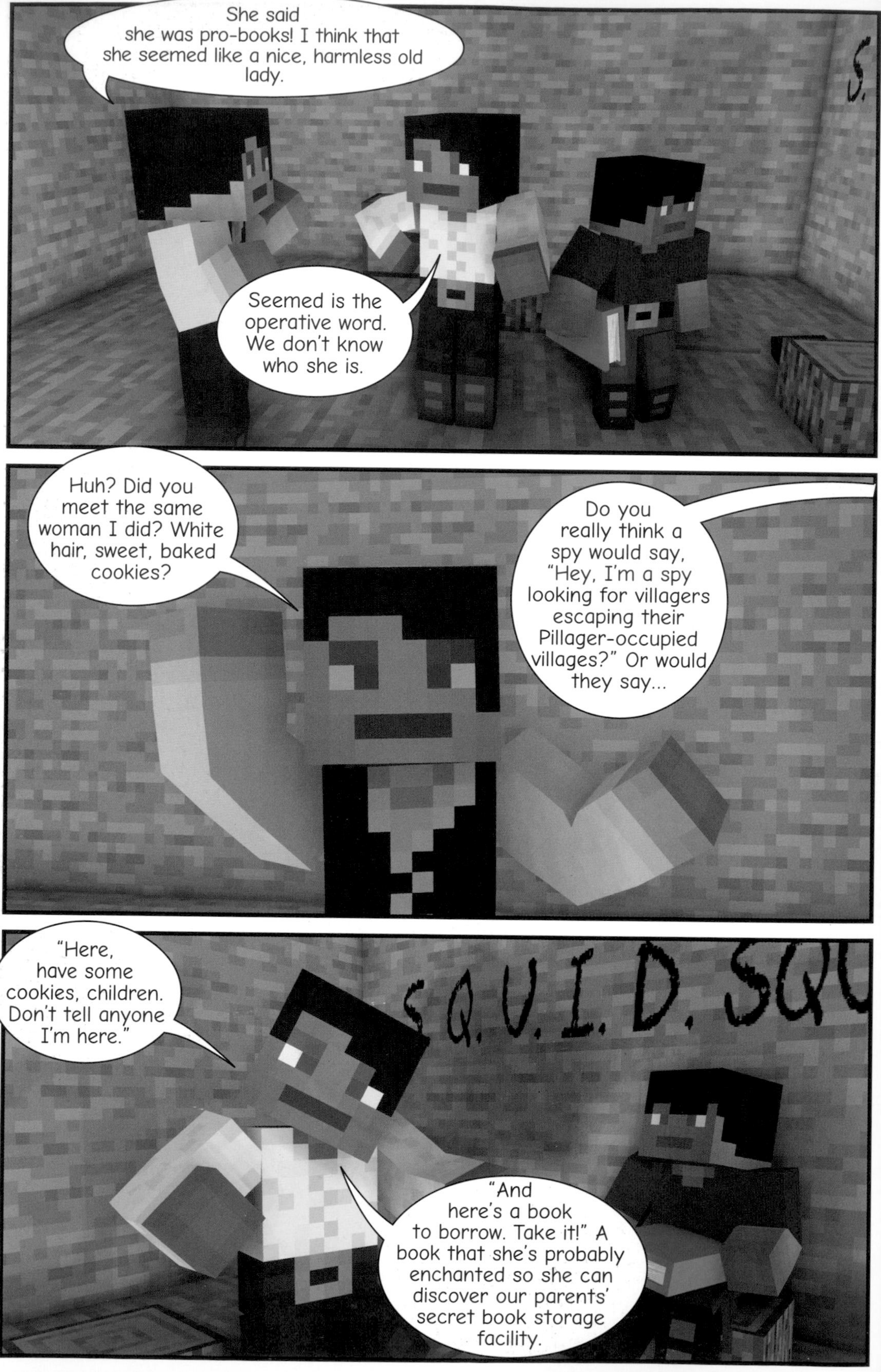
She said she was pro-books! I think that she seemed like a nice, harmless old lady.
Seemed is the operative word. We don't know who she is.
S.
Huh? Did you meet the same woman I did? White hair, sweet, baked cookies?
Do you really think a spy would say, "Hey, I'm a spy looking for villagers escaping their Pillager-occupied villages?" Or would they say...
"Here, have some cookies, children. Don't tell anyone I'm here."
S.Q.U.I.D. SQU
"And here's a book to borrow. Take it!" A book that she's probably enchanted so she can discover our parents' secret book storage facility.

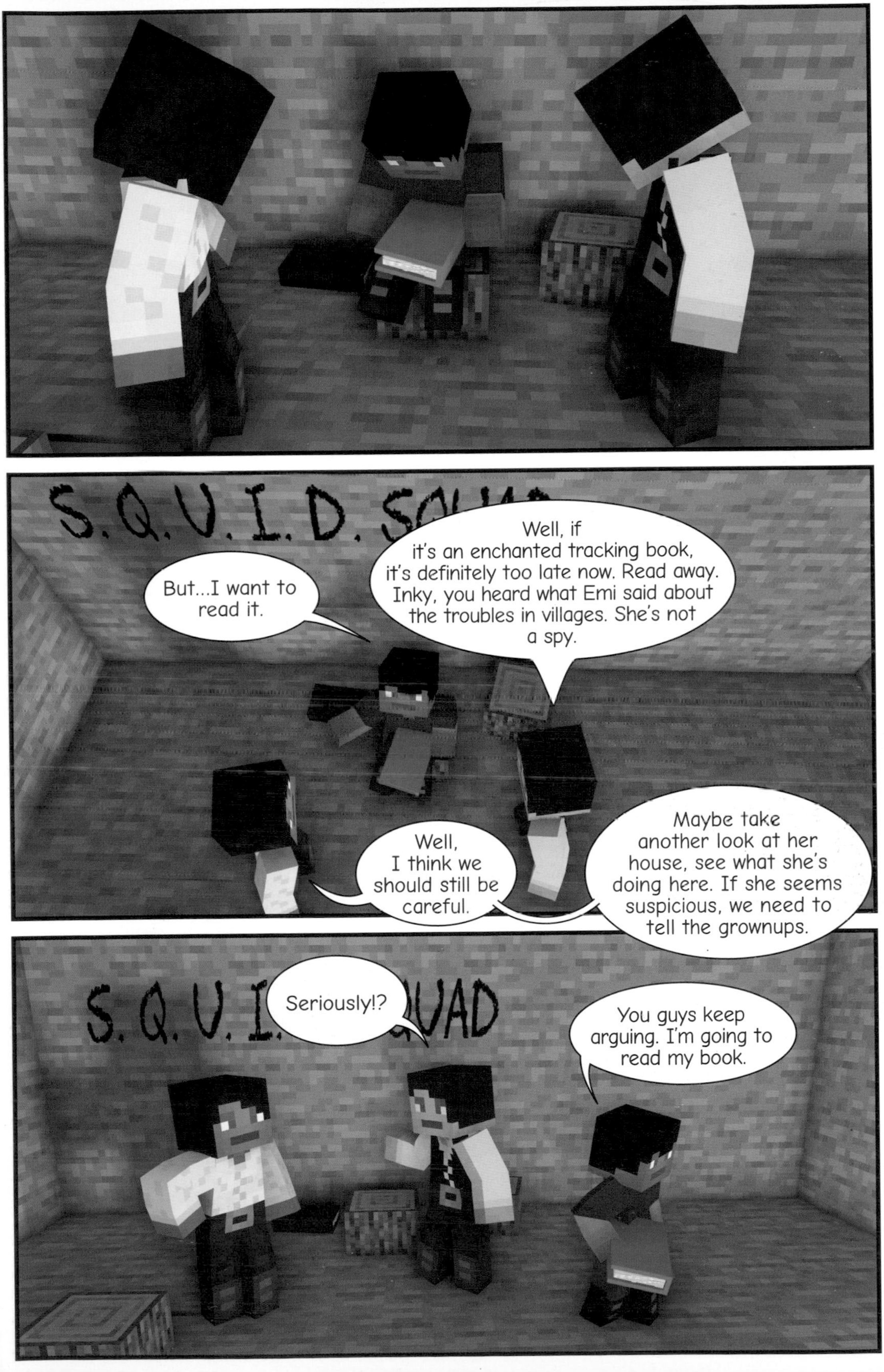
But...I want to read it.
Well, if it's an enchanted tracking book, it's definitely too late now. Read away. Inky, you heard what Emi said about the troubles in villages. She's not a spy.
Well, I think we should still be careful.
Maybe take another look at her house, see what she's doing here. If she seems suspicious, we need to tell the grownups.
Seriously!?
You guys keep arguing. I'm going to read my book.

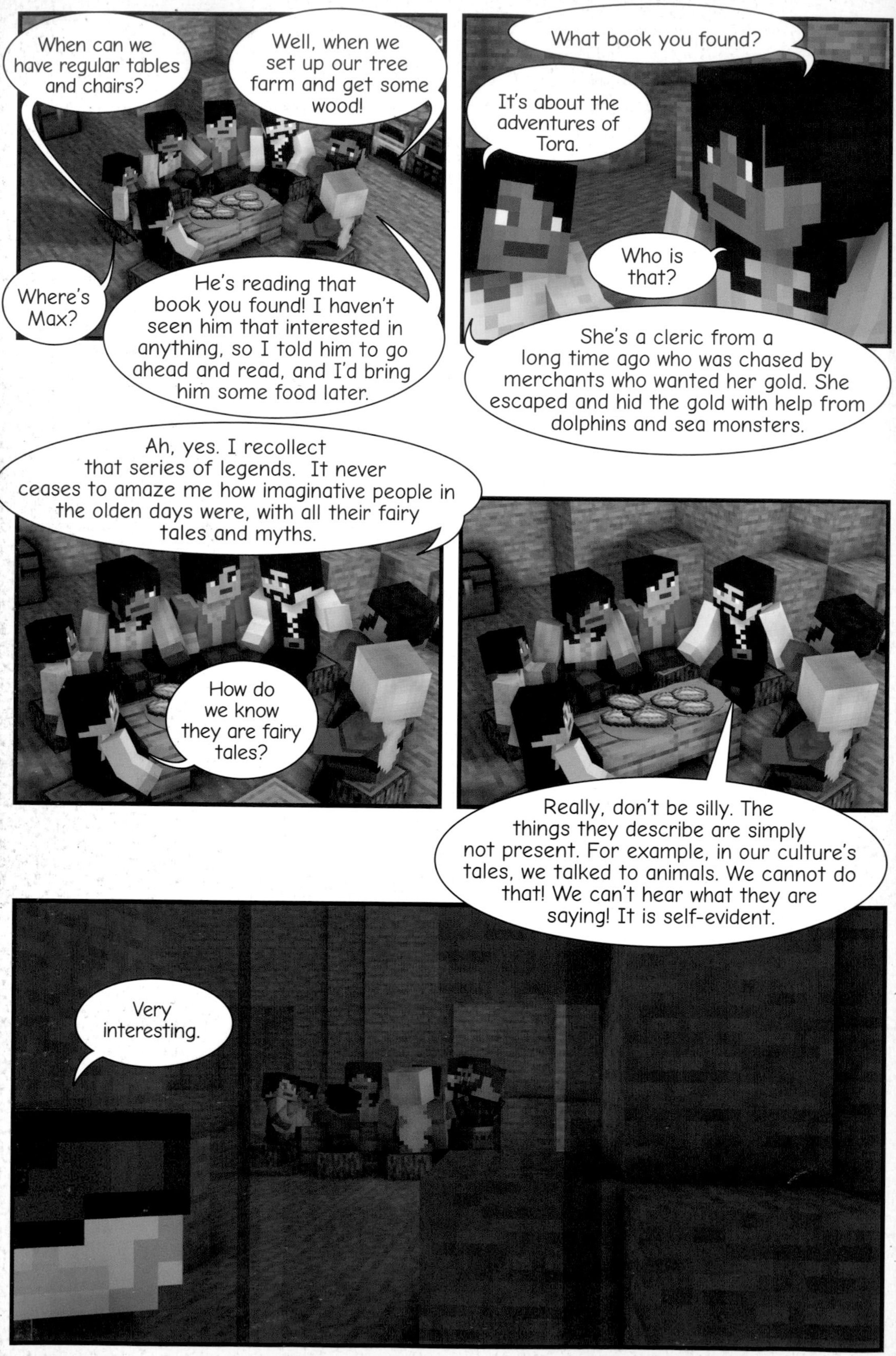
When can we have regular tables and chairs?
Well, when we set up our tree farm and get some wood!
Where's Max?
He's reading that book you found! I haven't seen him that interested in anything, so I told him to go ahead and read, and I'd bring him some food later.
What book you found?
It's about the adventures of Tora.
Who is that?
She's a cleric from a long time ago who was chased by merchants who wanted her gold. She escaped and hid the gold with help from dolphins and sea monsters.
Ah, yes. I recollect that series of legends. It never ceases to amaze me how imaginative people in the olden days were, with all their fairy tales and myths.
How do we know they are fairy tales?
Really, don't be silly. The things they describe are simply not present. For example, in our culture's tales, we talked to animals. We cannot do that! We can't hear what they are saying! It is self-evident.
Very interesting.

Chapter 7
Secret Escape

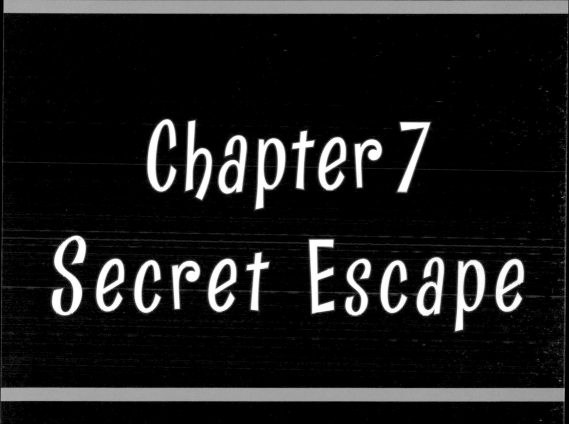

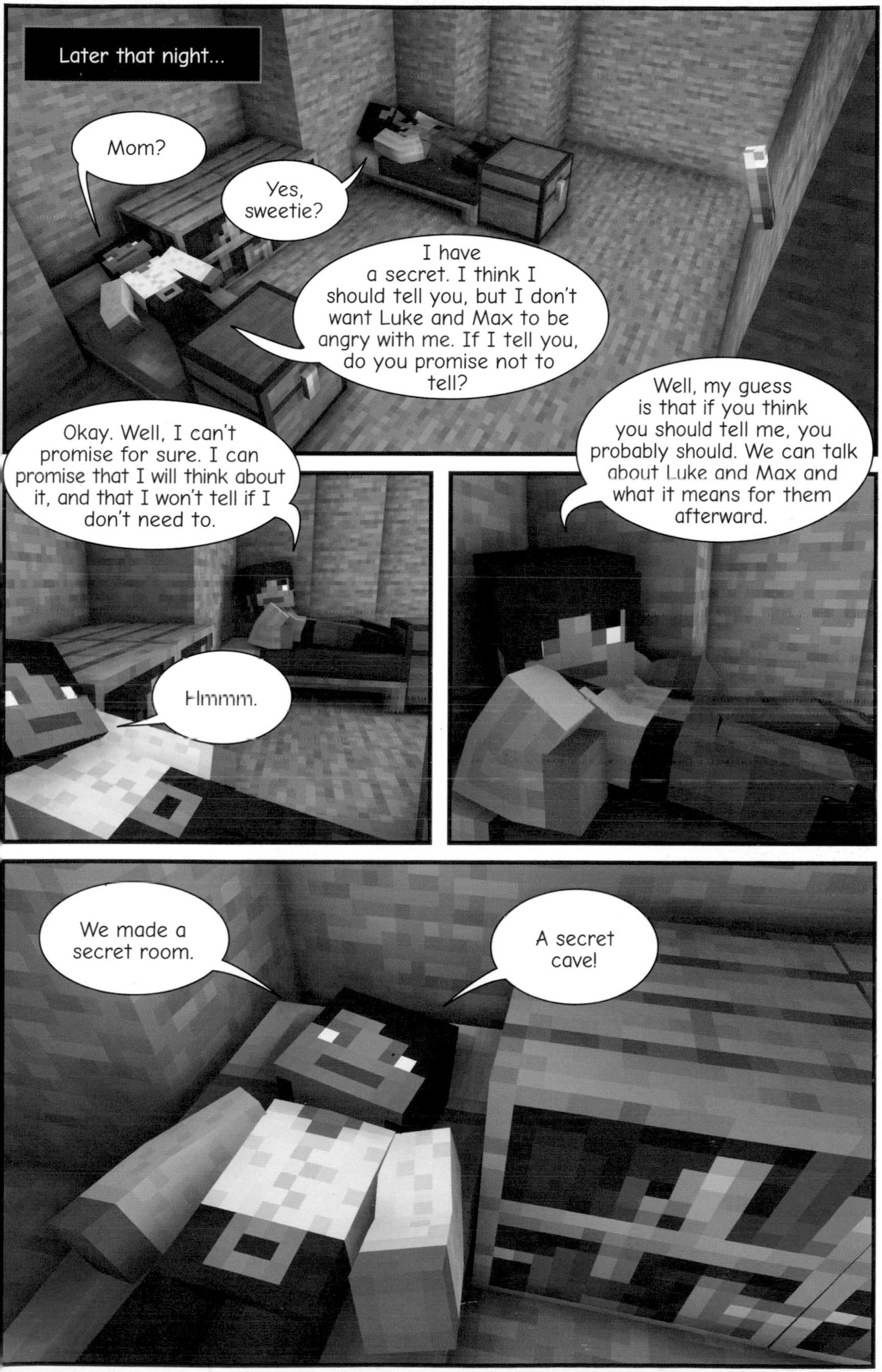

Later that night...
Mom?
Yes, sweetie?
I have a secret. I think I should tell you, but I don't want Luke and Max to be angry with me. If I tell you, do you promise not to tell?
Okay. Well, I can't promise for sure. I can promise that I will think about it, and that I won't tell if I don't need to.
Hmmm.
Well, my guess is that if you think you should tell me, you probably should. We can talk about Luke and Max and what it means for them afterward.
We made a secret room.
A secret cave!

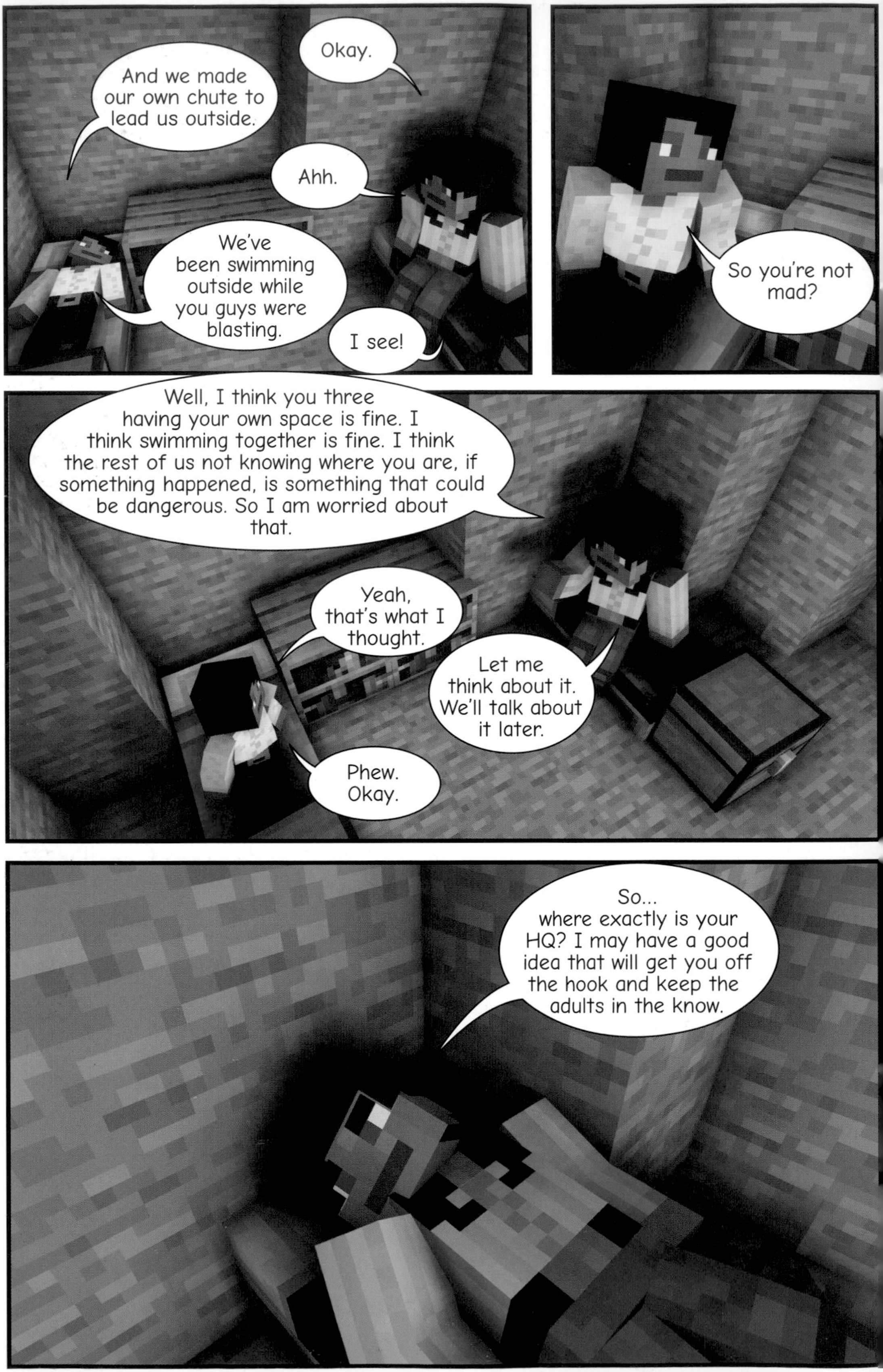
And we made our own chute to lead us outside.
Okay.
Ahh.
We've been swimming outside while you guys were blasting.
I see!
So you're not mad?
Well, I think you three having your own space is fine. I think swimming together is fine. I think the rest of us not knowing where you are, if something happened, is something that could be dangerous. So I am worried about that.
Yeah, that's what I thought.
Let me think about it. We'll talk about it later.
Phew. Okay.
So... where exactly is your HQ? I may have a good idea that will get you off the hook and keep the adults in the know.

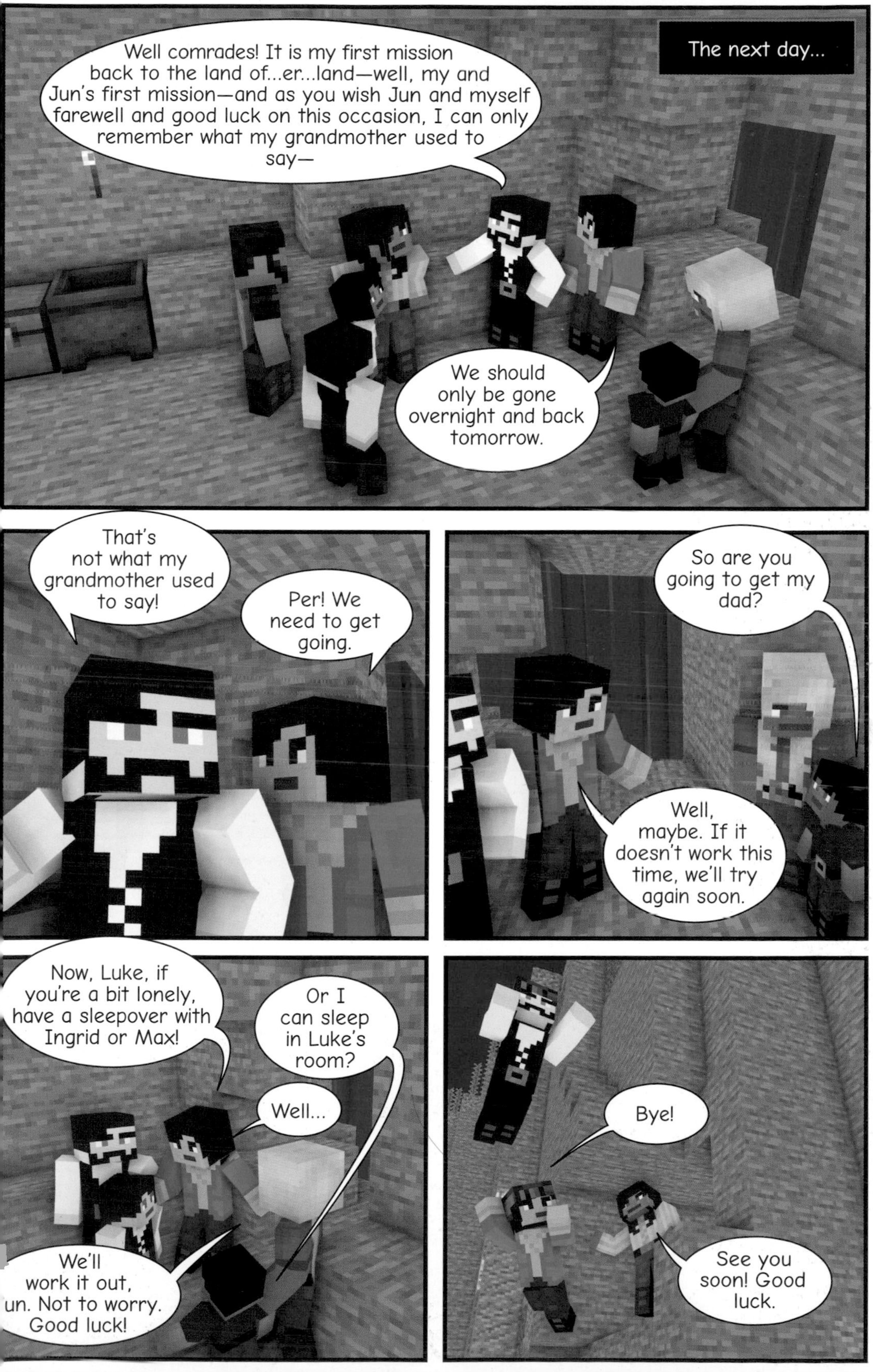
The next day...
Well comrades! It is my first mission back to the land of...er...land—well, my and Jun's first mission—and as you wish Jun and myself farewell and good luck on this occasion, I can only remember what my grandmother used to say—
We should only be gone overnight and back tomorrow.
That's not what my grandmother used to say!
Per! We need to get going.
So are you going to get my dad?
Well, maybe. If it doesn't work this time, we'll try again soon.
Now, Luke, if you're a bit lonely, have a sleepover with Ingrid or Max!
Or I can sleep in Luke's room?
Well...
We'll work it out, un. Not to worry. Good luck!
Bye!
See you soon! Good luck.

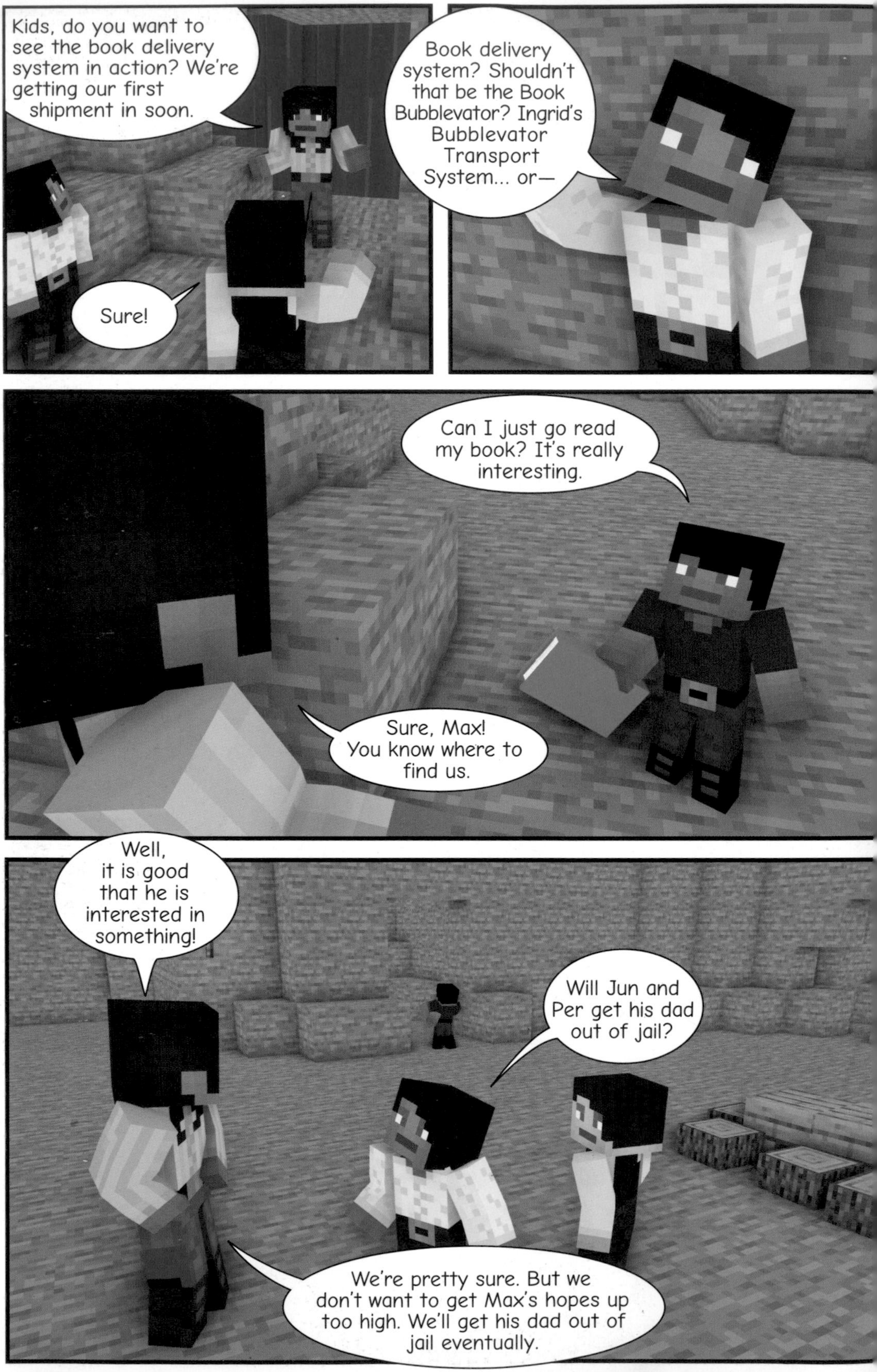
Kids, do you want to see the book delivery system in action? We're getting our first shipment in soon.
Sure!
Book delivery system? Shouldn't that be the Book Bubblevator? Ingrid's Bubblevator Transport System... or—
Can I just go read my book? It's really interesting.
Sure, Max! You know where to find us.
Well, it is good that he is interested in something!
Will Jun and Per get his dad out of jail?
We're pretty sure. But we don't want to get Max's hopes up too high. We'll get his dad out of jail eventually.

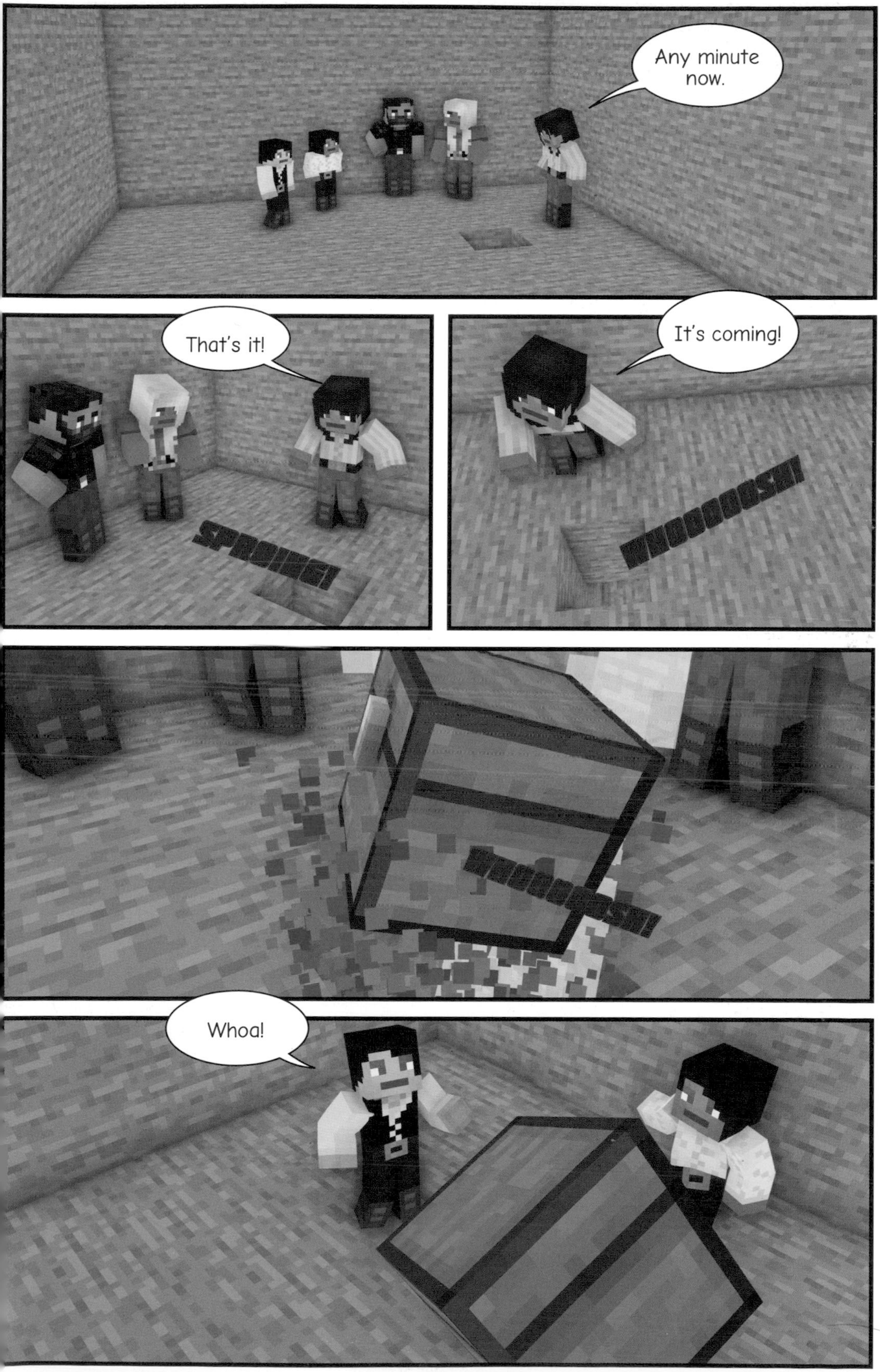
Any minute now.
That's it!
SPROING!
It's coming!
WHOOOOSH!
Whoa!

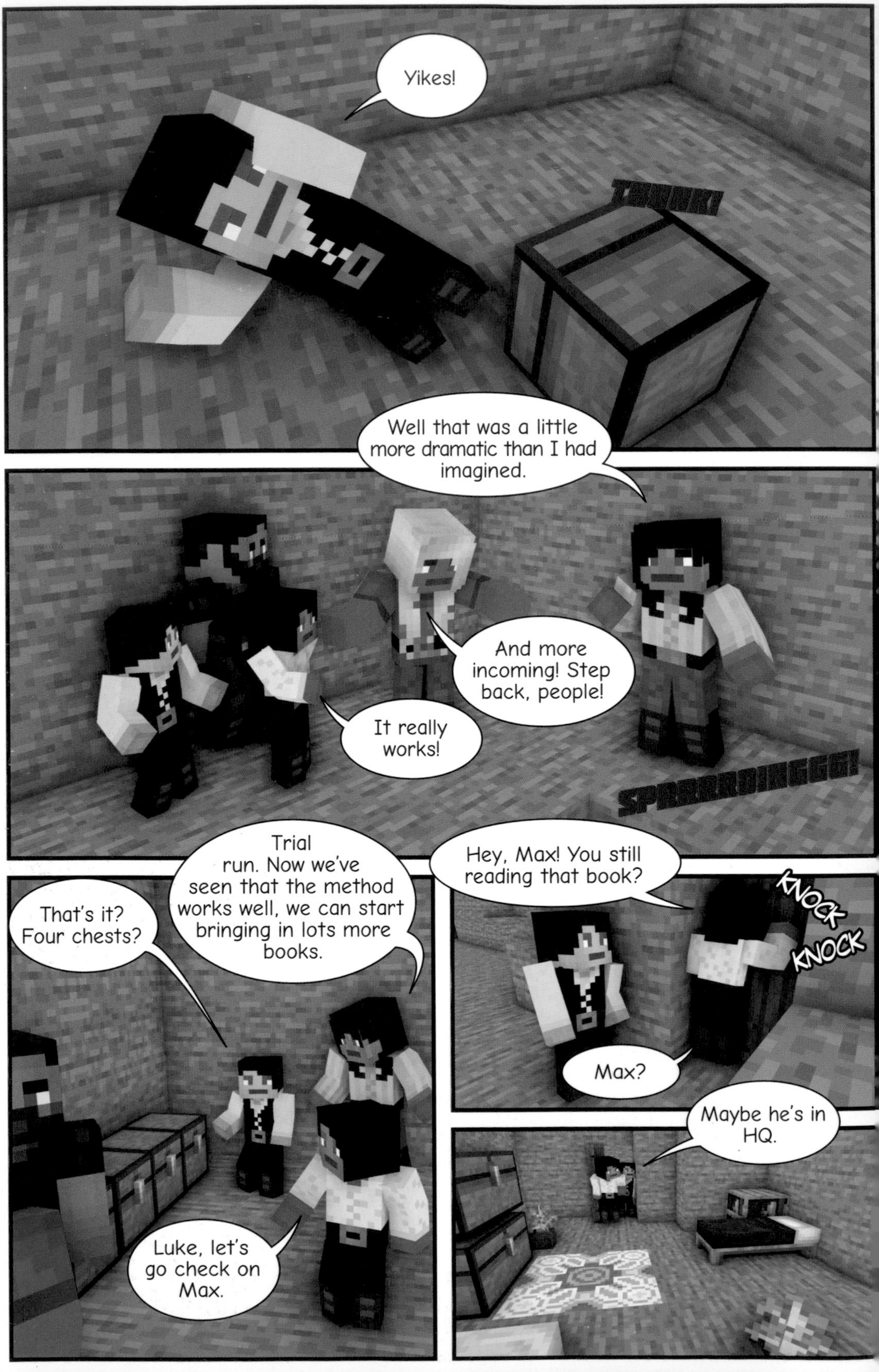
Yikes!
Well that was a little more dramatic than I had imagined.
And more incoming! Step back, people!
It really works!
SPRRROINGGG!
That's it? Four chests?
Trial run. Now we've seen that the method works well, we can start bringing in lots more books.
Luke, let's go check on Max.
Hey, Max! You still reading that book?
KNOCK KNOCK
Max?
Maybe he's in HQ.

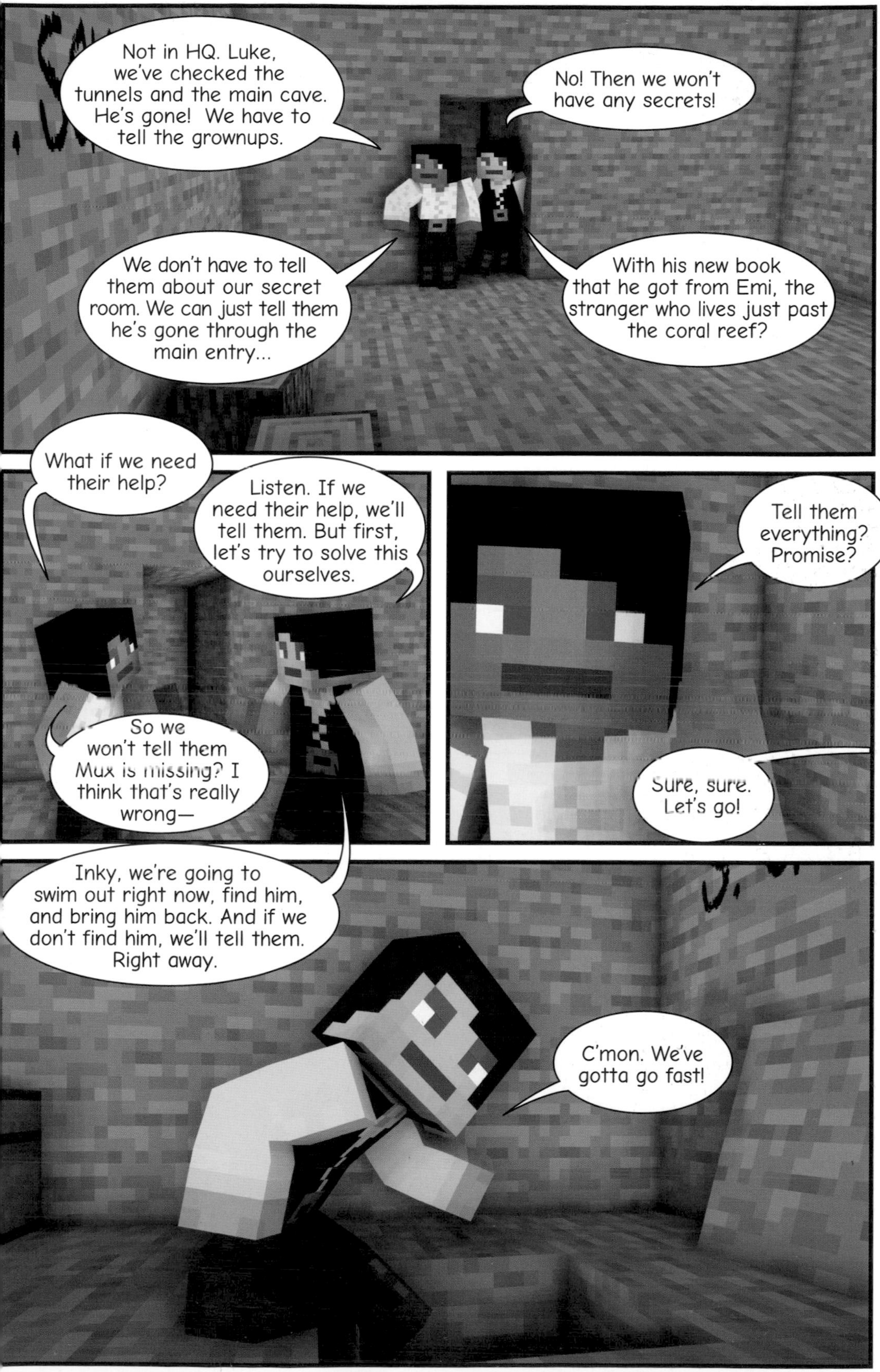

Not in HQ. Luke, we've checked the tunnels and the main cave. He's gone! We have to tell the grownups.
No! Then we won't have any secrets!
We don't have to tell them about our secret room. We can just tell them he's gone through the main entry...
With his new book that he got from Emi, the stranger who lives just past the coral reef?
What if we need their help?
Listen. If we need their help, we'll tell them. But first, let's try to solve this ourselves.
So we won't tell them Max is missing? I think that's really wrong—
Tell them everything? Promise?
Sure, sure. Let's go!
Inky, we're going to swim out right now, find him, and bring him back. And if we don't find him, we'll tell them. Right away.
C'mon. We've gotta go fast!

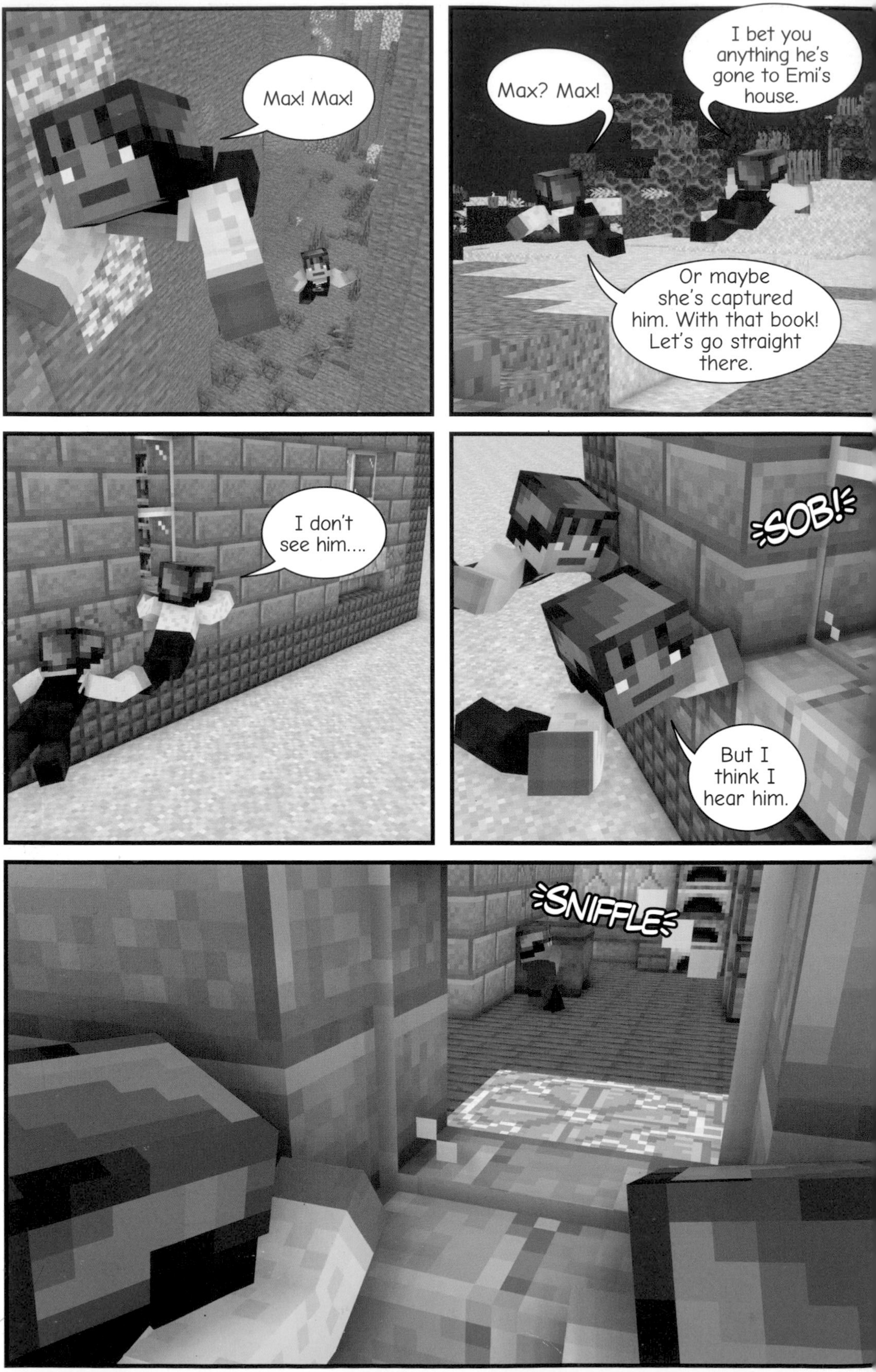
Max! Max!
Max? Max!
I bet you anything he's gone to Emi's house.
Or maybe she's captured him. With that book! Let's go straight there.
I don't see him....
SOB!
But I think I hear him.
SNIFFLE

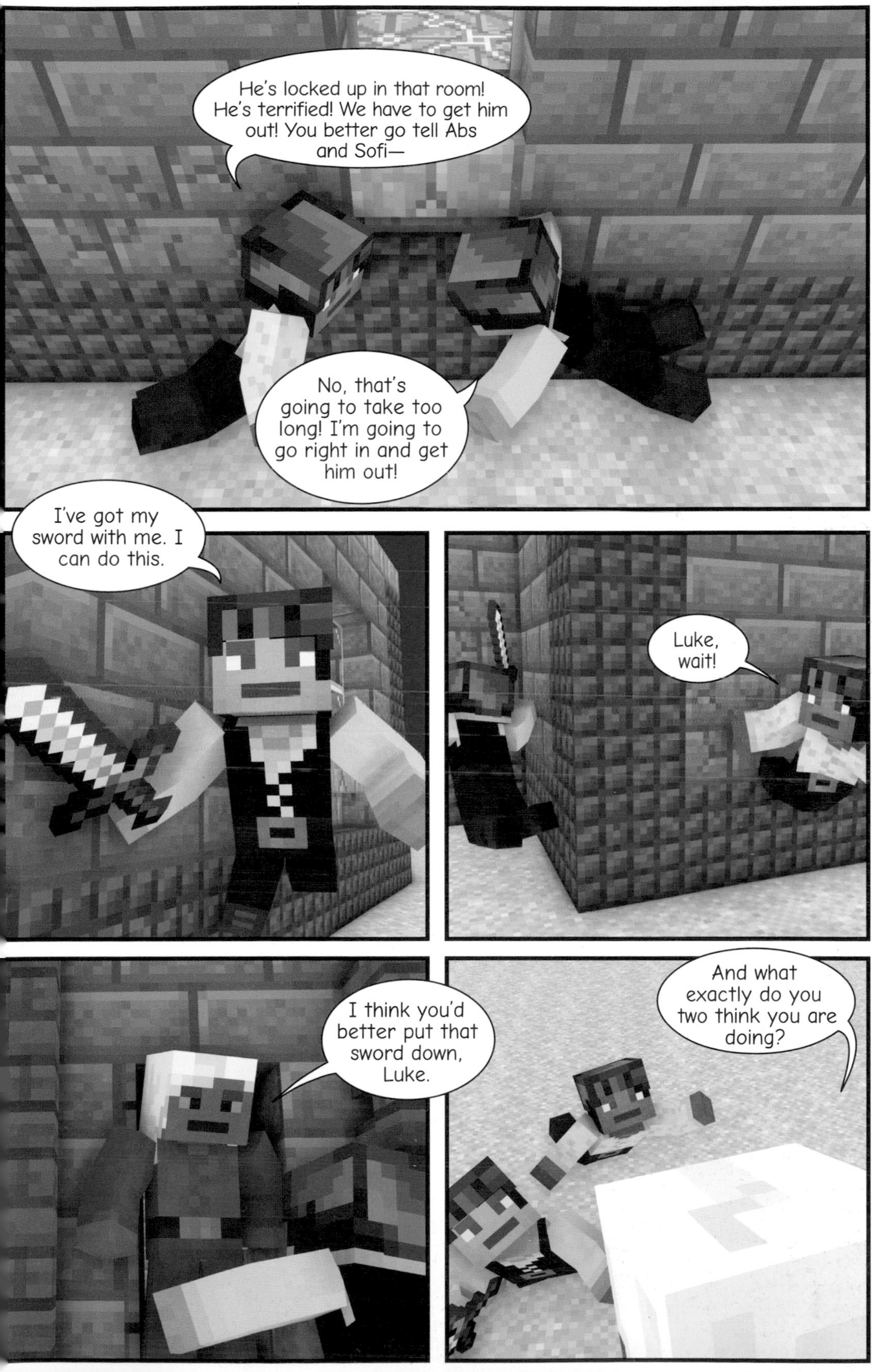
He's locked up in that room! He's terrified! We have to get him out! You better go tell Abs and Sofi—
No, that's going to take too long! I'm going to go right in and get him out!
I've got my sword with me. I can do this.
Luke, wait!
I think you'd better put that sword down, Luke.
And what exactly do you two think you are doing?

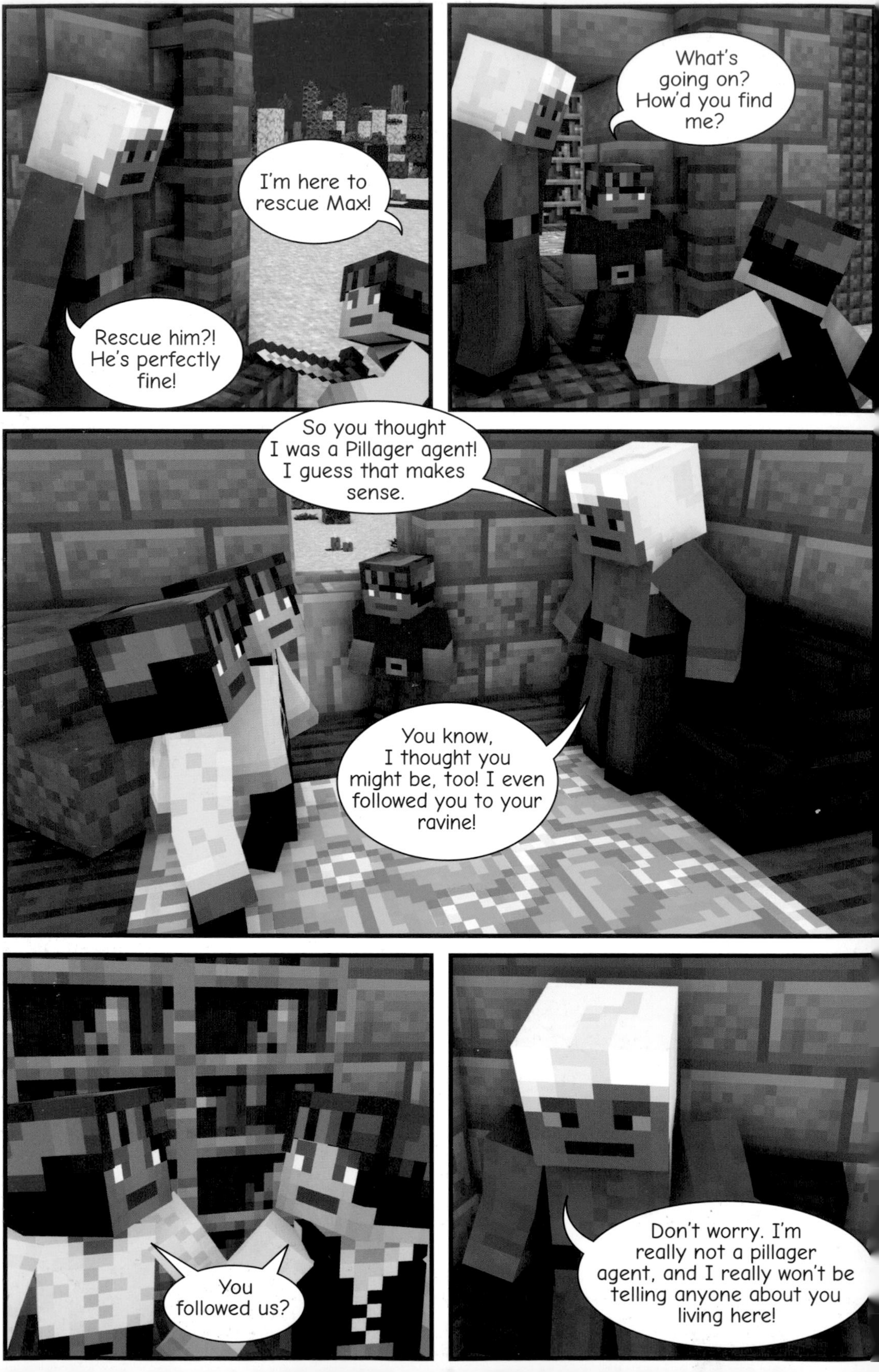
I'm here to rescue Max!
Rescue him?! He's perfectly fine!
What's going on? How'd you find me?
So you thought I was a Pillager agent! I guess that makes sense.
You know, I thought you might be, too! I even followed you to your ravine!
You followed us?
Don't worry. I'm really not a pillager agent, and I really won't be telling anyone about you living here!

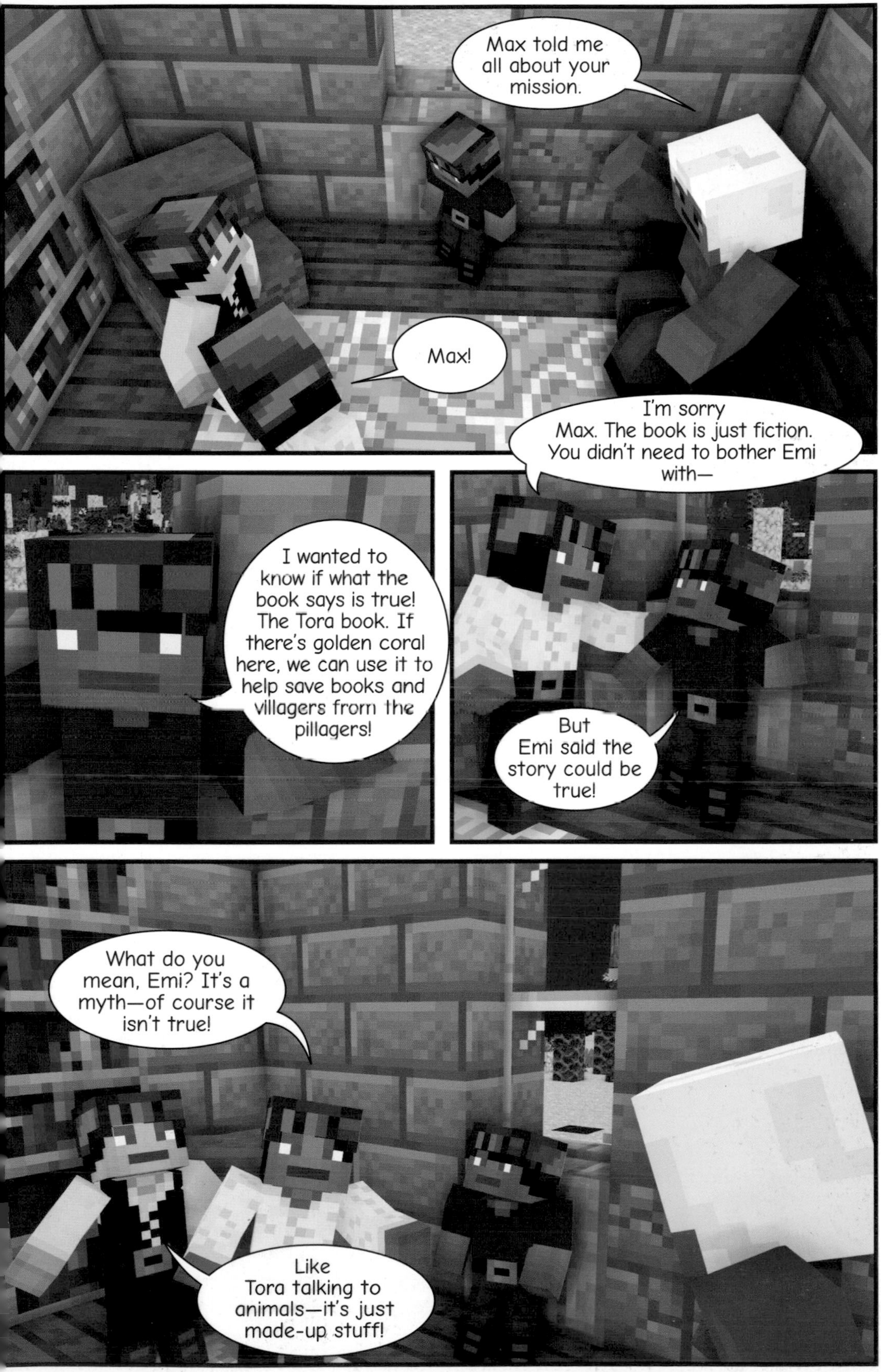
Max told me all about your mission.
Max!
I'm sorry Max. The book is just fiction. You didn't need to bother Emi with—
I wanted to know if what the book says is true! The Tora book. If there's golden coral here, we can use it to help save books and villagers from the pillagers!
But Emi said the story could be true!
What do you mean, Emi? It's a myth—of course it isn't true!
Like Tora talking to animals—it's just made-up stuff!

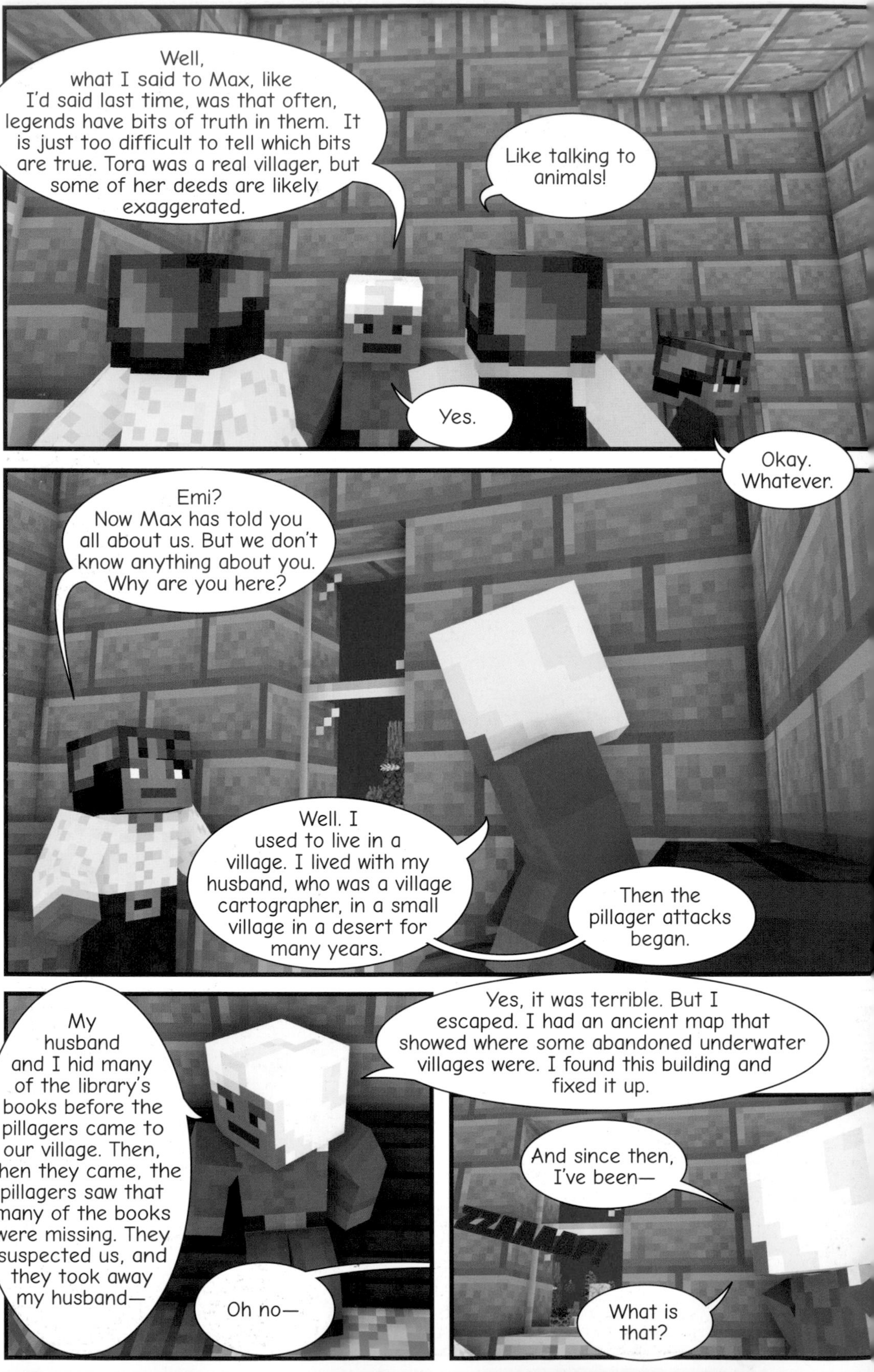
Well, what I said to Max, like I'd said last time, was that often, legends have bits of truth in them. It is just too difficult to tell which bits are true. Tora was a real villager, but some of her deeds are likely exaggerated.
Like talking to animals!
Yes.
Okay. Whatever.
Emi? Now Max has told you all about us. But we don't know anything about you. Why are you here?
Well. I used to live in a village. I lived with my husband, who was a village cartographer, in a small village in a desert for many years.
Then the pillager attacks began.
My husband and I hid many of the library's books before the pillagers came to our village. Then, when they came, the pillagers saw that many of the books were missing. They suspected us, and they took away my husband—
Yes, it was terrible. But I escaped. I had an ancient map that showed where some abandoned underwater villages were. I found this building and fixed it up.
Oh no—
And since then, I've been—
What is that?

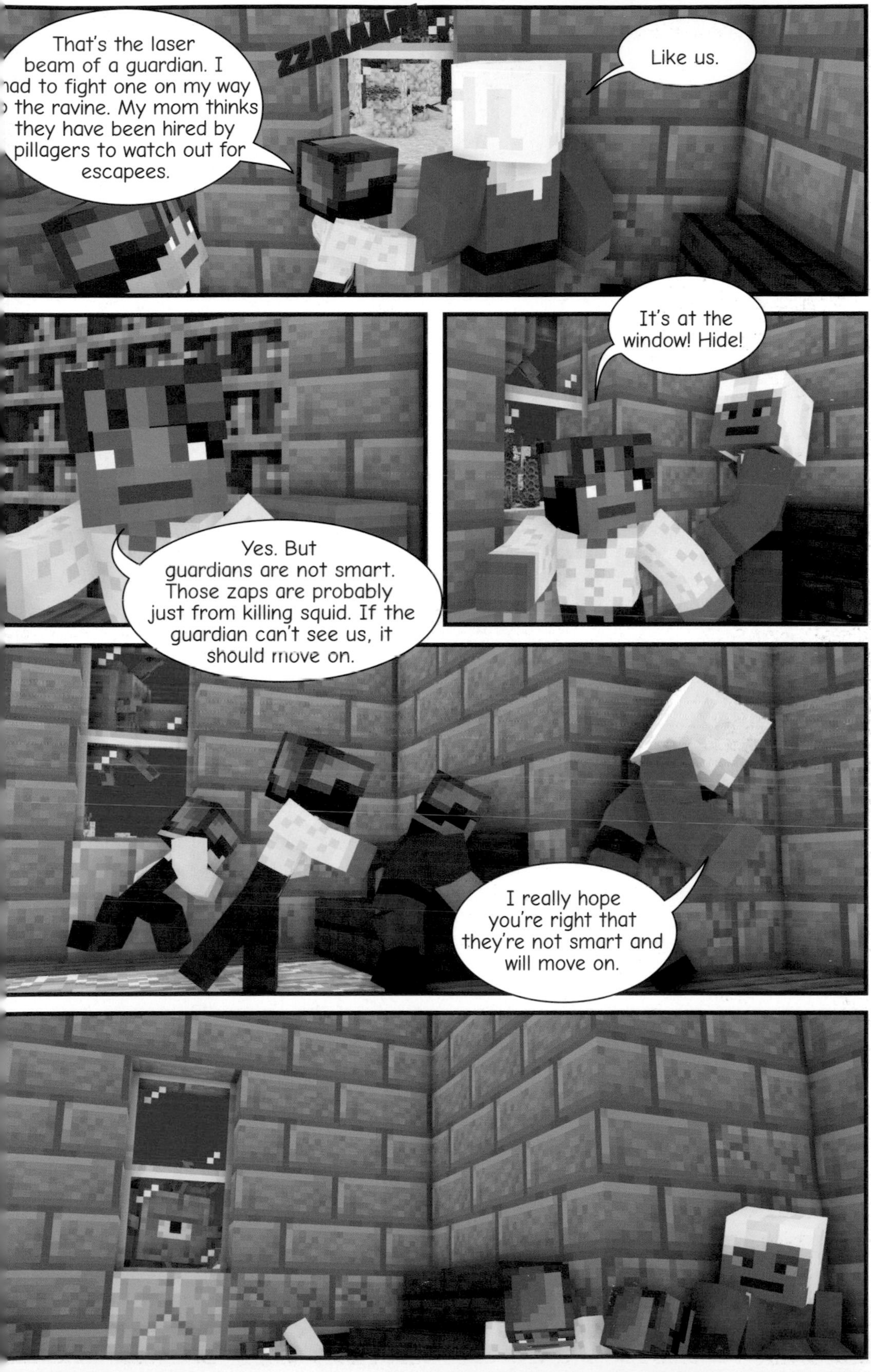
That's the laser beam of a guardian. I ad to fight one on my way the ravine. My mom thinks they have been hired by pillagers to watch out for escapees.
Like us.
Yes. But guardians are not smart. Those zaps are probably just from killing squid. If the guardian can't see us, it should move on.
It's at the window! Hide!
I really hope you're right that they're not smart and will move on.

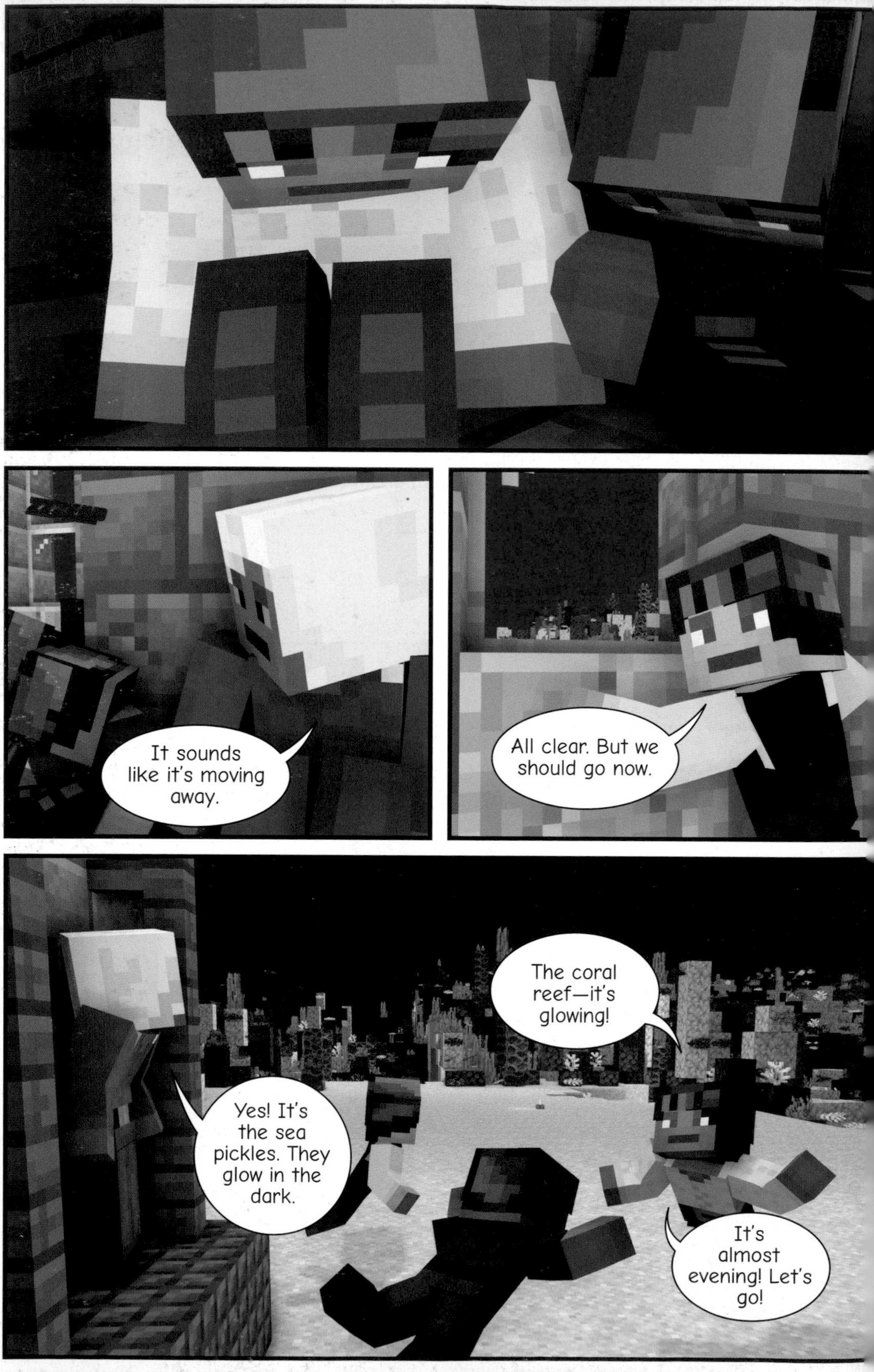
It sounds like it's moving away.
All clear. But we should go now.
The coral reef—it's glowing!
Yes! It's the sea pickles. They glow in the dark.
It's almost evening! Let's go!

Chapter 8
The Clue to Gold

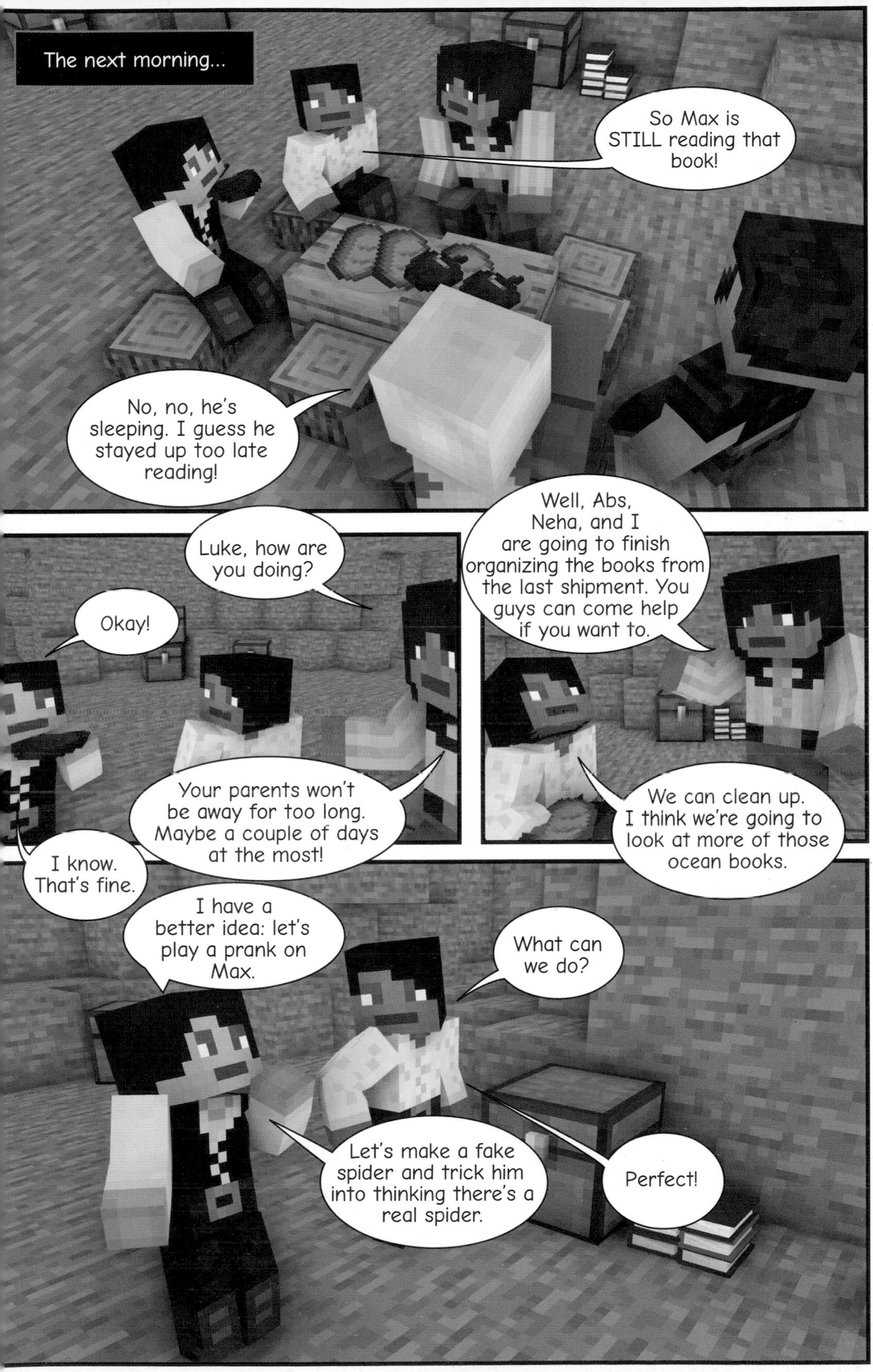

The next morning...
So Max is STILL reading that book!
No, no, he's sleeping. I guess he stayed up too late reading!
Luke, how are you doing?
Okay!
Your parents won't be away for too long. Maybe a couple of days at the most!
I know. That's fine.
Well, Abs, Neha, and I are going to finish organizing the books from the last shipment. You guys can come help if you want to.
We can clean up. I think we're going to look at more of those ocean books.
I have a better idea: let's play a prank on Max.
What can we do?
Let's make a fake spider and trick him into thinking there's a real spider.
Perfect!

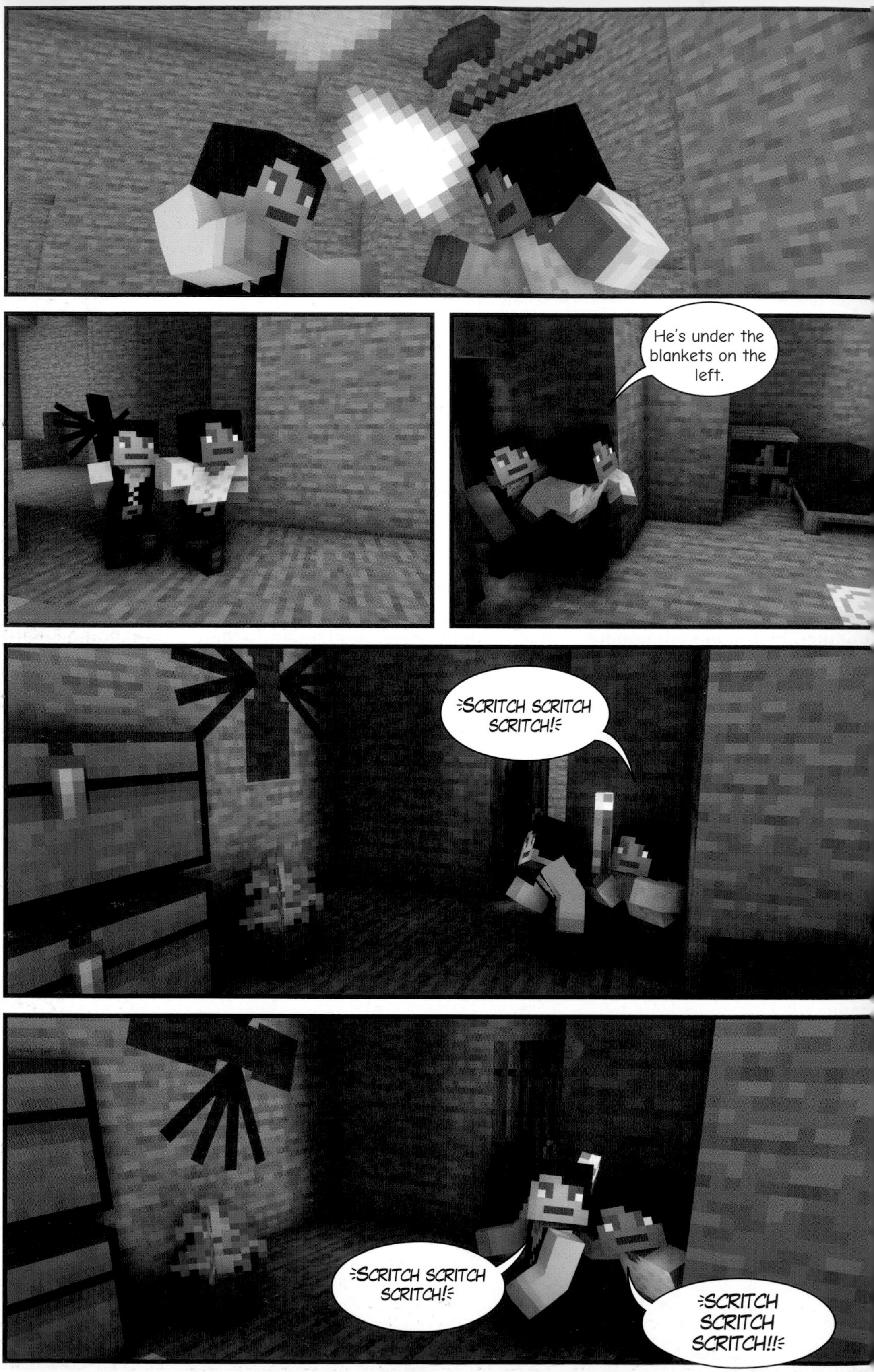
He's under the blankets on the left.
SCRITCH SCRITCH SCRITCH!
SCRITCH SCRITCH SCRITCH!
SCRITCH SCRITCH SCRITCH!!

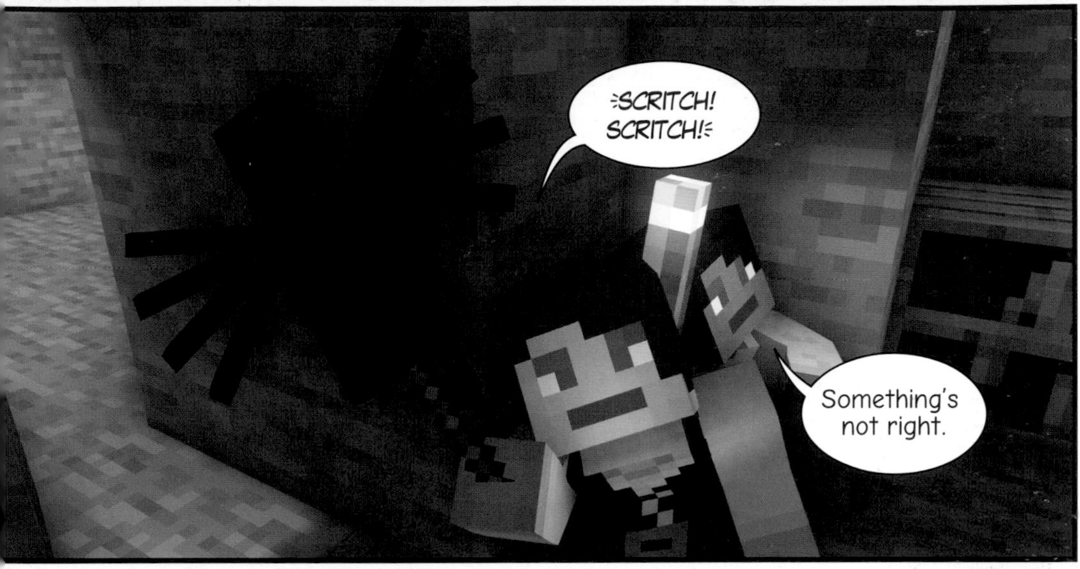
SCRITCH!
SCRITCH!
Something's not right.

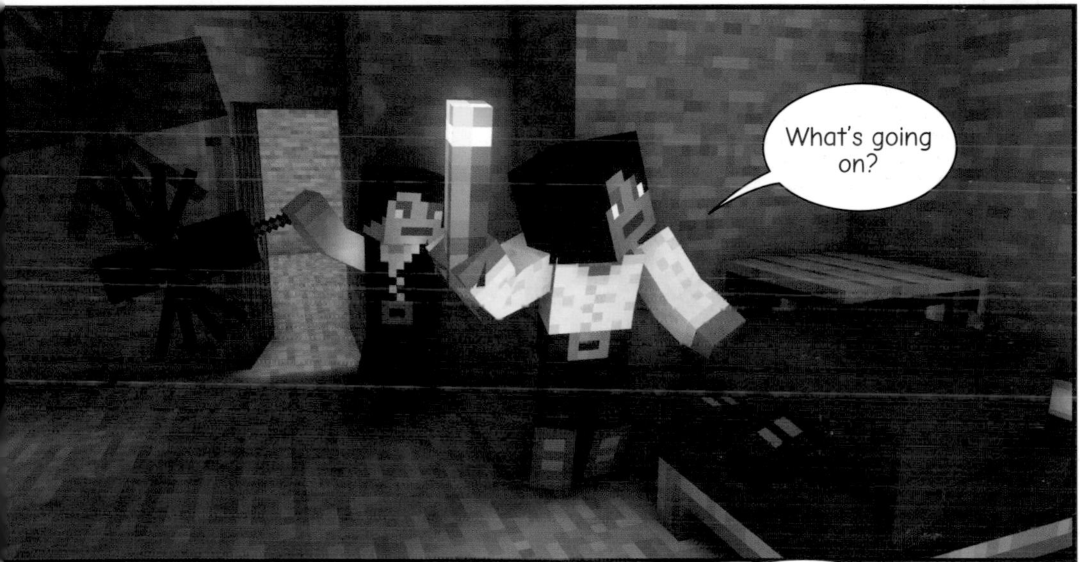
What's going on?

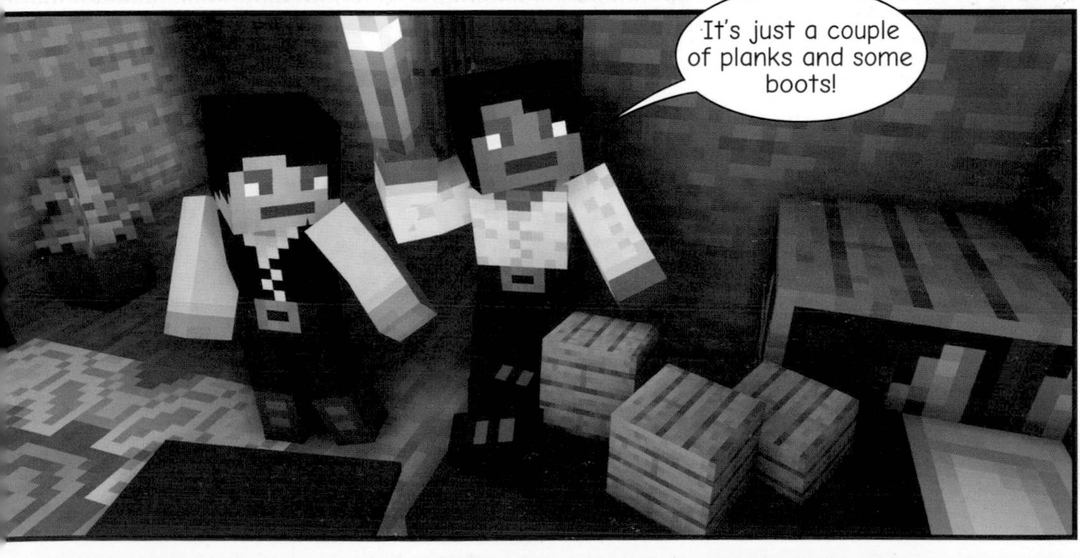
It's just a couple of planks and some boots!

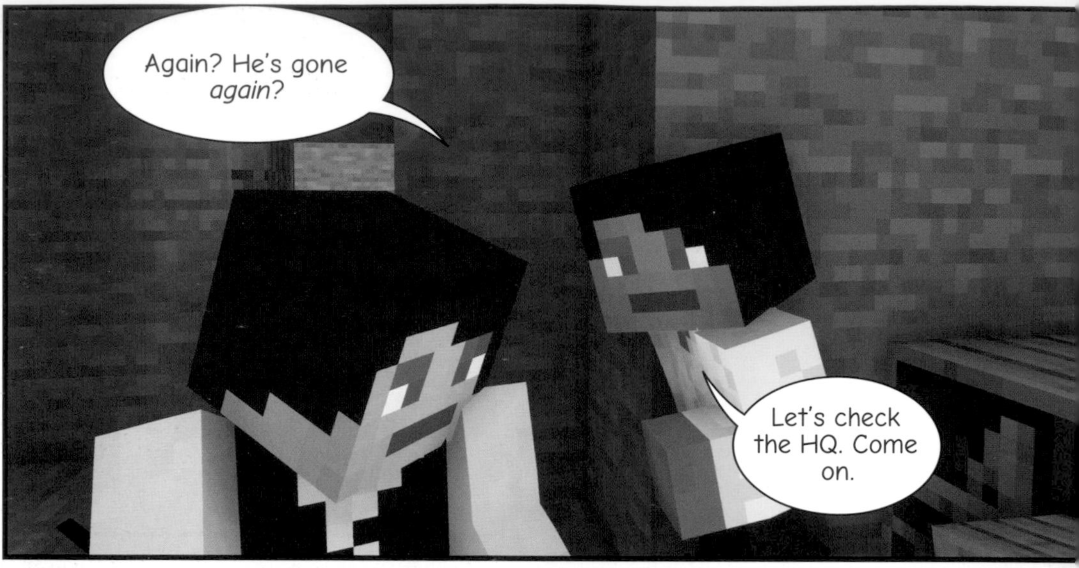
Again? He's gone *again*?
Let's check the HQ. Come on.

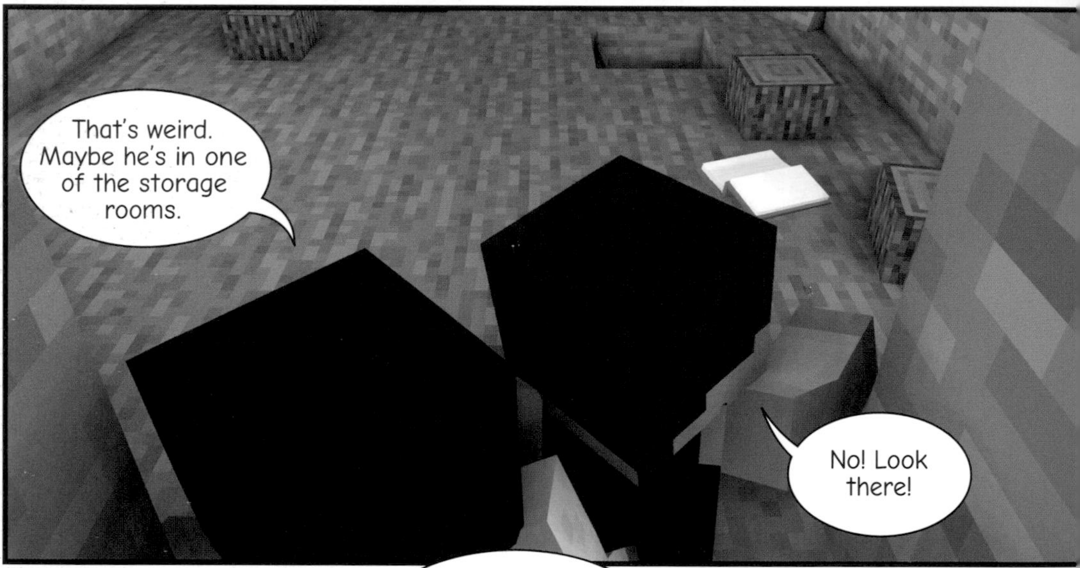
That's weird. Maybe he's in one of the storage rooms.
No! Look there!

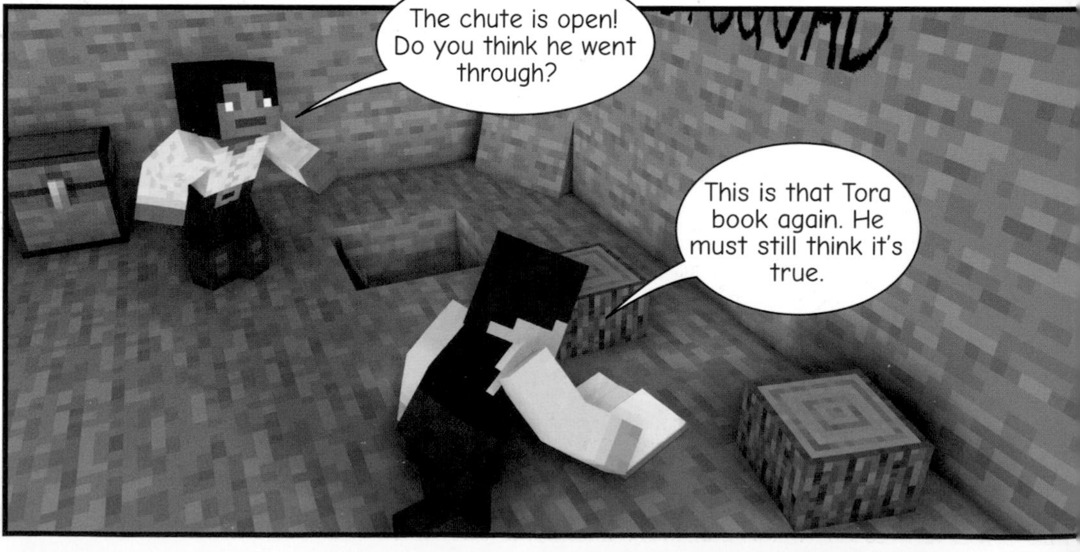
The chute is open! Do you think he went through?
This is that Tora book again. He must still think it's true.

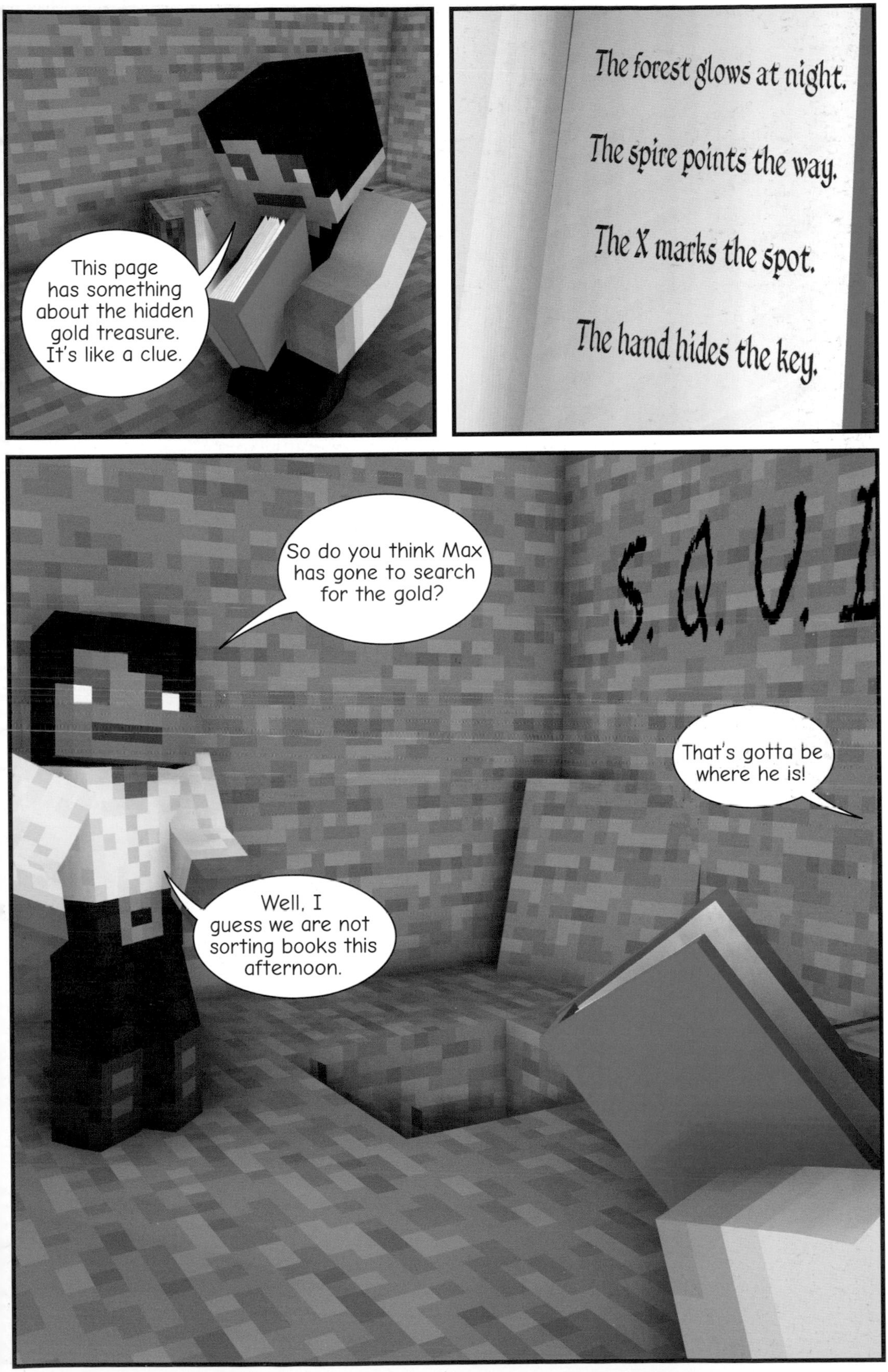
This page has something about the hidden gold treasure. It's like a clue.
The forest glows at night.
The spire points the way.
The X marks the spot.
The hand hides the key.
S. Q. U.
So do you think Max has gone to search for the gold?
That's gotta be where he is!
Well, I guess we are not sorting books this afternoon.

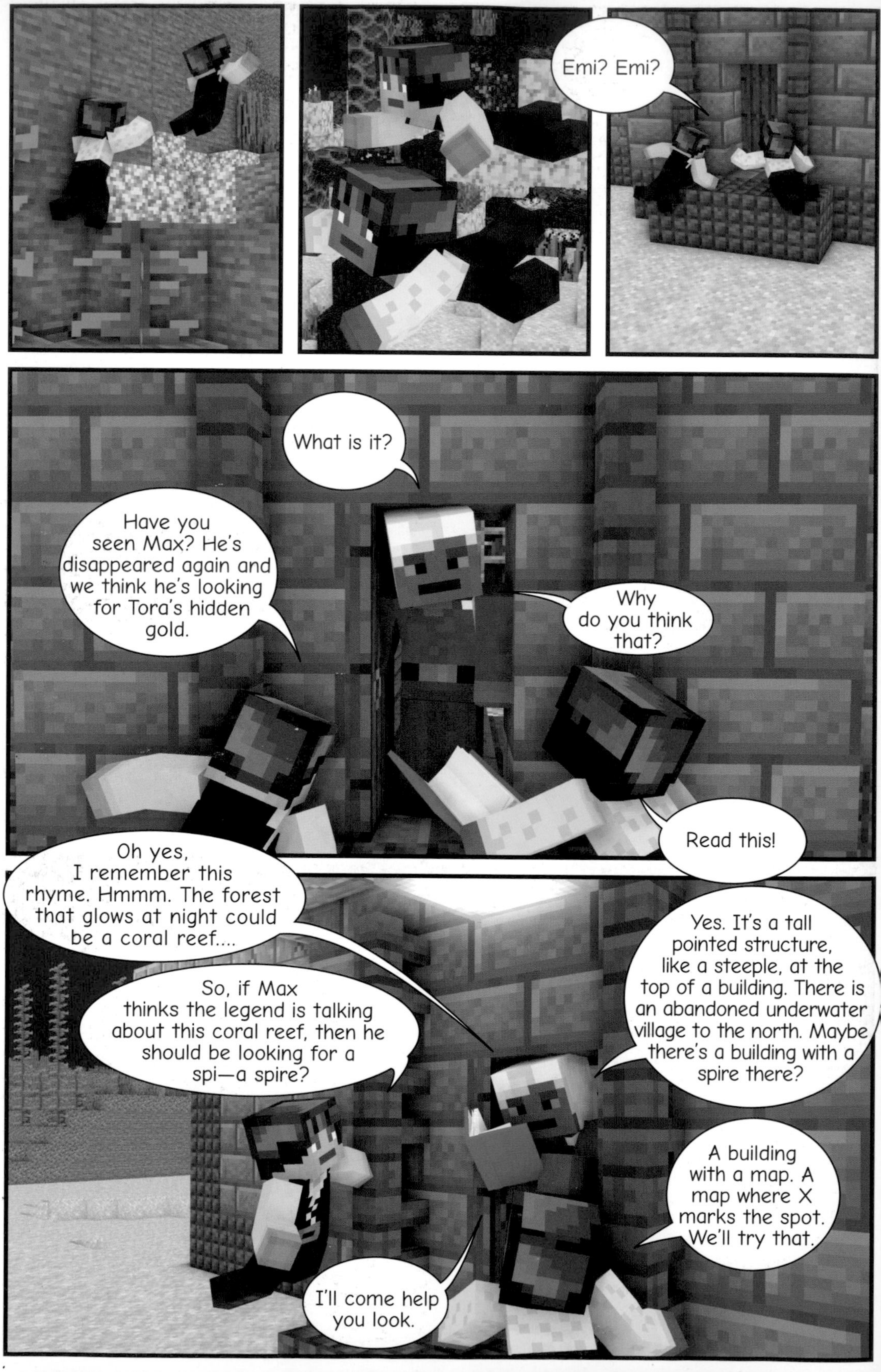
Emi? Emi?
What is it?
Have you seen Max? He's disappeared again and we think he's looking for Tora's hidden gold.
Why do you think that?
Read this!
Oh yes, I remember this rhyme. Hmmm. The forest that glows at night could be a coral reef....
So, if Max thinks the legend is talking about this coral reef, then he should be looking for a spi—a spire?
Yes. It's a tall pointed structure, like a steeple, at the top of a building. There is an abandoned underwater village to the north. Maybe there's a building with a spire there?
A building with a map. A map where X marks the spot. We'll try that.
I'll come help you look.

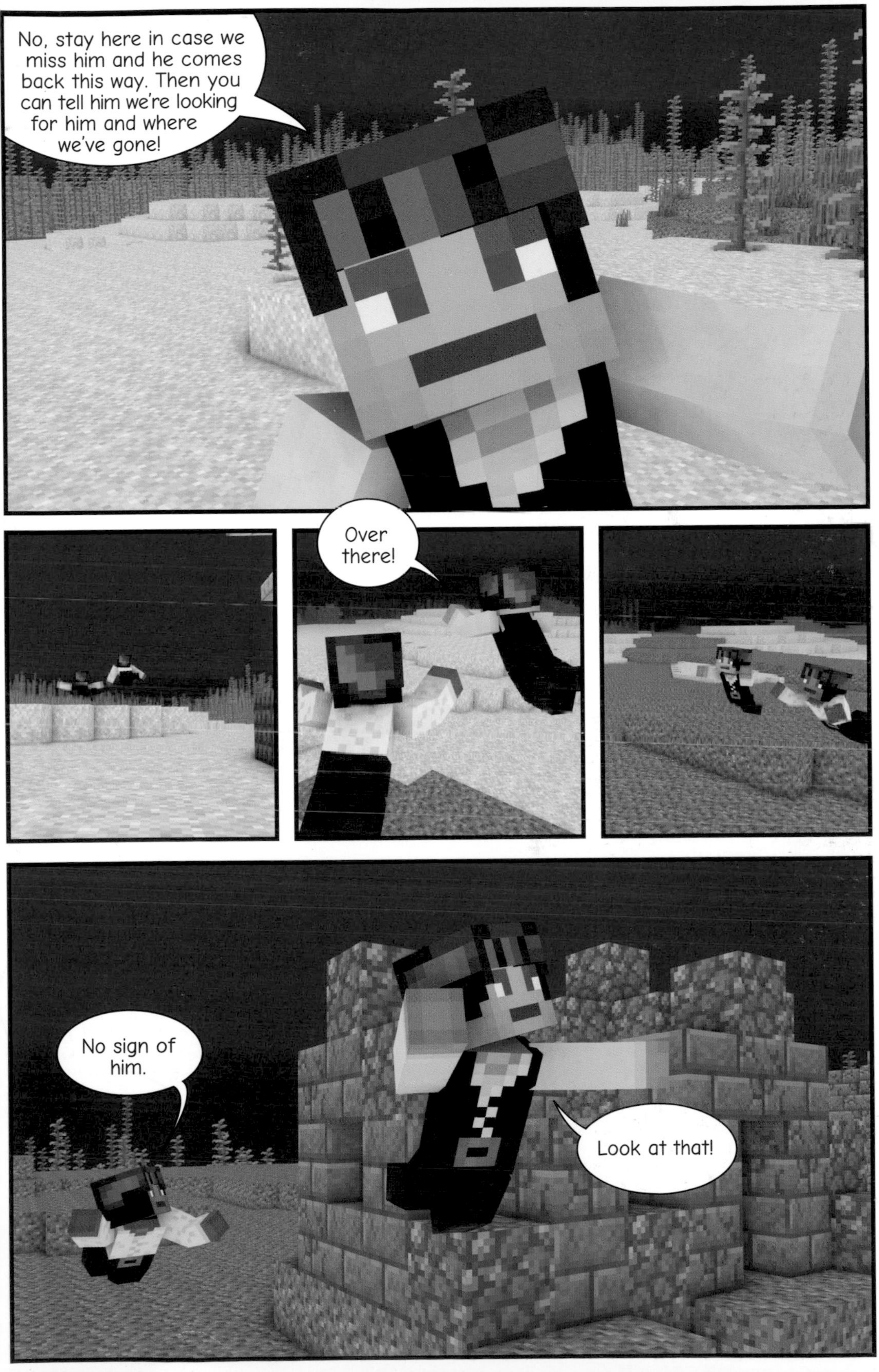
No, stay here in case we miss him and he comes back this way. Then you can tell him we're looking for him and where we've gone!
Over there!
No sign of him.
Look at that!

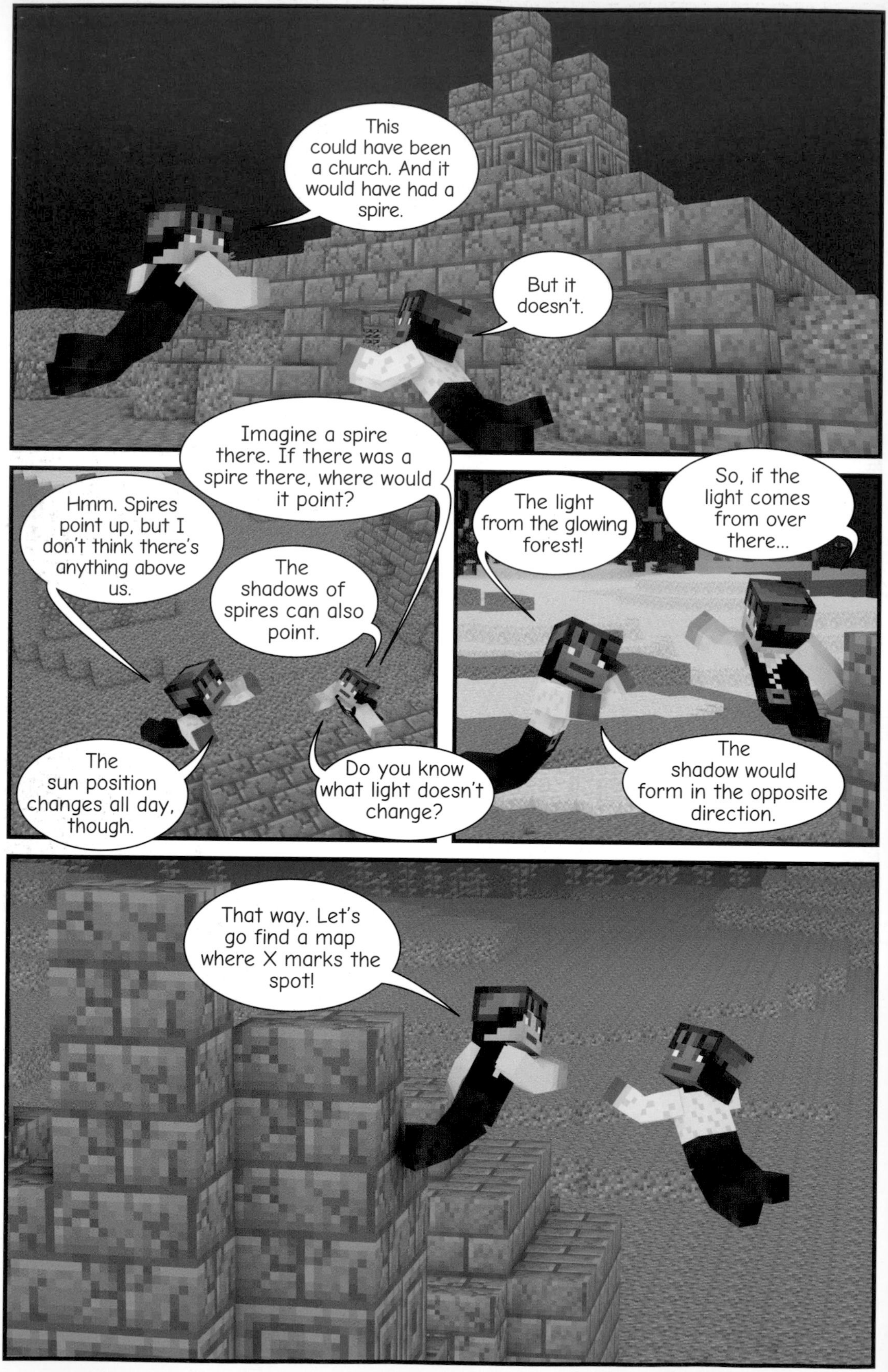
This could have been a church. And it would have had a spire.
But it doesn't.
Imagine a spire there. If there was a spire there, where would it point?
Hmm. Spires point up, but I don't think there's anything above us.
The shadows of spires can also point.
The sun position changes all day, though.
Do you know what light doesn't change?
The light from the glowing forest!
So, if the light comes from over there...
The shadow would form in the opposite direction.
That way. Let's go find a map where X marks the spot!

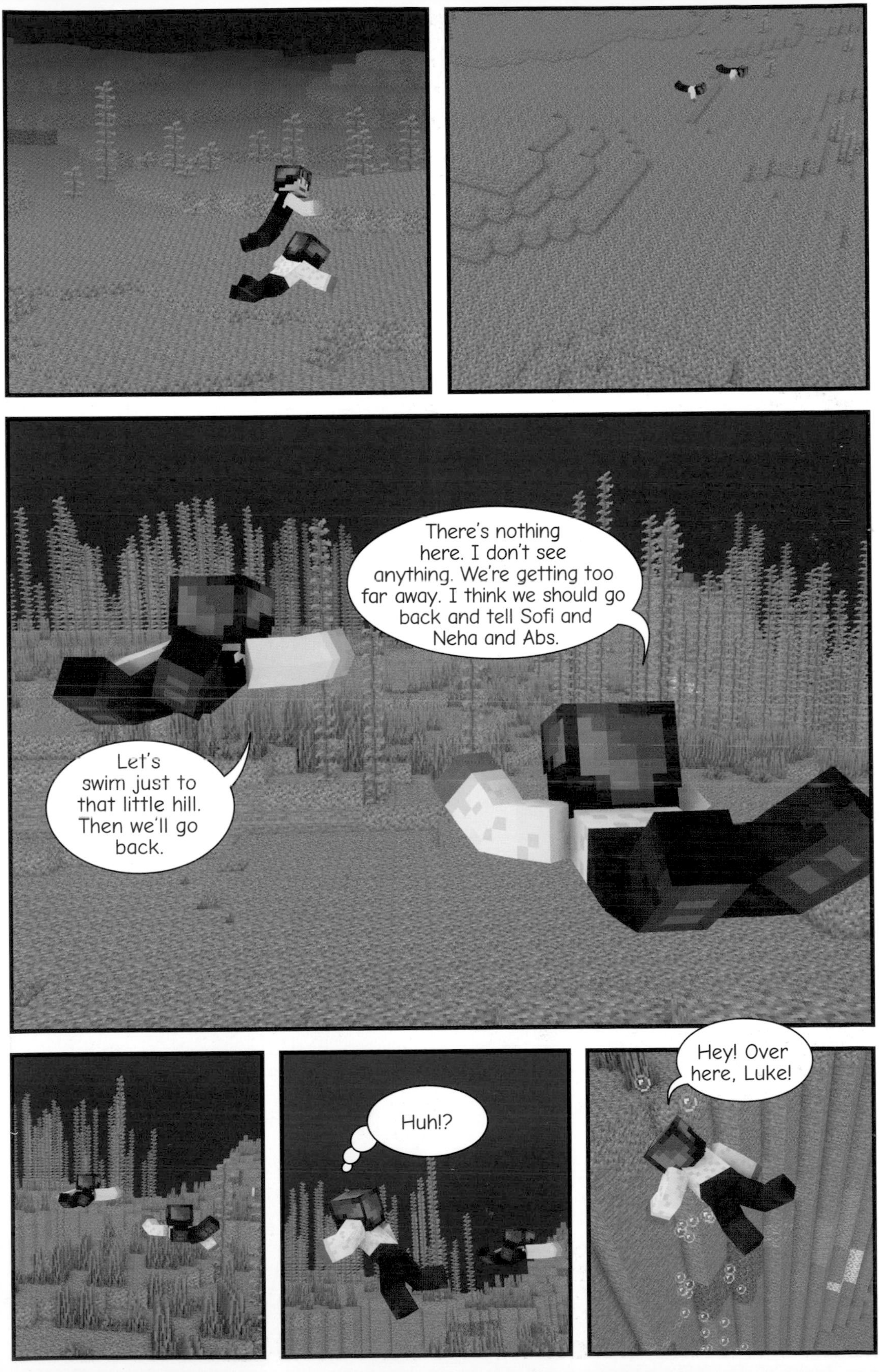
There's nothing here. I don't see anything. We're getting too far away. I think we should go back and tell Sofi and Neha and Abs.
Let's swim just to that little hill. Then we'll go back.
Huh!?
Hey! Over here, Luke!

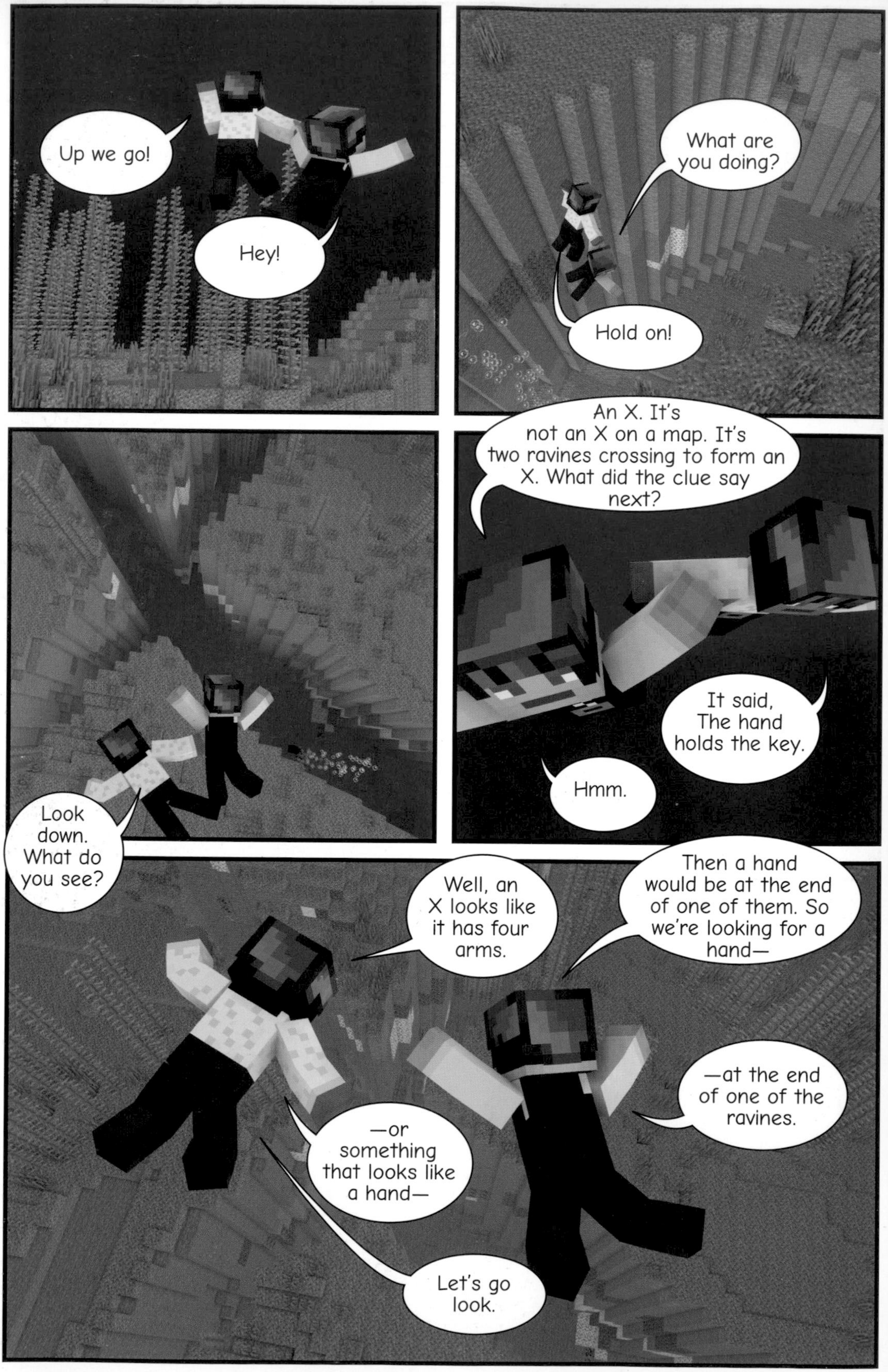
Up we go!
Hey!
What are you doing?
Hold on!
Look down. What do you see?
An X. It's not an X on a map. It's two ravines crossing to form an X. What did the clue say next?
It said, The hand holds the key.
Hmm.
Well, an X looks like it has four arms.
Then a hand would be at the end of one of them. So we're looking for a hand—
—or something that looks like a hand—
—at the end of one of the ravines.
Let's go look.

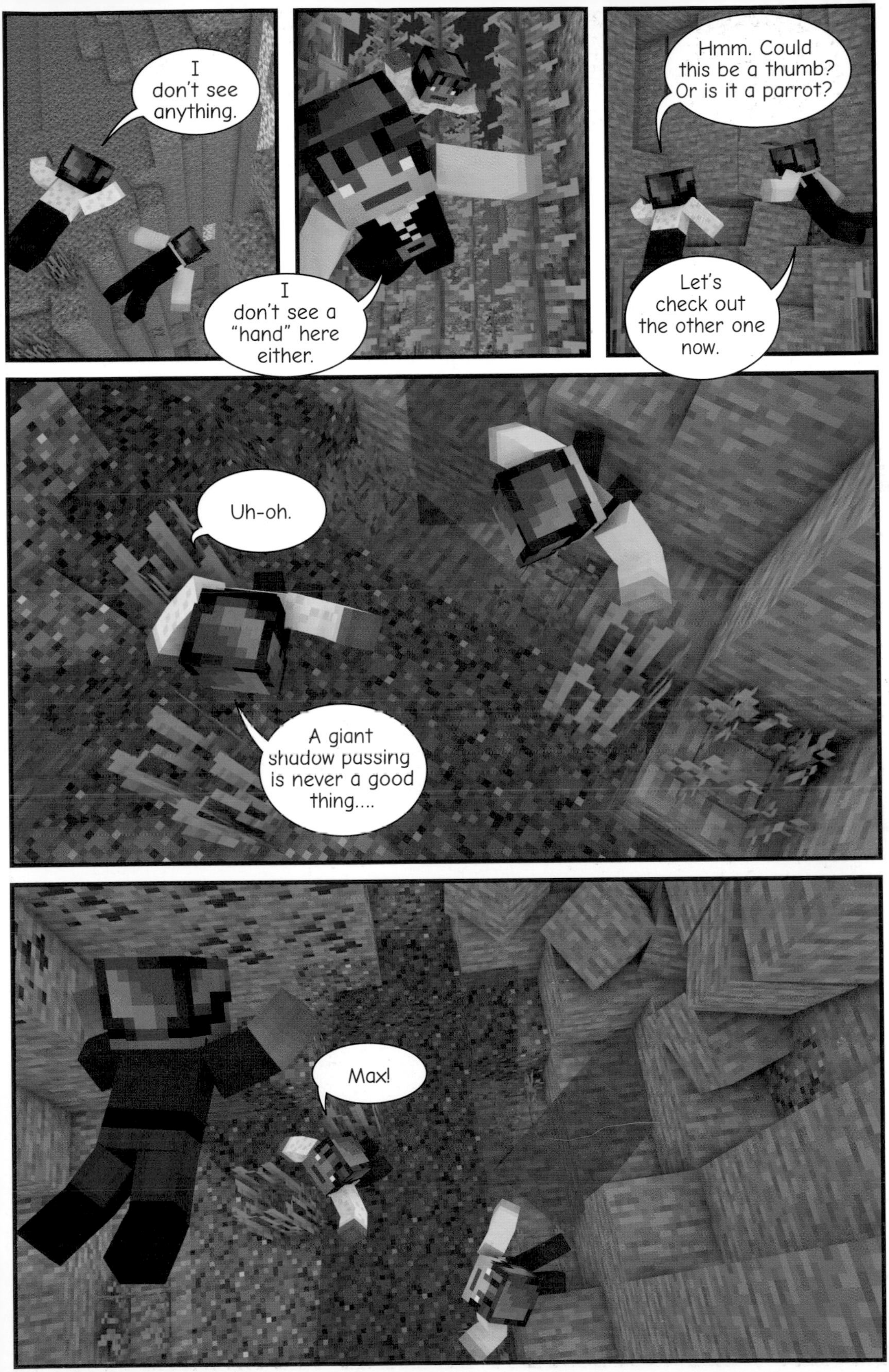
I don't see anything.
I don't see a "hand" here either.
Hmm. Could this be a thumb? Or is it a parrot?
Let's check out the other one now.
Uh-oh.
A giant shadow passing is never a good thing....
Max!

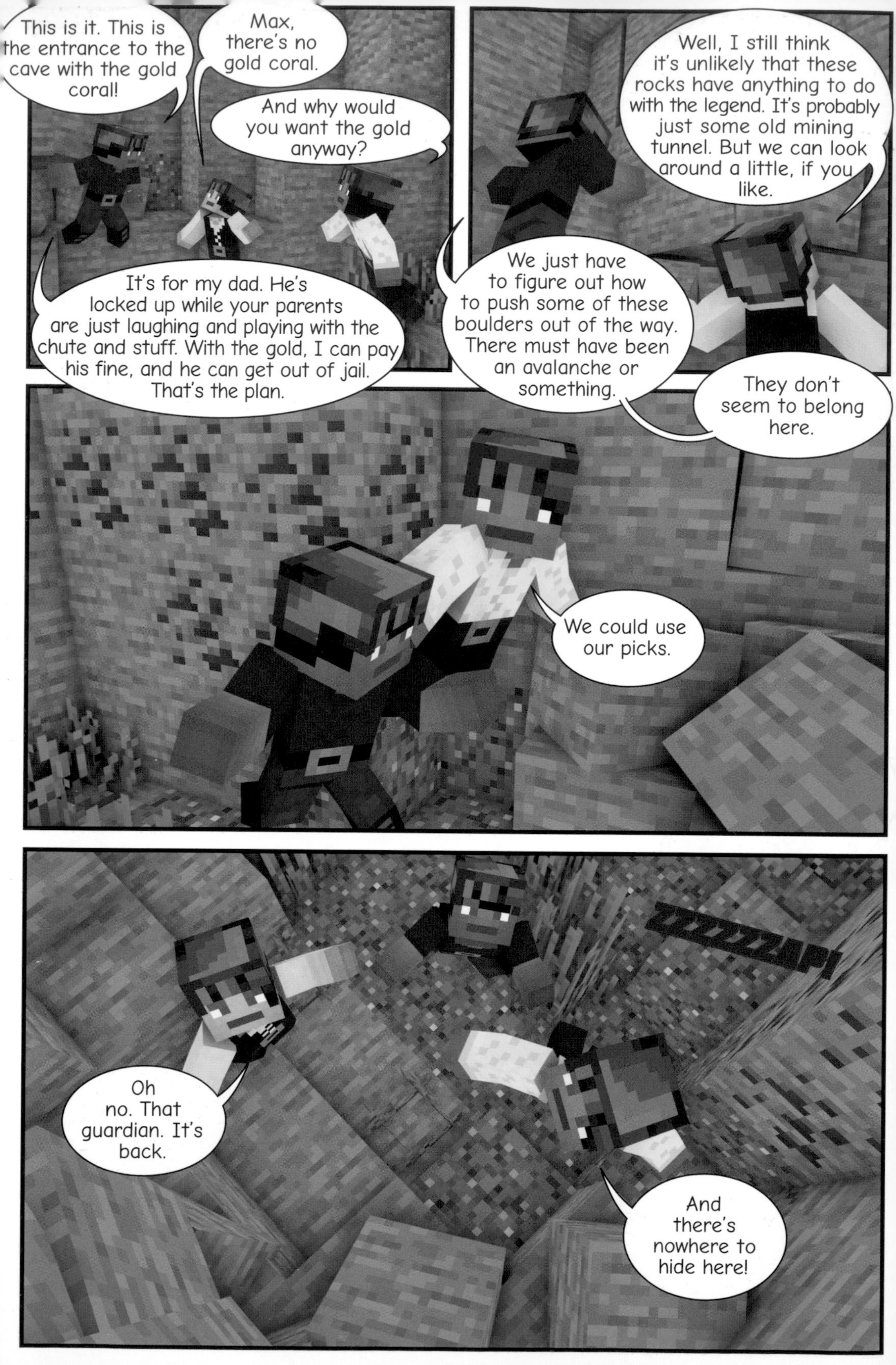
This is it. This is the entrance to the cave with the gold coral!
Max, there's no gold coral.
And why would you want the gold anyway?
It's for my dad. He's locked up while your parents are just laughing and playing with the chute and stuff. With the gold, I can pay his fine, and he can get out of jail. That's the plan.
Well, I still think it's unlikely that these rocks have anything to do with the legend. It's probably just some old mining tunnel. But we can look around a little, if you like.
We just have to figure out how to push some of these boulders out of the way. There must have been an avalanche or something.
They don't seem to belong here.
We could use our picks.
ZZZZZAP!
Oh no. That guardian. It's back.
And there's nowhere to hide here!

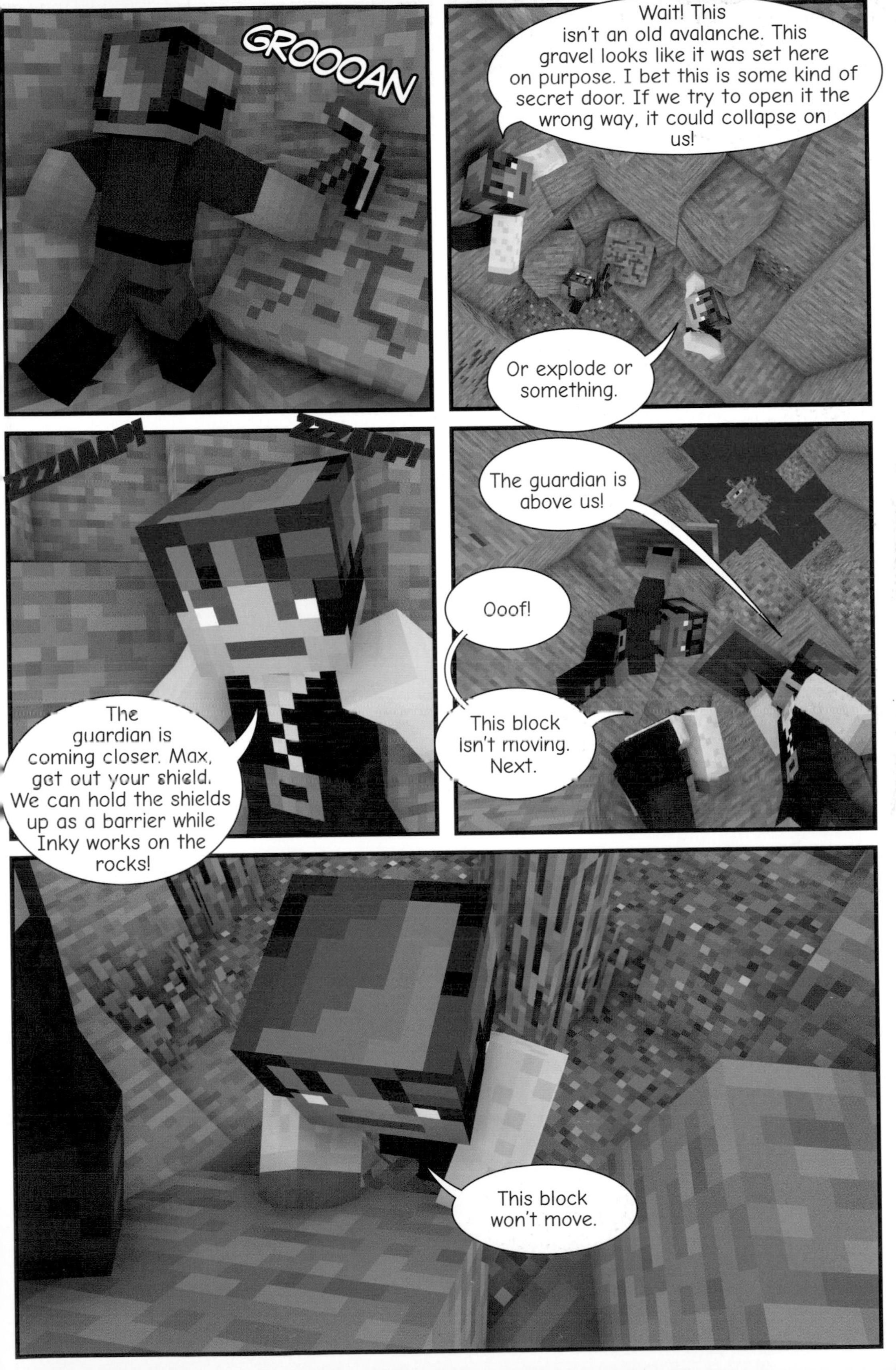
GROOOAN
Wait! This isn't an old avalanche. This gravel looks like it was set here on purpose. I bet this is some kind of secret door. If we try to open it the wrong way, it could collapse on us!
Or explode or something.
ZZZAAAP!
ZZZAPP!
The guardian is coming closer. Max, get out your shield. We can hold the shields up as a barrier while Inky works on the rocks!
The guardian is above us!
Ooof!
This block isn't moving. Next.
This block won't move.

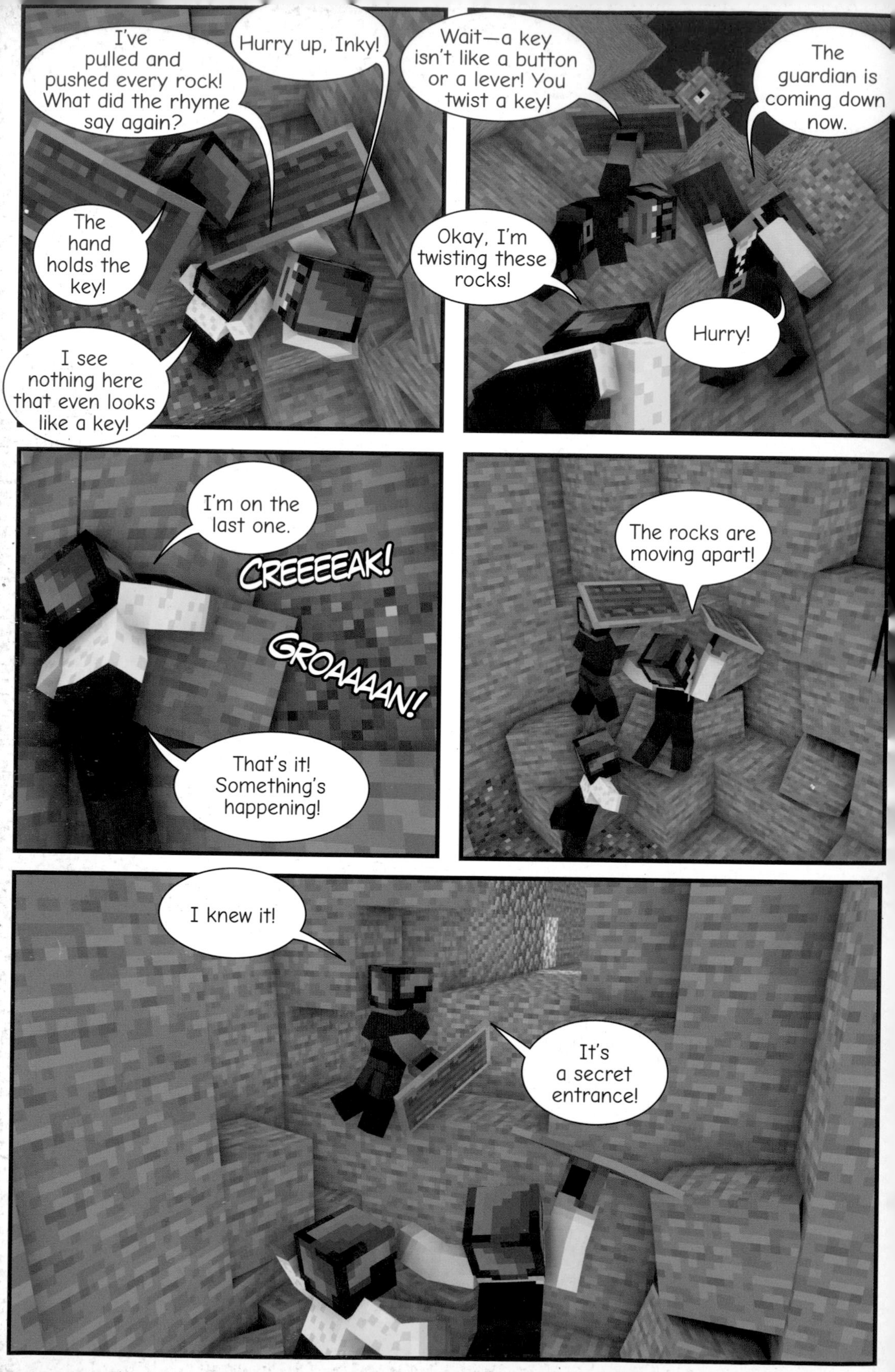
I've pulled and pushed every rock! What did the rhyme say again?
Hurry up, Inky!
The hand holds the key!
I see nothing here that even looks like a key!
Wait—a key isn't like a button or a lever! You twist a key!
The guardian is coming down now.
Okay, I'm twisting these rocks!
Hurry!
I'm on the last one.
CREEEEAK!
GROAAAAN!
That's it! Something's happening!
The rocks are moving apart!
I knew it!
It's a secret entrance!

Chapter 9
A Cave of Golden Coral

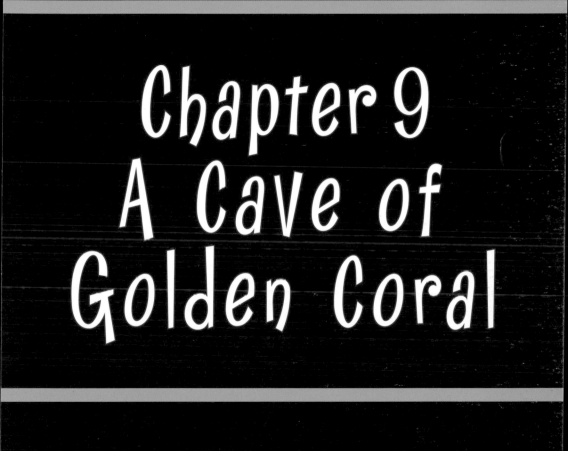

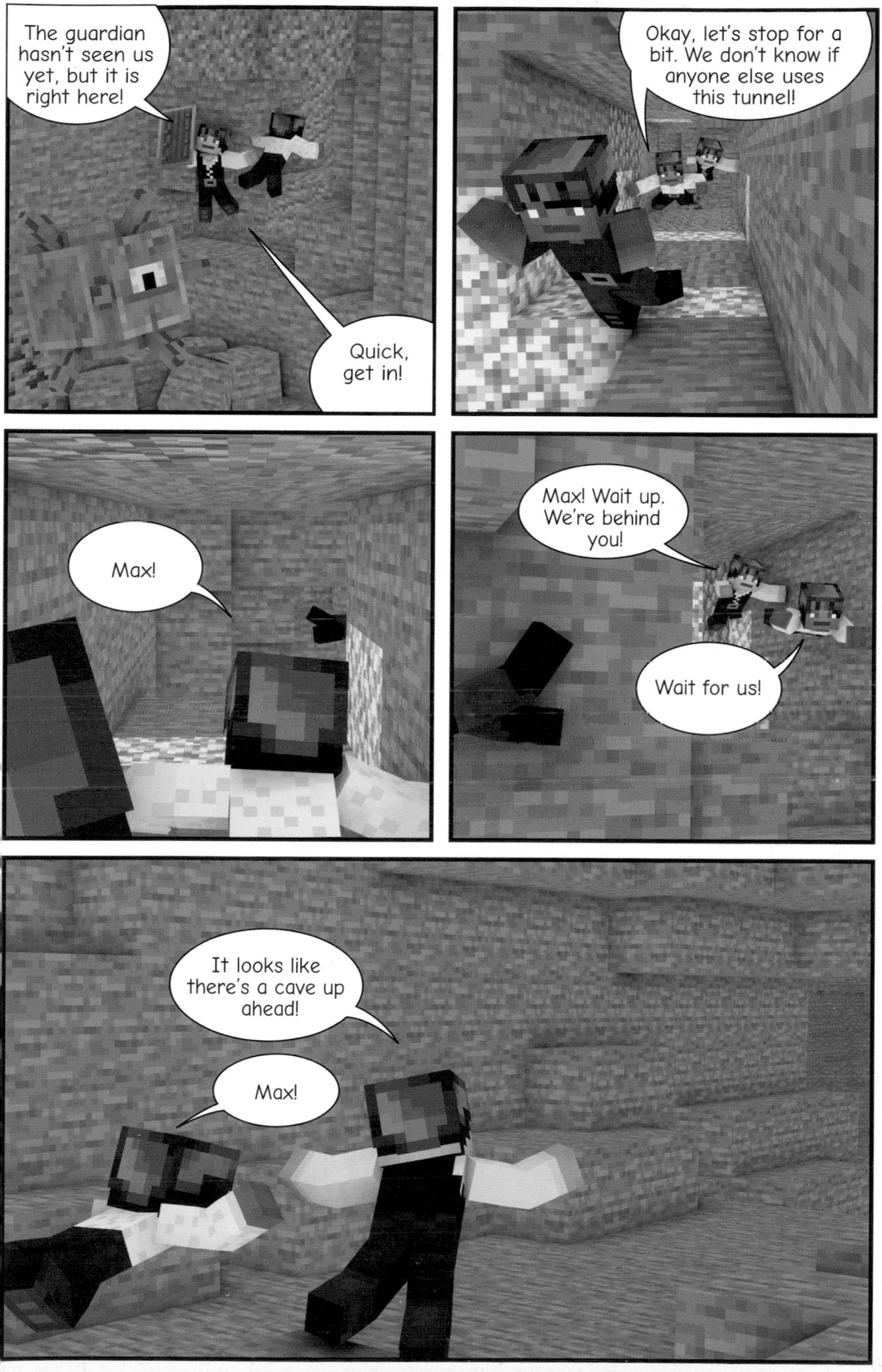
The guardian hasn't seen us yet, but it is right here!
Quick, get in!
Okay, let's stop for a bit. We don't know if anyone else uses this tunnel!
Max!
Max! Wait up. We're behind you!
Wait for us!
It looks like there's a cave up ahead!
Max!

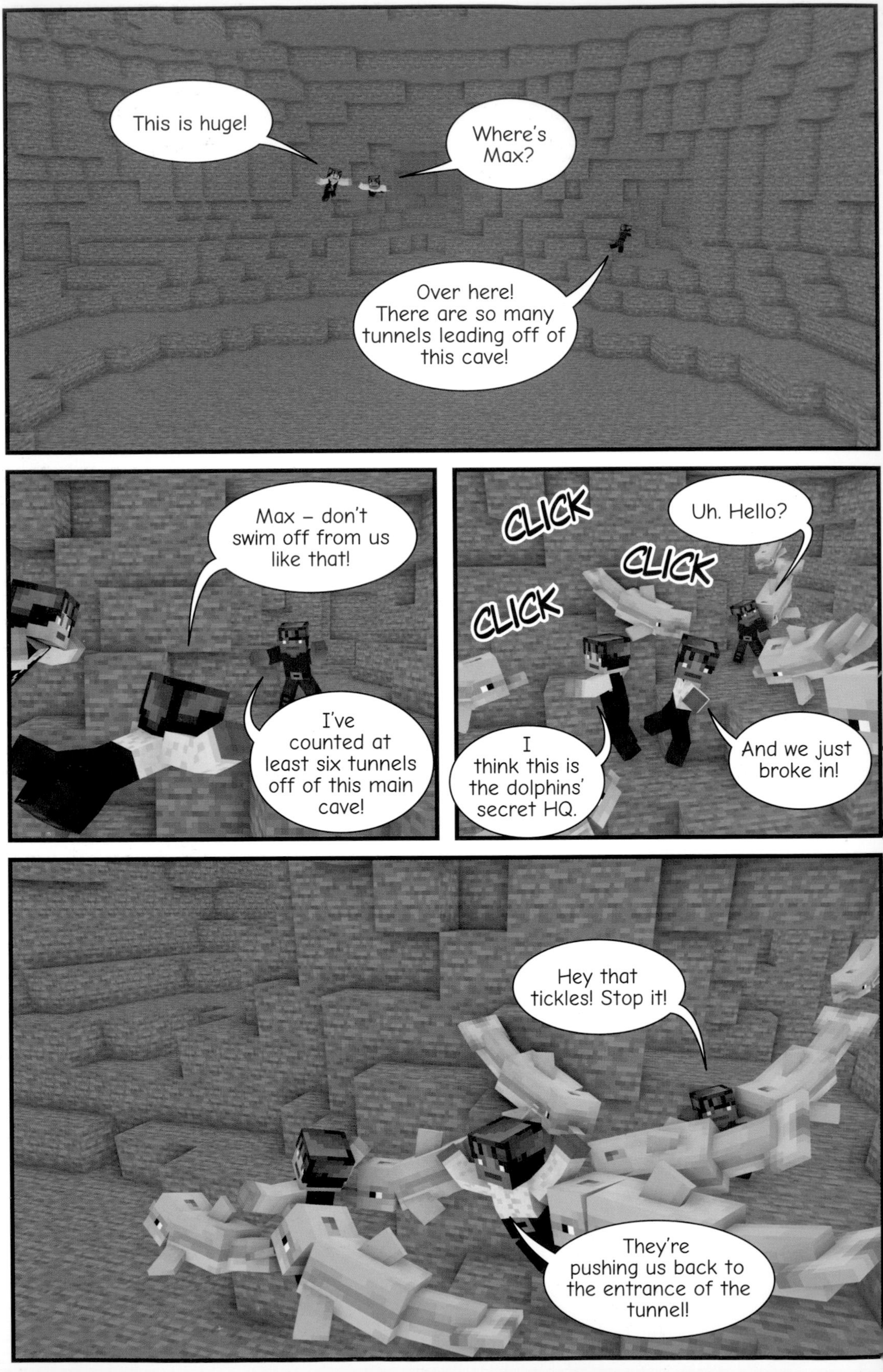
This is huge!
Where's Max?
Over here! There are so many tunnels leading off of this cave!
Max – don't swim off from us like that!
I've counted at least six tunnels off of this main cave!
CLICK
CLICK
CLICK
Uh. Hello?
I think this is the dolphins' secret HQ.
And we just broke in!
Hey that tickles! Stop it!
They're pushing us back to the entrance of the tunnel!

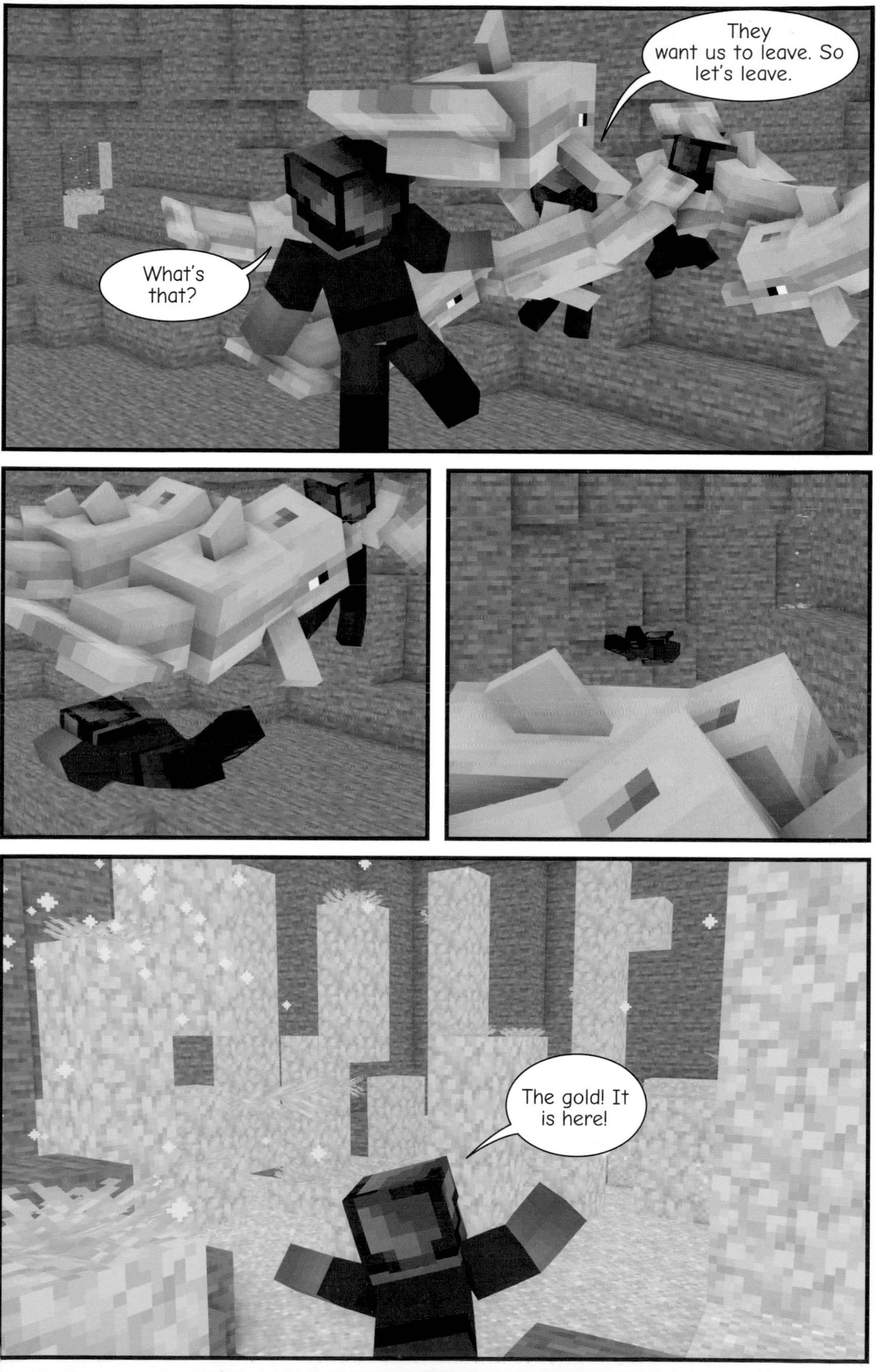
They want us to leave. So let's leave.
What's that?
The gold! It is here!

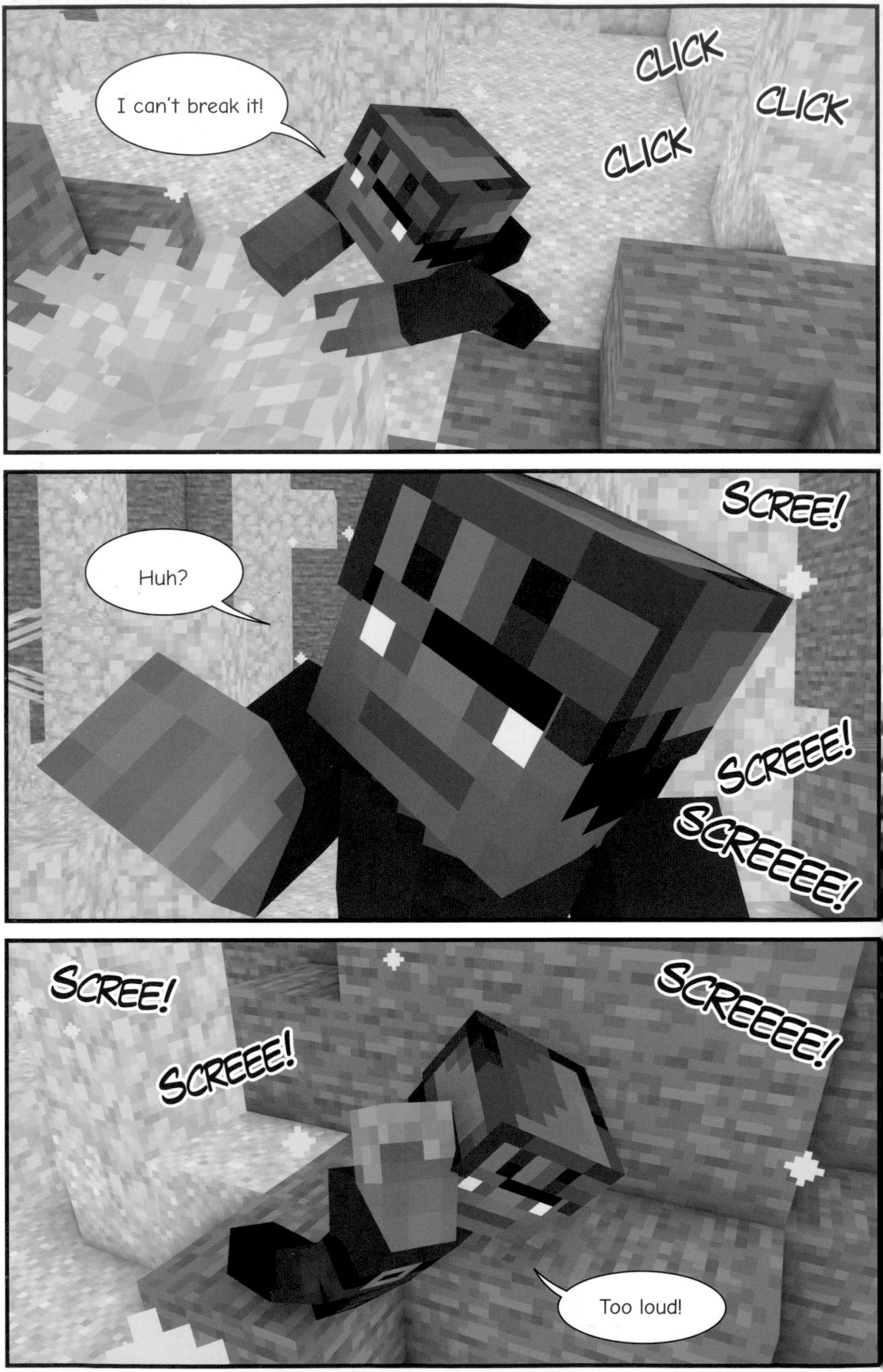
I can't break it!
CLICK
CLICK
CLICK
Huh?
SCREE!
SCREEE!
SCREEEEE!
SCREE!
SCREEE!
SCREEEEE!
Too loud!

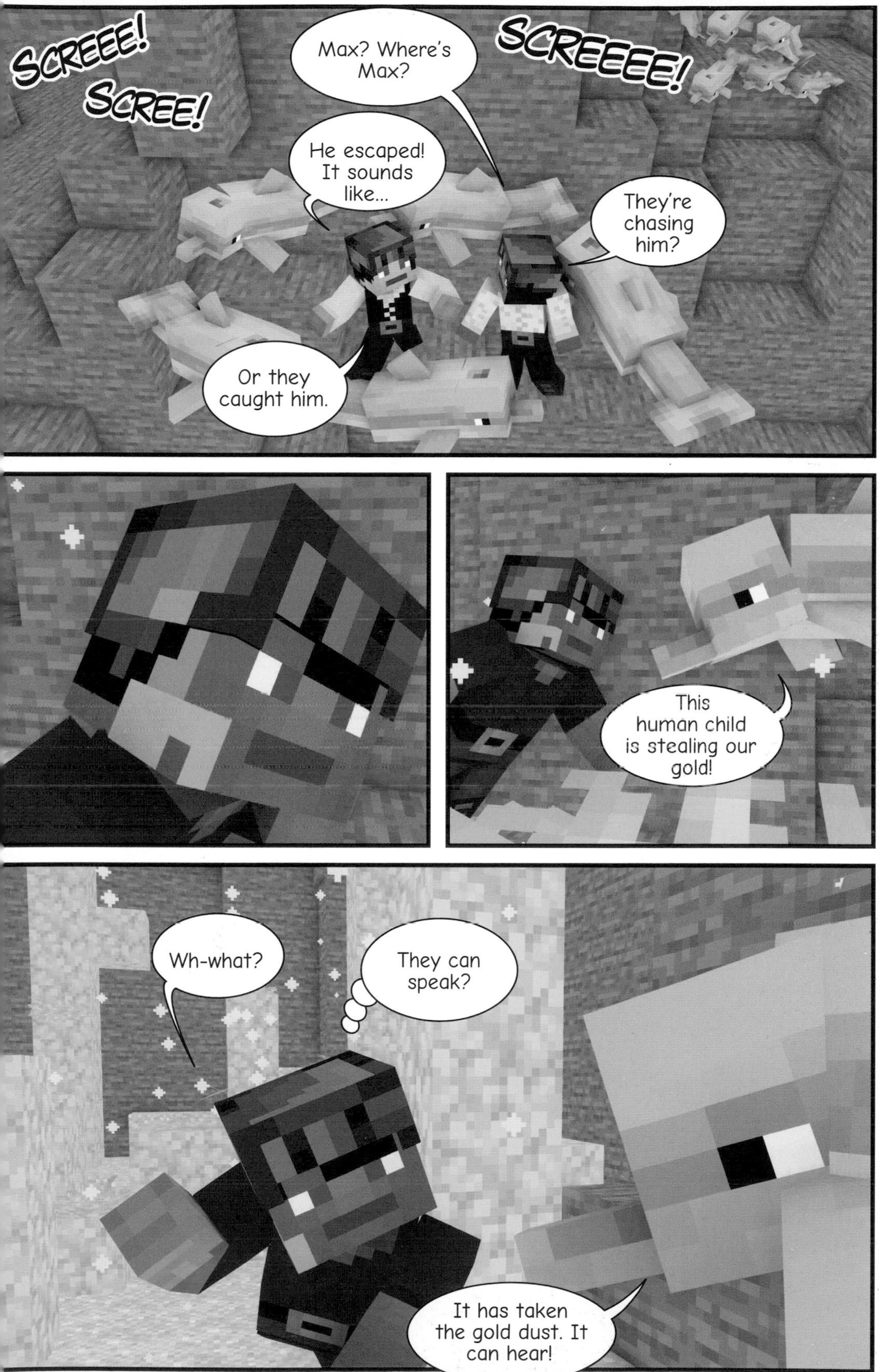
SCREEE!
SCREE!
Max? Where's Max?
SCREEEEE!
He escaped! It sounds like...
They're chasing him?
Or they caught him.
This human child is stealing our gold!
Wh-what?
They can speak?
It has taken the gold dust. It can hear!

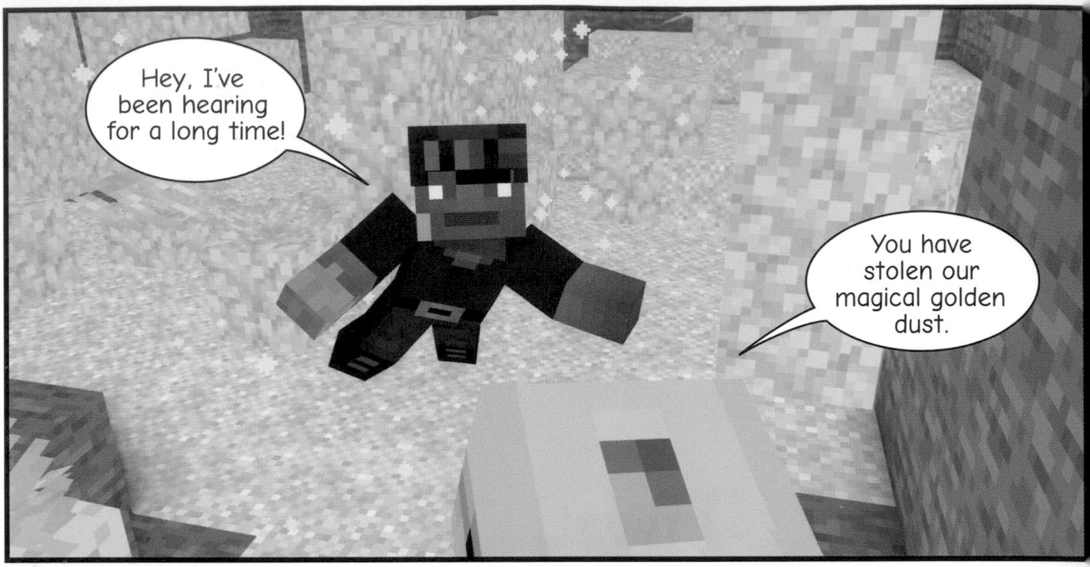
Hey, I've been hearing for a long time!
You have stolen our magical golden dust.

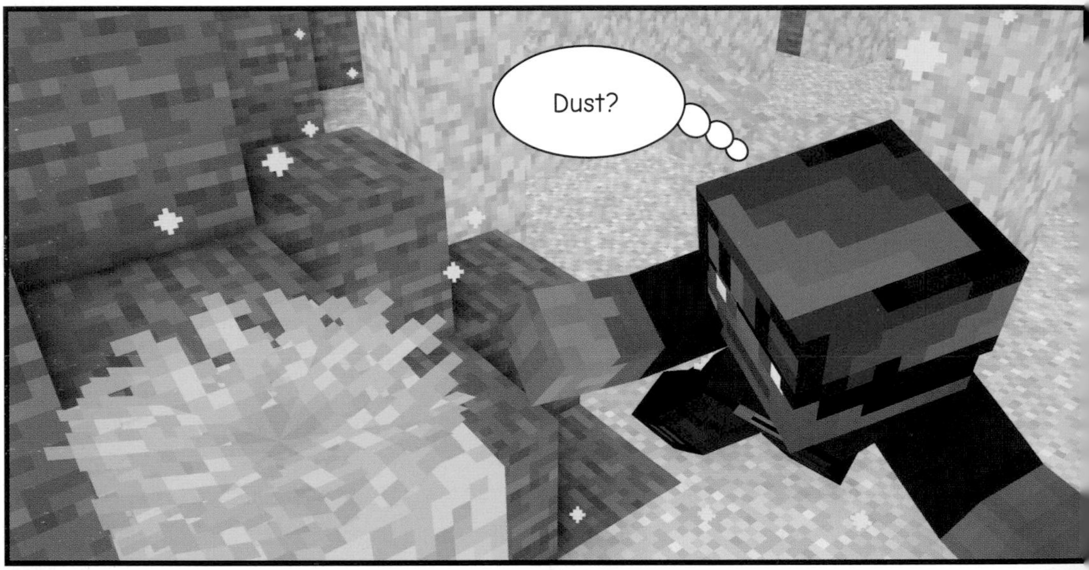
Dust?

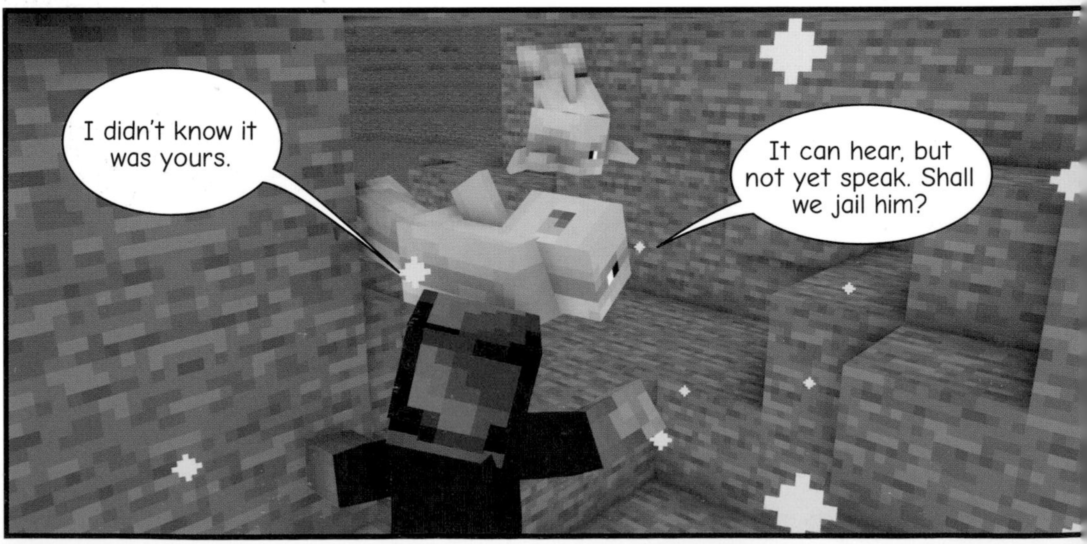
I didn't know it was yours.
It can hear, but not yet speak. Shall we jail him?

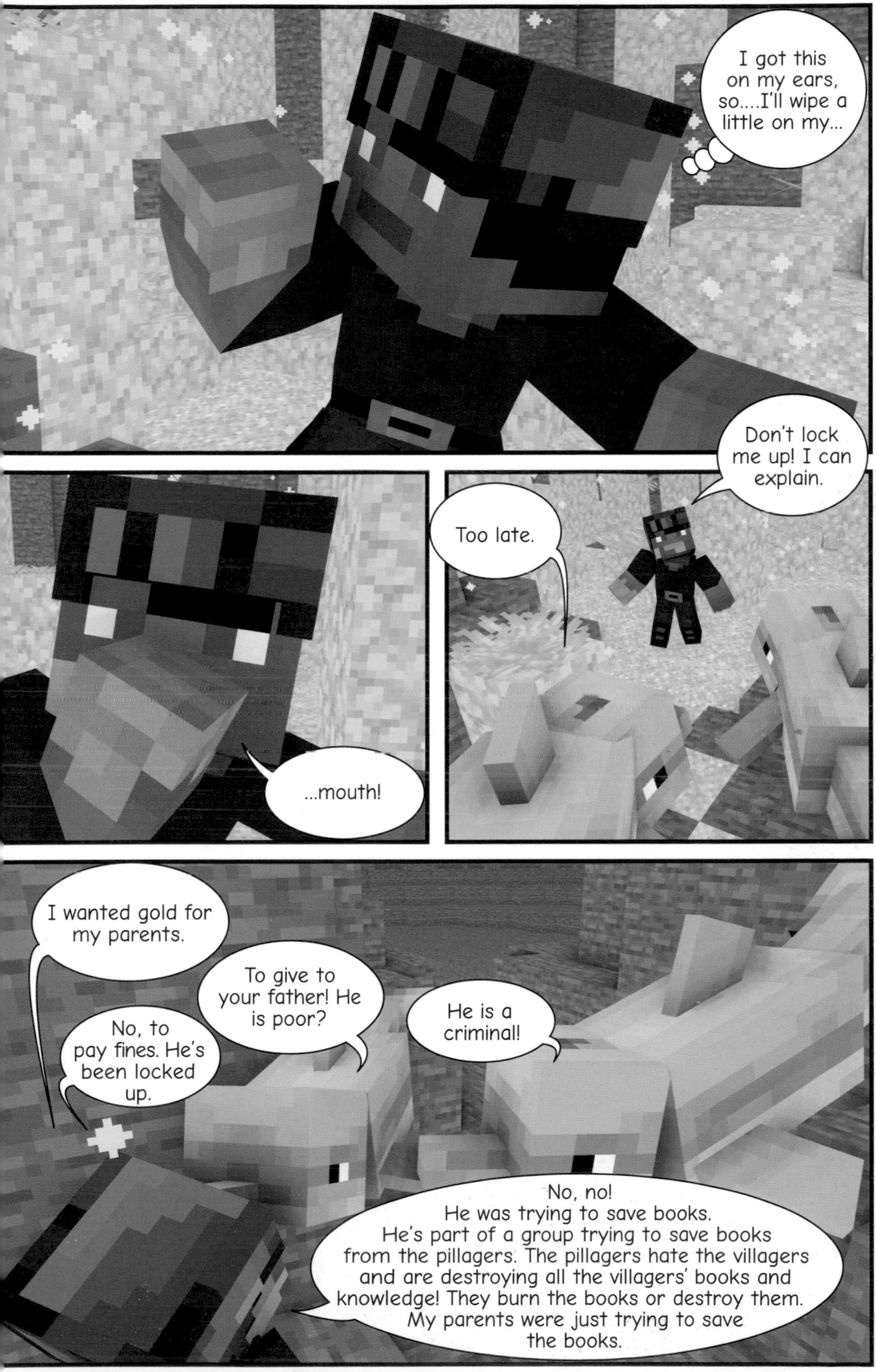
I got this on my ears, so....I'll wipe a little on my...
...mouth!
Don't lock me up! I can explain.
Too late.
I wanted gold for my parents.
To give to your father! He is poor?
No, to pay fines. He's been locked up.
He is a criminal!
No, no! He was trying to save books. He's part of a group trying to save books from the pillagers. The pillagers hate the villagers and are destroying all the villagers' books and knowledge! They burn the books or destroy them. My parents were just trying to save the books.

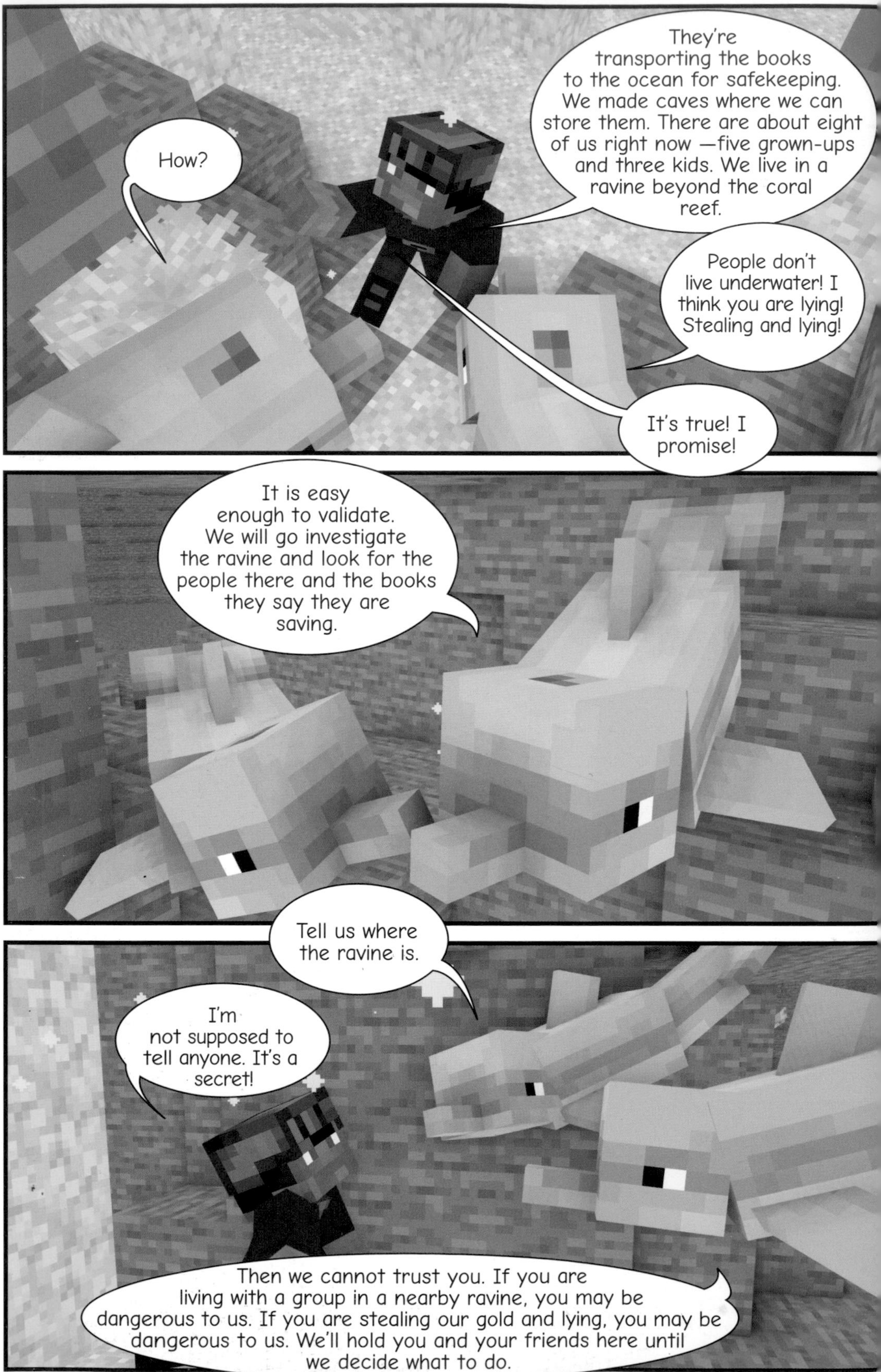
How?
They're transporting the books to the ocean for safekeeping. We made caves where we can store them. There are about eight of us right now —five grown-ups and three kids. We live in a ravine beyond the coral reef.
People don't live underwater! I think you are lying! Stealing and lying!
It's true! I promise!
It is easy enough to validate. We will go investigate the ravine and look for the people there and the books they say they are saving.
Tell us where the ravine is.
I'm not supposed to tell anyone. It's a secret!
Then we cannot trust you. If you are living with a group in a nearby ravine, you may be dangerous to us. If you are stealing our gold and lying, you may be dangerous to us. We'll hold you and your friends here until we decide what to do.

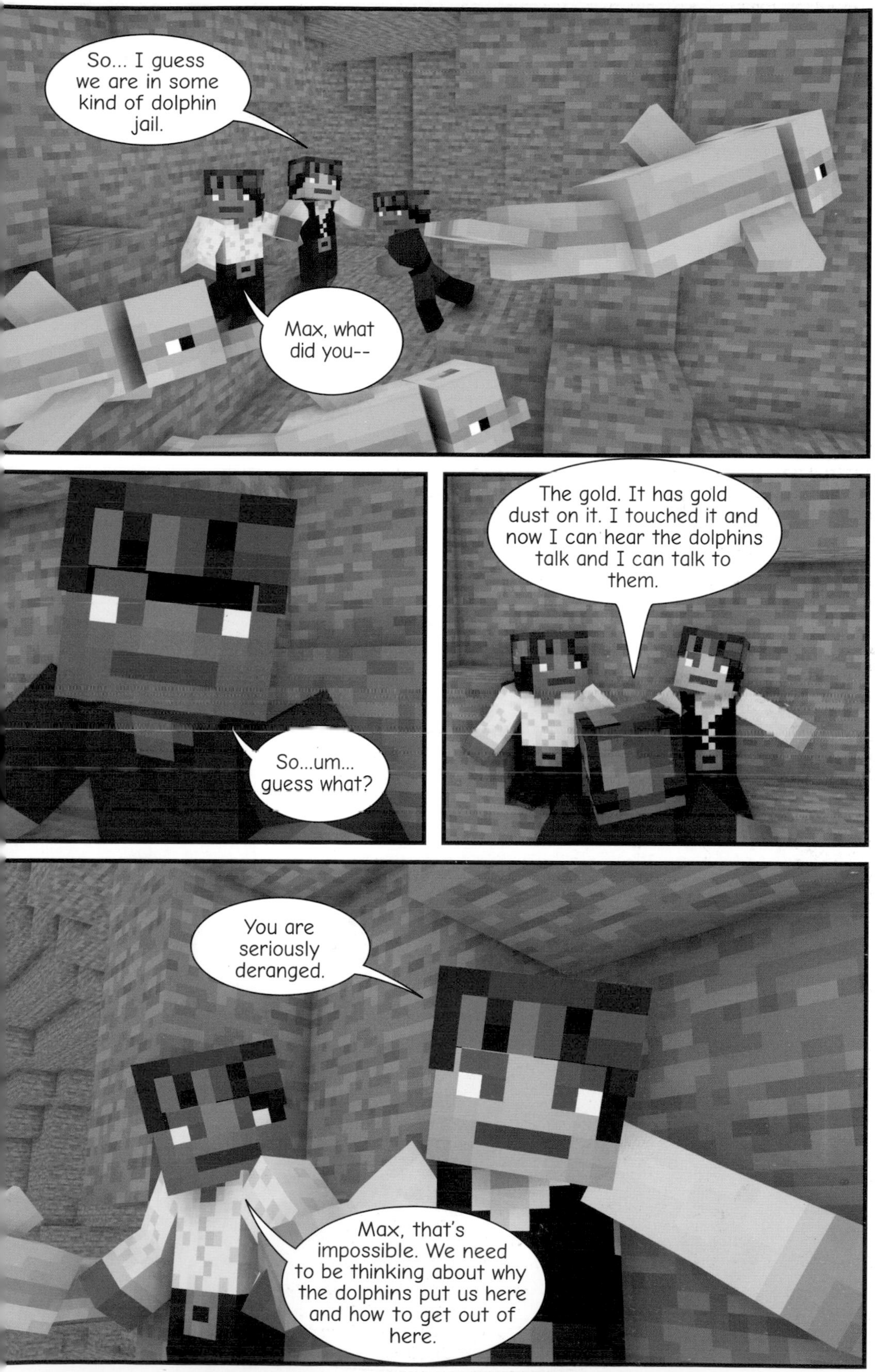
So... I guess we are in some kind of dolphin jail.
Max, what did you--
So...um... guess what?
The gold. It has gold dust on it. I touched it and now I can hear the dolphins talk and I can talk to them.
You are seriously deranged.
Max, that's impossible. We need to be thinking about why the dolphins put us here and how to get out of here.

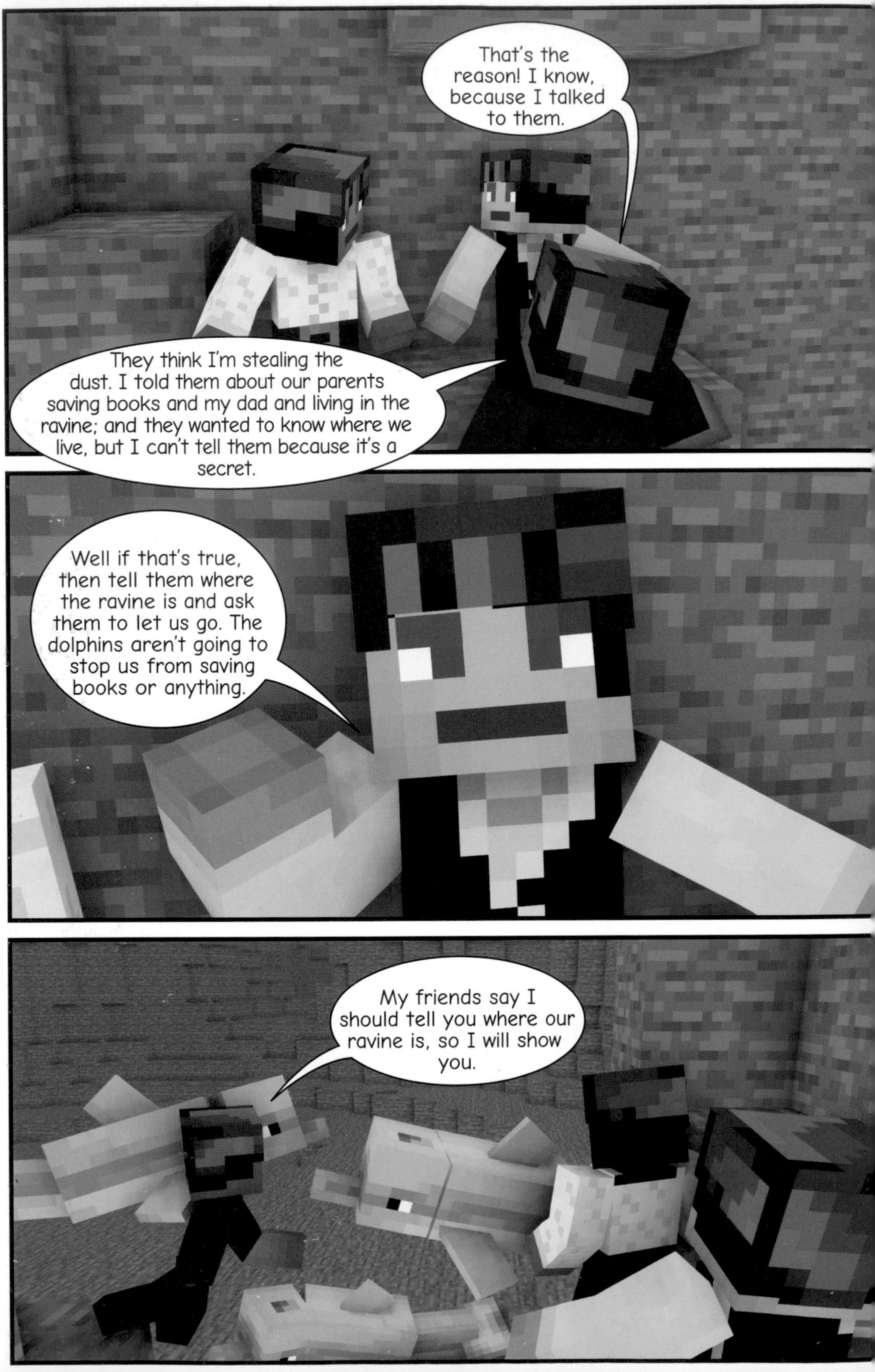
That's the reason! I know, because I talked to them.
They think I'm stealing the dust. I told them about our parents saving books and my dad and living in the ravine; and they wanted to know where we live, but I can't tell them because it's a secret.
Well if that's true, then tell them where the ravine is and ask them to let us go. The dolphins aren't going to stop us from saving books or anything.
My friends say I should tell you where our ravine is, so I will show you.

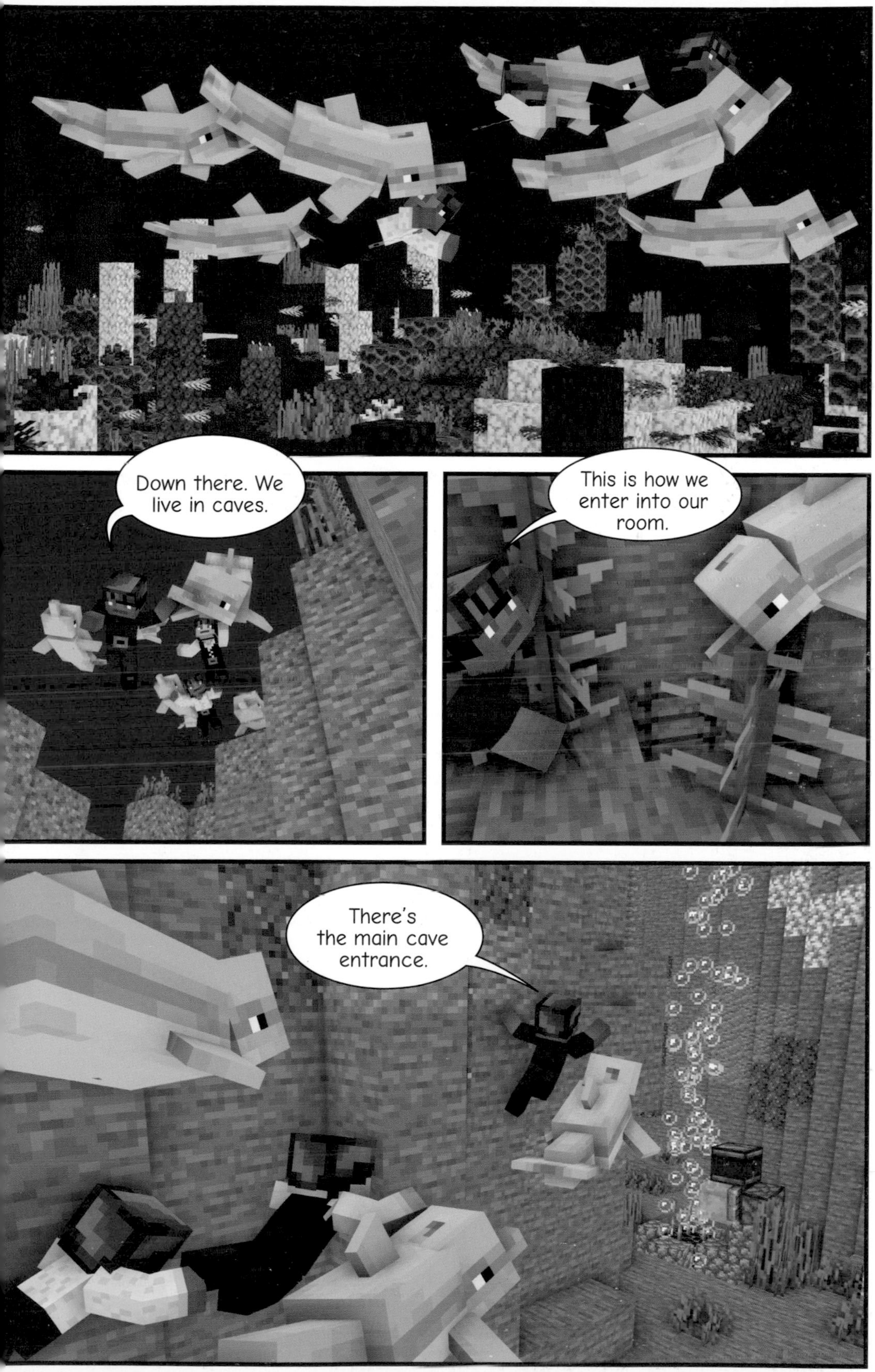
Down there. We live in caves.
This is how we enter into our room.
There's the main cave entrance.

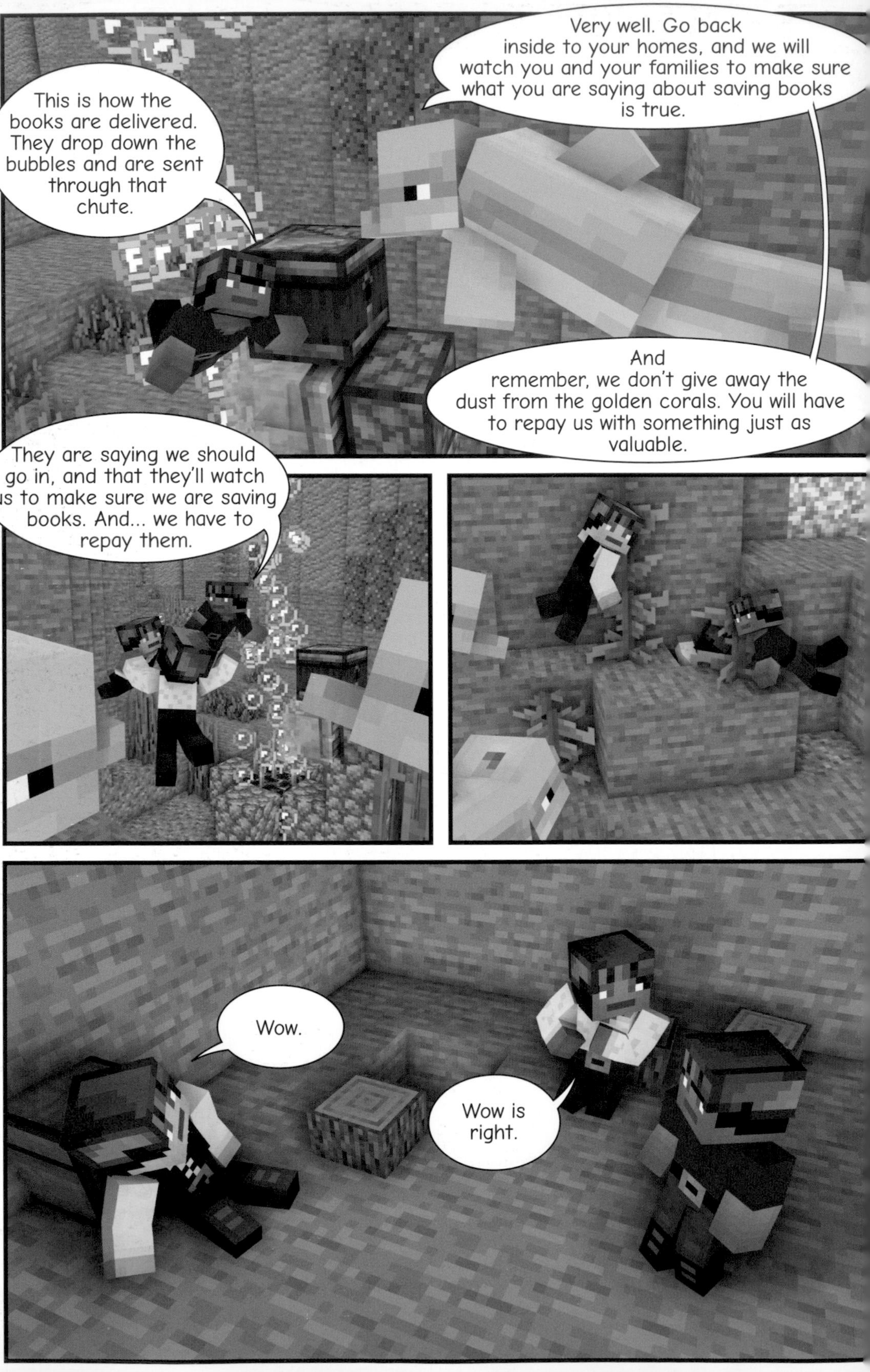
This is how the books are delivered. They drop down the bubbles and are sent through that chute.
Very well. Go back inside to your homes, and we will watch you and your families to make sure what you are saying about saving books is true.
And remember, we don't give away the dust from the golden corals. You will have to repay us with something just as valuable.
They are saying we should go in, and that they'll watch us to make sure we are saving books. And... we have to repay them.
Wow.
Wow is right.

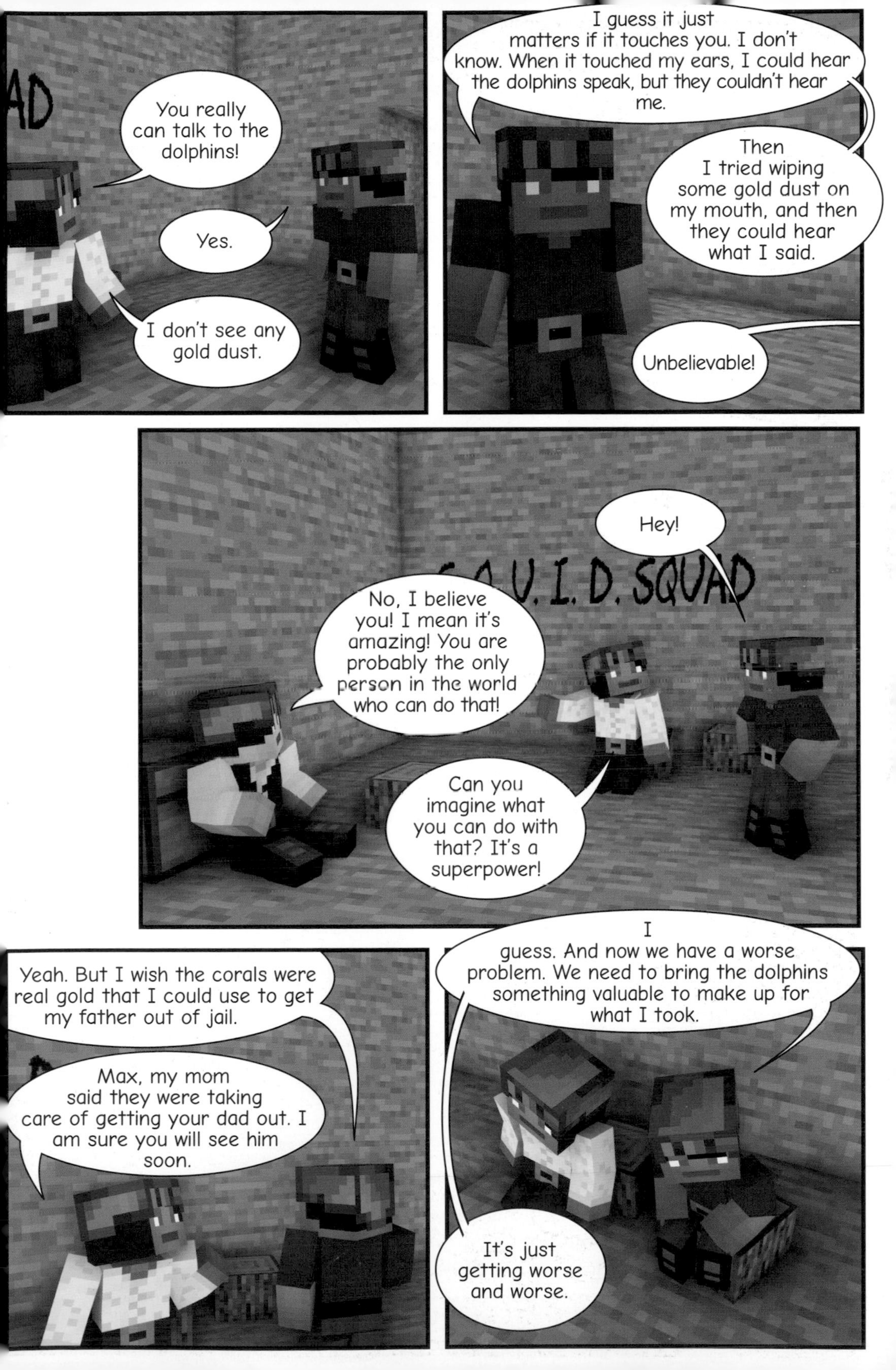
You really can talk to the dolphins!
Yes.
I don't see any gold dust.
I guess it just matters if it touches you. I don't know. When it touched my ears, I could hear the dolphins speak, but they couldn't hear me.
Then I tried wiping some gold dust on my mouth, and then they could hear what I said.
Unbelievable!
Hey!
S.Q.U.I.D. SQUAD
No, I believe you! I mean it's amazing! You are probably the only person in the world who can do that!
Can you imagine what you can do with that? It's a superpower!
Yeah. But I wish the corals were real gold that I could use to get my father out of jail.
Max, my mom said they were taking care of getting your dad out. I am sure you will see him soon.
I guess. And now we have a worse problem. We need to bring the dolphins something valuable to make up for what I took.
It's just getting worse and worse.

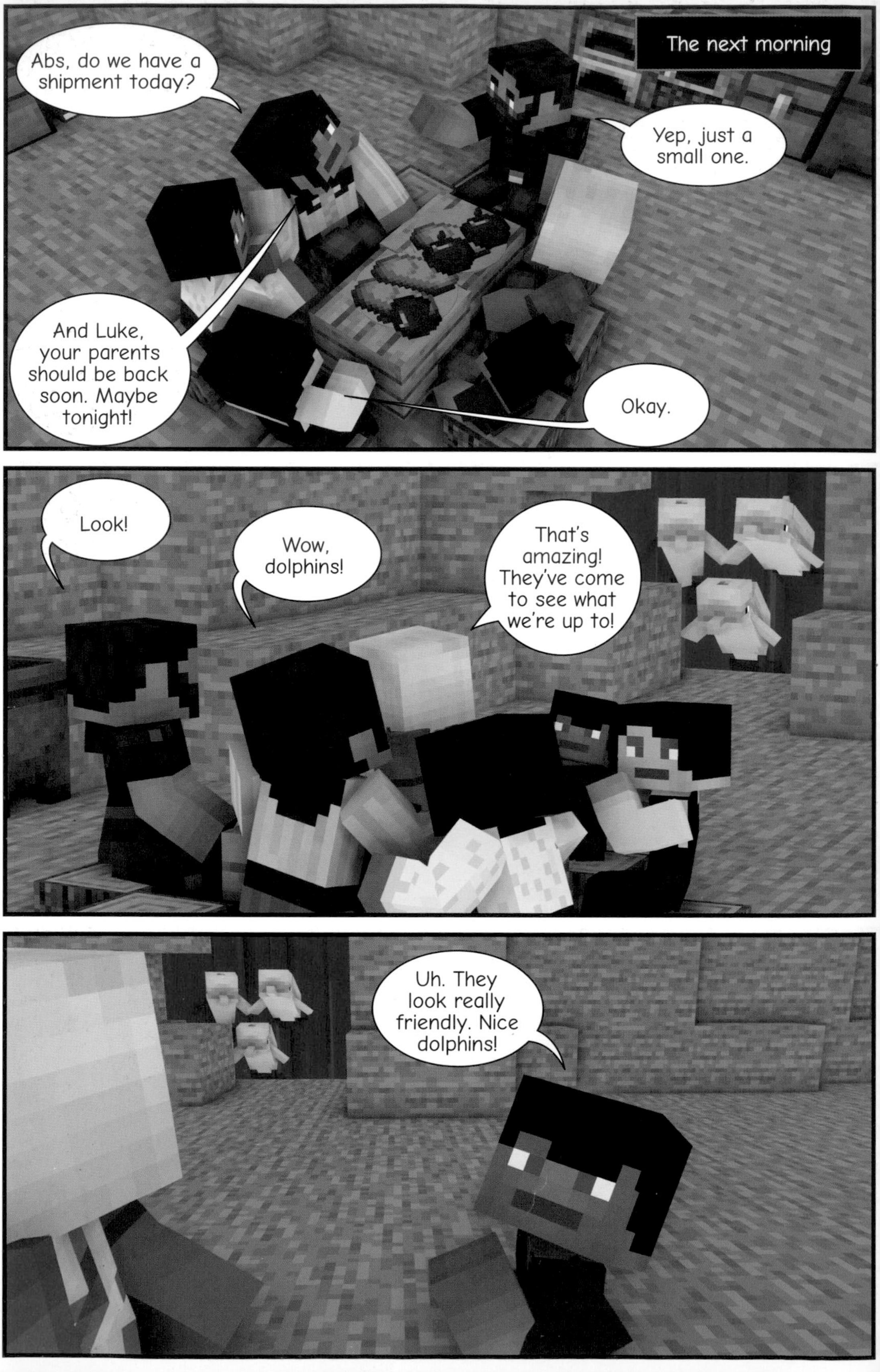
The next morning
Abs, do we have a shipment today?
Yep, just a small one.
And Luke, your parents should be back soon. Maybe tonight!
Okay.
Look!
Wow, dolphins!
That's amazing! They've come to see what we're up to!
Uh. They look really friendly. Nice dolphins!

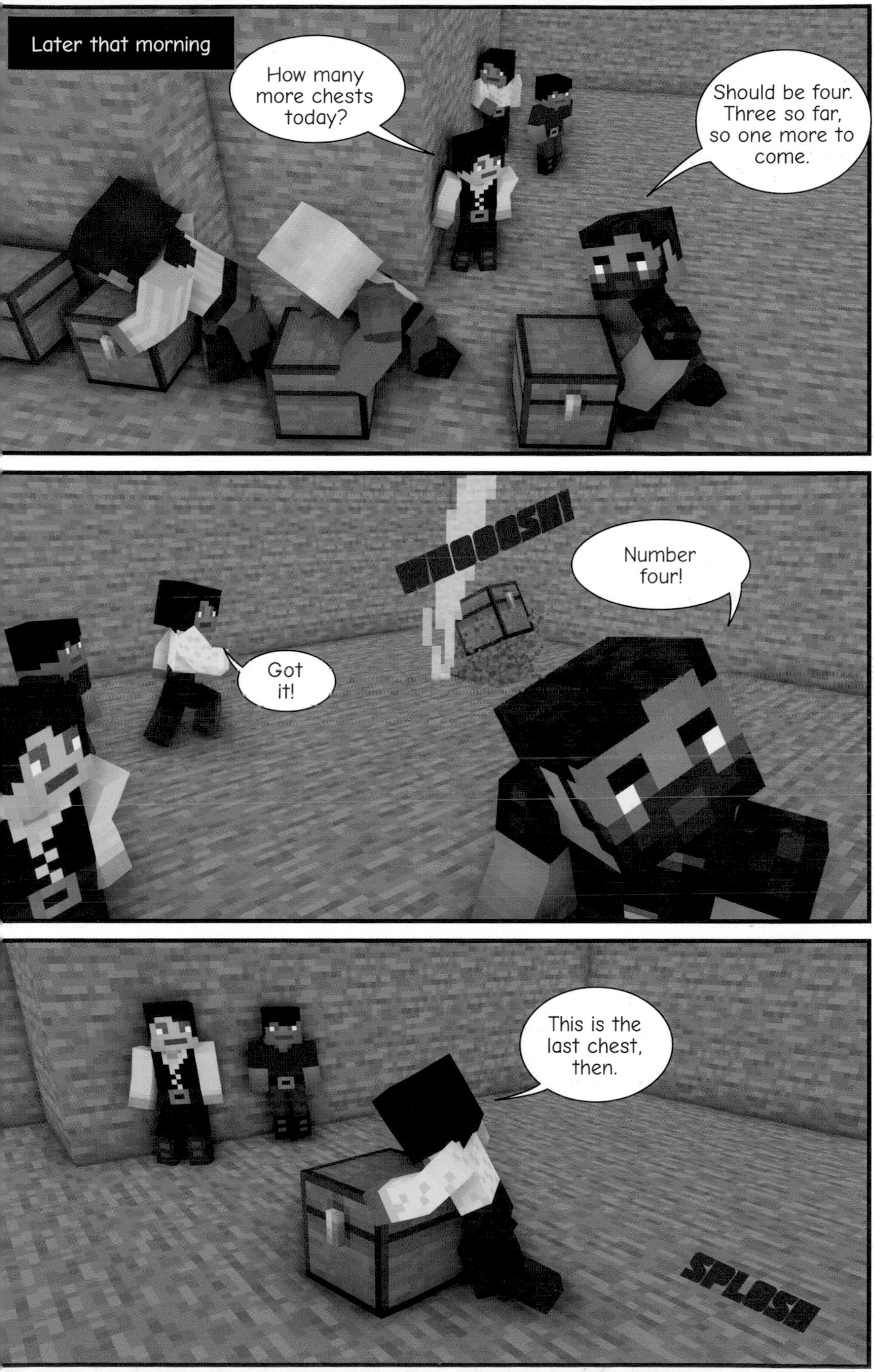
Later that morning
How many more chests today?
Should be four. Three so far, so one more to come.
Number four!
Got it!
This is the last chest, then.
SPLOSH

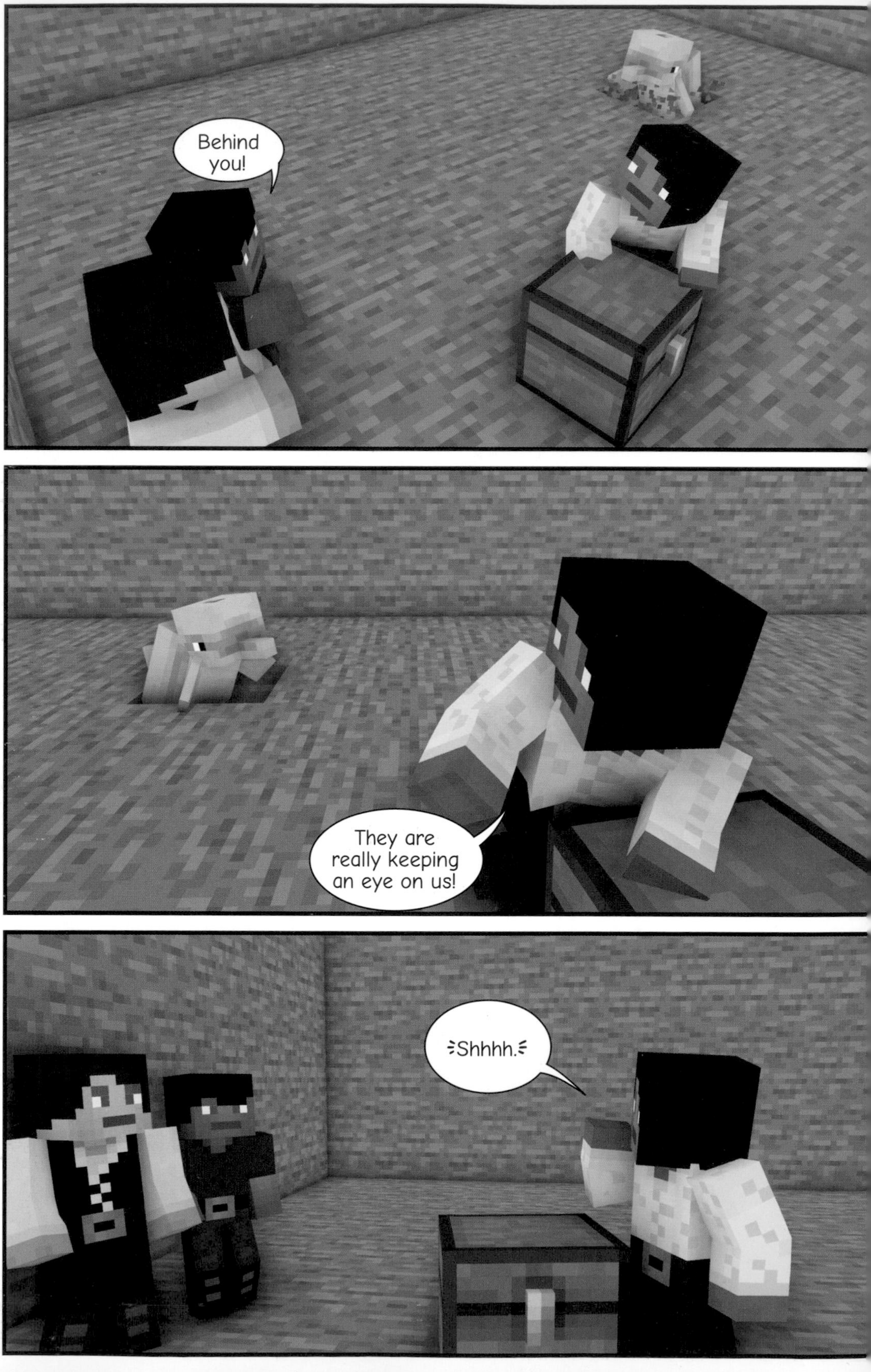
Behind you!
They are really keeping an eye on us!
Shhhh.

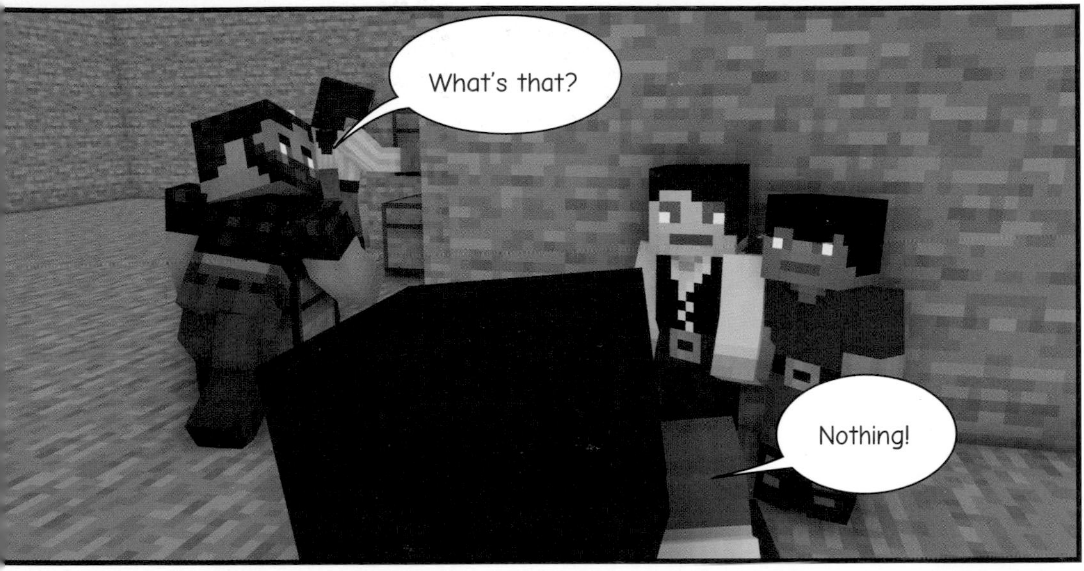
What's that?
Nothing!

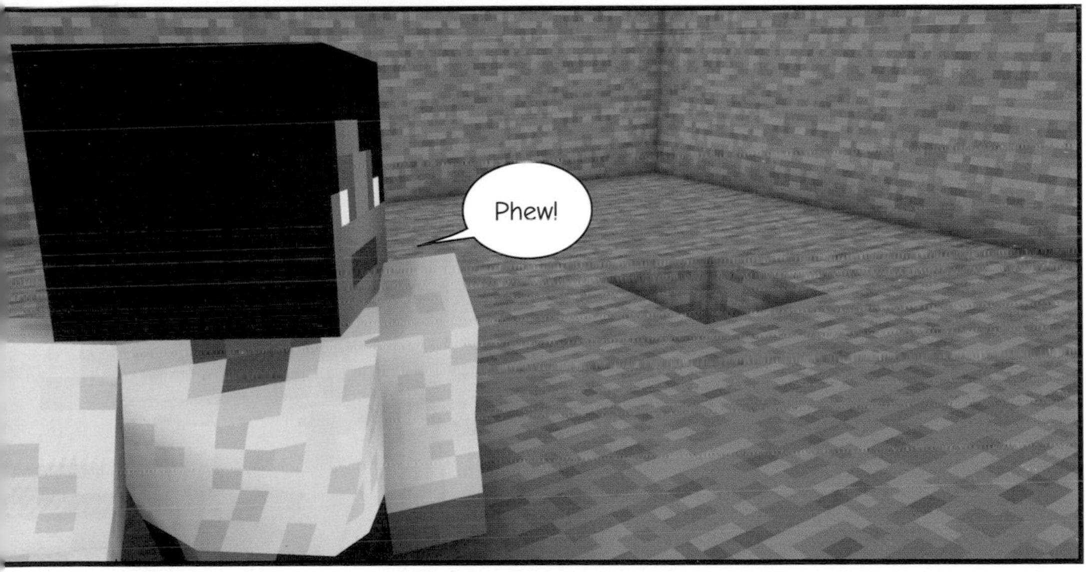
Phew!

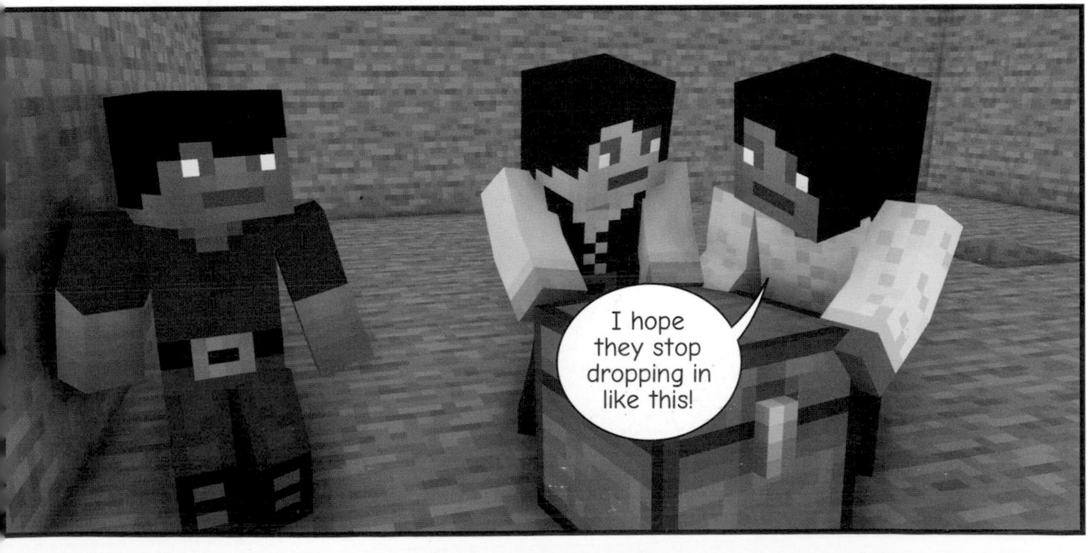
I hope they stop dropping in like this!

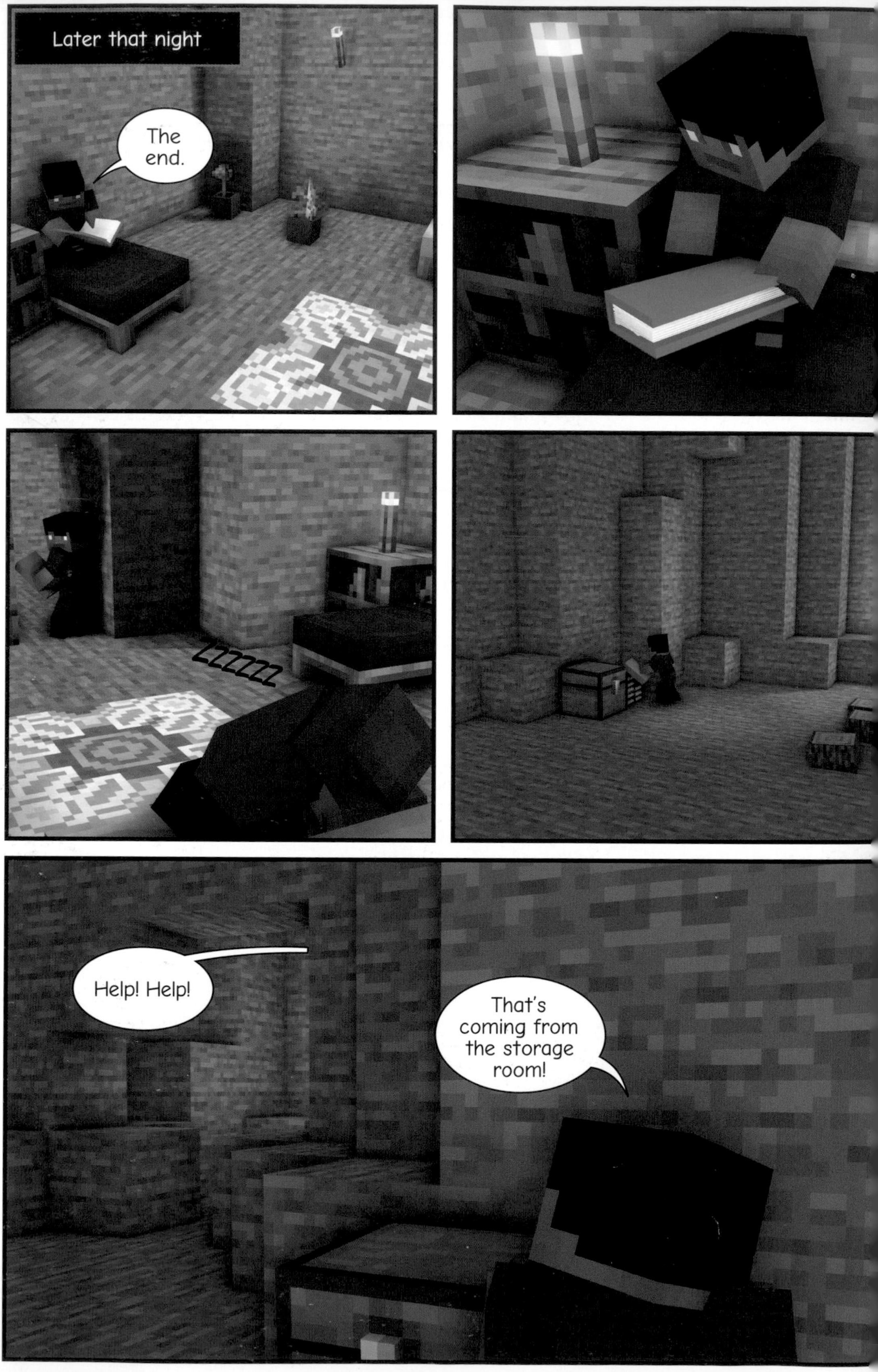
Later that night
The end.
ZZZZZZ
Help! Help!
That's coming from the storage room!

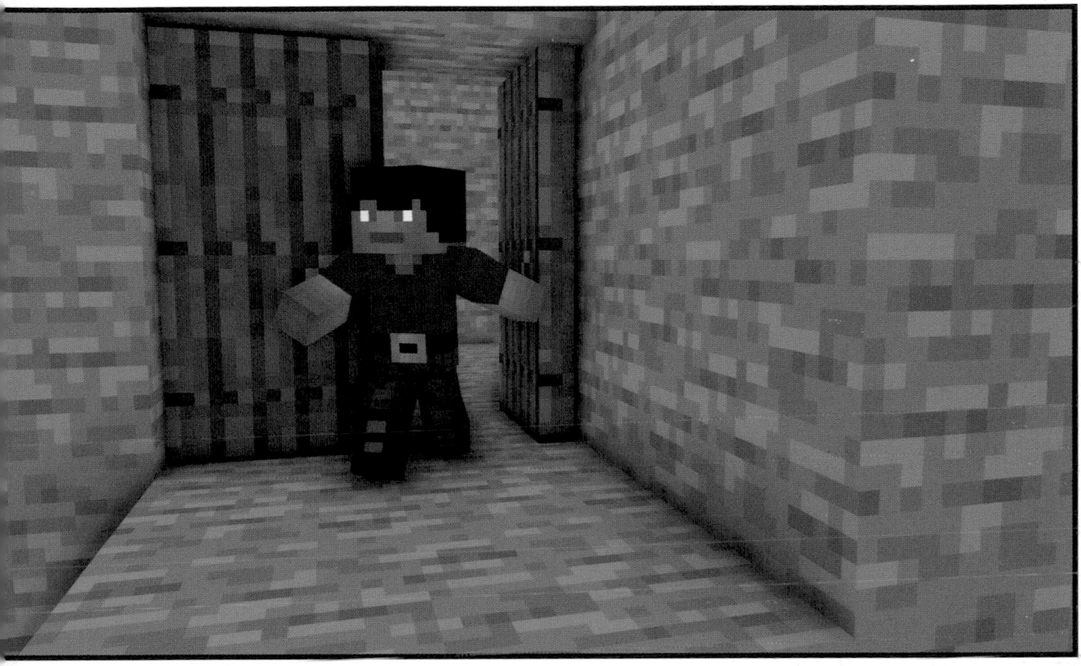

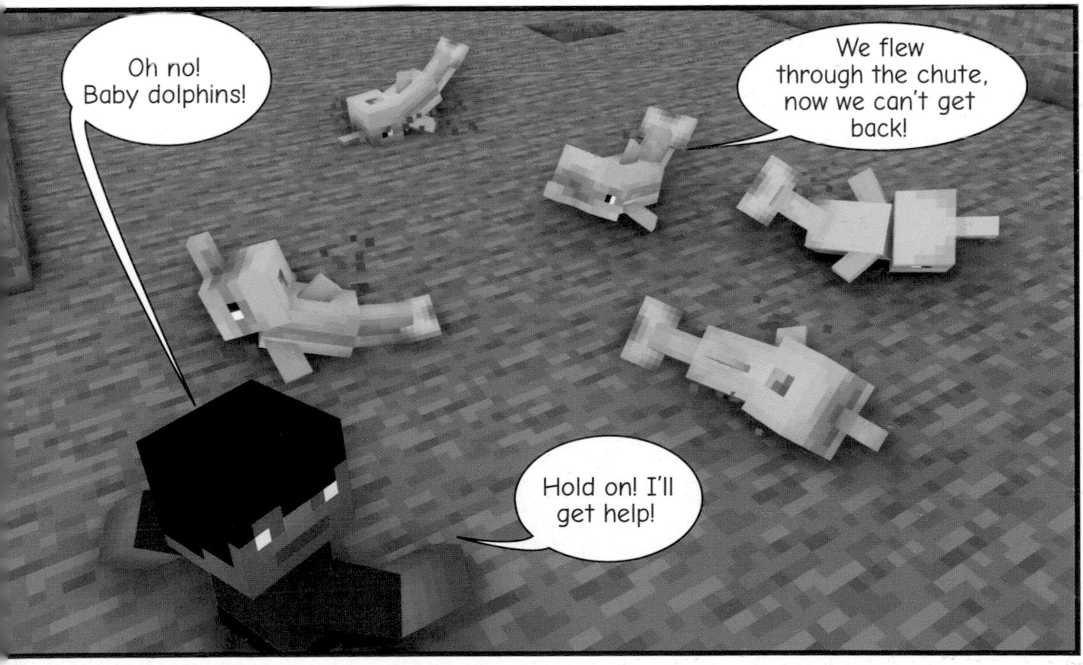
Oh no!
Baby dolphins!
We flew through the chute, now we can't get back!
Hold on! I'll get help!

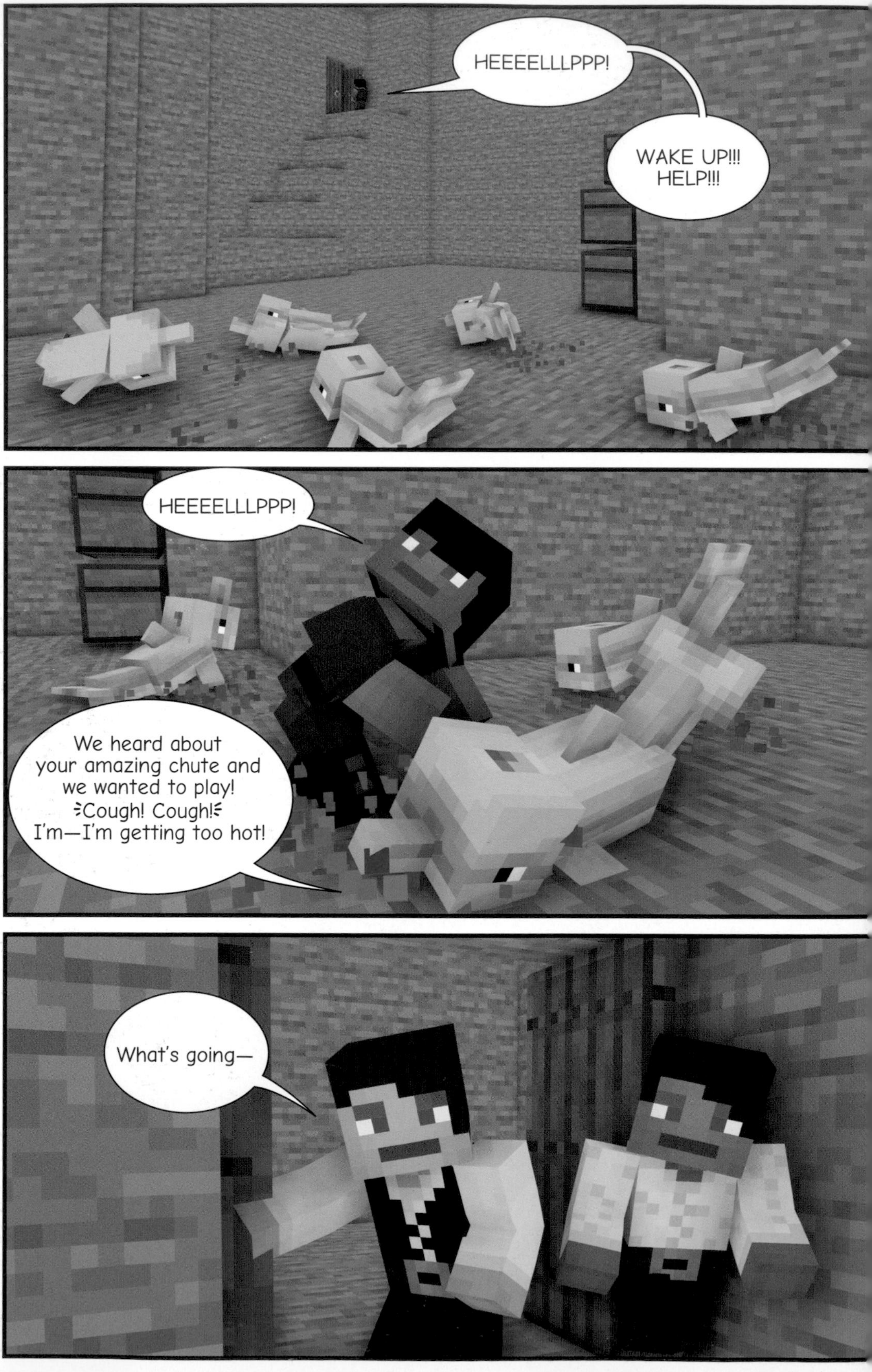
HEEEELLLPPP!
WAKE UP!!! HELP!!!
HEEEELLLPPP!
We heard about your amazing chute and we wanted to play! Cough! Cough! I'm—I'm getting too hot!
What's going—

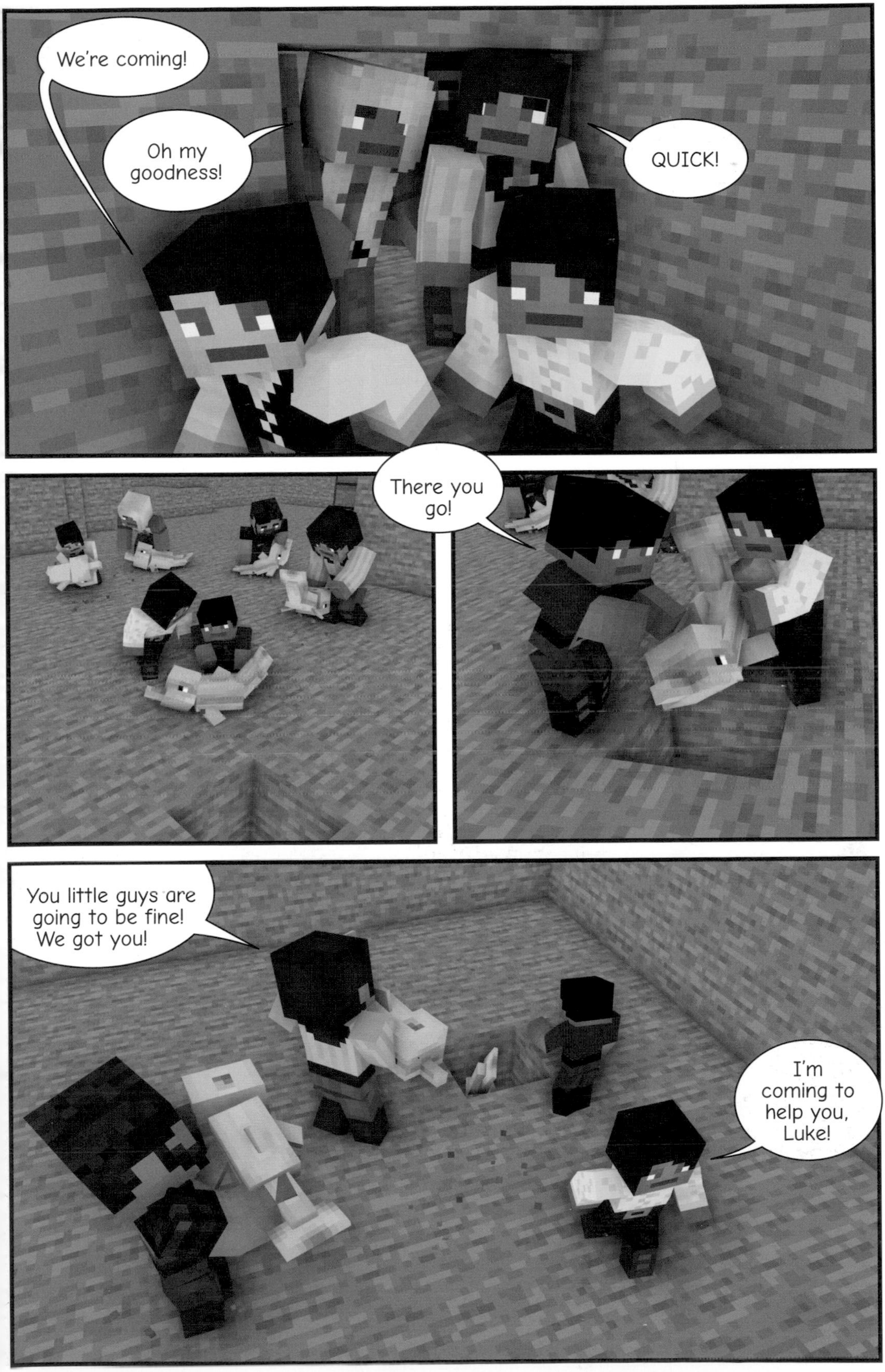
We're coming!
Oh my goodness!
QUICK!
There you go!
You little guys are going to be fine! We got you!
I'm coming to help you, Luke!

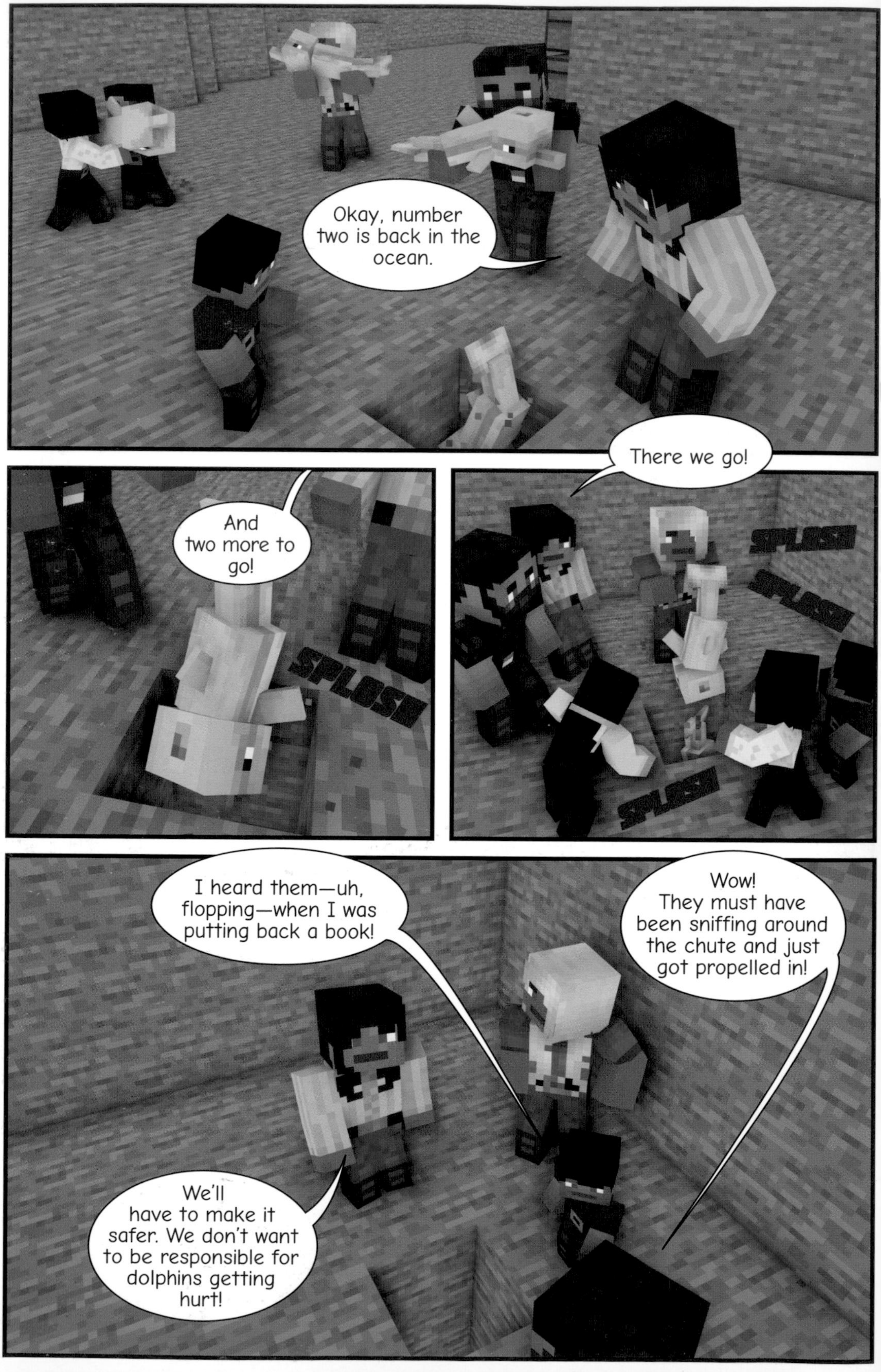

Okay, number two is back in the ocean.
And two more to go!
SPLOSH
There we go!
SPLOSH
SPLOSH
SPLOSH
I heard them—uh, flopping—when I was putting back a book!
Wow! They must have been sniffing around the chute and just got propelled in!
We'll have to make it safer. We don't want to be responsible for dolphins getting hurt!

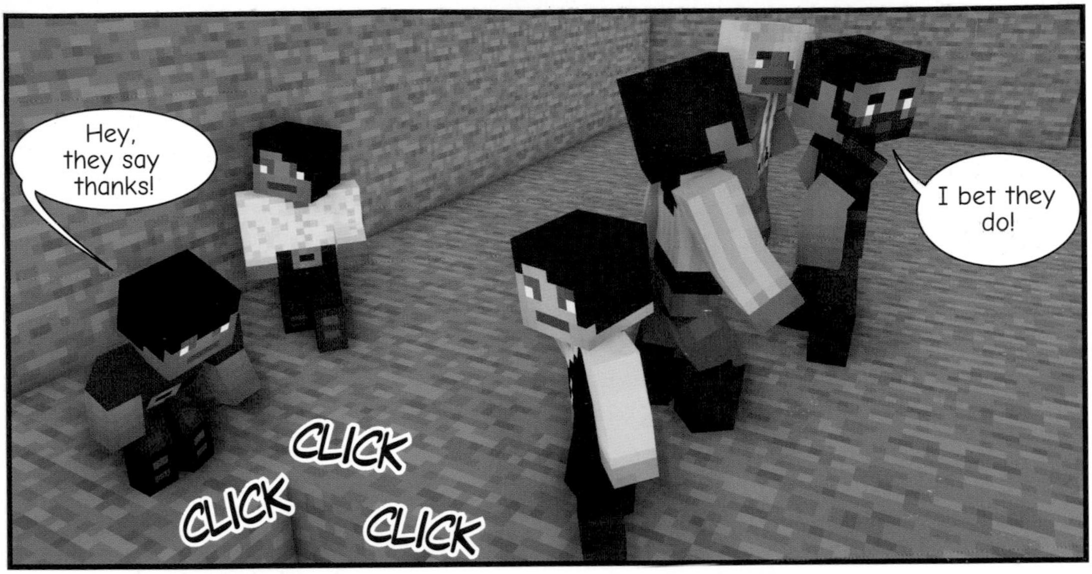
Hey, they say thanks!
I bet they do!
CLICK
CLICK
CLICK

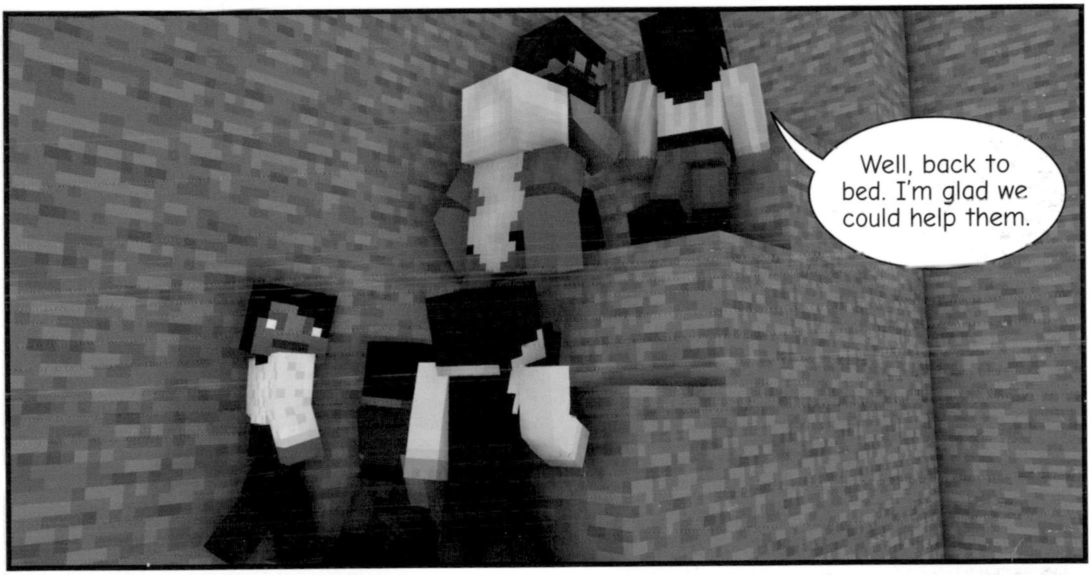
Well, back to bed. I'm glad we could help them.

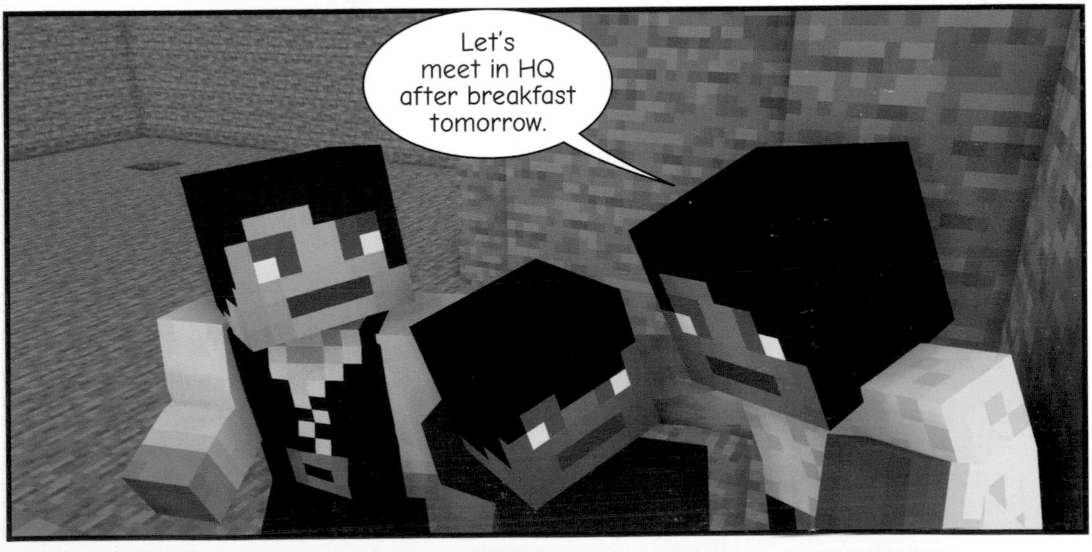
Let's meet in HQ after breakfast tomorrow.

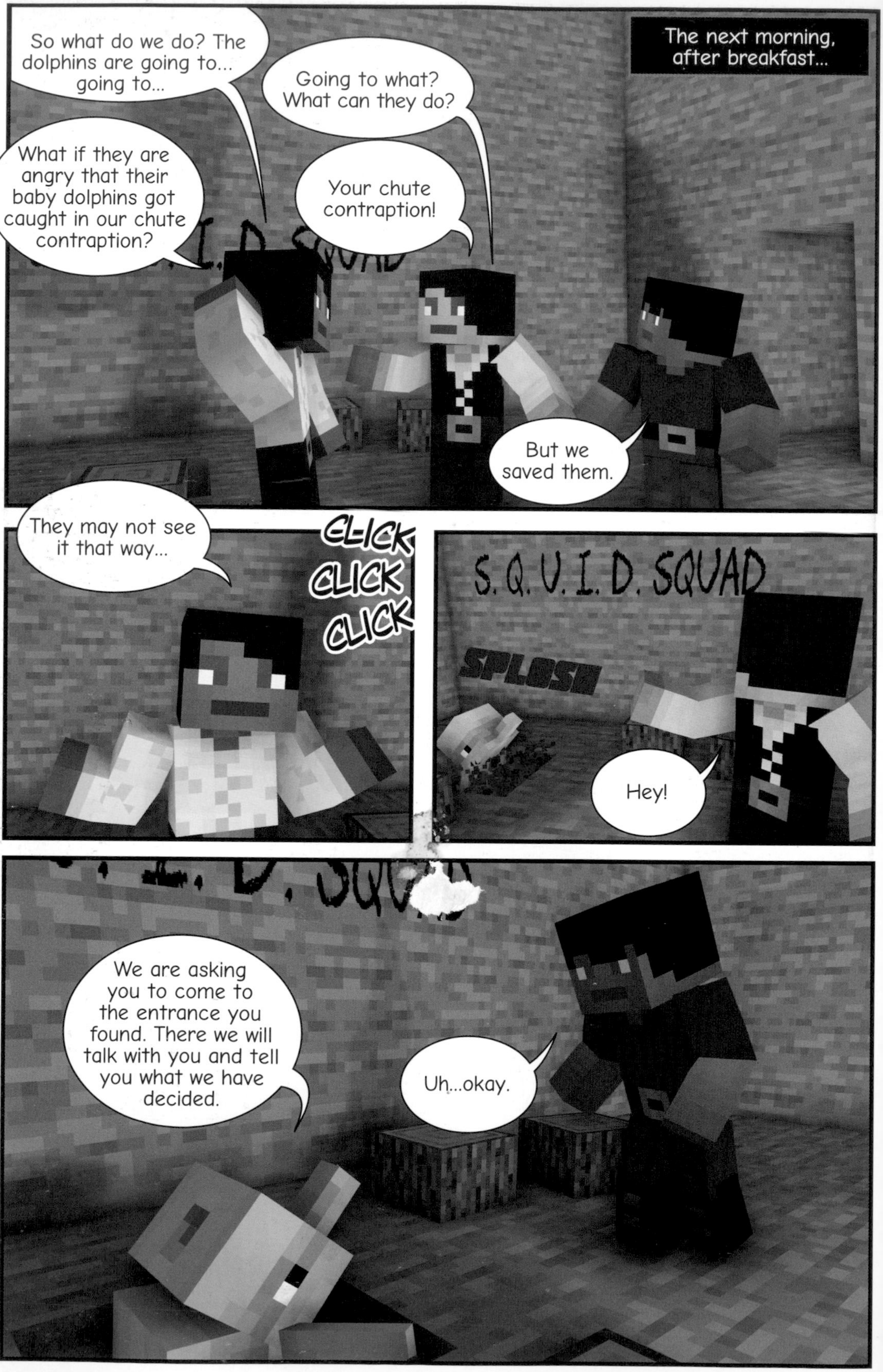
The next morning, after breakfast...
So what do we do? The dolphins are going to... going to...
Going to what? What can they do?
What if they are angry that their baby dolphins got caught in our chute contraption?
Your chute contraption!
But we saved them.
They may not see it that way...
CLICK
CLICK
CLICK
S. Q. U. I. D. SQUAD
SPLOSH
Hey!
We are asking you to come to the entrance you found. There we will talk with you and tell you what we have decided.
Uh...okay.

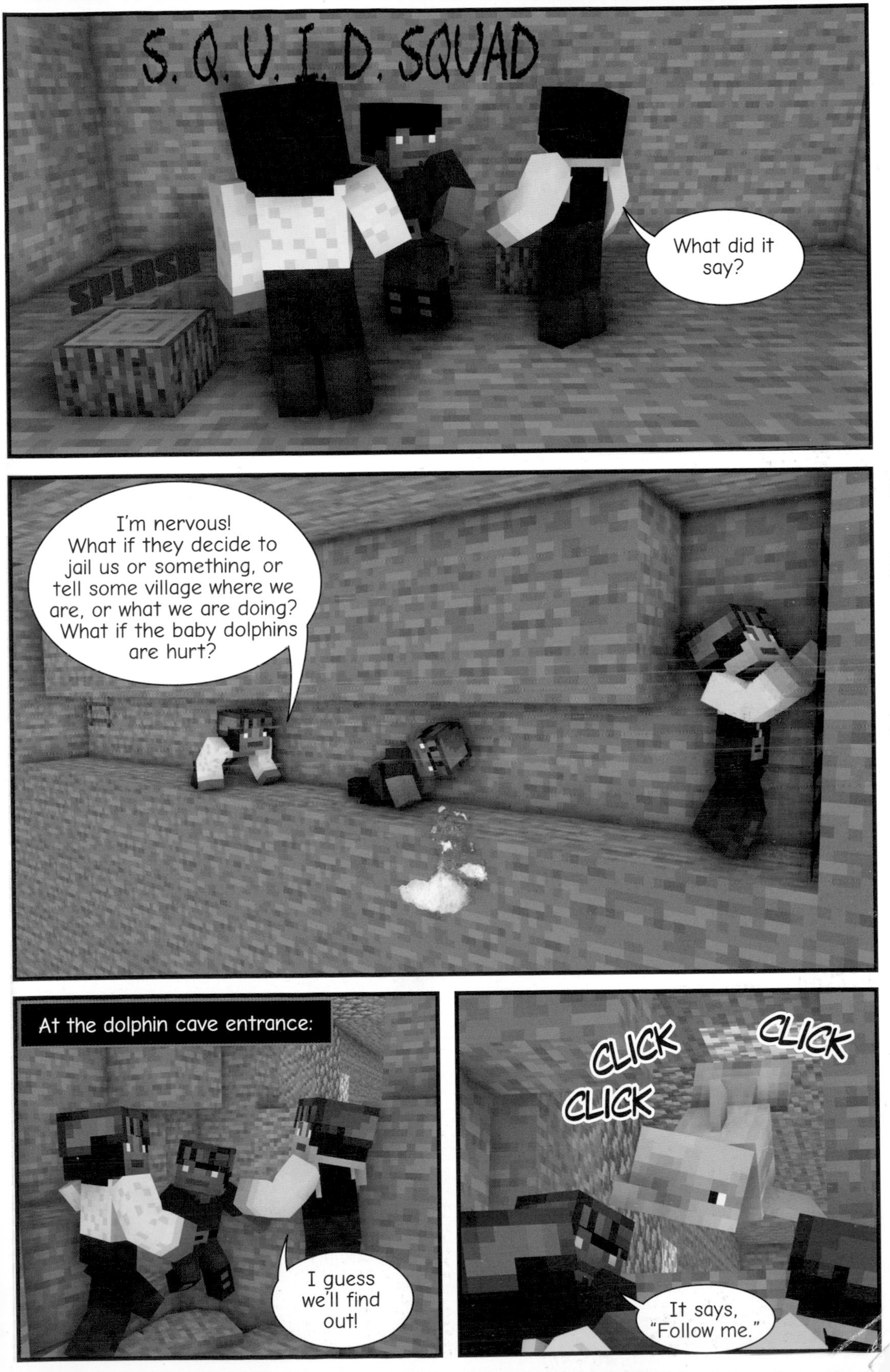
S. Q. U. I. D. SQUAD
SPLOSH
What did it say?
I'm nervous! What if they decide to jail us or something, or tell some village where we are, or what we are doing? What if the baby dolphins are hurt?
At the dolphin cave entrance:
I guess we'll find out!
CLICK
CLICK
CLICK
It says, "Follow me."

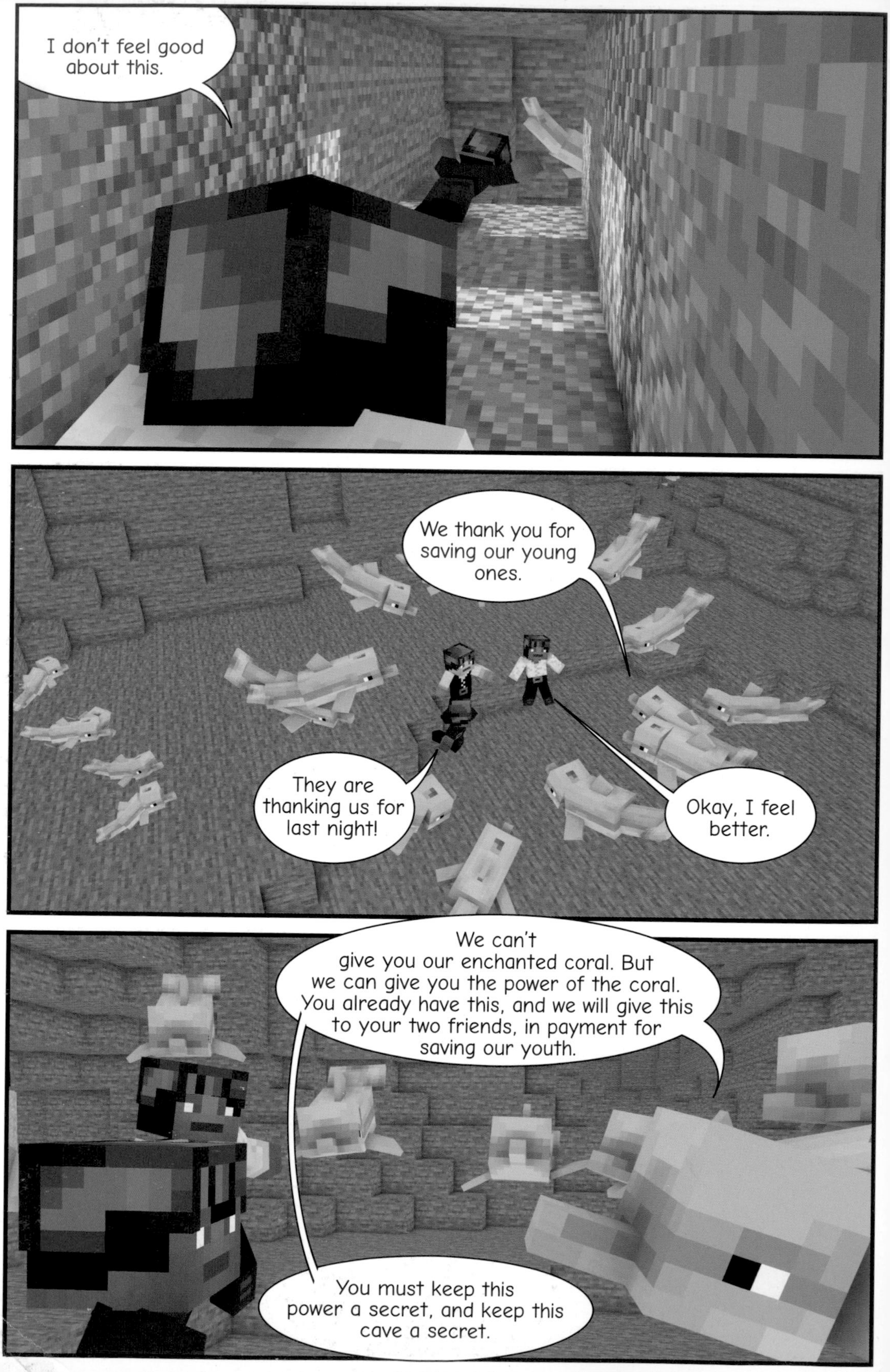

I don't feel good about this.
We thank you for saving our young ones.
They are thanking us for last night!
Okay, I feel better.
We can't give you our enchanted coral. But we can give you the power of the coral. You already have this, and we will give this to your two friends, in payment for saving our youth.
You must keep this power a secret, and keep this cave a secret.

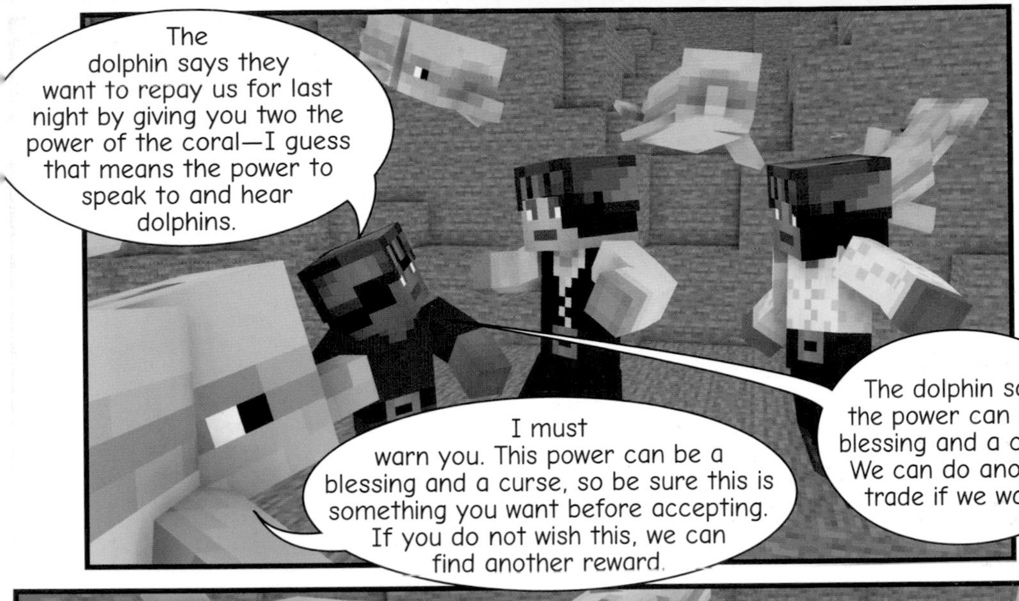
The dolphin says they want to repay us for last night by giving you two the power of the coral—I guess that means the power to speak to and hear dolphins.
I must warn you. This power can be a blessing and a curse, so be sure this is something you want before accepting. If you do not wish this, we can find another reward.
The dolphin says the power can be a blessing and a curse. We can do another trade if we want.

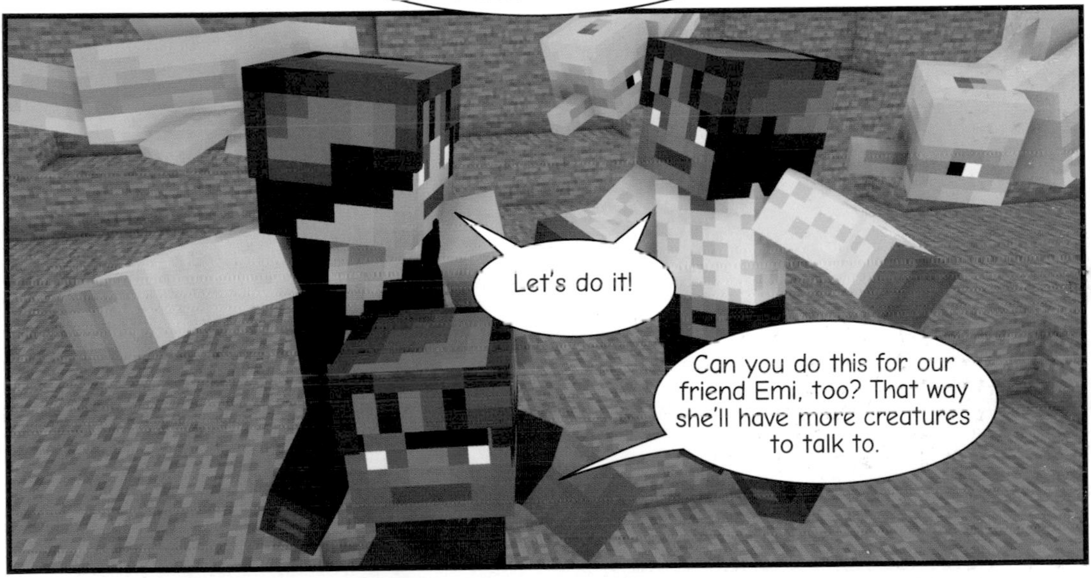
Let's do it!
Can you do this for our friend Emi, too? That way she'll have more creatures to talk to.

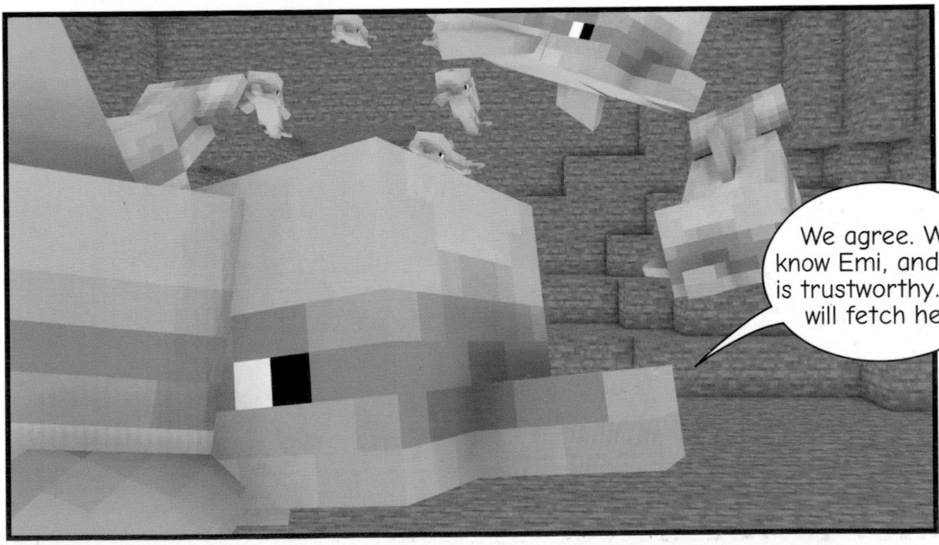
We agree. We know Emi, and she is trustworthy. We will fetch her.

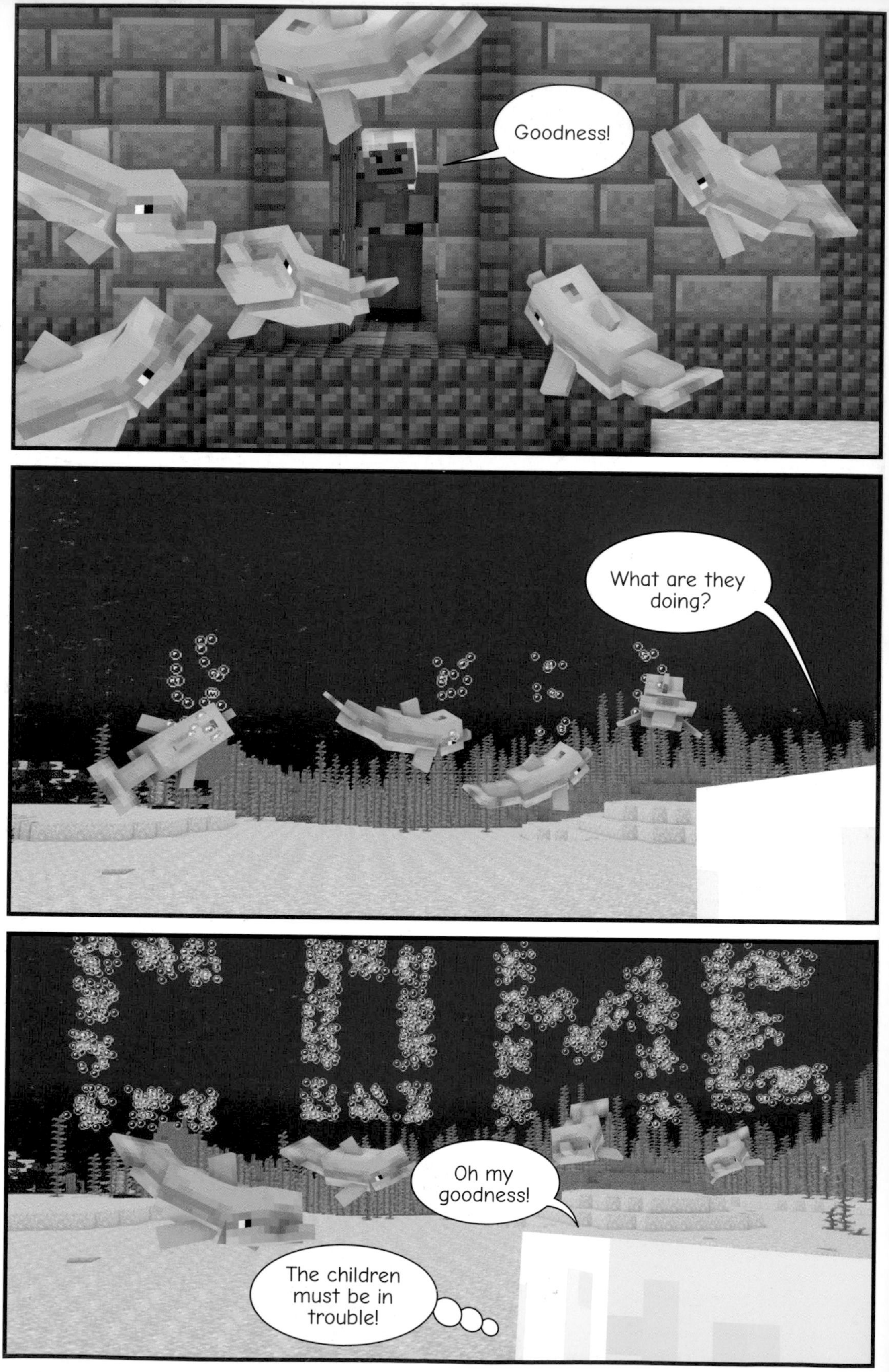
Goodness!
What are they doing?
Oh my goodness!
The children must be in trouble!

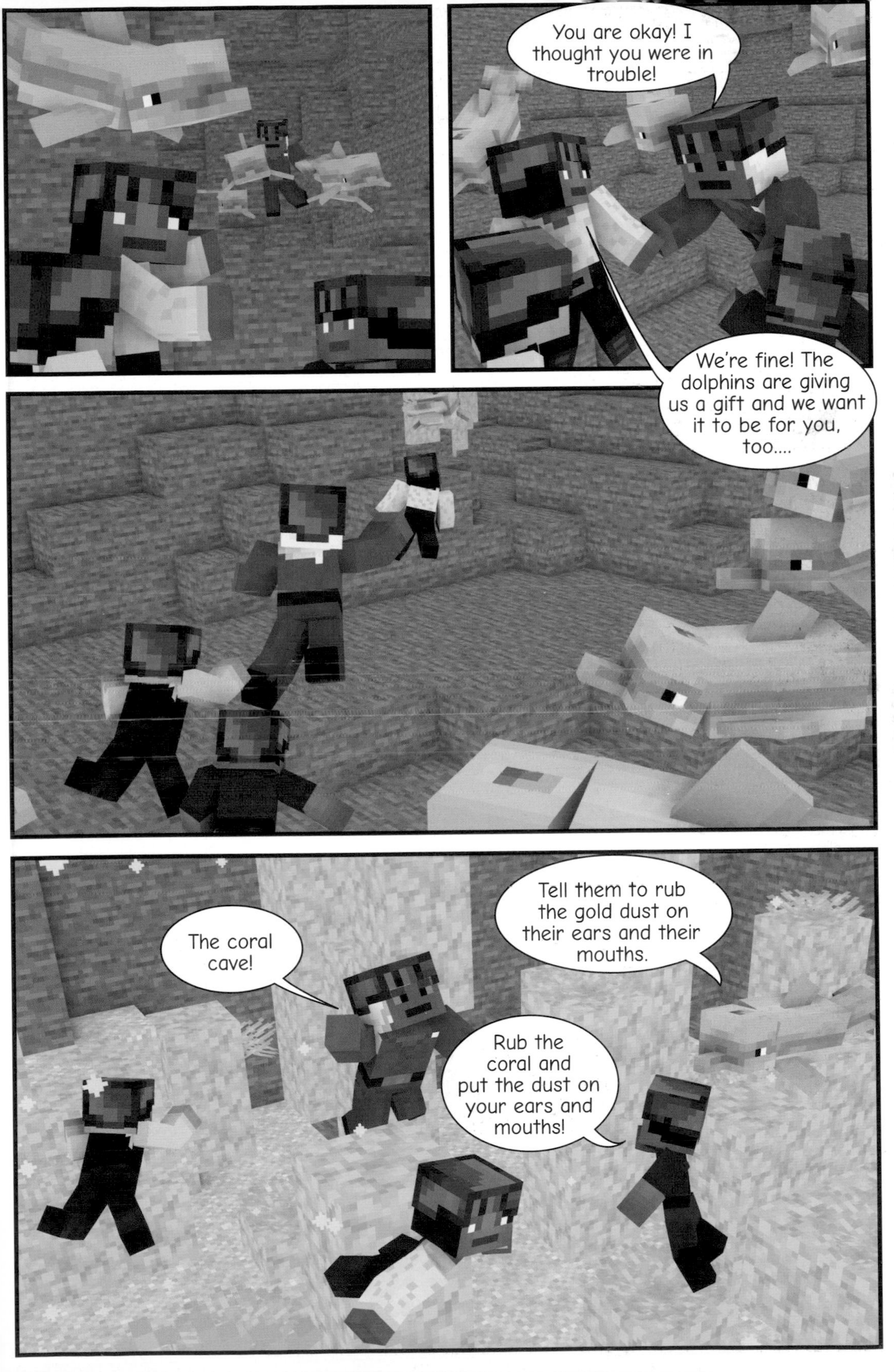
You are okay! I thought you were in trouble!
We're fine! The dolphins are giving us a gift and we want it to be for you, too....
The coral cave!
Tell them to rub the gold dust on their ears and their mouths.
Rub the coral and put the dust on your ears and mouths!

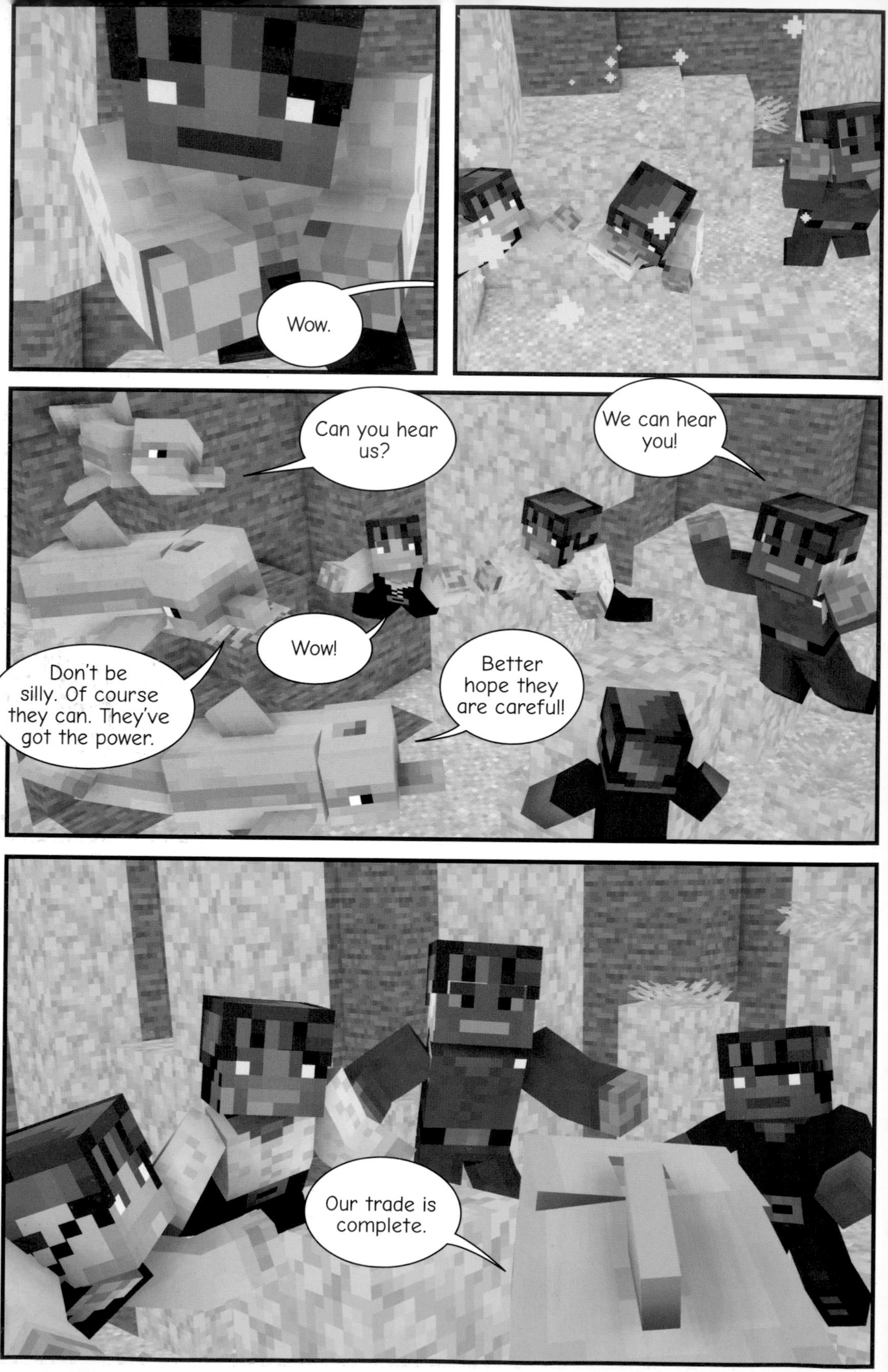
Wow.
Can you hear us?
We can hear you!
Wow!
Don't be silly. Of course they can. They've got the power.
Better hope they are careful!
Our trade is complete.

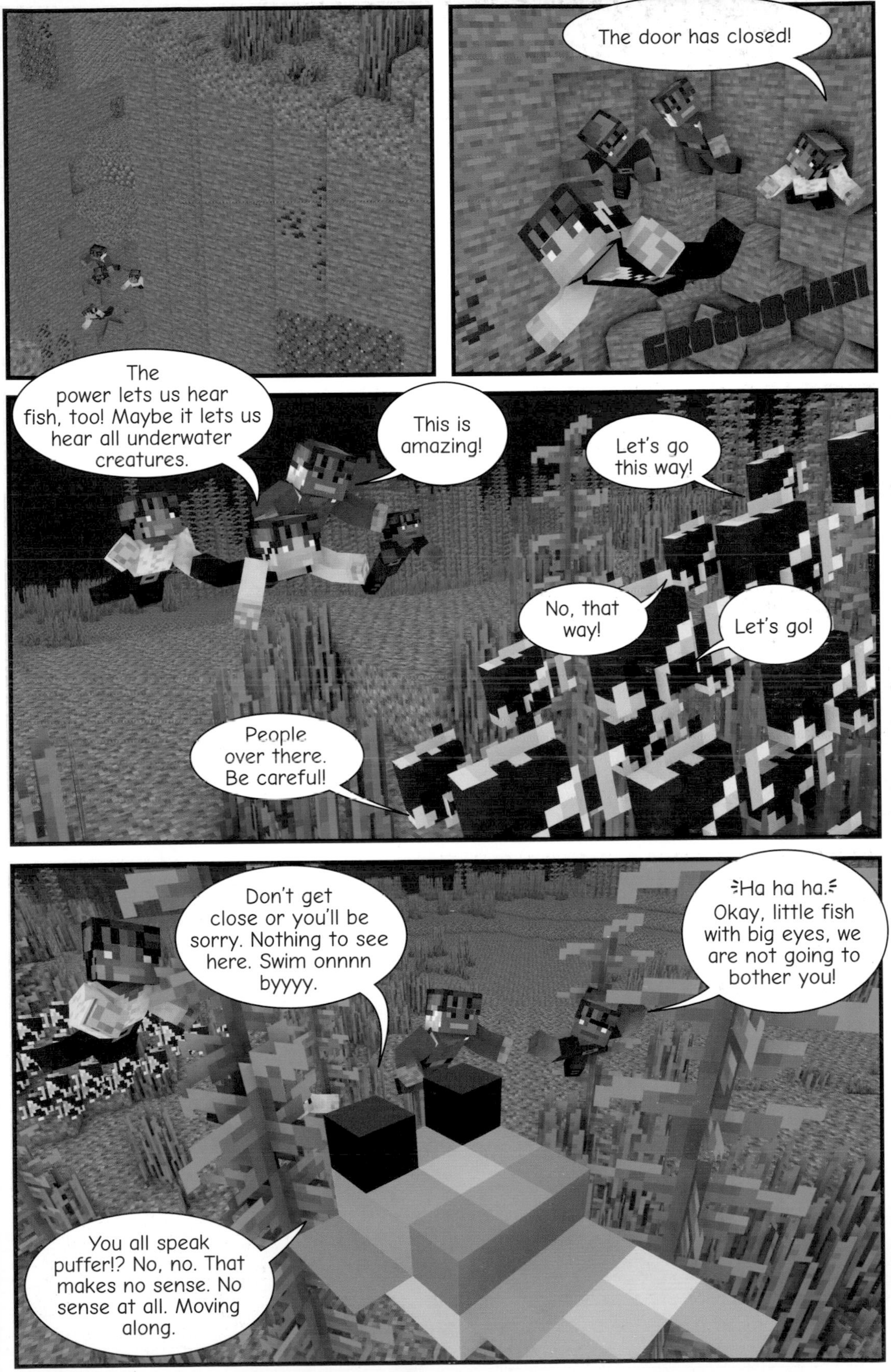
The door has closed!
The power lets us hear fish, too! Maybe it lets us hear all underwater creatures.
This is amazing!
Let's go this way!
No, that way!
Let's go!
People over there. Be careful!
Don't get close or you'll be sorry. Nothing to see here. Swim onnnn byyyy.
Ha ha ha. Okay, little fish with big eyes, we are not going to bother you!
You all speak puffer!? No, no. That makes no sense. No sense at all. Moving along.

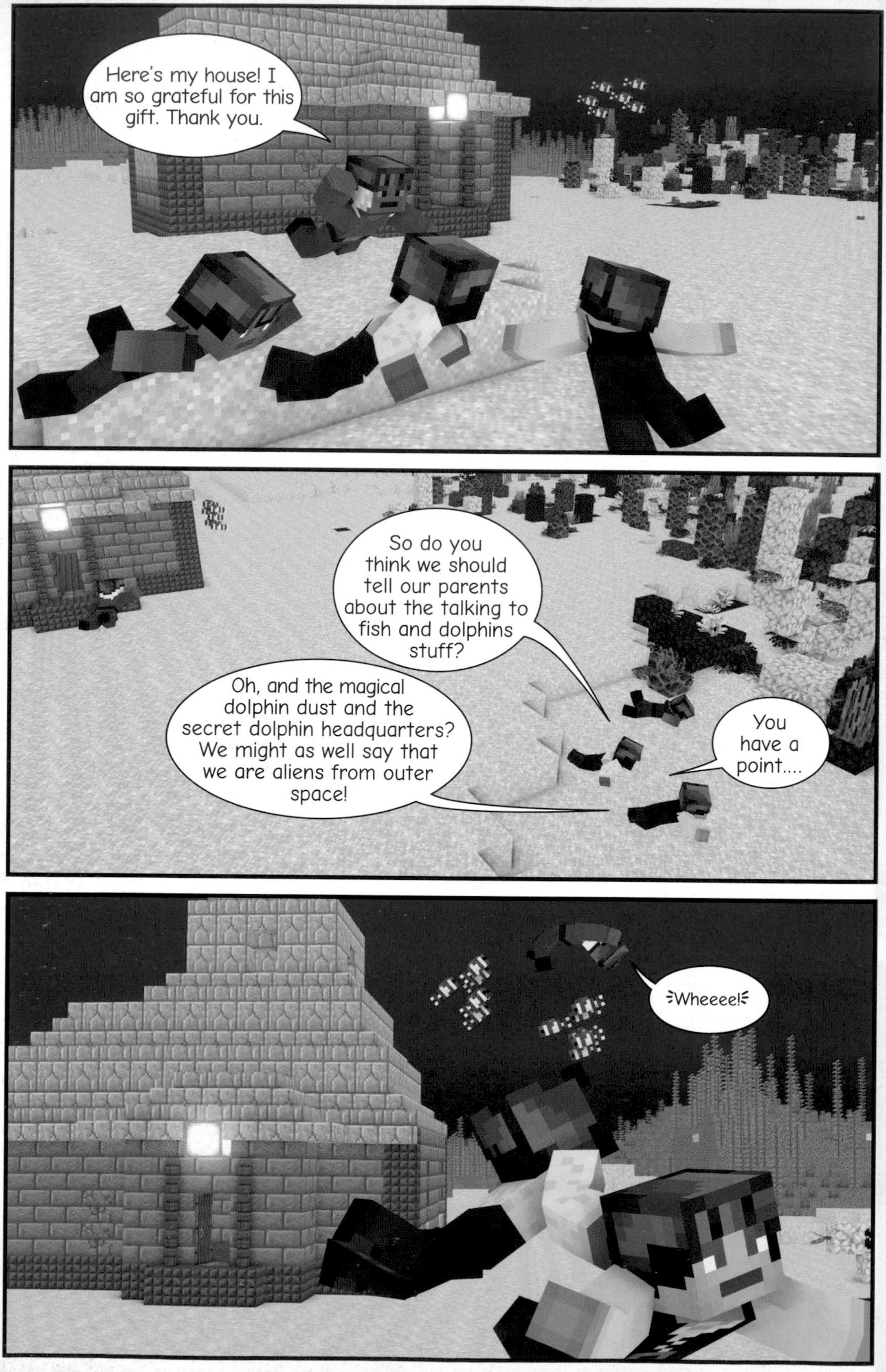
Here's my house! I am so grateful for this gift. Thank you.
So do you think we should tell our parents about the talking to fish and dolphins stuff?
Oh, and the magical dolphin dust and the secret dolphin headquarters? We might as well say that we are aliens from outer space!
You have a point....
Wheeee!

Chapter 10
From Squid
to Squad

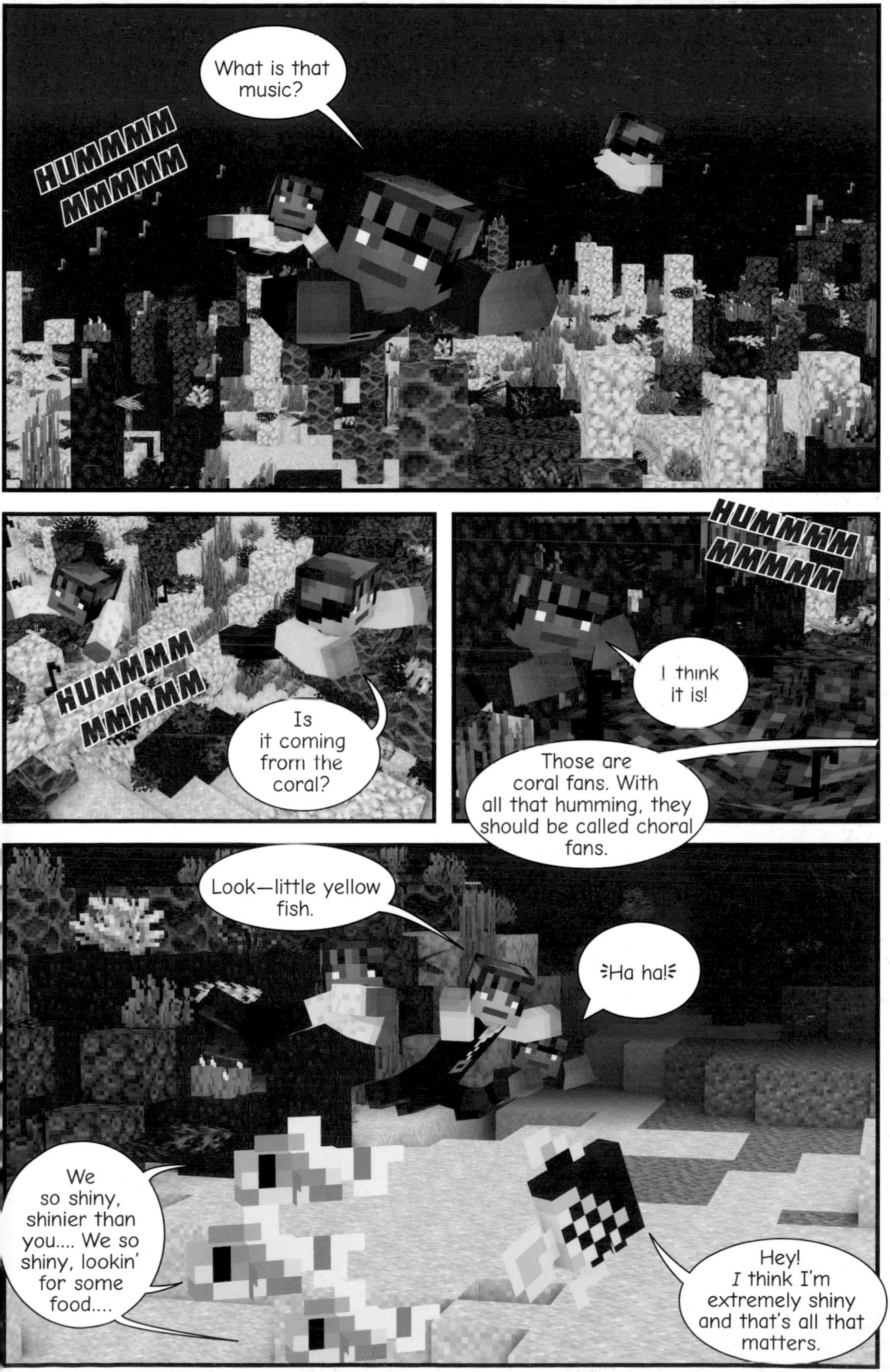
What is that music?
HUMMMM MMMMM
HUMMMM MMMMM
Is it coming from the coral?
HUMMMM MMMMM
I think it is!
Those are coral fans. With all that humming, they should be called choral fans.
Look—little yellow fish.
Ha ha!
We so shiny, shinier than you.... We so shiny, lookin' for some food....
Hey! *I* think I'm extremely shiny and that's all that matters.

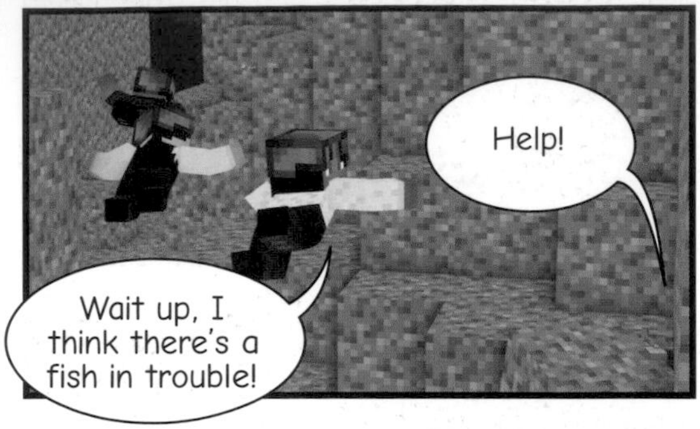
Help!
Wait up, I think there's a fish in trouble!

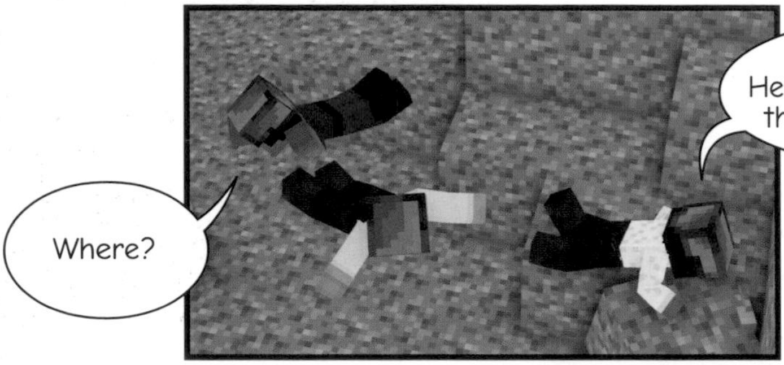
Where?
Here! Help me pull this gravel away!

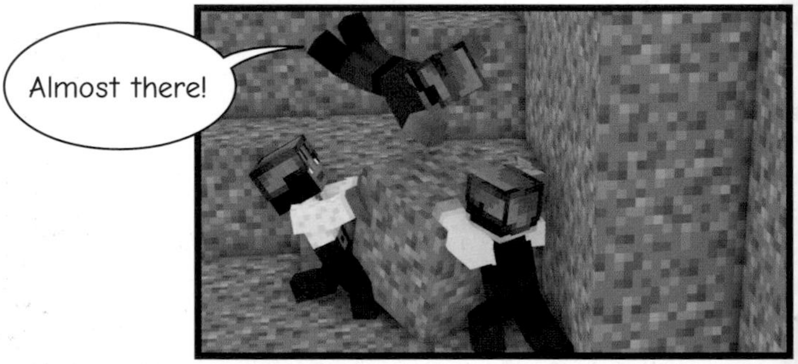
Almost there!

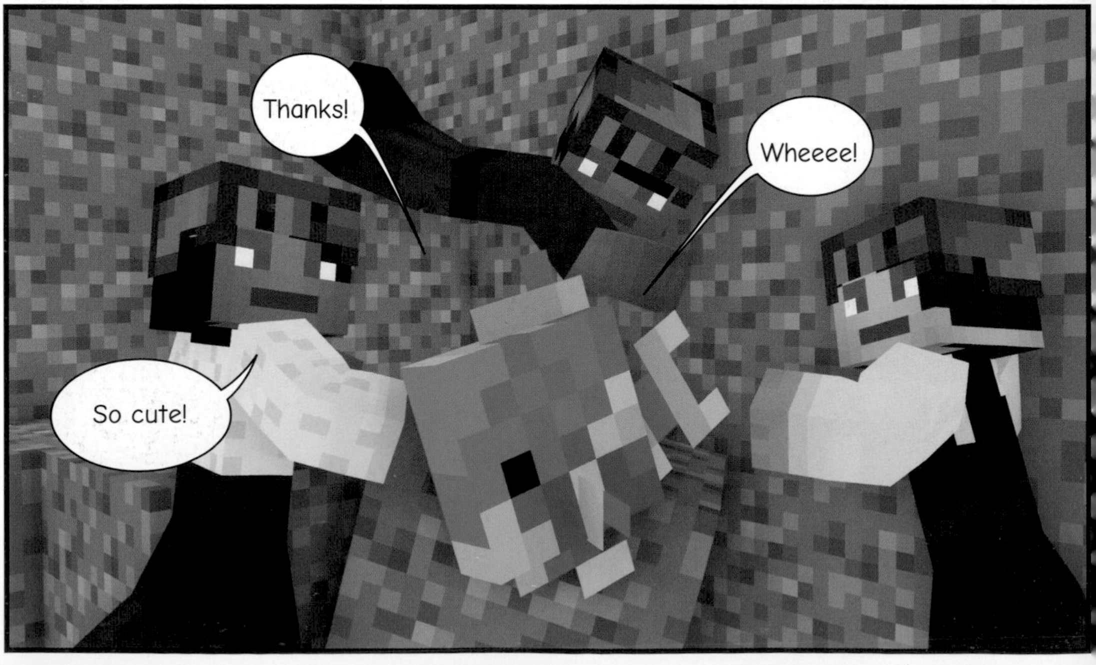
Thanks!
Wheeee!
So cute!

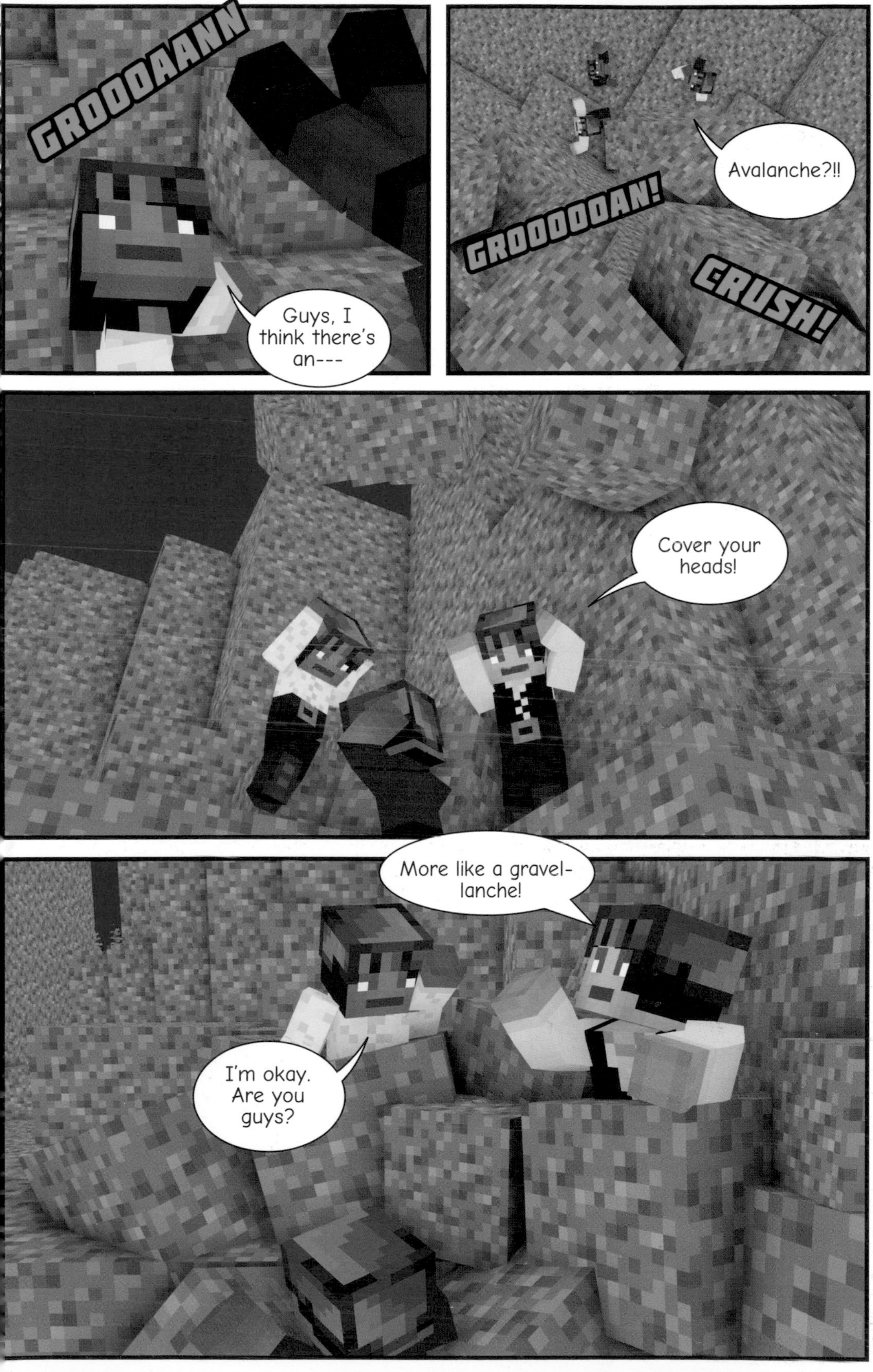
GROOOAANN
Guys, I think there's an---
Avalanche?!!
GROOOOOAN!
CRUSH!
Cover your heads!
More like a gravel-lanche!
I'm okay. Are you guys?

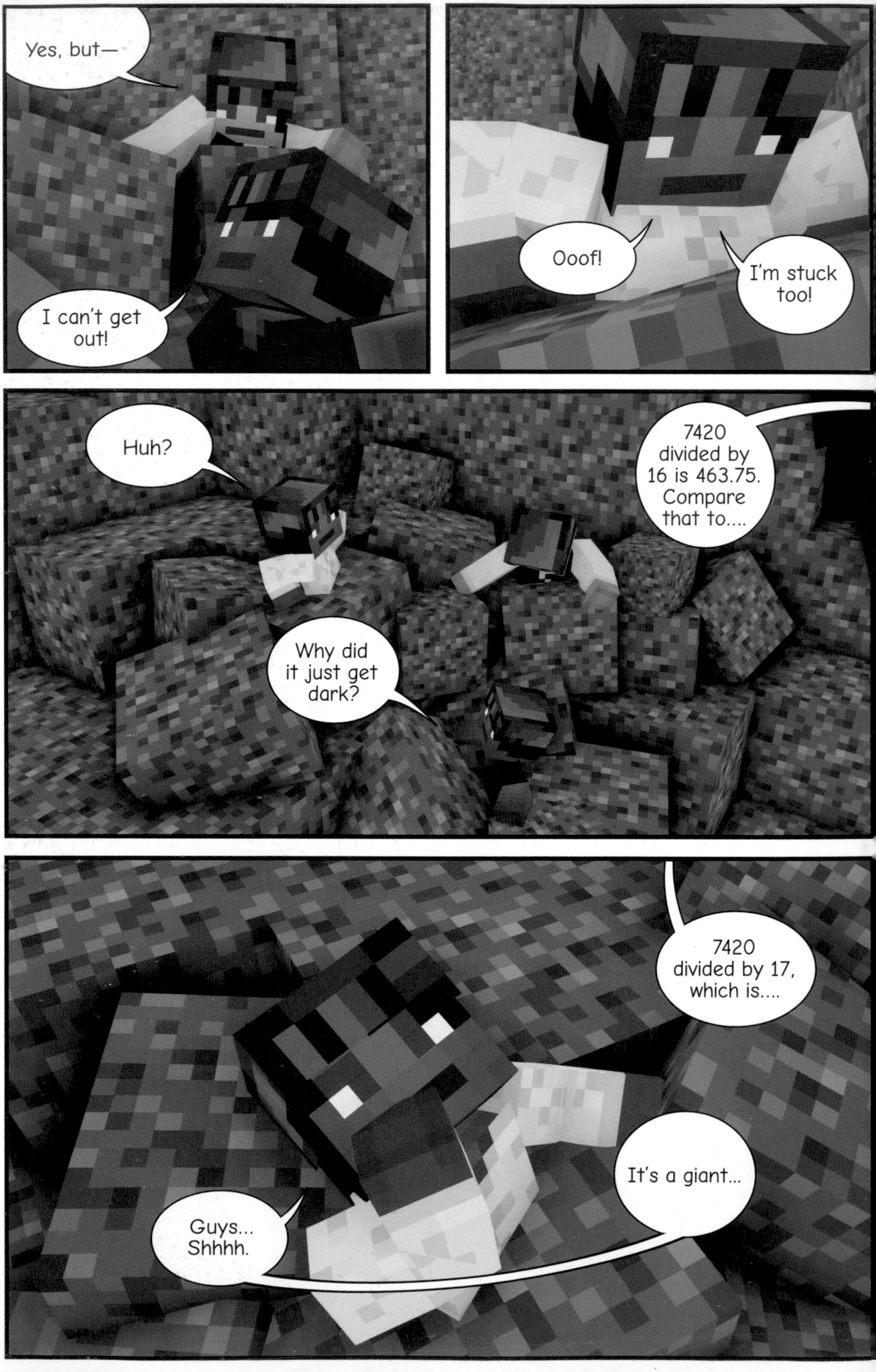
Yes, but—
I can't get out!
Ooof!
I'm stuck too!
Huh?
7420 divided by 16 is 463.75. Compare that to....
Why did it just get dark?
7420 divided by 17, which is....
It's a giant...
Guys... Shhhh.

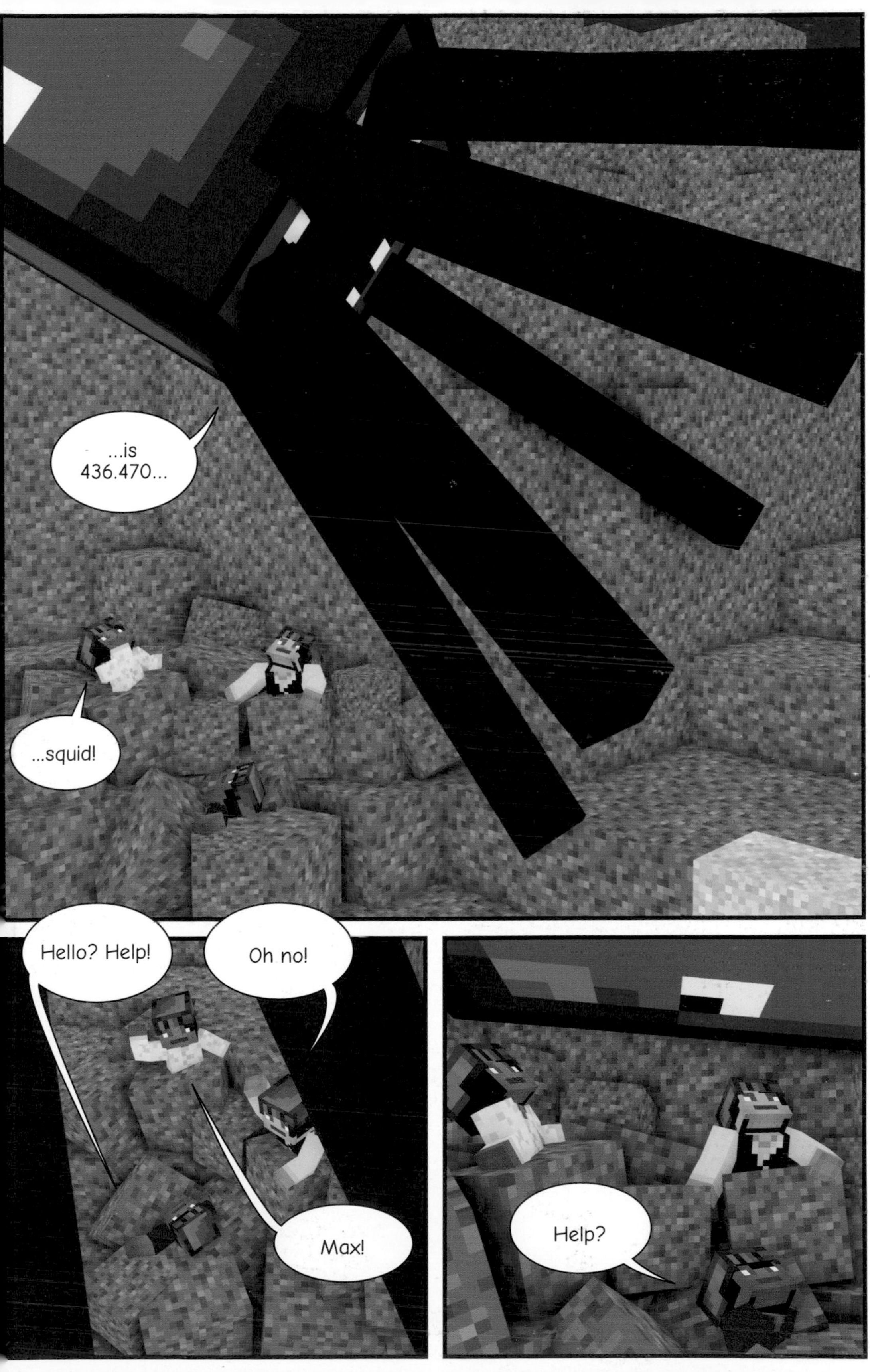
...is 436.470...
...squid!
Hello? Help!
Oh no!
Max!
Help?

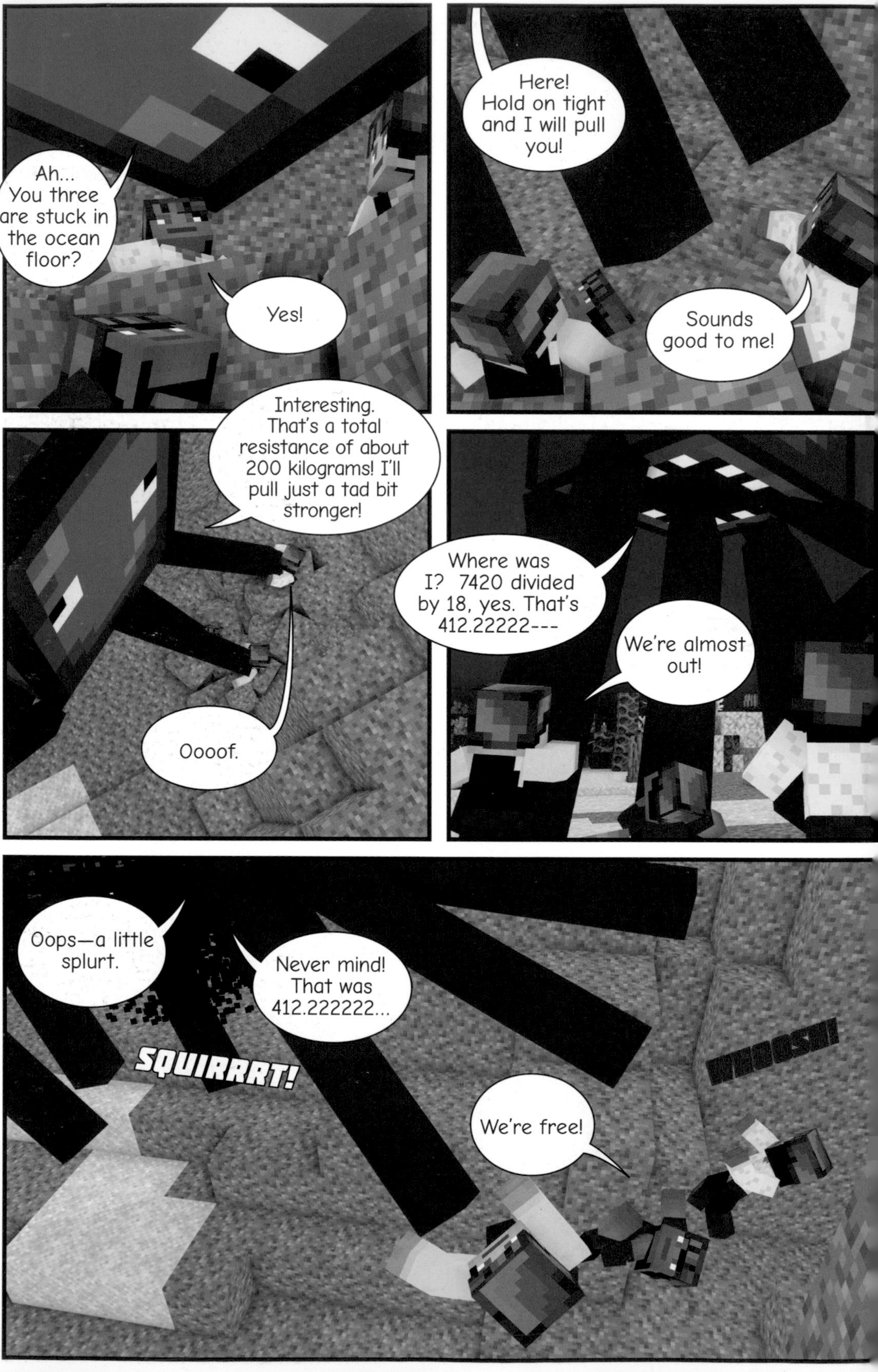
Ah...
You three are stuck in the ocean floor?
Yes!
Here!
Hold on tight and I will pull you!
Sounds good to me!
Interesting. That's a total resistance of about 200 kilograms! I'll pull just a tad bit stronger!
Oooof.
Where was I? 7420 divided by 18, yes. That's 412.22222---
We're almost out!
Oops—a little splurt.
Never mind! That was 412.222222...
SQUIRRRT!
WHOOSH!
We're free!

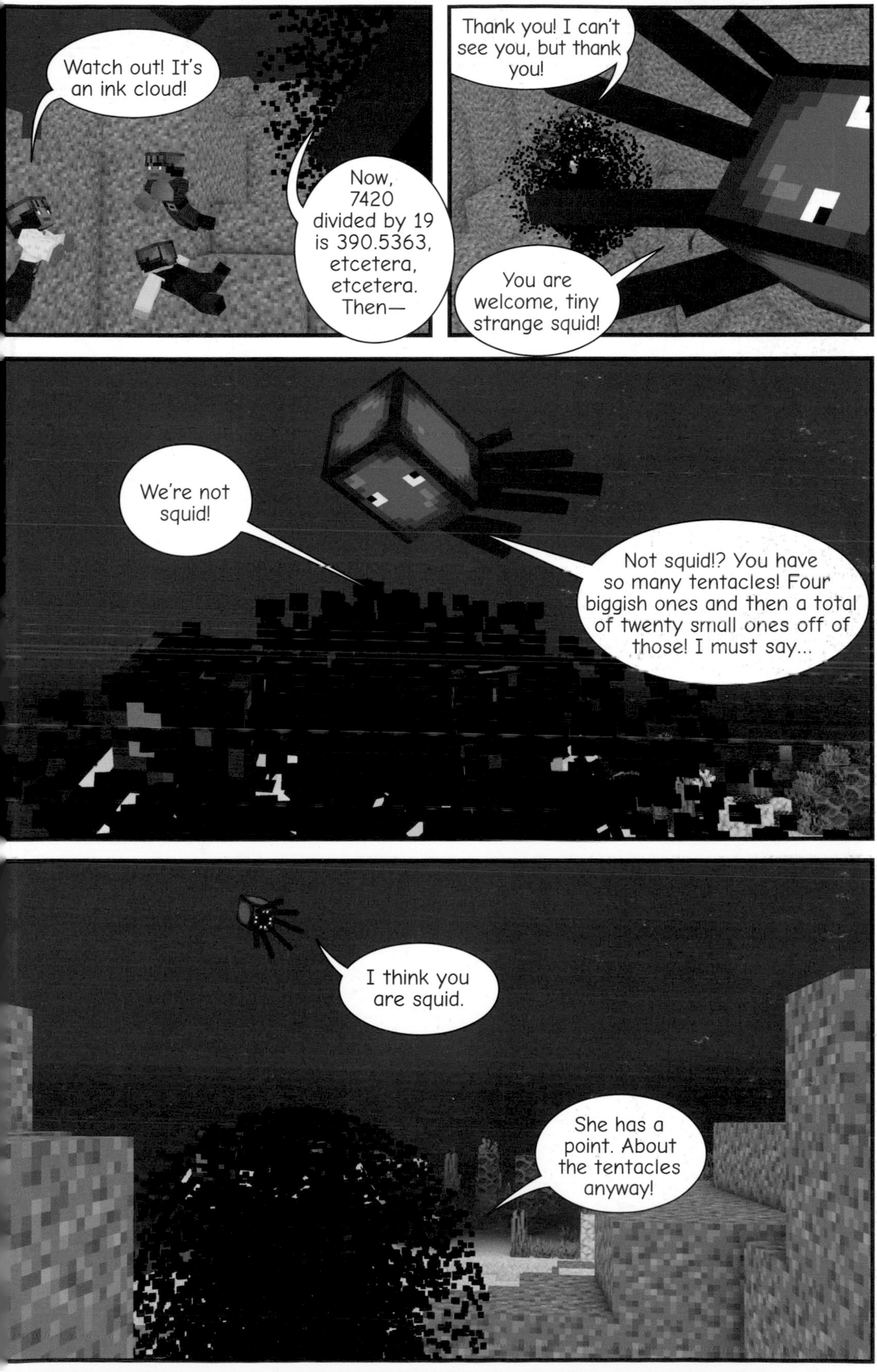
Watch out! It's an ink cloud!
Now, 7420 divided by 19 is 390.5363, etcetera, etcetera. Then—
Thank you! I can't see you, but thank you!
You are welcome, tiny strange squid!
We're not squid!
Not squid!? You have so many tentacles! Four biggish ones and then a total of twenty small ones off of those! I must say...
I think you are squid.
She has a point. About the tentacles anyway!

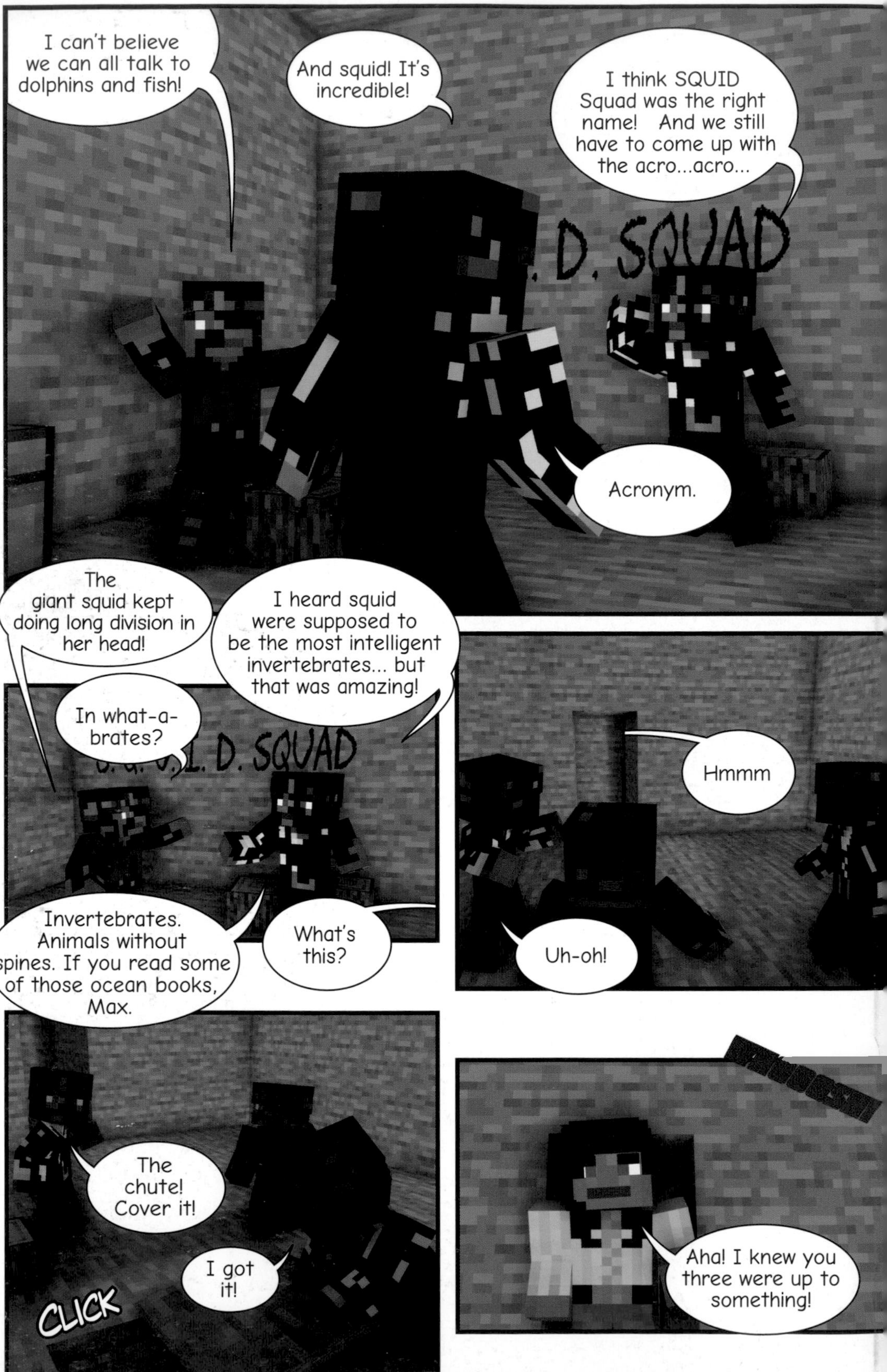
I can't believe we can all talk to dolphins and fish!
And squid! It's incredible!
I think SQUID Squad was the right name! And we still have to come up with the acro...acro...
Acronym.
The giant squid kept doing long division in her head!
I heard squid were supposed to be the most intelligent invertebrates... but that was amazing!
In what-a-brates?
Invertebrates. Animals without spines. If you read some of those ocean books, Max.
What's this?
Hmmm
Uh-oh!
The chute! Cover it!
I got it!
CLICK
Aha! I knew you three were up to something!

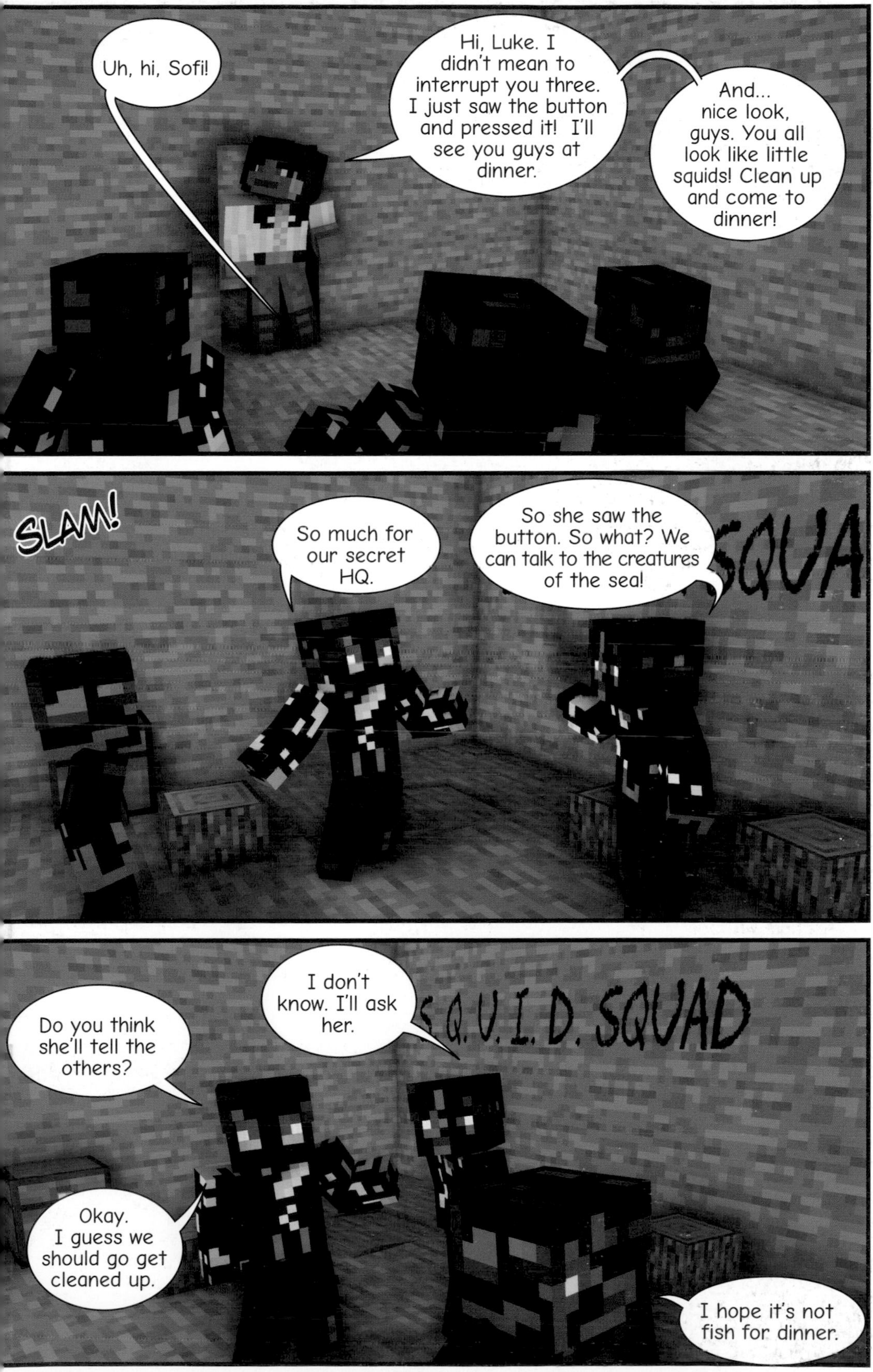
Uh, hi, Sofi!
Hi, Luke. I didn't mean to interrupt you three. I just saw the button and pressed it! I'll see you guys at dinner.
And... nice look, guys. You all look like little squids! Clean up and come to dinner!
SLAM!
So much for our secret HQ.
So she saw the button. So what? We can talk to the creatures of the sea!
Do you think she'll tell the others?
I don't know. I'll ask her.
S.Q.U.I.D. SQUAD
Okay. I guess we should go get cleaned up.
I hope it's not fish for dinner.

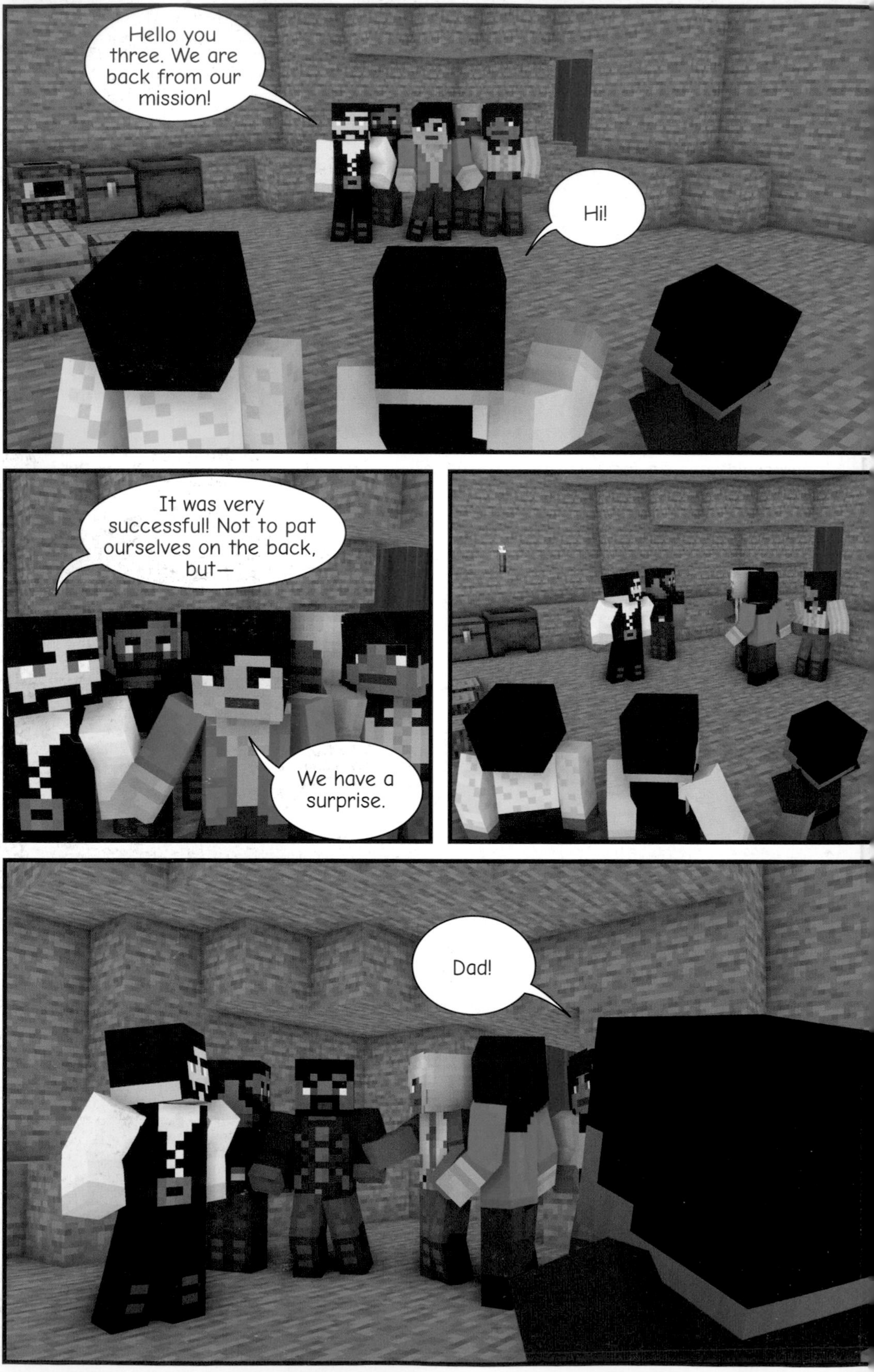
Hello you three. We are back from our mission!
Hi!
It was very successful! Not to pat ourselves on the back, but—
We have a surprise.
Dad!

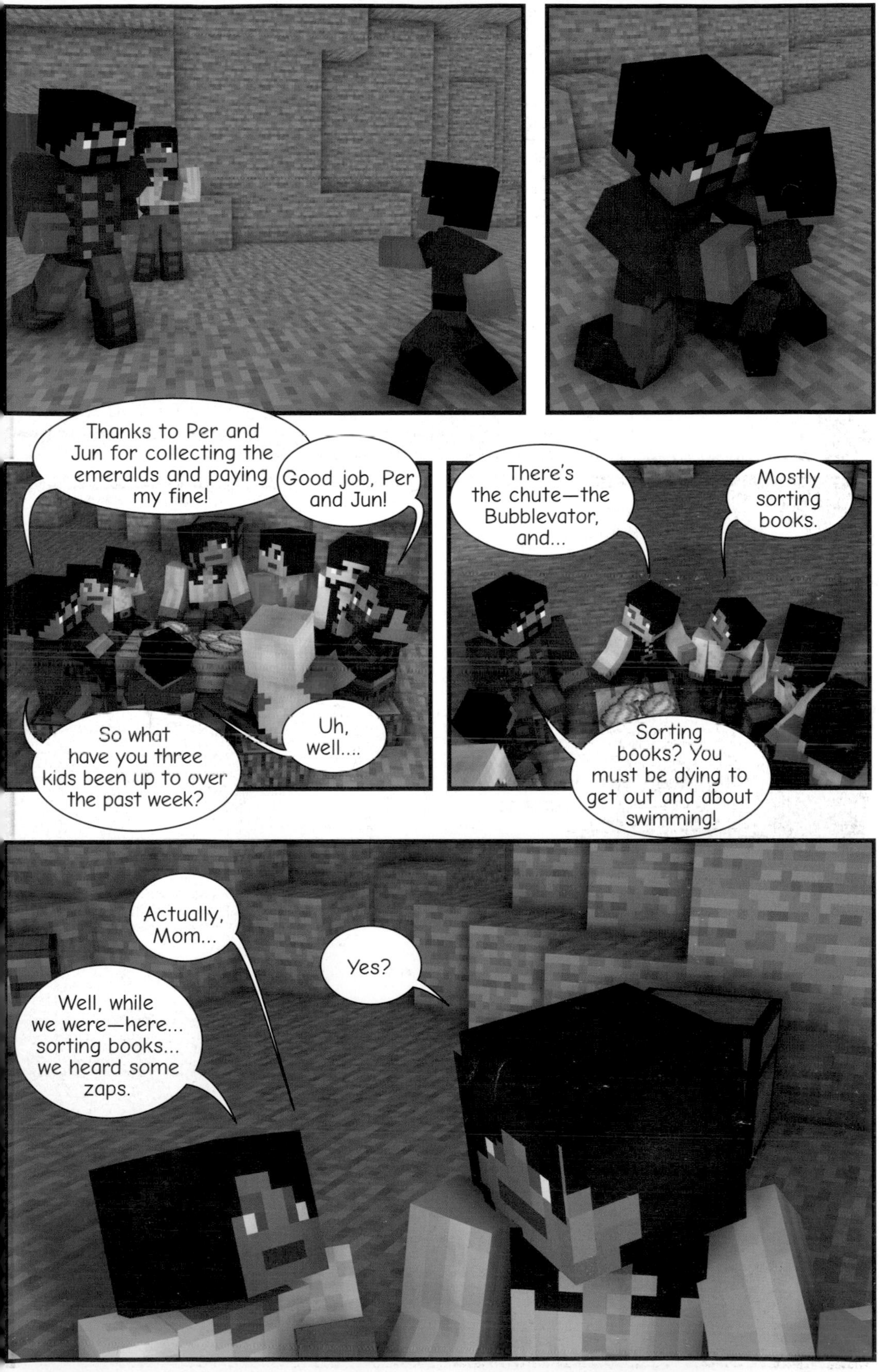
Thanks to Per and Jun for collecting the emeralds and paying my fine!
Good job, Per and Jun!
So what have you three kids been up to over the past week?
Uh, well....
There's the chute—the Bubblevator, and...
Mostly sorting books.
Sorting books? You must be dying to get out and about swimming!
Actually, Mom...
Yes?
Well, while we were—here... sorting books... we heard some zaps.

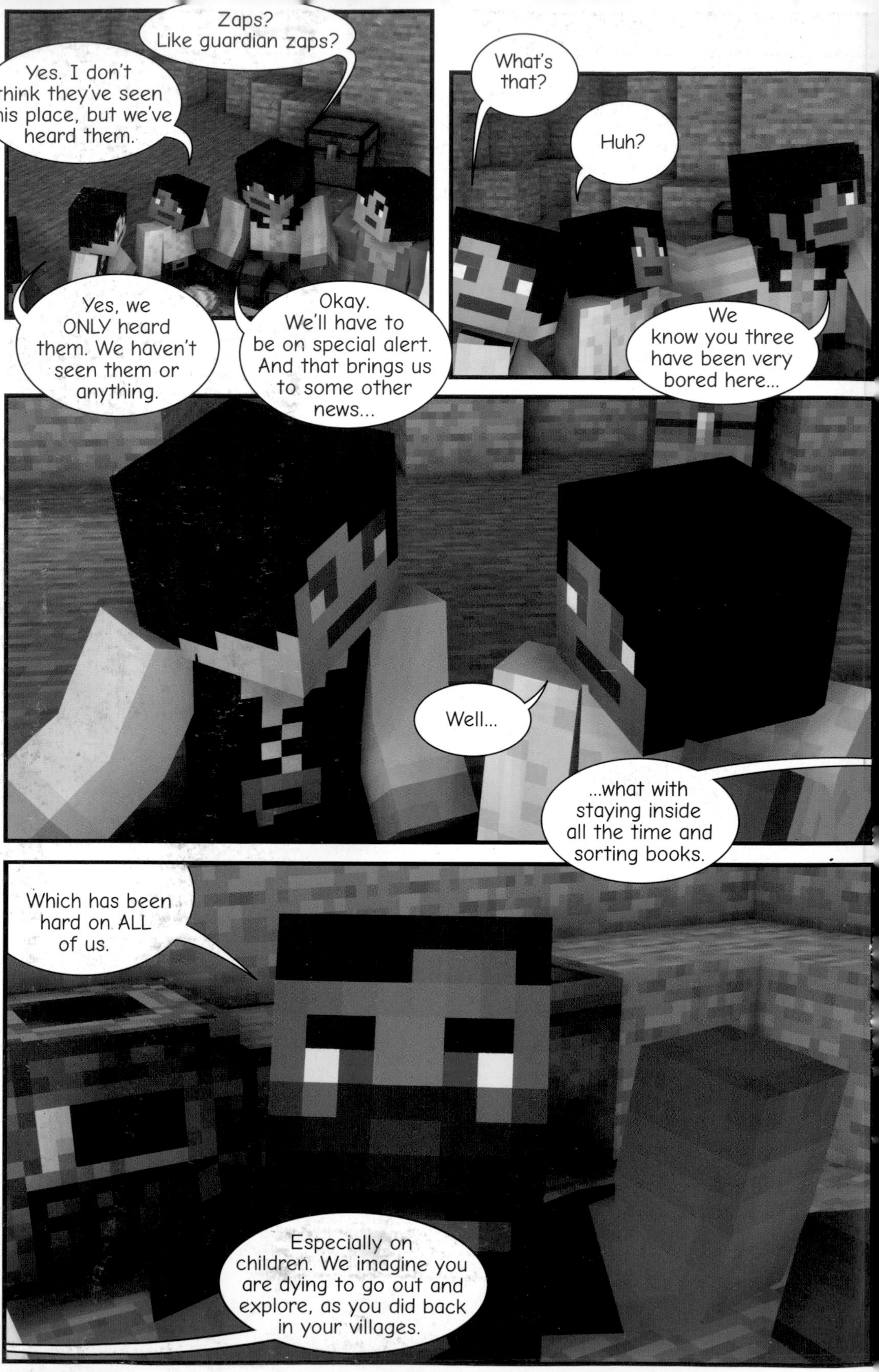
Zaps? Like guardian zaps?
Yes. I don't think they've seen this place, but we've heard them.
Yes, we ONLY heard them. We haven't seen them or anything.
Okay. We'll have to be on special alert. And that brings us to some other news...
What's that?
Huh?
We know you three have been very bored here...
Well...
...what with staying inside all the time and sorting books.
Which has been hard on ALL of us.
Especially on children. We imagine you are dying to go out and explore, as you did back in your villages.

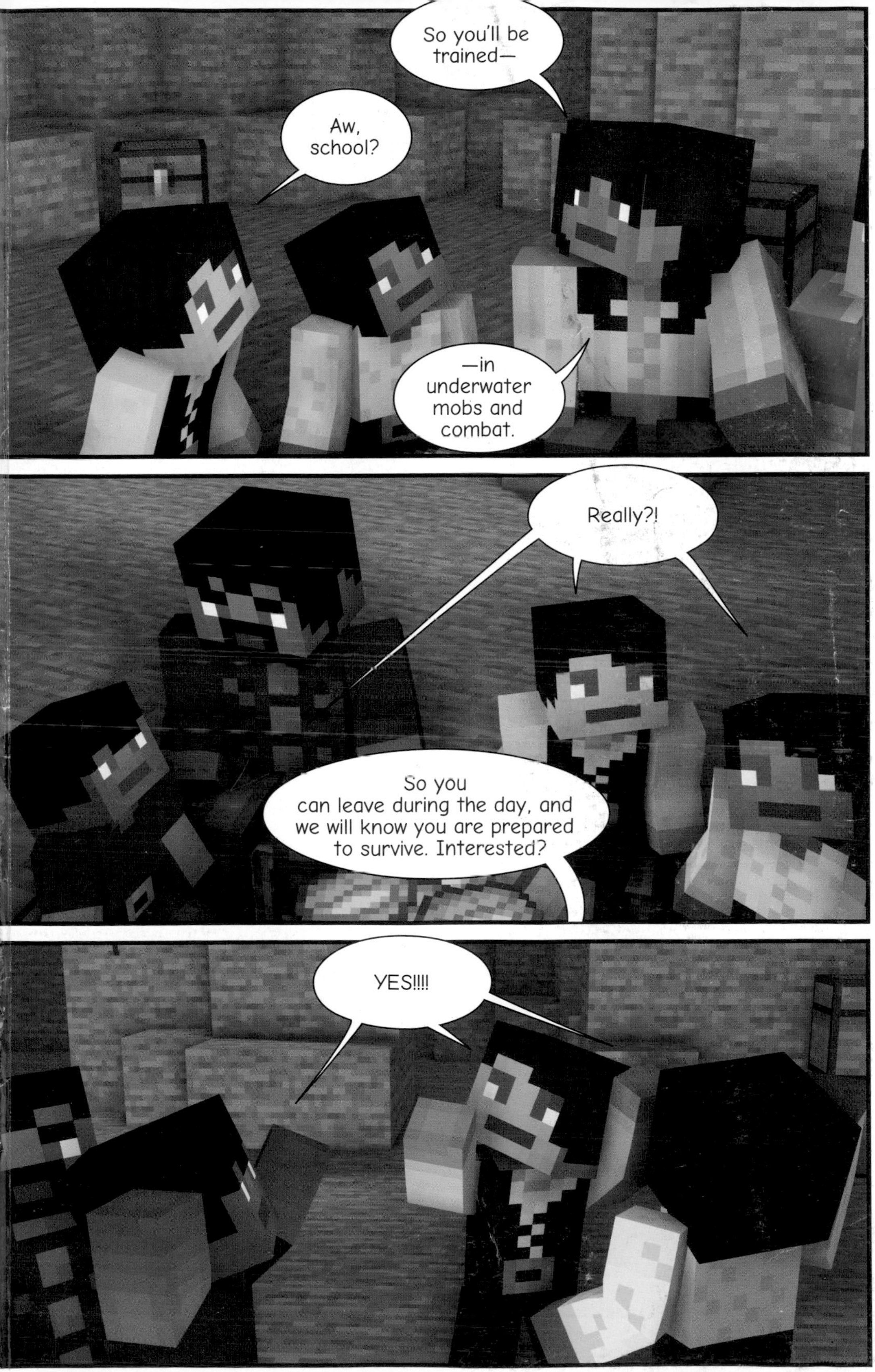

So you'll be trained—
Aw, school?
—in underwater mobs and combat.
Really?!
So you can leave during the day, and we will know you are prepared to survive. Interested?
YES!!!!

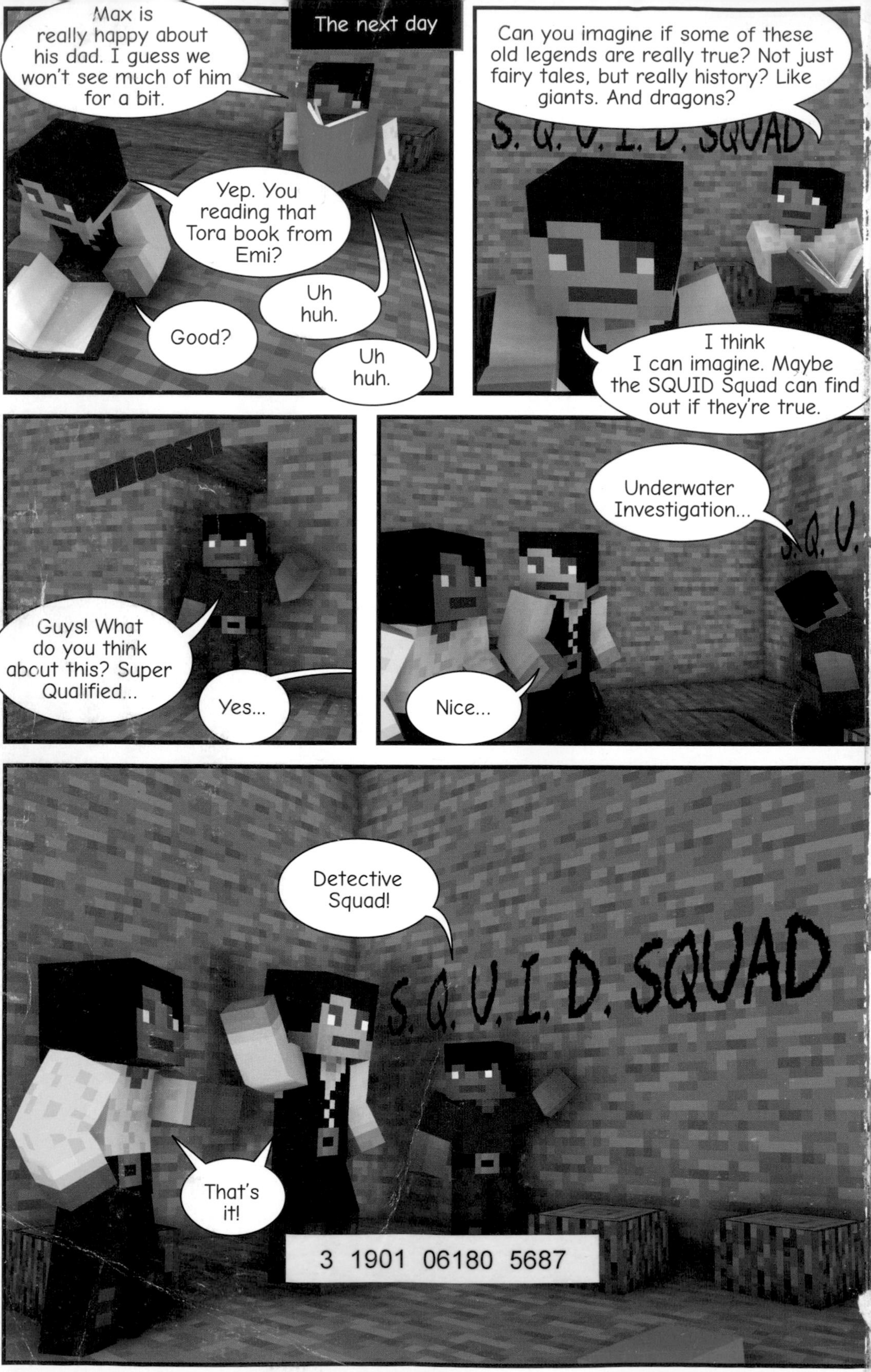
The next day
Max is really happy about his dad. I guess we won't see much of him for a bit.
Yep. You reading that Tora book from Emi?
Uh huh.
Good?
Uh huh.
Can you imagine if some of these old legends are really true? Not just fairy tales, but really history? Like giants. And dragons?
S. Q. U. I. D. SQUAD
I think I can imagine. Maybe the SQUID Squad can find out if they're true.
Guys! What do you think about this? Super Qualified...
Yes...
Underwater Investigation...
Nice...
S. Q. U.
Detective Squad!
S. Q. U. I. D. SQUAD
That's it!